M000231497

✡✡✡✡✡✡✡

The
Armies
of Gog

A novel by
R.K. Sparks

ISBN 978-1-64515-275-0 (paperback)
ISBN 978-1-64515-276-7 (digital)

Copyright © 2019 by Reginald Kensington Sparks

All rights reserved. No part of this publication may be reproduced, distributed, or transmitted in any form or by any means, including photocopying, recording, or other electronic or mechanical methods without the prior written permission of the publisher. For permission requests, solicit the publisher via the address below.

Christian Faith Publishing, Inc.
832 Park Avenue
Meadville, PA 16335
www.christianfaithpublishing.com

Printed in the United States of America

To my family who have supported me in my brightest days and my darkest hours. They are a shinning example of pure, unconditional love. Thank you all. Love you all.

Special thanks to God, Kristy and Rachel. Couldn't have done it without you.

*"And now I have told you before it comes to pass,
that when it comes to pass, you will believe."*

—John 14:29

PROLOGUE
✡✡✡✡✡✡✡

As I waited my turn in the long line of unfortunate souls, I reflected on the past ten or so years. What I was back in 2022 was lost, out of control, with no sense of right or wrong. No sense of what side I was on, because I had played on all sides. The world allowed it. My job demanded it.

The sounds in the near distance were horrifying. None of us dared look that way. I could hear a lot of praying and praising. I was doing both, but also reflecting. Up until the summer of 2022, the world was a pretty normal place. Yes, as in all of man's history, there was chaos—in pockets. The Chinese and Russians had been saber-rattling since the election of Donald J. Trump in the 2016 Presidential election. He was an enigma, a non-politician, and no one knew what to expect. Since then, it seemed the US, the world, and most of mankind was on edge—expecting the worst but always avoiding it somehow. My native land of Israel was no different.

The Arabs and the Jews had squared off a dozen times in Israel's short history since re-establishing national status in '48. The theme always seemed to be the same, at least up until 2022. It had been building—the coalition, a group of countries who were anti-Israel and anti-Jew. In 1948, '67, '70, and '73, it seemed the surrounding Arab countries wanted their land back and Israel out. This time it was very different. This time they wanted to wipe Israel off the map.

The coalition narrowed to a dozen countries with Persia and Russia leading the way. And all of that, the war that followed, and the peace that followed that, had led to this—me, a former agnostic, half-Jew, half-Palestinian NSA operative turned Jesus-follower, standing in a line of fellow believers to face a twenty-first–century guillotine and certain death. I now knew my destination and embraced the outcome, if not the path. Having been awakened by the Great War and seeing the miracles of fulfilled prophecy, I had pledged my allegiance to Christ just after the great disappearances.

At the very best, I would be a tribulation saint, living in the "Time of Jacob's Trouble"; the great tribulation spoken of in the Bible and the most terrifying time on earth. My thoughts were interrupted by the decisive clash of a sharp blade to the throat of one of my fellow saints. Our archenemy, Satan, had decided to put these victims on their backs, so that they could watch the blade descend on them—how thoughtful. What he didn't realize was that he was giving them one last earthly look at their future home. Refusal to take the mark of the Antichrist, whom we now know as Lech Manevetski, resulted in facing this certain death.

The public spectacle, broadcast live to audiences throughout the world, was deemed appropriate incentive to others who rebelled against the power of the new world leader. The Great War had paved the way—it was all predictable and laid out in dramatic accuracy within the pages of the Bible. Prior to my salvation and subsequent transformation, I knew it only as: "Basic Instructions Before Leaving Earth"—a manual for those who were not intelligent enough to figure it out on their own. Back then, the Bible was a mystery to me; nothing more than a glorified paper weight.

Academia had no use for it. Governments ran from it, men and women fought against its basic principles of love, redemption, law, and peace. In America and in the world, what people wanted was auton-omy—to follow his or her way. The Bible was counter to that and Jesus was viewed as a divider. Oddly, that was true. He had not come to unite, but to divide. He claimed to be Truth and that got in the way of most people's view of what was good for them and what they wanted.

What had intrigued me most was the accuracy and depth of the prophecies in the book. Once that was revealed to me, I could place on a calendar the events to come. But by then, it was too late. Now my life was about to end. I was keenly aware that all these in line with me looked forward to their destination. But no one wants to die, and the sound of death, the blade, the thud of the head hitting the ground in a pool of blood and the audible anguish of those close to the front was difficult at best.

Since I have some time, I want to go back several years and share my story. It is a life lesson and it impacts all of us. Since the invention of the Proto-Cloud and the ability to preserve my story, notes, and memoirs for generations, you are now reading selective events of the end days, and can most assuredly benefit from them. It just may save your life. I understand that all of the prophecies, all the indicators, point to this inevitable outcome. But I didn't see it until it was too late. Perhaps I can assist some willing souls in seeing the facts and making valued eternal decisions.

chapter
ONE
✡ ✡ ✡ ✡ ✡ ✡

My name is Jeremy Stone, but that is just one of my twenty-three aliases, and the one I use when I am at home in Annapolis, Maryland. My real name is Eliezer Abdullah Grollenberg, the only son of a Jewish father by my same name and my Palestinian mother Norra who insisted I receive some semblance of Arab inclusion in my life. 1975 was a tumultuous time in Tel Aviv, my birth city. It would be safe to say it was a case of fatal attraction, the unlikely union of a Jew and Arab in war-torn Israel. I had no control of those circumstances or of the death of my mother, soon after my birth.

So fractured was my father over the death of his cherished wife that he left Israel for the United States and never looked back. Determined to keep my mother's heritage alive in me, my father hired an Egyptian nanny who taught me three Arabic dialects and English to go with the Hebrew we spoke every day. My father utterly hated the God of Israel, and was furious at Muhammed, who had written laws dictating the death of a Muslim married to any infidel, especially a Zionist.

Too young to remember, and only late in life told of all of this, I grew up in a tiny house in Front Royal, Virginia, went to school, and lived my life as an American boy. My father proudly became a US citizen and eventually married my nanny who, for all intents and purposes, had raised me.

I was a slight kid, olive-skinned and a bit feminine. Of course, I never gave it much notice because my dad told me that tom-boys turned into beautiful brides and men with a bit of femininity made wonderful fathers. That stuck with me and, though I was teased a bit, even bullied, I always prevailed in the fight and proved I was all man. This detail would also play into three of my aliases which were women—attractive women at that. I could pull it off flawlessly with my chameleon abilities. By my second year of college, I was fluent in nine languages and poised to enter the Naval Academy where I would be groomed into a valuable asset for the NSA.

My final year at the Academy was eventful and transformational as we all watched the fall of the Twin Towers. My passion had been for Near- and Middle-Eastern studies, but now a shift was required, and, well—as the story goes—I could tell you but I'd have to kill you. Suffice to say, I was thrown into the spy business and overwhelmed with everything from dissecting and interpreting high-value intel to deep-cover missions inside Iran.

I mastered martial arts and high-tech weapons training. It seemed that every kind of advanced tech device was forced down my throat. It was for my own good, and I could never have imagined how valuable the training was for both my NSA career and my future work as a tribulation saint. Of course, the latter was evolved out of both a spiritual passion and pure survival. In many ways, I felt I had been much more valuable serving Jesus than I was at any time serving my country. I think Solomon adequately summed it up; the pursuit of worldly things, "vanity of vanities…"

Things really began to heat up after the Trump election in 2016. I can say this now; the former president—well, everyone in the agency would have loved to take him out. Secretly, of course. His Presidency had been and would prove to be the most detrimental eight years of human history. Yes, I said it; not American history, but human history. He put us on the brink! Trump came in with his hands full of every kind of trouble. First, a third of America hated him and it was hard to understand. We had gone so far left and it made sense that it could not continue to move that way. Once, on a trip to the Smithsonian, my father had shown me a giant pendulum. "What goes out here eventually will swing back there," he explained.

So what were all these people mad about? I guess it was the autonomy thing. Boys wanted to be girls, girls wanted to be boys. Men wanted men rather than women. People sought relationships with dogs, cats or pigs rather than their human counterparts. Despite people's perceived happiness, the suicide rates were growing by leaps and bounds.

A large group of ticked-off Americans wanted what they wanted— freedom to do anything. They wanted to get high, stay at home and collect entitlements of all kinds—it was crazy. And Trump tried to reel it in. He did a lot of things right, as far as I was concerned, and it mostly made sense. But things that took decades to evolve could not be changed overnight.

Then, there was the fact that everyone was hell-bent on tolerance to the point of intolerance and globalization, even though none of the globe could get along. Throw in a super-dose of political correctness— the Left embraced it, the Right and Donald Trump were opposed and hell-bent on changing it. Frankly, it had to change. It was destroying families, society, and dividing all of humanity from almost every perspective.

The Alt-Left, as they had been named, could not go back, and near the end of the President's first term, chaos erupted. It began as a peaceful protest in Detroit over union teachers whom Trump had fired because they simply refused to return to work after a failed strike. Of course, Trump could not fire state employees, but he did cut off federal funding by executive order. It was well known that recently deceased billionaire Gregory Boros was still funding violent protests by way of his evil successor, thought to be Bob Edmonds. He would fly professional protestors in, masked and marching in all black. Their purpose was to stir up trouble, suck the police in, and begin anarchy.

The Alt-Right had its own anti-semitic and anti-government groups. There was one example of the tension, played out in Charlottesville, Virginia where clashes erupted injuring many and killing a young woman. After this incident, both sides retreated and laid low waiting for better protest opportunities.

On the occasion of the Detroit protest, that is exactly what transpired. What they hadn't expected was the huge militant force of suburbanite vigilantes who engaged the Boros teams with clubs, batons, and eventually, guns. The melee brought in gangs, drug dealers, mobsters, and anyone else who was chomping at the bit. As the police stood down, urban Detroit became a war zone. Trump stepped in with military force and the war was on. On prime-time TV, Detroit looked like Beirut in the eighties. From there, people came out of the woodwork, looting, beating, shooting, burning, and pillaging. The images were just too much for the pent-up observers in cities across the country and it spread quickly.

Gun battles, hand to hand combat, and general lawlessness erupted in twelve US cities. Those mayors who had a good handle on the citizens avoided major issues, but chaos ensued in Baltimore, Detroit, Chicago, New York City, St. Louis, New Orleans, San Francisco, Los Angeles, Seattle, Houston, Miami, and Washington, DC. The cities burned and were like war zones. Both sides were fed up, both wanted the end of the other. It would be ugly. Battle lines were drawn, sides taken, and the animalistic nature of man kicked in.

The Trump White House had planned for such an incident. Trump called it his "war on lawlessness". What he couldn't have known was the depth of the indoctrination that had been going on in the public schools, universities, and inner cities for years. It was a conditioning of the soul. Evolution taught the idea that there are no eternal consequences in life, and when it ends you just go in a box. If we evolved from animals, we are expected to act like animals. The process of revisionist history removed the greatness of this truly great country. Then there was dependency—on the government, on drugs, on rent subsidies and support of all types. The government had built power on the backs of its people, stripping the taxpayer and redistributing for the purpose of dependence.

For sixty years, immigrants without documentation had sneaked across the borders and, in some cases, been invited to do so. As Trump complained against these issues, the Left lost it, to a point that the former president, in an effort to get then-candidate Hillary Clinton elected, actually went on a Latin TV Network and encouraged undocumented immigrants to vote illegally. It didn't matter, Trump won and the power had swung to the Right. Now, the philosophy had broadly switched from "give a man a fish" to "teach a man to fish." It really was as simple as that, but a tough sell.

Trump gutted some bloated government agencies, eliminated others, and created millions of new jobs. The potential was extraordinary, yet a segment of the people didn't want that. We had created an entitled society and the incentives to get off the sofa or the street were not that attractive. So they resisted—everything. Even things that would benefit them, they resisted. Oddly, they were resisting the only thing that could save them. The delusion was wide and deep. The dependency and the moral depravity were pervasive. Something was going to give, and Detroit was it.

As Trump's war on lawlessness began, the twelve host cities burned and rioting was widespread. Trump's first tactic, since the rioters had a head start, was to let it burn itself out. Like a fully involved house fire, sometimes nothing could be saved but lives and resources, so you let it burn, controlled but complete. The stores were stripped bare, the crowds raucous and rebellious. With no law enforcement in sight, families and the elderly were fleeing and were being rescued at the perimeters. But inside it was chaos.

As for me, I was hunkered down in a bunker just outside Damascus. I watched it all unfold along with my team, a mix of NSA, CIA, and Mossad guys all poised to act quickly. My first thought was to get my dad and mom out of Annapolis where they were living in my home. Calls and emails were 100 percent a no-go in this location, so I had to hope they were far enough from DC to be okay. Plus, I had friends in high places that knew and loved my folks. They would look out for them and tell them to head to the lake house if things got bad.

Knowing what I knew, even then, was enough to warrant preparations for "end times" scenarios. The lake house was much more than a vacation home. On the surface, yes. But it would serve all of us well in the difficult years to come. Looking back, I could feel it, a force working in me, causing me to think ahead, investigate unique things and follow through on others. Now I know it was the One who holds it all together. He was then. He is now.

Most thought the protests would die out with time. After three weeks of bedlam, the real war of lawlessness began. The troops went in to find booby traps, ambushes, and fortified outposts. The inner-city rebels had taken over Wal-Mart, Target, Safeway, and other huge distribution centers. They had guns, ammo, food, water, and armies in the hundreds of thousands willing to fight for the cause. They wanted their lives of leisure, drugs, and freedom back. If they had only put this much effort into opening a business or driving a truck, all would have been well. But their sports, drugs, and video games were calling. For them, quitting or conforming was not an option. Their lifestyles were their idols. So they dug in for the long haul. It was as if they had planned this over many years.

In the meantime, the US government had its hands full of Iran and their race to get an Israel-destroying nuclear bomb. China was pushing to establish itself as a naval power, Russia was working hard to restore its diminished status, and Israel was holding its collective breath. The intent of the Islamic world was unanimous and well-known: wipe the little Satan, which is Israel, off the map and then destroy the great Satan, the USA, in order to usher in Islamic end times.

My role played right into the Middle-East conflict. We knew who the bad actors were and had eyes and ears on them. I had worked my way covertly into Iran's supply chain. Acting as a Morocco-based small arms dealer, my company provided new smart grenades and stinger, shoulder-fired rockets. We assembled some slick prototypes and demonstrated them to the Iranian Republican Guard (IRG). They were all in. There was one caveat—the company was low on price, high on quality, and very slow to deliver. It was a purposefully built-in caveat to help us gauge the Iranian timeline for attacking Israel.

The Iranian Republican Guard did not bat an eye at sixteen-month delivery times, so we knew there was some long-term strategy going on. Of course, the US was now headed into an election and Iran was hoping for any alternative to the current president. They knew a second term may be trouble for them and their evil plans. Way back in 2009, Mahmoud Ahmadinejad had bragged about lighting up the sky over Israel on August 22 to show the power of Iran's nuclear program. The date was a significant one in Islamic lore, and it was fundamental to Islamic end times.

Even though the specific year was in question, I considered the attacks of 9/11 as America's warning. God gave the people of Nineveh twenty years to repent and return to His ways, and then He allowed for their judgment. Using that logic and other Bible verses dealing with nations and cities in disobedience, I felt the US was due its just reward. For Nineveh and cities like Sodom and Gomorrah, it was complete destruction. For Israel it had been nations God had allowed to come against them—the Babylonians and Assyrian empires. Iran, it's coalition and the much anticipated caliphate, were perfect examples.

One thing was certain to me, America was in line for some chastisement and we had received the warning. Perhaps the civil war was part or the beginning. Jesus told us to watch for the signs. Israel was also watching, knowing that it was squarely in the coalition crosshairs.

chapter
TWO
✡ ✡ ✡ ✡ ✡ ✡ ✡

As far back as 2008, the agencies were keeping careful watch as Iran developed a proactive strategy of preparing to wipe our ally Israel off the map. Iraq was off the grid for now, Syria was moving into a protracted civil war, and most of the Arabic nations surrounding Israel were sure to join in. After the devastating wars, this was nothing new to Israel. The mix of countries had changed from war to war, but the theme was always the same: say goodbye to Israel.

As we watched the coalition build and Russia come into the picture, things got very interesting. Our team was positioned in a bunker deep below the city of Damascus, Syria monitoring the events of the ever-expanding civil war. Our team of spies was tasked with intel evaluation and covert missions to both disrupt and gather information on the coalition as it developed. John Reynolds, a Christian team member shared with me two very interesting stories in the Bible. That is what I equated anything that came from the Bible to—a story. But this had some meat. He began with a bizarre account of a pile of bones coming back to life.

"Can these bones live?" was the very silly question.

Then God spoke to the prophet, "Prophesy to these bones and say to them, 'Oh dry bones, hear the Word of the Lord! Thus says the Lord God to these bones; Surely I will cause breath to enter into you, and you shall live. I will put sinews on you and bring flesh upon you, cover you with skin, and put breath in you; and you shall live. Then you shall know that I am the Lord.'"

He continued to read the story: "So I prophesied as I was commanded; and as I prophesied there was a noise, and suddenly a rattling; and the bones came together, bone to bone. Indeed, as I looked, the sinews and the flesh came upon them, and the skin covered them over; but there was no breath in them."

I stared at John like he was nuts but asked him to go on.

"Also, He said to me, prophesy to the breath, 'Thus says the Lord God: Come from the four winds, Oh breath, and breathe on these slain so they may live.' So I prophesied as He commanded me, and breath came into them, and they lived, and stood upon their feet, an exceedingly great army.

"Then He said to me, 'Son of man, these bones are the whole house of Israel. They indeed say, 'Our bones are dry, our hope is lost, and we ourselves are cut off!' Therefore, prophesy and say to them, 'Thus says the Lord God: Behold, O my people, I will open your graves and cause you to come up from your graves, and bring you into the land of Israel. Then you shall know that I am the Lord, when I have opened your graves, O my people, and brought you up from your graves. I will put My Spirit in you, and you shall live, and I will place you in your own land. Then you shall know that I, the Lord have spoken it and performed it, says the Lord.'"

My friend paused so all this could sink in. "You see, God made a promise to His people that He would bring them back into the land after their punishment had ended. It ended 907,200 days later, on May

14, 1948." My friend John smiled, and then it was like a lightbulb went off inside my head.

"When was this written?" I asked John.

"Around 550 BC by Ezekiel, the Prophet."

I swallowed hard, felt some sort of strange connection to those bones, and closed my eyes. I knew Israel's history; how complex the process was to re-establish the Hebrew language, get through two World Wars, and battle every kind of foe to get to May 14, 1948.

"The very day?" I asked John.

"The very day. I can show you the math, it's amazing..." he explained.

"Not necessary. I believe you, for some strange reason."

"It's the Spirit. The very same Spirit that breathed life into the nation of Israel. And there is more—so much more," John said. I was in shock, my mind racing. I felt like one of those in the great army of revived souls.

John got up and returned with a cup of coffee. I smiled, knowing that he had read my mind. "What else have you got, John? You have my attention."

"Only a small matter, a coalition forming—a strong coalition against Israel. Iran, Lebanon, Syria, Somalia, Libya, Yemen, Turkey... and Russia." He paused.

"In the Bible. All that is in the Bible?" I asked.

"Yes, and much more—detail, motives, even a clue to the timing of such an event."

"You're kidding. It feels like we are living it."

"I wouldn't kid. This is serious stuff and it is evolving as we watch from our bunker."

"All right, you have my attention. Let's hear it."

"We'll start with another unique but, I believe, connected prophesy in the book of Isaiah."

"Fair enough," I answered.

"Okay, here we go! 'Behold, Damascus will cease from being a city, and it will be a ruinous heap. The royal power of Damascus will end. All that remains of Syria will share the fate of Israel's departed glory, declares the Lord of Heaven's Armies,'" John read.

"Wow, Damascus—gone?"

"Gone, sheep grazing on the land, gone…"

"When was that one written?" I asked.

"Around 580 BC by Isaiah the prophet. It is an end times prophecy, as is Ezekiel."

"Why, what makes you say that?"

"Well, Damascus is one of, if not *the*, oldest continually inhabited cities in the world."

"So you're saying it's still to come?"

"Yes. And now Israel is back in the land, which opens the door for virtually all end-times prophecy."

I stopped, took a sip of my coffee and looked into John's very serious eyes. John Reynolds was not a nut case. In fact, he was second in his class coming through the Academy and had always been a 100 percent straight shooter.

"Stone, these are not stories. These are prophecies, and Bible prophecy has proven out 100 percent so far. Nostradamus is hitting like 30 percent!"

"The NSA does not equate the Bible to useful or even marginally reliable intelligence. You know that. What are we supposed to do with this?" I asked.

"The US won't do anything with it." John said. "But the Mossad can and will." His pause for effect was powerful. Or maybe it was the words registering in some previously unknown compartment of my brain. "I can assure you that the Israelis consult the Bible on all these matters."

"Does it say how Damascus is destroyed?" I asked.

"No, and it's not just Damascus, it is several Middle Eastern countries. There are clues, but the greatest clues concern the coalition that is forming to come against Israel– The War of Gog and Magog."

"Magog?"

"That's it for today. This is mind-blowing stuff and your mind has already been blown."

"Okay, then take me through the math to May 14, 1948."

"Later, we have work to do."

"This could be work."

"Yes, but Jake and Alex will be back soon and we have intercepts to sift through."

Already over-burdened, I had to agree and I wasn't about to argue with John. John was a beast of a man at 6'5", 265 pounds of solid muscle. He played fullback at the Academy and beat Army every year he played. Oh, I could probably take him, you know, with my speed and agility. But I wasn't in the mood to tick him off today and he was right, we had a lot to sift through. This was all new for me. I had never had a spiritual moment in my life prior to that day.

A week later, news came to the bunker via an NSA coded alert. Russian bombers were on the ground in Iran and one of their anti-quated carriers was on the way to the Mediterranean with a flotilla of escort ships. The coalition was strengthening and both the US and Israel were on high alert. John decided it was time to get to the proph-ecy before it unfolded right in front of us. Looking back, I see that none of these details were so small as to overlook. I hadn't noticed at the time, but it began to become clearer when I dove into a very detailed history book on the nation of Israel.

The book began with a man named Eliezer Ben Yehuda who sud-denly decided to revive the Hebrew language back in 1881. He relo-cated to Jerusalem and set out to revive a truly dead language. The first Aliyah, that is, a movement of Jews from Europe and other nations back to the homeland, began in 1891 and launched the Zionist move-ment. Of course, the Palestinians were not excited to see Jews overrun-ning their land. But the Jews had cooperation from the Turks who had control of the land at that time.

It took World War I to wrestle the land of Palestine from the Ottoman empire and into British hands. But that is just the short ver-sion. The book is full of events, both positive and negative for Israel. For instance, the Palestinians gave the Jews useless desert and swamp-land. In a few short years, they had those trash-lands producing crops, grains, fruits, and nut trees while their economy grew. They build houses and started businesses. I had another one of those spiritual moments—some power, outside of their own, was orchestrating events, actions, outrageous coincidences. It was obvious—at least to me.

Another example: prior to the British invasion, General George Allenby had his troops positioned in the Sinai of Egypt. The British were getting valuable troop movement information from Jewish spies. One of these spies, Aaron Aaronshon, had new and strategic information to share with Allenby but could not get it out to the General. In an odd twist, Aaronshon, a botanist and inventor of weather resistant wheat, was called by the Palestinians to go to Egypt and sort out a huge locust invasion originating from the Sinai area. With a Palestinian escort, he delivered the intel to General Allenby and solved the locust problem at the same time.

These and many more spectacular events, too numerous to count, were throughout this history book. It was written by a secular professor who failed to make any biblical connection. I certainly did. These things were too "out there" to be purely coincidence. So John had my attention and our only delay was the presence of Jake, our Mossad buddy, and Alex, the CIA agent we worked with. But somehow, they both had an assignment and we were left alone. Another strange coincidence.

"Funny how that worked out," John said.

"I am becoming a believer," I said.

"Not yet..." John smiled, "Let's get started. Okay, this comes from the prophet Ezekiel and it follows the dry bones prophecy. Israel, as we will see, is back in the land and this is a future—that is, an as yet not fulfilled prophecy. Now, we will have to do some work to identify some of these names, but I have put the work in. I'll explain on the fly. Here we go from Ezekiel 38: 'Now the Word of the Lord came to me saying; Son of man set your face against Gog, of the land of Magog, the Prince of Rosh, Meshech and Tubal and prophecy against him.'

"Okay, we see here a leader of a land named Magog. The Lord refers to him as Gog—could be a name, but probably a title, like an emperor, czar, or pharaoh. This figure is definitely a military and political leader as well as a coalition builder, much like Hitler prior to World War II. He is of the land of Magog. Gotta dig deep here—the Great Wall of China along the border of Russia was first called the Wall of Magog. A group called the Scythians settled north of the Black and Caspian seas in the region we now know as Russia."

John continued because I was looking quite interested and I could tell he was dying to share it with me or someone. "There are more clues we will pick up as we go deeper into the text. Ezekiel tells us that the armies of Gog will come out of the remotest parts of the North."

"Sounds like Russia…" I chimed in.

"Yes, a logical conclusion. Flavius Josephus, the first-century historian and writer, calls the descendants of Noah's son Magog *Scythians*. So in my mind, what we have here is a leader from Russia whom the Lord tells Ezekiel to set his face against. With me so far?" John asked.

"I know there is more, so yes…"

"'Set your face against Gog of the land of Magog the prince of Rosh, Meshech and Tubal, and prophesy against him, and say; Thus says the Lord God: 'Behold I am against you, Oh Gog, the prince of Rosh, Meshech and Tubal. I will turn you around, put hooks in your jaws and lead you out, with all your army, horses, and horsemen, all splendidly clothed, a great company with bucklers and shields. Persia, Ethiopia, and Libya are with them, all of them with shield and helmet; Gomer and all its troops; the house of Togarmah from the far north, and all its troops—many people are with you.'

"We have a few additional countries to identify and a huge horde of armies set for war. The Lord is going to cause them to come—draw them in."

"The hook in the jaws—like they do with swine."

"Exactly. The first three are obvious, except that territories have changed much in twenty-five hundred years."

"Well, Persia we know," I said. "Iran…"

"Yes, and Libya and Ethiopia are pretty straightforward, but I think that those two made up most of North Africa back then." John added. "Now, some Bible versions use Cush, Put, and Beth Togarmah. Again, names used over the centuries to coincide with modern Turkey, Sudan, Algeria, Syria, Lebanon. You get the idea."

"Yes, essentially the mostly Islamic, anti-Semitic and anti-Israel countries. But what about Egypt and Babylon? Aren't they historic enemies of Israel?" I asked.

"Yes, but they are not mentioned as part of the coalition," John concluded.

"Interesting," I said as I scratch my chin. "Neither are really in a position to come against Israel—Jordan or Saudi Arabia either," I offered.

"That's correct. And when brought into the context of present day, they are not a part of the real, developing group," John added.

"What about Tubal and…what did you say?"

"Cities in the land of Magog. One could narrow it down, I suppose. I think at this point we just have to go with the six to ten coalition countries and match it up with present time."

"I'll go for that—right now. But I am curious. We just may run out of time before it really goes down. What do you suppose the hook in the jaws could be?" I asked.

"Good question. How about a preemptive strike against Iran's nuclear program and Syria's stockpile of chemical weapons?"

"Logical. I'm not sure Israel will wait much longer. The next nuclear test-induced earthquake could be it," I said.

Just then, the screens lit up with alerts and the sat-phone rang. Iran had just fired a test ICBM and it was in-path at that moment. John answered the phone.

"Someone just blew the thing up..." He said.

We were both shaking our heads in disbelief.

chapter

THREE

✡✡✡✡✡✡✡

Our study of Gog and Magog was put on hold as we held our collective breath and furiously began to dissect email and cell phone intercepts out of Iran. I can't tell you much about that, but suffice to say it moved Israel into a Defcon 1 level of preparedness. Israel's short history of war was, if nothing else, consistent. The enemy would gather, building at the borders, trying to act like it was all normal. Preemptive actions helped Israel move quickly and decisively against their foes. None of us expected anything less this time.

As we assembled our reports it became obvious that the coalition was solidifying and focus was pointed directly on the biblical area described. A month previously, Algeria's long-time president, Abdelaziz Bouteflika, had died. Iran now had multiple groups of the IRG moving in for the final take over. The Algerians seemed to side with the Iranians and small rebel groups, funded and armed by the IRG, fought and won several small battles against both ISIS and the Muslim Brotherhood. It appeared that the final key coalition member was now in place.

To say that Israel was now on edge would be putting it lightly. Interestingly enough, Jake our Mossad agent, had a strange confidence about him. In a quiet moment in the bunker, I asked him how he was doing.

"Oh, fine," he responded. "It is all coming together." His smile left little doubt, he was not only familiar with the text in Ezekiel, he was counting on it.

I went ahead and prodded, "What do you mean, Jake? It seems the entire Arab world is coming at your land."

"Yes, as it is foretold. It is quite exciting to me. But I still have concerns. Even with God's protection, many will die. Israel *will* be victorious, but it will come at a high cost."

"Okay, I'll bite. Where is all this foretold?" I asked.

"The Tenach."

This caught me off guard. "The Tenach?"

"Yes, the Jewish Old Testament—Ezekiel to be exact. He was a prophet."

"So what we are seeing is Jewish prophecy?"

"More like world history prophecy. The coming war will shape the end times and bring us closer to Messiah's return."

"You mean Jesus?" I asked.

Jake took a long, hard look at me. We had never talked as openly as this about anything.

"Are you a believer, Jeremy?" He asked.

A pause hung in the air as John and Alex reentered the room

"I guess I need to think about that one," I said quietly.

Jake shook his head in acknowledgment. Both of us knew we had more to discuss.

Our small group was joined by Major Stu Kanaly, our team leader, for a quick debriefing. A flood of sat-phone calls and emails between Iranian president, Hassan Rouhani, and Russian foreign intelligence head Alexi Dimitri had our crew stumped. A brand-new encryption method had been implemented just prior to the launch and teams in the US as well as local intelligence were busy scrambling to break it. What was obvious was that Russia knew of the launch, anticipated a response and was ready for the next step.

The next bit of news was both reassuring and frightening. Israel's state-of-the-art Iron Dome missile system had effectively intercepted and taken out the Intercontinental Ballistic Missile that was headed out to sea for yet another test. The US flotilla just off the coast of Israel and in full readiness hadn't even attempted to lock onto it. Nothing had hit the press, but Benjamin Netanyahu was furious and the evil coalition was, no doubt, aware of this.

Caught up in an ugly civil war, America had reached a point of complacency regarding Israel. Despite the definitive steps by the President to recognize Jerusalem as Israel's capital and the move of the US embassy to the capital city, the US was distracted by its own issues. The show of force was there, but was the resolve of both the President and the people of the US solid or in question? Major Stu promised pizza and beer to the team able to break the new encryption and a major full-scale calamity of epic proportions if we didn't. It also could show America was still in the game if we could solve the riddle. Everyone was on edge. The coalition and the tension was building.

Our crew, at least John and I, had been in this bunker on and off for over a year now. I had been blessed to breeze in and out under two of my aliases. I was about ready to arrange shipping on the huge arms cache posing as Said Imam, my French-Syrian coffee trader alias. I could go into great detail about how the NSA set up multiple layers of cover for these faux people, but then again, I would have to kill you. Suffice it to say that my three most effective were Said Imam, Jeremy Stone, and my heroine, Deandrea Perone. I must say she is a knock-out and totally believable, but I have found myself in more near-compromising positions playing Miss Perone. She even has her own alias, one of Samantha DeVoss, an Egyptian-Indian with a Masters in International Finance from New Delhi University.

Honestly, I amazed myself at how I could pull off such a sham with the level of confidence I did. I had walked up to John two years ago as Sam DeVoss and he had no idea it was me. In fact, he later bragged at how he had made a huge impression on this super-hot Indian lady. I never told him. At the present, operating from Damascus, Deandrea was back-dooring high-end, non-hackable laptops to any Islamic terrorist group who had the money. And of course, that was all of them. Deandrea was a very fickle woman, however, and drove a hard bargain. She (I) purposely tacked on extra costs and minimum unit purchases to weed out the want-to-be terrorists. We were, however, able to get these high-tech wonders into the right hands, but sadly, they were only partially unhackable. Only the NSA had access to their hard drives. We could get the info out, but now we had this new Russian encryption to deal with. Everyone was competing for the high-tech advantage and the stakes were high.

Said Imam left the Damascus Hotel to meet with the Iranian buyer. The shipment was coming, but it had been delayed a bit. The depth of the cover and the trust I had built with my contact, Aharon Hadad, was paying off and I was able to get a clear picture of the evolving timeline. The Iranians had tested the ICBM for two purposes. First, how would the IDF respond and second, how would the US Navy respond? Both were negative and Iran was happy with that. I was confirming, at least in my own mind, the timeline that I had worked out.

My mission done and the contacts made, we settled into the work of the encryption. This is where Jake really shone—well, we all did, but Jake would be the one to crack it. We were able to confirm the purpose of the test, postpone our arms shipment and gain a better sense of the timeline. It was becoming very obvious how patient the Islamic community was when it came to implementation and that they wanted to be sure Israel and America were both toast when they hit.

The civil war had reached its peak just prior to the November elections, and the vice president delivered an impassioned prime-time speech to America. The country was torn apart and many wanted to hear some reassuring words. Anyone who could get to a TV was tuned in. "My fellow Americans. We are on the brink of disaster... Many have been killed, injured and displaced from their homes. Cities, businesses, schools, infrastructure and homes have been decimated. What we have experienced is pure evil. Following the attacks on 911, people flocked to churches and experienced a revival of patriotism not seen since World War II. Sadly, it did not last. What we need now is a resurgence of that Spirit.

My goal today is to interject some sound wisdom from our moral source. This is from the Holy Bible, God's direct words. "If my people who are called by my name will humble themselves and pray and seek my face and turn from their wicked ways, then I will hear from heaven, and will forgive their sin and heal their land." The truth is that when we have experienced disasters of various kinds, from hurricanes, to tornados, to earthquakes, to the attacks on 911, we have bonded and come together. This requires us to put aside our sin, pride, prejudice, hate, and selfishness long enough to deal with the issues at hand. It works amazingly well for a time. Then we go right back to our sin.

From God's words, we can assume that if we can stop sinning and pray, he will forgive and heal. If we sin and do not pray, then he will not. Let's face facts, there are consequences for our sin and efforts to push our Creator away. He can and has brought judgment to our land just as he did in the Bible. We must consider that 911 was just a warning. The civil war, the deadly storms we have experienced, and our division are signs that we will soon suffer huge consequences for our sin. Consider this. The ancient city of Nineveh was warned of impending destruction, and they repented of their evil ways. As a result the great city was spared. The city later reverted back to their sinful ways and ignored God's warning. Twenty years later the city was destroyed. Soon, we will reach that twenty-year milestone in America. We would be wise to consider how we are living our lives and how our actions affect others. God's promises are true and he will pass judgment on us. It is coming.

Let me expand on a key point. The answer to every question, and every problem can be found in the Bible. Simply open it up and God will guide you to all of the answers. We can also pray individually, and collectively as a country, for our needs. It is not too late! I implore you to carefully consider your life and actions. It is a choice each one of us must make."

Washington DC, Miami, St. Louis, and New Orleans had been taken back by the government forces. Detroit, New York, Seattle, and Houston were basically wastelands, burned to the ground in most of the downtown areas and abandoned. No one wanted to go back in for any reason. Los Angeles, Chicago, San Francisco, and Phoenix, who joined after a flood of Central and South Americans poured in to take up the cause, were all war zones. Most of the Phoenix combatants were cartel members that had been deported by the government forces.

Every law-abiding citizen in all of those cities was long gone, moved out to small towns away from the chaos. Everyone had underestimated the size and ferocity of the combatants on both sides. The civilian death toll as of Christmas was 62,870 with another 200,000 injured. Of those, 2,619 were law enforcement losses. There were to be no winners in these battles and the entire country had paid a huge price. Before the end of the war and the last bullet was fired in, of all places, Compton, California, another 5,230 civilians would die. Yes, the militants were gone, but the morality of the country seemed to be locked in a free fall. Loss of real property was in the trillions and all of the insurance companies were bankrupt. Rebuilding the fallen cities would simply not be a priority.

The great second civil war of America ended two years and fourteen days after the first shots were fired in Detroit. We all agreed that America would never recover and had only hurt itself in the process. If Iran, Russia, China, Japan, or North Korea had designs of taking us down, the United States was prime for the taking. Equally, if not more, importantly was the fact that we were left impotent, broken and even more divided. A presidential election was held amid protests from the Democratic Party. With the cities in chaos, their constituents would be severely disenfranchised. Despite legal challenges, the President claimed victory and another term.

As we watched the president speak of victory over lawlessness from the blackened shell of Trump Tower, evil of a far more serious kind was brewing on our video feeds and intercepts. The Ezekiel coalition was now complete and ready to move. While we worked frantically to expose more details of the coalition's plans, John and I studied the chapters verse by verse for any hidden clues.

"So we are pretty sure we have the Gog coalition set," John said. "Iran has full control of Syria, Libya, and Algeria, Russia's influence over Turkey, Lebanon, Yemen, and the rest of Northern Africa completes the group. The UN is firmly on the side of Palestine, with the former president's puppet Lech Manevetski about to be sworn in and no fewer than a hundred anti-Israel resolutions on record."

"Yes, and the US is pretty much impotent," I add.

"Well, the prophecy is clear about one thing," John said. "No one but God Himself will come to the defense of Israel. I would say the timing is just about perfect."

"The scene is set, the actors dressed and in position, and the curtain is about to go up."

"So any time now?" John asked.

I had never disclosed my thoughts on the date to anyone. I had been looking for any intercepts that would lend specifics to a time frame. One thing was clear, the Russians and the Iranians wanted Israel to think it was coming at any moment. Of course, I wouldn't be surprised if Jake and the Mossad were holding back critical data. Given the state of America, who could blame them. John and I had both considered the possibility of getting the axe. Then again, it was entirely possible that no one except for an elite handful of insiders at NSA knew we existed and how we were funded.

I suspected that it was the enormous profit from the computers, sat-phones, and illegal arms deals that created the revenue for our meager salaries and outrageous bonuses.

"John, do you think the Mossad is holding cards?" I asked in earnest.

"No doubt. Wouldn't you? I mean, the US cannot really be an asset in this."

"So you think the Mossad reads Ezekiel?"

"I know it. I know they are busy praying to the God of Abraham right now. Some in the agency are expecting God to tell them when to set the hook in the jaw."

"I always thought it would be a response based on a test or confirmed, rock-solid intel. Isn't that more logical?" I ask.

"To a non-believer…yes…"

My look was crestfallen, but he was right. I didn't even know what it would be like to be a true believer.

"Don't worry chameleon, God knows your true identity and He needs to call you. I would pray about it and keep reading."

I paused. Had he read my mind?

"Gift of discernment, my Jewish friend."

I about fell out of my chair. Only my father and step-mother knew the truth about me. I said nothing.

John knew it was a good time to change the subject. "Let's dive into Ezekiel further. We see God instructing through the prophet: 'Get ready; be prepared. Keep all the armies around you mobilized and take command of them.'"

"I think the coalition's armies are ready, don't you?" I offered.

"No doubt. Now look at what's next: 'A long time from now you will be called into action.'"

"It's been about twenty-five hundred years, I guess that equates to a long time," I added laughing.

John continued, "'In the latter years you will swoop down on the land of Israel, which will be enjoying peace and recovering after its people have returned from many lands to the mountains of Israel.' Okay, let's try to unpack that..."

"Okay, John, but I have a thought."

"What?"

"I believe we need to get Jake involved in our discussion."

John looked surprised, but broke easily. "You're right. I too am becoming a little unnerved by our location—Isaiah 17 and all."

"Affirmative. I believe he may be the only real way out of here." We both smiled, but not from joy. I think more out of desperation.

chapter

FOUR
✡✡✡✡✡✡✡

J ake, John and I sat in control room 6 in the joint NSA-Mossad bunker located in Damascus, Syria. Even though we were well outside of the city limits, a hundred feet underground and without a doubt unknown to the outside world, we all had that uncomfortable feeling. With my increased knowledge of Bible text and prophecy coming to life in front of me, I was seeing things from a completely new perspective. I hoped that in today's rare time the three of us could spend together, we could quell, to a degree, my angst.

Both John and I wanted to tread lightly based on Jake's faith and the simple fact that he worked for the Mossad. Allies, yes. In reality, we were two countries with common enemies yet unique perspectives of war. For Israel, this was life or death. Surrounded by their enemies and squarely in the cross-hairs of this new coalition, the next war could very well be their final war. Of course, we had another connection—John and Jake were both born-again Christians. Well, Jake was a Messianic Jew, but still a Christ-follower. I was on the outside and looking for more direction, despite a huge tug on my heart.

John broke the ice. "Jake, what is your view of Isaiah 17?"

A safe Old Testament question, I reasoned.

"Any moment now," Jake stated without expressing a bit of concern.

"Can we survive it?" John asked.

"Initially, yes. Long-term, no. Six months to a year, depending on how many are here at the time. But that really isn't the issue."

"What is?" I asked.

"What would we be surviving for? The prophecy is clear—gone. The entire city—gone!"

"Fair enough," John chimed in. "What about Ezekiel 38, 39?"

Jake took a moment to assess. He knew I wasn't a believer and I was pretty sure he knew John was. He also knew our time was in days, not years. He decided to press on.

"There is no question—we are there. Just waiting for the first move," Jake said.

"Which is?" I ask.

"First strike—retaliation to the next Khorram—shahr launch or a big earthquake. I think Israel has to go on either."

"What about the new Thaad Anti Ballistic Missile systems? Won't the IDF want to see them tested first? With all the test launches we've had, it may pay to see it in action," John said.

"Oh, we'll see it in action all right. And they already know the Arrow III and Iron Dome are solid, even with these new course-changing ballistic missiles. We just witnessed its effectiveness." Jake added.

"What about the whole 'God' thing, Jake?" I asked.

"God's purpose in all this is clearly stated. After this the nations will know Him. Israel will be outnumbered, surrounded, facing long odds for survival, and no country will step up to help. It's a million to one proposition with Israel on the short end of those odds. Except for one thing."

"And that is?" I asked.

"The 'to one' is God. We are told of His purpose, His victory, His dealing with the armies, the leaders, the governments of Israel's foes. I am convinced there will be little left of Islam, countries that support radical Islam, and all the combatants in the Magog war," Jake stated solemnly.

"Including Syria—and more precisely the city of Damascus?" John asked.

"Yes. Russia and Iran have both invested heavily in Syria. Then, there is the chemical weapons component." Jake added.

There was a long pause.

"Then what?" I asked.

"Well, Israel prevails. But like all our wars, Jews will be lost—perhaps in big numbers," Jake said with a grimace.

"Does this open the door for the next round of prophecies?" John asked.

"Such as?" Jake responded.

"Daniel's seventieth week, the antichrist, the two witnesses, Armageddon?"

"I believe so. Let's look at the aftermath of Ezekiel's prophecy, keeping in mind that Ezekiel 40 and on is about the Kingdom."

"The Millennial Kingdom?" I asked.

"One in the same," John said.

"I would agree," Jake added. "So, let's go back to Ezekiel 38 and 39. Can you read it John?"

"And it will come to pass at the same time, when Gog comes against the land of Israel," says the Lord God, "that My fury will show in My face. For in My jealousy and in the fire of My wrath I have spoken: 'Surely in that day there shall be a great earthquake in the land of Israel, so that the fish of the sea, the birds of the heavens, the beasts of the field, all creeping things that creep on the earth, and all men who are on the face of the earth shall shake at My presence. The mountains shall be thrown down, the steep places shall fall, and every wall shall fall to the ground.' I will call for a sword against Gog throughout all My mountains," says the Lord God.

"And you, son of man, prophesy against Gog, and say, 'Thus says the Lord God: "Behold, I am against you, O Gog, the prince of Rosh, Meshech, and Tubal; and I will turn you around and lead you on, bringing you up from the far north, and bring you against the mountains of Israel. Then I will knock the bow out of your left hand, and cause the arrows to fall out of your right hand. You shall fall upon the mountains of Israel, you and all your troops and the peoples who are with you; I will give you to birds of prey of every sort and to the beasts of the field to be devoured. You shall fall on the open field; for I have spoken," says the Lord God.

Ezekiel 38:18-21; 39:2-5

"Okay, we have an earthquake—a big one that causes the hordes to turn on themselves. Terror will ensue on all sides—even the animals and the fish of the sea will quake in terror. He will disarm the arrows. I have to believe it means rockets and missiles will fail, or fall back on the attackers. I also assume that the Israeli defenses, the IDF, the Iron Dome, and the Arrow will all do their jobs," Jake explained.

"Still, thousands or even hundreds of thousands of Israelis could perish," John added.

"Okay, I missed something. What do you believe is the 'hook in the jaws'?" I asked.

Jake was thinking, having to backtrack his thoughts. "Preemptive strikes on Iran's facilities, bases, leadership, and Syrian stockpiles of chemical weapons. We know where they are and that they have been moving them into Lebanon and the Sinai. We have been surrounded for several years," Jake sighed.

"Yes, and the chapter 39 references are indicative of chemical or even local nuclear weapons," John added.

"I do believe Israel will wait until the last minute, as they did in Iraq, to try to avoid civilian casualties and then go full in with a pre-emptive strike." Jake said emphatically.

"The hook in the jaw. That will draw them out, but we all know Israel can't take all the weapons out on a first strike."

"Not without the US. Even then, President Trump would be reluctant to go preemptive. It's very risky. The world would condemn them."

"Okay, Jake. I agree with all that. When?" I asked.

"Jeremy, we need to keep an eye on Sulaman."

"Qussam Sulaman, the commander of the Iranian Republican Guard?" I asked.

"Yes, he is the key. He is a twelver and reports directly to Kahmenei," Jake added.

"He's not supposed to be allowed out of Iran, but our operatives have tracked as many as six high-level meetings in Russia where he was flown by a private jet," Jake said.

My mind was racing. What was a twelver and how did that fit into the timing of the war? Could the Magog war have a far deeper meaning on the Islamic side? Questions were going off like light bulbs and I was beginning to feel a little uncomfortable in Damascus.

"Jake, where did Sulaman fly and who did he meet with?" I asked.

"Let me pull up the map…" Jake went to the computer and pecked away. "Roslavl, an airport located in a small town with the same name. It is situated half way between Moscow and Minsk, forty-five miles from the Belarus border."

There was a pause as he stared at the screen.

"Wait a minute," Jake said, snapping his fingers, "remember Sergey Kisylak, the Russian Ambassador to the US?"

"Yes, he died in New York shortly after Trump took office," John chimed in.

"The very one. He has a home near this airport. A very nice summer home that is often used by the Kremlin elites. It's in a tiny, obscure province called…Rosh."

"Prince of Rosh. Sulaman was meeting with the Prince of Rosh! Who is the prince of Rosh?" I asked.

Now we were fired up. None of us felt that Putin could be Gog. But what about a puppet master, Putin's secret boss—an Oligarch in the shadows?

"It makes sense," Jake says, "But could Kisylak's death be related? Perhaps there was friction between Putin and this guy."

Jake was busy typing. "Here it is; it gives his KGB name: Yuri Ovetchkin, age sixty-six."

Now we were all standing behind Jake, looking at a picture of this guy.

"He doesn't look evil," I say.

THE ARMIES OF GOG

Jake and John both looked at me with that sideways look. We were on to something—we may have found the Prince of Rosh.

"So what do we know about Yuri Ovetchkin?" I asked.

"Wait, wait, wait!" Jake said. "Do you remember that Uranuim 1 deal?"

"The US sold uranium to Russia on the former president's watch. HC was Secretary of State. The deal was investigated and buried." John added.

"Yes, but we know the real story, and it was likely hatched at Kisylak's summer home near Roslavl. One of Sulaman's illegal visits."

"That's right Jeremy, and it likely accelerated the Iranian nuclear program exponentially."

"I wonder what the Mossad knows?"

John and I stared down Jake who was not flinching.

"I know nothing, but we are likely to see another test, and soon…"

"So what's next?" I asked.

"You need to confess Jesus in your heart, Jeremy. You can't afford to wait," Jake said.

"Now wait a minute. John said God would call me."

"And he hasn't?" John asked.

"Well, yes—a little. But I don't feel ready. Besides, we have time."

Both Jake and John snapped looks at me.

"What do you know about the timing, Jeremy?" Jake asked.

"I have a theory, that's all. From a spy's perspective. I'll share it with you, right after you tell me what a twelver is."

John headed for the coffee pot. It would be a long night. While John and I did NSA work, Jake set out to research Yuri Ovetchkin and shed some light on the relationship with Qussam Sulaman of the IRGC.

This former KGB agent was cut out of the mold of Vladimir Putin. But Putin was a dove, a moderate compared to this guy. Ovetchkin was a hardline communist who wanted the glory days back for Russia. With changes at the UN, the US in disarray, and Israel gone, he could almost tie a ribbon on his scheme.

From the time the former president left office, he had been working his way into global politics, first doing a binge-talk circuit pushing globalization, equality, and peace. He had been a lefty poster-child and, even more importantly, an American apologist. No one except him, his dead financier Gregory Boros, and his new-found protege Lech Manevetski knew what he was up to. It would all become very evident soon. His sway in the United Nations had virtually all the nations leaning left. It all sounded good: peace, disarmament, equal justice for all, wealth redistribution, and elimination of contentious religions which had little value in the modern world.

Sadly, only Christians, true Bible believers, saw through his phony talks and resisted. The world was headed where God knew it had to go. Practically the day the former president had left office, he was stirring up trouble for Trump and working his way into the ranks of the UN leadership. The UN saw him as a natural fit for their world agenda, so they welcomed him in and gave him a platform. He was now the forerunner.

Waiting in the wings was a man that could sway the world and fulfill prophecy. It had to come and it was slowly evolving. His name was Lech Manevetski. And as soon as he made his first public appearance, it was all but a foregone conclusion—Lech Manevetski was the Antichrist foretold in the Bible.

Jerusalem: Time of Jacob's Trouble

My thoughts were suddenly interrupted by the sound of the metal knife-edge meeting yet another Christian throat. I swallowed hard, yet refused to look down the line toward the ungodly machine. I should have known I could be caught and killed. I wouldn't be lucky enough to live through the tribulation and see Jesus come in my fleshly body. But I would be coming back with Him and enjoy what I had discovered to be the greatest event to occur in history prior to His return. That would be the Marriage Supper of the Lamb. The blade would only be for an instant, but my life in heaven was eternal—a solid trade off, I thought.

Barring some miraculous rescue in the next thirty minutes, I could count on the white robe and the heavenly feast. Tanner, my good friend and accomplice since the disappearances, had preceded me to heaven by just two days, a spectacular shootout on the streets of Jerusalem. I counted him as the lucky one, a bullet to the forehead. No changing all of that now. Even so, I was looking for a way out.

chapter
FIVE
✡✡✡✡✡✡✡

"Islam has two major sects," John explained. "The largest group are the Sunni and they inhabit Iraq, Egypt, Syria, Yemen, and much of Northern Africa. The Shiite are found in most every country as the minority, except in Iran which is 89 percent Shia. Each has its own eschatology and holy sites. They also share some historical sites like Mecca, Medina, and Jerusalem. ISIS is a mix of these two with a lot of extremism thrown in. Their goal is to form the Caliphate, or a world-wide jihad against infidels—convert or die."

John took a sip of coffee and Jake began, "The Caliphate is key to ushering in the return of the Islamic Messiah, the twelfth imam, also known as the Mahdi. The Mahdi will return when the world is cleansed of infidels. Also, according to Islamic eschatology, Jesus will return with the Mahdi, but will subordinate all power to Mahdi and proclaim Islam as the true religion. Within the Shia leadership is a group of men called Twelvers—followers of the Twelvth Imam who is considered the equivalent of the Christian Messiah. These men are set apart to facilitate the removal of the satans—that is, Israel and the US—who have been the biggest deterrents to Islam's world domination. Others, like France, Germany, and the UK have been sufficiently infiltrated and are ready to fall. For the US and Israel, a massive jihad is needed. This is why the Twelvers exist and why the coalition exists. It is a logical first step to the world wide Caliphate," Jake concluded.

John picked it back up, "The reason Islam has so many conflicting sects—the Kurds, the Houthies, ISIS, al Qaeda—is that they simply can't get along or agree on anything. Each seems to have its own ideas about how to pave the way for the end times. The one thing they have in common is the Koran, and even that and its teachings are splintered. You could say that about Christian sects as well," John concluded.

"I believe that all of Islam is, to a degree, perverted from Muhammad's original writings. You know, it is easy to attach our own skewed views and stray from what the original intent of the writings infer. It is also the most logical reason that all the various factions of Islam exist, for fifteen hundred years the Muslims have been at war with each other. They need something to bring them together. The Jews have only been a small sore to them. Now they are an island of God's will that is opposed to Islam. The end result is fireworks," Jake explained.

About that time, alerts filled the screens and alarms broke our conversation. It was another missile launch, this time from North Korea. Despite the extensive talks between the president and North Korea to disarm and make peace, Kim Jong Un was a wild card in all of this and the US had done its best to build a political barrier of sorts between the North and South. Thankfully South Korea approved and installed the newest Thaad system provided by the US and many of the South Koreans were cheering when the Thaad went into action. The sophisticated BPI (Boost Phase Intercept) system detected the launch and destroyed it just forty seconds into its flight—during the boost phase.

We watched in awe as the news coverage rolled on. The new South Korean President, Lo Yan Ing, had not hesitated to launch a counter-measure to Pyong Yang's brazen test. Of course, the testing wasn't new, but the missile was—a newly designed Pho-Yang MBS which could, theoretically, avoid anti-missle technology. Well, it seemed the test was a success for South Korea as the Thaad BPI system functioned just as it was supposed to. It was not only a success at proving the Thaad effective, but it was a huge political victory as well. Deployment of the Thaad system had not only been shunned, it seemed that no one wanted it anywhere near their city, town, or village.

Finally, a farmer on the northern border welcomed the system and donated the land. At first, every country was angry at the US. Our allies and North Korea were mad, China was mad, Japan was torqued, the Philippines, Vietnam, and India were mad. And Russia was angry at all of them and us. But to us in the bunker, it was laughable. The Thaad system was unproven, yet did its job. In fact, it was so quick and precise that much of the debris landed in North Korea, killing hundreds of civilians. The US at least for now had been vindicated.

"Being evil has consequences…" stated John as we watched the coverage. It was obvious that the Pho-Yang was a promising new technology that had promised avoidance of anti-missile batteries. And fortunately the Chinese, who had sold the technology and much of the components, would be back to the drawing board. Even they had discouraged the rebel leader from a premature launch.

Probably the only ones who were smiling after the launch was Israel. Thaad had just proven itself and the Iron Dome system was equally effective on short-range incoming missiles. It had to be a bit of light as the darkness closed in around them. As the Syrian civil war raged on above us, none of us were very comfortable. It took about three months for the intel to die down enough for us to have our next in-depth discussion.

It was Shavout, also known as the Christian Pentecost, and the Jews were gathering in Jerusalem for the festival which had been celebrated in one form or another for over three thousand years. Tensions were high and friction from the recent annexation of the Golan Heights back into Israel was still grating on the Palestinians and Hamas. None of the big players in the coalition were happy, but it simply wasn't time yet. Of course, Israel could only view its preparedness one way—they had to be ready 100 percent of the time.

Saturday morning, the Sabbath and a time of gathering in Jerusalem, was the opportunity Hamas had been waiting for. On their own, they launched hundreds of Russian-made missiles at Tel Aviv and Jerusalem. It was chaos as IDF F-22s launched a counter-attack on the launch sites and the Iron Dome AMD's kicked in. Waves and waves of Katushas and Kassam missiles rained down over Israel and as the anti-missile banks were reloaded, a few stray rockets got through. It seemed God stepped in and they fell short of their desired targets.

The assault was a precursor to the future pounding Israel would face, but for now they held their own and managed to infuriate the Hamas fighters. The IDF F-22s had a field day wiping out launch batteries as they became exposed. "Aggression has consequences," John would later say. As if nothing happened, the festival of Pentecost went forward with hundreds of thousands of Jews worshiping in the Holy City.

"I almost expected the two witnesses to show up..." said Jake.

"What are you talking about?" I asked.

"Time for another lesson," Jake announced.

With that and a fresh pot of coffee, we gathered for another lesson on Ezekiel 38 and 39.

"Okay, so we see Israel living in relative peace in unwalled cities. This is another confirmation that it is an end-times prophecy. Walled cities were a requirement until the late 1600s," John says, "and while Israel deals with rockets and terrorist attacks, they are not at war—at least not now."

"We also see the intent of the invading forces to take booty, to strip the nation of its resources," Jake adds. "We know that Israel has amazing nuclear weapons and nuclear power technologies. But we also know the real reason: the Arabs want Israel done so that Palestine can have its own land and Islam can claim victory over the little Satan... the first step. They also want Jerusalem as their exclusive holy place, with no sign of the Jews remaining. The ultimate victory in the Islamic mindset is Allah winning out over the god of the infidels."

"I never mentioned a date, but I have come to some conclusions in my own mind."

"Let's hear it, Mr. Stone," Jake said.

"Back in 2009, Mahmoud Ahmadinejad, Iran's president, spoke to a UN audience in New York City and said the Iranians would light up the sky over Israel and show the capabilities of the Iran nuclear program on August 22. He didn't mention a year. I think that was on purpose, but it was the highlight of his rant against Israel."

"So you think August 22 is the day?" Jake asked.

"Well, we would need to see it on an Islamic calendar, but it is a significant date. It is thought to be the date of Muhammad's night journey from Makkah to the farthest mosque in Jerusalem. The date would have broad significance."

"Yes, I remember now. That is a key date and a fitting event to launch a knock-out punch," Jake said.

"Still, something must draw them out. Could easily be this year or next, or even a dozen years from now." Jake added.

"Do you recall God sent Jonah to warn the people of Nineveh and they repented? Twenty years later—gone!" I say emphatically. "I believe 9/11 was our warning."

"I don't see the connection," John said.

"I spent some time last night studying the warning to Nineveh by Jonah and it's ultimate destruction twenty years later. It is clear that God is a compassionate and caring creator. He shows respect for life in the people and the animals. But He is not your Uncle Joe who winks and says 'boys will be boys'. He instead, offers a stern warning and an opportunity to leave the folly and come back into His will. You see, Nineveh, like Sodom before it, was the complete antithesis of what God desires for us. Jonah delivered this message, although reluctantly—He could see their ways and felt they deserved the wrath of God.

Twenty years—He gave them twenty years and then, done. He is a loving God but a just God who sees the perverting influences of a nation and has no choice but to step in. We are certainly there. We were adequately warned on 9/11. Next is the judgment.

Islam sees the US as the big Satan, the source of all perversion in the world.

"Strike the big Satan—leave them impotent, then crush the little Satan while the big Satan is weak. God has the timing, Nineveh is just an example of the timeline," I say.

"It is true," John added, "that all the answers to our questions can be found in the Bible."

"Plus, it feels close. August 22 and any year now. Like 9/11, it has meaning all the way around. Nothing is by coincidence in God's will…" Jake said.

"So we have a year, maybe two, and sometime around August 22, we could see something—an earthquake, Iran doing something provocative?" John asked.

"That's the way I see it right now," I said.

"It's also not actionable intelligence. It's just a guess, albeit a very good one," Jake added.

"I'm not sure how much more Israel can take of the constant barrage of rockets," I said. "I guess when the rockets stop, that's when Israel should worry?"

"Could be a good indicator. Hamas won't want to use up their inventory close to attack time," Jake added.

"Now, when are we doing the delivery of the weapons cache?" John asked.

"Delivery date will be June 8. We are all going in and we should get some good intel. We will be delivering into the belly of the beast," I said.

"Who's we?" John asked.

"You, me, Jake, Alex, Biggs, and Rolf. Six in all—me and my delivery team. It's to a warehouse in Tehran."

"Sounds sticky. What kind of backup do we have?" Jake asked.

"Working that out now, but at least one stealth drone and a deeply implanted extraction team."

"Sounds thin—razor thin," John says with a grimace.

"It is razor thin. But we have one thing that cannot be gauged or undervalued. It is the same power the nation of Israel has been protected by all these years. And even if we fail, our destination is determined—or at least, *ours* is..." John said, glancing at me.

"I know, I know. I need Jesus in my life," I say.

"You have Jesus in your life. You need him in your heart," Jake said.

"Amen, Brother!" John added.

"Besides, none of our missions are ever routine. We have it hanging out there all the time. We're not exactly safe, even in this well-protected bunker. So between now and June 8, we need to be praying for God's will in our lives," Jake said.

"Good call. Now, back to the study," I said.

"The rest of chapter 38 is an overview of God's sovereign protection and deliverance of Israel. It also says He will rain down on Gog and his troops—great hailstones, fire, and brimstone. They will have no chance," Jake said.

"And then God restates His purpose—'to magnify Myself and sanctify Myself.' What does that mean exactly?" I asked.

"To prepare or set apart for holy use. He is showing the nations His power, sovereignty, and protection of His chosen people. Also, sanctify means to establish union with Christ by faith. His stepping in will be a 'sign' to the nations," John said.

"And a clear message to those unbelievers. His actions will deal with the Jews and the enemies of Israel. Remember Jesus' words in

Luke 13:34: 'Jerusalem, how I wanted to gather you like a hen gathers her chicks under her wings, but you would not!'" Jake added.

"Wow, what a perfect metaphor for God's love for the Jews," I said.

"Yes, Jeremy, and for you!" Jake concluded.

There was a long pause as that painful yet accurate volley hit me right between the eyes. I could feel in my heart that Jesus was talking to me, through the Word, through these men, and through my life experiences. My being in this room with these men, one a Jew like me, one a Gentile believer, was part of my education. Slowly, I guess because of my Jewish heritage, I was being trained. My mind went back to boot camp, weapons training, endless hours on the range, PT's, hours of classroom and tech training, even the hand to hand combat and martial arts. I was in a whole new training and I hadn't even decided what side I was fighting for in this spiritual war.

"The important thing is that Jesus knows," John said in a soft voice as he laid a hand on my shoulder. This man and I had gone through hell together, special ops missions, near-death experiences, more than I wanted to remember. But he was showing me what I really needed. "Obstinate and stiff-necked", that is what Moses had called the Jews. I was that, with the Palestinian stubbornness thrown in. If this man, this Word, and these circumstances could not change me, what could?

"I think we need more coffee..." Jake stated as he headed out the door.

"Don't worry, Stone...your heart may be made of it, but God can soften even the hardest stones. He can even turn them into bread, the bread of life!" He flashed me a reassuring smile and suddenly, the coffee sounded like a good idea. Jake came in with our three cups and my favorite add-in: Italian sweet cream.

"I thought this may cheer you up. Nothing like a little Syrian coffee and Italy's sweetness…" Jake said with a smile.

"So God magnifies Himself among the nations and deals with Israel's enemies the same way he dealt with Nineveh, Sodom, and Gomorrah. It will be ugly," John said.

"Yes, and there is much more valuable detail in chapter 39. So let's go there," Jake added. "God begins 39 with words to Ezekiel: 'Prophecy against Gog.' Then he adds this: 'Then I will knock the bow out of your left hand and cause the arrows to fall out of your right hand.' I suppose that means He will disarm Gog's armies prior to them shooting their 'arrows'. Could be they have a few of those shoulder-launched RPG's that Jeremy sold them. What was the guarantee on those, Stone?" John said jokingly.

"Guaranteed not to work—just as designed." I said. We all laughed.

"I sure hope they don't want a field demo when we deliver them…" Jake added.

"Oh, we have a couple of good crates, just in case," I said.

"Look what God tells Ezekiel next: 'I will give you to birds of prey of every sort and to the beasts of the field to be devoured.' He must be talking about those packs of hyenas that have been multiplying east of the Jordan," John said.

"Then He confirms it, as only God can—His stamp of assurance, if you will: 'For I have spoken, says the Lord God.'" Jake concluded.

"Now we see detail on God's judgment of Gog: 'And I will send fire on Magog and on those who live in security in the coastlands.

Then they will know that I am the Lord.' For what purposes? 'To make His holy name known in the midst of My People, Israel, and I will not let them profane My Name anymore.' Do you realize that Israel as a nation is something like 90 percent secular? They have forgotten God!" Jake exclaimed. "My people have forgotten God in a single generation since He so graciously returned them to their land."

"That He gave them and then restored!" I added.

"Again, He confirms it: 'Surely it is coming, and it shall be done, says the Lord God. This is the day of which I have spoken,'" John read.

"Now this is where it gets a little weird. We see clues here to the type of battle and armaments that are used," Jake says.

"'Then those who dwell in the cities of Israel will go out and set on fire and burn the weapons, both the shields and bucklers, the bows and arrows, the javelins and spears, and they will make fires with them for seven years.' First, we must realize that the prophet is describing here the tools of the trade of war in 580 BC. He would have no way to understand guns, grenades, RPGs, and the like. But still, it is odd that they would use them as fuel," John commented.

"Yes, and as you read on, it's like the weapons are used for heat and cooking—as fuel—no need to cut trees or even go into the forest. Odd. But there may be an explanation. Back in the eighties, a man in the Netherlands invented a product called Lignastone, a plywood-like laminated composite that is formed under tremendous pressure. The result is a light wood-like product that is machineable and very dense. Like carbon fiber, or Kevlar, the composite design creates a super strong material that can be used as armor on tanks, hum-vee's, and soldier's helmets. It can also be substituted for metal in guns, knives, grenades, and rockets. It is stealthy, can pass through the x-ray, and can't be picked up by metal detectors or on radar."

"The Russians began using the product as tank and vehicle armor. When they perfected Lignastone guns, they bought the factory and moved it to Moscow. Since the company was small and the Russians acted quickly, they went dark with it. It is suspected that much of their modern weaponry and armor is Lignastone," I contributed.

"Well, they did a good job. Mossad knows little about this, especially about the origin," Jake added. "Thank you for that tidbit, Jeremy."

"Here is the most interesting part. The one unique characteristic of Lignastone is that it burns better, hotter, and longer than coal," I added.

"Wow! That would explain a lot…" John said.

"Okay, so Lignastone is a possible explanation to that one. This must have had commentators scratching their heads for fifteen hundred years," Jake said.

"At least…" I added, "And the coffee is first-rate, thank you Jake…"

"They will also plunder and pillage. I assume that means they will commandeer all their tanks, vehicles, airplanes, etc. But bigger than that, I believe Israel will take their land, like they have every war since they came back into the nation," John said.

"And I believe they will need it because it says in verse 27 that He is gathering all His people back from their enemies' lands—that is a lot of people. Jews from all over the world will return to the Promised Land. But I am getting ahead," I said.

"Yes," Jake chimed in, "We still have a lot to cover regarding the clean up after the war and the parallels to the final war—Armageddon,"

Jake stated excitedly. It was clear that all of us were getting caught up in this great and swift victory, delivered by the Lord.

"Before our shift ends, let me point out a big item, then we can pick it up tomorrow. Look at verse 21: 'I will set My glory among the nations; all the nations will see My judgment which I have executed, and My hand which I have laid on them.' Guys, God wants the world to *see*. This is one of only two places in the Bible where it says *see* rather than *hear*. How else but by worldwide satellite coverage could the world see this event happen? The world will see it and the world will recognize the miracle that only God is capable of—simply amazing…" Jake concluded with a deep sigh.

It had been an amazing day of discovery and I felt closer to God than I ever had. It wasn't a bond yet, but I could feel His power and His grace. I knew, just like John and Jake knew, that this event would be transformational, yet the least of those transformed would be the Jews.

chapter
SIX
✡ ✡ ✡ ✡ ✡ ✡ ✡

O ur off-time at the bunker consisted of emails from our superiors and intel updates. It left me lots of time to ponder my life as a Jew, my life as a Palestinian, and my life as an American. It all led me back to the Bible and various passages that were being revealed to me. John told me it was hard for Arabs and Jews to accept Jesus as God. And the testimonies I found posted online supported that. For Muslims, it was visions of Christ in bizarre moments that changed their minds. For Jews, it was appearances of Moses or Elijah who swayed them. I wondered how it would happen for me.

I kept being led to Romans 10:9: "If you confess with your mouth that Jesus is Lord and you believe in your heart God raised Him from the dead, you will be saved." Could it be that easy? It wasn't for me. I was still waiting for the vision or Moses. Would I know him?

I got a message from John: "Oh, I forgot to tell you the difference between the Magog war and the Armageddon events. There are several differentiating keys. First, Magog is a coalition of specific countries against Israel. Armageddon is the entire world coming against Jesus. Second, there are clearly at least seven years after the war of Magog. After Armageddon, only the millennial Kingdom follows. Next, Magog is fought on the borders while Armageddon is in Jerusalem and on the plain or valley of Megiddo, also known as the Jezreel valley. There is more, but that is a start. Goodnight, buddy."

I thought about that for a moment, logged it in, and pondered my love life, or lack of it. I lingered on Stephanie Skater, my high school sweetheart whom I loved but never was good at showing. Steph was tall, slender, cute as a button, and a great kisser. Boy, would I give an arm and a leg for a Steph kiss! NSA agents are not reliable or consistent in any way, and not what any decent woman would be interested in. On this last assignment, I hadn't spoken to my folks in nearly seven months. Yep, my love life was a total loss with no chance for a win. But still, Steph was on my mind and I had to smile.

As my thoughts lingered on what could have been, I was reminded of the present reality. My stepmother had been a strong influence in my life. She had done her best to keep me grounded in some bit of faith. I felt a pull to my Jewish roots and a strong attraction to Jesus. I knew it was no accident that John was my best friend and a strong Christian. Jake was now also a strong influence on the Jewish side. As he explained in detail, the Messianic Jews had a special place in Judaism and in Christianity. But as he had explained, Heshem, which is how he referred to the Father God (it means "The Name"), was dedicated to each of us in His own special way through His Son. As John had explained it; "Jesus' church is a church of one, just you and Jesus in close relationship. We are abiding in Him, walking in His light where there is no darkness. Each of us yoked equally with Him. When we gather as a group it is fellowship between individuals of one accord, all uniquely connected to our Savior.

With the end of days bearing down on us, we all felt the division between the lost and the saved—the wheat and the tares, the sheep and the goats. We had all been allowed to exist together in this melting pot of the world. Yes, Israel was back in the land and God would deal with the Jews, as promised in Daniel's "seventieth week". I needed to get a lesson on that. He would also deal with the churches. I knew that the final book in the Bible, the Revelation of Jesus Christ, was the apostle John's way of communicating to us the end times. It appears he addresses the churches, and then moves on to deal with Antichrist and the events of the great tribulation. The church is gone early in John's account—I assume by way of the Rapture, God removing His elect prior to chaos. I needed sleep before our next work session, but there was no way. I opened the Bible and it fell open to Matthew 1.

I had always been fascinated by the Hebrew names. Now, I was looking at the genealogy of Jesus Christ, the son of David, the son of Abraham. "Abraham begot Isaac." The father of the Jews, the man who stepped out in faith, had a son, Isaac. That was a true miracle in itself, Abraham being a century old and Sarah being ninety. Then the long list of men and women bearing sons until it came to Jacob, who begot Joseph, the husband of Mary, of whom was born Jesus who is called Christ. I suddenly realized that God had orchestrated all of this so that Jesus could be born the Son of David, the son of Abraham, descending from the Jewish patriarchs.

But why did I need to know this? There was a reference note: Luke 3:23–38. I went there. Another genealogy, this one by Luke, and very different from Matthew's. It was reversed from Matthew's version, beginning with Jesus, the son of Joseph, and back to Abraham—and beyond. Luke's account went all the way back to Adam. I read through the names and recognized many from Matthew's account. "Why so different?" I asked myself. For some reason, I needed to know. Then I slept like a baby and woke up refreshed. I was anxious to hear what my two friends had to say about the Matthew and Luke genealogies.

The first two hours of our shift were frantic. We had a flurry of intercepts and only time for coffee. It was becoming obvious, at least to the three of us, it was all coming and soon. A huge breakfast was delivered and Alex was called to another control room. We had our lesson opportunity. Each of us had spent some time in the Bible the night previous and had revelations of sorts to share. I was chomping at the bit and they graciously allowed me to go. They both had a lot to share on the genealogies of Matthew and Luke.

Jake began, "Well, you see, Matthew was a Jew writing to a primarily Jewish audience. The entire concept of Jesus was new to the Jews. His family tree begins with Abraham, the father of the Jews. Every one of these men and women in Jesus' line were meaningful to the Jews. Abraham, Isaac, Jacob, Joseph, Tamar, Rahab, David, Solomon, Uzziah, Hezekiah, Josiah. All had played major roles in Israel's history. The gospel of Matthew was written by Levi, the tax collector and Jesus' disciple. His account was first hand, first person, walking with and being ministered to by Jesus Himself.

"Matthew would have known the value of connecting the patriarchs, kings, and leaders all the way to Jesus. You see, God raised up Abraham to raise up Israel to raise up Jesus. The Jews world began with Abraham and would end in 70 AD with the destruction of the Temple and their dispersion out to many nations. For these first-century Jews, Jesus had not or could not be Messiah because they were left out. They wouldn't recognize that Jesus came for a specific purpose or that Israel's punishment had not yet been fully lived out. I believe Matthew is pointing his intended audience to the New Testament and ultimately to Jesus. Some would catch it and others would not."

John picked up from there with fresh coffee all around. "Luke, on the other hand, wrote a gospel from an entirely different point of view. Most historians believe Luke was a Gentile physician who followed Paul, joining him on his second mission trip and working closely with him in ministry. Not that it matters a lot, but my own personal view is that Luke wrote his gospel to Paul and for Paul."

Jake was particularly intrigued with this idea. "What do you mean, John?" he asked.

"Well, we see that Paul had his gifting as the minister to the nations, but mostly to the gentile nations. In Galatians, Paul calls the message 'his Gospel.' It was the gospel of grace and grace alone. One did not have to become a Jew, experience circumcision, or go through the process of becoming a proselyte. The Gentiles were grafted into the church by God's grace and nothing more. Now, he got some pushback on this from many, including Peter and James, Jesus' half-brother and head of the Jerusalem church. They got it worked out at the Council at Jerusalem in AD 49 or 50. The thing was that Paul had his hands full with dealing with the churches. For gosh sakes, he wrote thirteen or possibly fourteen of the twenty-seven books in the New Testament.

"Paul was also there, through Jesus' years of ministry, at the feasts and the crucifixion. Yes, he was on the other side, but still a unique and valuable witness to Jesus' life and message. We can also suppose that in those three years he was in Arabia, he most likely sat, figuratively at the feet of Jesus in his preperation to minister to the world. Paul was well suited to be a gospel writer, but Jesus had not gifted him to do so. Instead, He gifted Luke to work alongside Paul in his ministry, to be a gifted writer, educated, a physician and well-respected in the world as they knew it."

John took a deep breath and smiled. We could tell he had studied this, put his heart and soul into it and probably had some revelation from the Holy Spirit regarding this. I was anxious for him to continue.

"Luke begins his gospel with a determinate message: his desire to 'set in order a narrative', his qualifications as one 'having had perfect understanding of all things from the very first.' Then he addresses it to 'most excellent Theophilus.' Most assume he is writing to a person named Theophilus. This could be, but let's break it down. *Most excellent*—this is obviously a high and lofty personality and someone looked up to. His greeting in the book of Acts is also to Theophilus. Let's look at the name. *Theo* is God and *philus* is Greek for love, as in *phileo*. 'Most excellent God-lover.'

"I believe that God has revealed to me that Luke was writing not only to but for his God-loving companion, Paul. I think Paul would love to have written the accounts of Jesus' life and the Acts of the Apostles. But God entrusted Luke to do it," John concluded with a confident smile.

"I received that!" Jake said.

"Me too!" I agree. "I'm blown away. But we still have to get to the genealogy."

"So this is all related to the genealogy," John continued. "What we have is an account of Jesus' life, taken from firsthand accounts of eyewitnesses, Paul, Luke himself possibly, and other writings that were circulating. I believe God ordained Luke, a Gentile, to write this gospel with a Gentile audience in mind—that is, the world in general.

And what does Luke's gospel do? It takes us from Jesus back to David, Abraham, and beyond, all the way to Adam, the son of God.

"I believe that Luke is pointing the Gentiles back to the Torah, to Genesis and to the ancients of Israel. Look at what Luke does: in Acts he connects Jesus to Israel and all their history in the accounts of Peter's sermon, Stephen's address, and Paul's sermon to the people of Athens," John stated confidently.

"Then, that would mean that Matthew would be pointing the Jews to the New Testament while Luke points the Gentiles back to the Old. Jesus did not come to destroy the law, but to fulfill it!" John said.

"Wouldn't you know it, I just read this quote online: 'The Old Testament is the New concealed. The New Testament is the Old revealed,'" Jake stated.

"Wow! That hit me like a ton of bricks," I say. "What else have you got, Jake?"

"Okay, so it's about the churches and Daniel's seventieth week. You needed a lesson on that, right Jeremy?"

"Yes. That is a mystery to me."

"The seventy weeks prophecy is found in the book of Daniel, ninth chapter, and requires a bit of math and interpretation. Let's start in verse 24: 'Seventy weeks are determined for your people and your holy city, to finish the transgression, to make an end of sins, to make reconciliation for iniquity, to bring in everlasting righteousness, to seal up vision and prophecy, and to anoint the most holy.'

"As you can see, this is a bit convoluted. So let's lay some groundwork first. The Torah has these words to Moses from God: If you do not carefully observe all the words of the law that were written in this book, then the Lord will uproot you from the land. Then the Lord will scatter you among them, from one end of the earth to the other. I'm paraphrasing a bit, but you get the idea. Obedience is key to inhabiting the land on an ongoing basis. This warning plays into a major fulfillment in the seventy weeks prophecy.

"Now, Daniel was writing from Babylon and he was experiencing firsthand the first part of that fulfillment. The prophets had been warning the people of Israel ever since those first words to Moses. The Jews had been exiled to Babylon and only a remnant of Jews remained in Israel. They had been scattered, yet this was just the warning. This was not unusual. God had Jonah warn Nineveh of their judgment and hit pause for twenty years as they repented, got it together, then went right back to their disobedience. He is a patient, long-suffering God, but He is also just and Nineveh was eventually destroyed, fulfilling yet another prophecy.

"Daniel's prophecy is an over-compassing one. It talks about Israel's dispersion, the coming Messiah, the tribulation, and the end times as recorded in The Revelation of Christ. It also mentions the pause between the seven weeks, the sixty-two weeks, and then the huge pause prior to the seventieth week. The weeks are seven year periods—so seventy seven-year periods."

"Let me read from a great book that explains it much better than I can," John said, "From *Jerusalem Rising: Countdown to Armageddon*, a book by David Head. 'The prophet Jeremiah foretold of a Babylonian captivity that was to last for seventy years. In response to Daniel's inquiry following the completion of the seventy years, the Lord then pronounced another period of time upon the Jews, Jerusalem, and the Temple, of seventy times seven years, equaling 490 years. The prophecy included a timetable to the appearing of the Messiah (Jesus), the destruction of their second Temple (which at the time had not been built yet), the coming of the antichrist, the third temple to be built in the end times, and the judgment to be poured out upon the wicked during the great tribulation.'[1]

"You see," John continued, "the prophecy lays it all out, and part of this prophecy includes the judgment and punishment of Israel as a people and nation. I will explain that later. Let's go on with Head's book. 'The countdown on the 490 years was to begin when a certain decree would be issued by someone in power to restore the wall around Jerusalem that had been destroyed by the Babylonians in 586 BC. The rebuilding of the wall, we are told, is to occur during a troublesome time for the Jews."

"Let me interject," said Jake. "The seventy years of Israel's first punishment (the warning) is complete and the Lord is allowing, by decree, their return to Jerusalem. The dispersed Jews would begin the rebuilding process. Note that many did not return and rather, stayed in Babylon. And this displeased the Lord."

"The man sent to rebuild was Nehemiah and he met lots of resistance, both from the Jews who wouldn't leave Babylon and the nations around Jerusalem. We find this story in the book of Nehemiah—got it?" John asked. Both Jake and I nodded.

"Okay, let's keep going. From history, we know that this decree was given by the Persian king Artaxerxes exactly 483 years before the death of Christ. Let me continue with the Daniel 9 prophecy. I'll quote it from David Head's book since he interjects some valuable notes. Starting in verse 25, 'Know therefore and understand that from the

---

[1.] Head, David pp. 7,8

going forth of the commandment to restore and to build Jerusalem unto Messiah (Christ), the Prince, shall be seven weeks and threescore and two weeks (483 years): The street shall be built again and the wall (around Jerusalem), even in troublesome times.'

"Now to verse 26: 'And after threescore and two weeks (at the end of the 483 years), shall Messiah be cut off (death of Christ), but not for Himself (for He died for the sins of man): And the people of the Prince (Caesar/Satan), that shall come, shall destroy the city (Jerusalem, AD 70), and the sanctuary (Temple): And the end therefore shall be with a flood (of Roman soldiers) and unto the end of the war (between the Jews and the Romans, AD 66–70) desolations are determined (for the Jews, Jerusalem, and the Temple).'[2]

"With the death of Christ, the remaining seven years of the prophecy were put on hold until the time of the end, which will be the final seven years of human history, before Christ returns to establish the Kingdom of God on earth at His Second Coming."

"'Following the crucifixion of Christ, God gave the Jews a period of about forty years to accept Jesus as their Messiah through the ministries of the apostles of Christ. Afterwards, God lifted His protection and allowed Satan, the real (although invisible) Prince of the Roman Empire, to destroy Jerusalem and the Temple in AD 70.'"[3]

"Remember these words from Jesus in Matthew 24 in speaking of the Temple: 'Not one stone shall be left here upon another, that shall not be thrown down.' You see guys, all of this plays out and God's timeline and Daniel's unique prophecy lays it out in detail along with

---

[2.] Head, David pp. 7,8
[3.] Head, David, pp. 7,8

the end times. That is the seventieth week. The seventieth week is described in detail in the apostle John's Revelation of Jesus Christ, the final book in the Bible," John concluded.

"So Revelation, with all its seals and trumpets and calamity is the final week of God's judgment of the Jews," Jake finished.

"Wow!" was all I could say.

"Yes, wow! And Israel becoming a nation once again, the gathering of the Jews from the four corners of the world, is key to all of it. That is why what we are doing, what is, right now transpiring is the precursor to it all. Gog has to be enticed, Israel has to be attacked, and God needs to step in. He has to deal with Islam. He has to deal with the churches. And He has to show the entire world that He is God," Jake proclaimed.

"Wow again!" I said in awe. It was all unfolding in front of us, we had front row seats to the biggest events in human history so far. God had been busy orchestrating and the curtain was about to go up.

chapter

SEVEN

✡ ✡ ✡ ✡ ✡ ✡

O ur shift in the bunker was over, twelve hours of sifting through intercepts and only marginal results. We all knew it was closing in. The hook in the jaw was coming, but we still had work to do. The computers Deandrea had sold to the Iranians had been delivered and were yielding some interesting emails. It wasn't a coincidence that they were being used by the highest-ranking officials, and it was clear that the twelvers all had her communicators. Part-phone, part-tablet, part-computer, these tiny devices could do it all and deliver access to any source on any cloud or server from anywhere via secure satellite. They were the best of the best.

Of course, Miss Deandrea Perone had the connections and the deal. Not only that, she could deliver. And deliver she did. Now, we were reaping info on the twelver group and it was all coming together. What we wanted most at this point was to go back to our conversation. We did our shift-end debrief and moved to the small lunch room. We found ourselves alone and anxious to jump back into our study.

"In the Torah," Jake began, "God taught His people that whenever they sinned against Him, they would be punished, but He also promised them time to repent. Much like Nineveh, God sent Jonah, who really did not want to help them, but eventually did. The people repented and changed their ways—for a short time. Much like America after 9/11. You all flew flags, went back to church, and were very patriotic. But it didn't last. Nineveh was destroyed twenty years later, America was crushed by civil war, and may not be done with God's judgment yet. Israel would have time to repent also. It was a promise!

"God also told them that if they did not repent, the remainder of their punishment would be multiplied by seven. God told the prophet Ezekiel to lie on his side for 430 days to signify the 430 years they would spend in exile. Then He prophesied in Jeremiah 25:11 that the first seventy years of the 430 would be the Babylonian exile—the warning.

"In 606 BC the Jewish people were indeed taken off to Babylon for seventy years. This is the seventy years we spoke of earlier. Now comes the fun part. Paul Meier's book, *The Third Millennium* says, 'Take 430 years of exile, subtract seventy years of warning and multiply the remaining 360 years times seven as Moses instructed in the Torah. You will get 2,520 prophetic years of 360 days each, or 907,200 days from the day the seventy years ended with the decree of Cyrus to return to Jerusalem. 907,200 days of punishment [4]– 'If after all this, you will not listen to me, I will punish you for your sins seven times over' (Leviticus 26:18).

"Then this: this whole country will become a desolate wasteland and these nations (Judah, Israel, and the surrounding lands) will be dispersed throughout all the nations. So we do the math: 907,200 days on the 360 day Jewish calendar, factoring in for the one year between 1 BC and AD 1 (there is no 0 year), and it comes out to…ready? May 14, 1948[5]!"

---

4. Meier. p. 304
5. Jeffrey. Pp. 40–41

John and I stood with mouths open. We had heard some of this prior, but never so well put. One could only conclude that God delivers on His promises—and exactly on time! We began to realize that we could take the seventieth week at face value and that Daniel's prophecy for the end of days would manifest itself exactly as foretold in the Bible. The amazing thing was that it all was rolling out in front of us.

In the meantime, sections of New York, San Francisco, and DC were quickly being rebuilt. Trump was proud that his law enforcement troops had held strong in DC and saved the White House, most of the Capitol structure, and the Pentagon. The government, at least the federal government, was only wounded. Nearly twelve million people had been deported or incarcerated in makeshift prisons during the civil war. Much of the lawless troublemakers were gone and the rest anxious to rebuild. With the cities devastated, houses were going up in rural America and farms had new life. Infrastructure projects were abundant and the economy was on the mend.

As we closed in on our arms delivery date, we were prepping and fine-tuning our plan. With two weeks to go and our faux arms shipment sitting in an abandoned textile mill in the heart of Tehran, we began to get some disturbing intercepts. Something was going to go down. The messages were short, cryptic, and limited to e-mail. The phones and cloud traffic was almost nonexistent. It was obvious something was going to go down and we really did not want to be in transit when it did. Our plan was to leave Syria, work our way into Iraq, cross the border, and be air-lifted to Germany. Then, we would fly commercial to Marseille and gather as a group.

The Friday prior to Memorial Day was silent. No e-mails, phone calls, nothing. We let Langley know at 9:00 AM their time that something was up. We were assured that Trump was in Florida for the holiday, most of Congress and the Senate were gone, and all was quiet at the Pentagon. For me, it felt too quiet. Things were uneasy and our screens blank—a tell-tale sign of something big. We decided to fine tune our exit strategy from Tehran and try to convince Langley and the Mossad that we needed a much better plan B. John kept repeating, "Thin. Too thin. Razor-thin."

The news flash came on at 12:01. A Russian sub off the coast of Massachusetts had been under close monitoring. A distress call had come from the sub at 11:46 AM—"Mayday, mayday, mayday. Lost control of ship—mutiny!" At 11:55 AM four Russian nuclear-tipped missiles were launched with trajectories towards New York, DC, and Norfolk, VA. The two and a half minutes it took to track the four missiles was all they needed. The first hit the base of Freedom tower, the second the White House, the third the dead center of the Pentagon, and the last hit headquarters at the Norfolk, VA, Naval station.

Our government, military, naval, and financial centers were all obliterated with one Russian sub launch. Of course, the Russians said it was subversives who took over the sub and denied any responsibility. The US was stymied. Who was responsible, if not the Russians themselves? What could further pave the way for victory by Russia in the Middle East but neutering the biggest obstacle to their victory? It all pointed to Russia.

We watched in horror as news and weather drones made passes over DC and New York. Manhattan was a moonscape, the White House and a mile in every direction gone. The Pentagon was flat. Only an eerie black and grey shadow in the shape of the building remained. On heightened alert as they were, the place was loaded with high-ranking military leaders—all gone! We had Langley on the phone, confirming the destruction. The sub was blown up immediately by a shadow sub sent to monitor its activity. Too little, too late.

The answer to why the US was not going to be coming to the rescue of Israel was answered. Now the communicators, sat-phones, email, and internet were humming with activity. In the hours that followed it became clear: the Gog coalition had succeeded at step six on their list of things to do—neutralize the US. Check!

The news flowed into our bunker like a firehose. We all knew by protocol that Air Force One and Two would be headed, on very different courses, to Colorado. The destination was Cheyenne Mountain, Norad command and control. A thousand feet below the surface was a trillion dollars' worth of housing, offices, hospital and command center, built specifically for this kind of event.

The good news was that most of the operational government was alive. The bad news was that every other aspect of that government was gone. Banking and financial centers, military, and most importantly, the will of the people was lost. We were at war, but we weren't sure with whom. The Russians sure, but what if the sub *was* taken over by subversives? And did we want to counter against a country with more nuclear weapons than us? Donald J. Trump's priorities had just shifted. We were just beginning to recover from a brutal civil war and now this. But Jake, John, and I all agreed: God had put the US right where they needed to be to fulfill the Gog and Magog prophecy. For all intents and purposes, the US was a non-factor.

We had two sources of information coming in; first, we had the news feeds. The video from high above New York and DC coming from what were weather drones was unbelievable. These drones were used to provide traffic and weather info to TV and radio. They also served as chase and surveillance drones for police and temporary portable cell towers. Of course, that was not public knowledge. They flew a grid pattern and were launched from a regional airport somewhere well outside the cities. They had neither human pilots nor human control. They took off, landed, and flew their daily grid by computer 24-7.

What we saw and what we heard was overwhelming and heartbreaking. Millions dead, a radioactive cloud moving toward Baltimore and Annapolis, Long Island being evacuated and tough talk from the politicians who could be reached. The top-secret feeds were worse. Literally nothing survived in Norfolk or at the Pentagon. Thousands of high-ranking military officers, the Navy, and the command and control of much of our intelligence was lost. This did not bode well for us in Syria or for our mission. But honestly, we could not back out and the Iranians were now going to be anxiously awaiting the huge shipment of arms to finish off their biggest pain and impediment to the coming of the Mahdi.

Needless to say, the entire world was on high alert. A lot of finger-pointing and ugly accusations were being levied in all directions. Russia blamed al-Qaeda or ISIS infiltrators. They both blamed Iran in collusion with Russia. Donald J. Trump was deep inside the mountain with his finger on the launch button of thousands of nukes and we were at Defcon 1. I sent an apologetic email to Aharon Hadad saying that air travel and shipping had been disrupted. The shipment was on-time, coming and so was the delivery team. But anything could happen.

Hadad was unwavering—"June 8 or the deal is off." My response: "We'll be there." Now, I just had to figure out how to get my team to Marseille in time to make the delivery. What Hadad did not know was that the weapons were already in Tehran and had been for six months. We just needed them to believe that they were in transit. I simply could not put him off anymore and we all knew the big day was drawing near. I went to work on our plan for Marseille. I knew the IRG had ways to track our movements on commercial flights. These were not stupid people. Every one of our team had been vetted by the IRG. It was the only way. So we had to stay with the plan. Anything less would raise suspicions.

Every detail of this kind of mission was critical and had to be rehearsed. Even under the most stressful situations, we had to use our proper alias names and know how to answer key questions that would be posed to expose us. We had even come up with a brilliant explanation for why the munitions were in a warehouse and not on the dock as they would be expecting. To cover our tracks, we had a ship scheduled, trucks rented, empty boxes taken from the dock to the warehouse, all the paperwork to prove it, just in case. There were a lot of things that could go wrong. My job was to make sure it all came off well and we made it home alive.

There was another reason I wanted to get to Marseille—well, two really. I wanted to talk to my father, and I had done some homework on Stephanie. It was a long shot, but when your life could end at any time, what the heck! It had also been nearly a year since I had a conversation with my father. My Virginia connections had told me they were still at the lake house and that was good. With the DC radiation cloud moving due east, I knew their home in Front Royal would be fine. My home in Annapolis was lost forever and I was grateful the folks were at the lake house. It was far better equipped to endure pretty much anything short of a direct missile strike. I was told the Naval Academy and surrounding areas were red hot.

Alex Stillman and I pulled out the warehouse floorplan to review our plan. We weren't quite sure who the IRG would send to verify the cache of weapons. We were sure the inventory would be checked and several crates opened to confirm it was all there. We knew it was all there. And we had already received the $120 million wire to an offshore account. It was possible that Sulaman himself might come. This deal was huge for the IRG. The warehouse had been thoroughly vetted, set up, and staged by our team well in advance. These were fairly tedious, yet routine security measures for a black-market deal like this.

"Alex, are the fire extinguishers in place?" I asked.

"Yes." He pointed to nine locations on the map within the warehouse where they had been positioned. This was a former textile plant. The area in question would have been the receiving department where rolls of fabric would have been stored. It is where the crates would be opened and the products examined. The extinguishers were not what they seemed, but they had to be placed to look like they belonged and appear that they had been left behind when they closed the plant.

Our advance team had been in Tehran now for six months, setting up escape routes, building stairways to access the roof, and laying the groundwork for plan B, plan C, plan D, and on down. If all else failed, the extinguishers had the capacity to be our plan E. These amazing old fire extinguishers had been transformed into our safety net. If anything went wrong—and what could go wrong with six of us unarmed amid a group of, say, ten to twelve IRG with the latest Russian fully-automatic weapons? The extinguishers could be called into action by a single press of a button on my, John's, or Alex's belts. The reality was that if all else failed and we were going to die, all we had to do was give the command, hit the floor, and the extinguishers would do the rest. It was a last-ditch backup if all else failed.

This was really the least of our worries. If anything did go wrong, we would have to hit the roof and hope our boys showed up or, better yet, were already there in the brand-new Sikorski M63-D5CM helicopters. Tehran was not the best place for this, but Tehran was the drop point. It wasn't negotiable. Plan C was to escape to our secret base in Turkey, lay low for a few days, then head to the safety of one of our primo carriers parked in the Gulf. No problem. If everything went well, we would just drive away to our commercial flights, back to Marseilles, and be done.

The sheer beauty of this deal was that when these munitions got to the front line, they would jam, lock up, misfire, and basically explode in the operators' hands. People in the IRG were not going to be happy with us. We were counting on God to work out those details. Hopefully, we would all be far away from the Middle East. Well, all but Jake. He was here for the long run and would have a front-row seat. And so would we, if it went down soon. We worked out the final details, got confirmations on our new airline schedule to Marseille, and decided all was in-hand. It was really a straight-up, covert mission, not unlike many we had pulled off in the past. But Jake and John were pushing me to accept Jesus. I wasn't quite ready. They just shook their heads.

The United States of America was a mess. The carcass of Freedom Tower, which New York Mayor DeBlasio had called "indestructible" lay on its side, crushing a hundred buildings in Manhattan. For all intents and purposes, the tower was intact. The missile hit its base and incinerated the first twenty floors. It was like a tree had been chopped down and felled to make room for something else. Former mayor DeBlasio couldn't comment. He and about six million other New Yorkers were now dead. John took me back to Isaiah 9:8–12. Nine-eleven had just been the warning, the civil war a wake-up call. We didn't listen. Now the US was a nonfactor. Our arrogance, like Israel's, was stronger than our desire to be obedient to God.

The path was now clear for the armies of Gog to run their course, to make their move. The odds against Israel were long indeed. But we went back to Ezekiel 39: "I will set My glory among the nations; all the nations will see My judgment which I have executed, and My hand which I have laid on them. For I have poured out my Spirit on the house of Israel, says the Lord God."

"I see now that the promises are real, intact, and unwavering. All will happen just as it is prophesied by Ezekiel, Daniel, Isaiah, Jeremiah, and even Jesus in Matthew 24. How long have we been living with wars and rumors of wars, false Christs, extreme weather, earthquakes of ever increasing magnitude? In Matthew, the disciples ask, 'what will be the signs?' They have all been unfolding in front of us," John said.

"Yes," said Jake, "and it all began with that fateful event: May 14, 1948. Israel, a tiny nation, forgotten, purged from their land and their land made desolate, is now the pivot point and the focal point of all end times prophecy. Gog, Magog, Damascus, the Antichrist, the seventieth week, it's all about to go down with one goal in mind: Jesus' return to Earth."

"And somewhere amidst all of that will be the Rapture, the disappearance of perhaps a billion people from the earth. Even though it is a promise of God, many will chalk it up to an evacuation by UFO's or some strong disturbance in the universe. Anything but God taking His children home. Of course, there won't be many left to challenge these bizarre theories," Jake concluded.

We were all scratching our chins and evaluating the gravity of hundreds of millions of people, or perhaps a billion people just vanishing. I really had no idea at the time that I would live to see it, to be one of those left behind, trying to explain what had happened. These lessons were deep and, looking back, it would have been so easy. But that stiff-necked part of me would not allow me to confess with my heart that Jesus was Lord. I pray that someone has the opportunity to read this and make that pivotal choice. I pray for you, my friend!

chapter
EIGHT
✡ ✡ ✡ ✡ ✡ ✡ ✡

On June 6 at 11:00 AM, local time, our team gathered at the famous Notre-Dame de la Garde overlooking Marseille and the prison island of Chateau d'If, made famous by the Count of Monte Cristo. A ferry shuttled tourists out to the island and the views and the sky were spectacular. You could almost see the distant country of Algeria on the horizon.

I hooked up with Biggs first. Benjamin Biggs was a rock of a man. At forty-five, he could pound it with anyone. A former special forces commander, he helped lead Iraqi troops into Mosul against ISIS and was a key player in the push to rid Syria of the Islamic state for good. Biggs wore his scars, grey hair, and butch haircut with pride. I had never met a tougher man. He was a loner, no family, and was afraid of nothing. You could see it in his eyes. Not one to assume I had it under control, he was genuinely interested in our plan and exit strategy. I had a reputation for thoroughness, otherwise he wouldn't be here. We met with a firm handshake and a crooked grin.

"How ya been, Ben?" I always got him with that one!

"You never change, do you?" He said.

"No, not really."

"You gonna give me a shot to take out QS?"

I knew he meant Sulaman, whom he hated. "Could be. But that is not our mission."

"I know. I'm just messing with you!"

Next on the scene was Growler, aka Rolf G. Tiblin. His nickname came from his middle initial and the fact that he growled when he worked out or trained. Rolf was a compact man at 6' and 240 pounds. He was all muscle, strong as an ox and loved to show himself off in skin-tight t-shirts and cargo shorts. His thighs were as thick as my waist and he had the calves to match. Simply put, Growler was a beast. He was also a gentle soul who had two grown daughters and a huge crush on his ex-wife. He was so in love with Kathy, but he was never home. When the girls went off to college, Kathy flew the coop. I had never seen a man as heartbroken as Rolf was.

I could see John at the balcony overlooking the Mediterranean. He was lying low, waiting for the rest to arrive. Jake showed up next and had some new intel. The Iranian Republican Guard was chomping at the bit to get these arms. His take was that they were close to D-Day. Jake shook with the others as Alex came up the stairs. Alex was our aviation expert, could fly anything at all and was proud of it. An Air Force Academy grad, he now pledged his loyalty to the CIA, but was just a tad disillusioned by all the leaks and turmoil caused when Trump took office. He was a huge Trump supporter, a strong Catholic who John said needed to be a born-again Catholic. We were always happy to have Alex on the team. He could steal a chopper or a plane and have us gone in no time and had done it—twice!

Guys like these are legends, giving all to their country for the greater good. We had all worked together as a team on four missions, all nail-biters but we came out successful and relatively unscathed.

John joined us as we coordinated flights, schedules, went over communications and other details, then decided we were ready. Our aliases were solid, passports and covers deeply honed and really the only thing missing was my salvation and probably Alex's as well. But we would talk. The fact was simple and always present. Any and every mission was life threatening.

Biggs was our explosives expert and he took me through the extinguishers.

"Geoff Hess is in charge of the advance team, as you know. What you may not know is that he invented these monsters. He's also a hobby antique restorer. He made these look like they belong there," Alex explained. "Each of these thirty-two-inch long canisters hold ten charges that send out projectiles in a set pattern. Hanging on the wall in a bracket, like a fire extinguisher would, the charge pattern is from thirty-six inches off the floor to forty-eight inches above. He places them, then turns on a laser device that shows the pattern. That way they can cover a huge area. If twenty people are in the warehouse, as it is set up, everyone in the open area is hit by at least one projectile. The only safe place is the floor."

"So we have a single word command, everyone hits the floor, and blam, everybody else is dead?" I asked in rhetorical fashion.

"You got it!"

"That is one sick concept," I added.

"Yes, but when they have all the guns, it is our only out. Any mission of this nature can be a trap. You know that," Biggs said.

"What about extraction?" I asked.

"We have two outs—the roof and the mail truck. The driver is one of us and has been doing the mail route for seven months. Huge mail bags in the back for cover. But the roof is the first option," Biggs said.

"Yes."

We rehearsed our questions, got used to our aliases and had a subdued evening with pizza delivered in. My cover was Said Imam, Growler would be Roger Johanson. Alex would be Daniel Webster, Biggs was Jack Bonner, and Jake would be his Polish counterpart, Werner Stolman. John, as always, was Rudolf Menschke from Berlin. Of course, all these covers were real people with real jobs, real families, educations at specific schools, and connections that went way back. The ruse had to be perfect and deep. It was do or die.

Our code word for drop was "Wait!" It caught everyone's attention and people hesitated, waiting for something. We hoped it wouldn't have to be used, but you never knew. This was war. In twenty-four hours, we would be landing in Tehran and driving unarmed into a trigger-happy group of Iran's best trained fighters. There was simply no room for error.

As the evening wound down, the door for a Jesus conversation was opened by Biggs, of all people. "Hey Jake, you're a Jew, right?"

"Yes."

"Aren't you a bit worried now that the US is neutered and the noose is tightening around your neck? I mean, Iran wants these weapons and the bomb for just one reason!"

"Well, the situation is bleak at best. And I treat this mission as an intel mission, not one to help the other side. I want to know how close it is. But I believe God and His promises. You know, this is all in prophecy."

"What is?" Alex asked.

"The war that is coming, the countries who are involved, the purpose and the outcome, all spelled out."

"Really. Who wins?" Rolf asked.

"Good wins over evil," Jake proclaimed. "We have been in this place before, as you all well know. 1948, '67, '73—all losable wars, but we won and enlarged our territory."

John took the guys through Ezekiel 38 and 39.

"Wow. It's all there. Even the exclusion of Iraq and Egypt, which makes no sense even twenty years ago. It's eerie, really," Rolf said.

"I'm becoming a believer!" Alex said.

"Do you mean that?" John asked.

"Well, I am a Catholic," Alex said.

"Yes, but are you born again?" Jake asked, "And what about the rest of you? You know it is near the end. Jesus is busy preparing for the harvest…"

"Jesus?" Rolf asked. "Jake, you are Jewish!"

"Messianic."

"Really? This is getting interesting. What about you, John?"

"Born again."

"Biggs?"

"Raised Baptist. But we were military. Born in Hawaii, lived in six countries. Who has time for church?"

"Rolf?"

"Deist," Rolf said with a smile.

"What's a deist?" I asked.

"Oh, I believe that God created us, the world, the universe, but then left it up to us to figure it out."

"So you're lost…"

"Lost as the day is long!" Rolf said. "What about you, Stone?"

"Considering. I buy it all. I just don't feel fully compelled. I know I am headed there, I just hope I don't die first."

"Could be tomorrow…" John said.

"So half are lost and one may as well be…" Jake said.

"Hey!" Alex said.

"Truth hurts, man…" Jake concluded. "Look, if an obstinate, stiff-necked Jew can be saved, anyone can…"

"I'm ready," Biggs said. "I want to be sure."

"Okay. I'll lead us in prayer. Whoever wants to go—do it…" John offered.

We all took a praying stance and John led us. "Dear Heavenly Father, I know I am a sinner in need of a Savior. I believe your desire is for us to be saved and that your Son, Jesus, died on the cross to take away my sins. I receive the gift that you have offered. The free gift of salvation. Lord, give me eternal life with you. I pray in Jesus' name, Amen."

There was a very long silence. All was still. Alex was holding his breath. When he exhaled, it broke the silence.

"I did it!" Rolf said.

"Me too!" said Biggs.

We all looked at Alex.

"It felt very right. I have been a pretender for so long."

Now everyone was looking at me.

"Sorry guys, I'm just not ready…" I said.

"Well, at least we know we won't die tomorrow…" John said.

"What do you mean?" asked Biggs.

"Because God is not going to allow this man to go to hell. I guess that is our plan F."

We all smiled. At that moment, I felt silly and selfish. "I guess I really am mostly Jew."

Jake came and put his hand on my shoulder. "No doubt about it."

We all laughed. But it didn't feel like a laughing matter. We were headed into the lions' den. I needed what Daniel had.

Jerusalem—Time of Jacob's Trouble

I was doing my best to look heavenward as my position drew closer to the machine. There were still about a hundred ahead of me, and as we all moved closer to the blade, the number of Global Constables and the fervency of these men and women increased. They were all fitted with MA-67 machine guns which I knew from experience were hair-triggered. One false move could get several people shot very quickly. The crowds were thick, but well back behind a catch-fence. Beheadings had become a popular live sport and a highly rated reality show in this perverted world. Everyone was hoping someone would make a break for it or say something keenly profound—stir things of a bit for the audience.

The live crowds were on their best behavior—act up and they would join the line. It was that simple. The sick part was the mothers that were holding babies or infants. Of course, all the kids were taken up in the Rapture. But somehow, in all the chaos, people still thought it was okay to bear a child and bring it to such an event. Really, that was the least of the levels of perversion going on in the world. Once Lech Manevetski entered the Temple at the mid-point, no boundaries to perversion existed. That included mandatory worship of him and his effigy.

The true followers of Christ had gone along with all the children. The tribulation saints were on the run, in hiding, or in custody. I didn't have much to lose, so I kept a careful watch for any opportunity. The only ones I truly cared about were the ones in this line. They were due to die anyway. I prayed for an opening.

chapter
NINE
✡✡✡✡✡✡✡

At 1900 hours I got a call from our mission support commander, Frank Blankenship, who would be monitoring us from the carrier G. W. Bush in the gulf. "We're all with you Stone. Geoff has got a camera in the old steam heater directly above your demo spot in the warehouse. We'll be able to see and hear how it's going. We also have a dedicated sat and two drones for cover. The extraction team is seven minutes out and you have Emil outside in the mail truck. If we can't get you all the way out, we do have a safe house Emil can get you to. You'll be fine."

"Thank you, sir..."

I knew Blankenship and he was no politician. He would pull all the stops if he had to. I knew the best result was to walk out and drive away.

I still had two very important calls to make. Since I was scared to death to call Steph, I decided to call home. It was just after noon in Virginia and the phone at my lake house rang and rang. Then, I heard a familiar voice—mine. "This is Eli. As usual, I'm not in. Don't bother leaving a message, it doesn't matter."

That is truly awful, I thought.

Beep. "Dad, it's Eli. I know it's been awhile and things are chaotic there now. I will try to call day after tomorrow." I paused a long minute, thinking. "Love you two. Bye."

Why couldn't they be there? I wondered. Now I had the tough one. Probably not in either. Story of my life! I thought. I dialed the number. Two rings, three…

"Hello."

I swallowed hard. Her voice hadn't changed in thirty years.

"Stephanie?"

"Yes, this is Stephanie."

"This is Eli. Eli Grollenberg."

"Eli from high school?"

"Yes, the very one."

"Where in the world are you, Eli?"

"Right now, I'm in Marseille."

"Where have you been all my life?"

I chuckled. Then I swallowed hard. "You're kidding, right?"

"Well, you certainly haven't been here."

"No, but my folks still live there."

"And you never came to see me?"

"I'm sorry. I haven't been good about that kind of thing."

"What are you good at, Eli?"

As I paused to think of a good answer, she continued. "In addition to kissing, that is."

"You are the good kisser. You taught me."

"You mean that was your first?"

"Yeah. Remember, it was frowned on, but I think the principal felt sorry for me. Looked the other way!"

"Well it was memorable. I think of you often."

"Thank you, Steph. Yes, I remember it well."

"Eli, you must have an exciting life if you call me from France to tell me hello."

"Yeah, pretty much. But this has been on my list for a while."

"Thirty years?"

"Better late than never, right?"

"Yes, certainly. It's good to hear your voice."

Then we just talked and talked and talked. I was that high school boy again. It was like thirty years had vanished between us. She had gone to college in Aix-en-Provence, just an hour's drive from Marseille. She taught school in Arles and never married. It was an amazing experience and at two in the morning we said goodbye. Suddenly I had Front Royal, Virginia, on my travel schedule. What could I expect? What the heck, can't hurt.

I slept hard and dreamed like I had never dreamed before. I woke and could not remember even one of the dozens of mish-mash dreams, but Steph was in there. I showered, geared up, and met the team for breakfast. John prayed for our food, God's protection, and a safe return. We caught our plane and picked up rental hum-vees at the airport. We were in full mission mode now and I caught glances of Geoff as they shadowed us very carefully. We arrived at the warehouse right on time, opened up, and sized things up.

Six dark blue suburbans showed up five minutes after us and Aharon Hadad got out of the lead car and shook my hand. We slid the huge doors open, one of the suburbans pulled in, and we shut the doors. I had done a head count quickly on the entourage. Eleven guards, Hadad, another man in the lead car, and then the drivers. All of them, including the drivers, joined us inside. I made introductions to Hadad and he introduced us to Qussam Sulaman.

Their team spread out, checking for snipers, bugs, cameras, anything. I handed Hadad the inventory and custom tags. Our job was to help confirm the inventory, open crates as directed and show the goods if desired. I had an accomplished and valued resume. This was a formality. But with Sulaman here, Hadad was going strictly by the book. The sweep was over and we gathered in the open area. I opened the first crate: shoulder-fired grenade launchers. They were pretty and heavy, so the next box was opened. These were MA-112s, the latest in fully-automatic street fighter weapons.

"How many rounds?" Sulaman asked.

"Fourteen million rounds for the MA's. Twenty-two thousand additional grenades." I said.

"Very well, Mr. Stone. I bid you farewell."

As my team and I digested that Qussam Sulaman had just called me by my NSA name, he turned with Hadad and walked out. We heard a suburban start and drive away. The guys were flashing glances to one another in a panic. We were surrounded by seventeen IRG who were now pulling their side arms. I raised my hand. "Wait!"

All of us dropped and I hit the button. There was an extraordinary boom as we hit the floor and all extinguishers fired at once. I got up and grabbed the sidearm of the man next to me. None of the seventeen were moving. That was when the earth began to shake. We could barely stand, and the shaking was intensifying as we tried to remove ourselves from the blood bath. We all crawled toward the wall as parts from the heater unit in the ceiling began to fall. I had felt a few earthquakes in my life, but this was strong and throwing us around like ragdolls. Then, it tapered off and was over.

Geoff showed up at the door, looked at the scene and called the "all safe" in to Blankenship. They had watched it all go down from above.

"He called you Stone!" Geoff said. "Your cover is blown! Now, let's get out of here."

We each grabbed an MA-42 out of the good crate. Biggs and John each grabbed RPG launchers and filled their pockets with ammo.

"Grab the extinguishers!" Geoff yelled. "We can't let that technology get out." We did, and then headed for the roof.

We were met by an incoming helicopter all right, but the Sikorski had an Iranian police chopper on its tail and they were both coming in hot.

"I'll get this!" Biggs said as he set up the launcher. Geoff was on the radio. All hell was breaking loose. We hit the deck as Biggs took aim. We saw the chopper bank left, but the rocket was on its way. When the grenade hit, it was over, a huge explosion with the debris raining down. The Sikorski flew in hot, dived at the roof, pulled up hard, and sat down with a thud.

The Sikorski M-63 was an awesome bird, a gunship that made the Blackhawk look like a toy. It had the capacity to hold ten and could fly at nearly 200 mph. The pilot hit the deck, we piled in, and Geoff loaded the fire extinguishers, still smoking, into the cargo compartment. We settled into seats and put our com-sets on.

"Welcome aboard, gentlemen. We have clear skies over Tehran today. My name is Hellbent and I'll be your pilot today. We can expect some company prior to our arrival on the cruise ship. So buckle up tight and prepare for a show."

None of us were very amused, but it did give us a feeling of confidence. I noticed that Alex had slipped into the co-pilot's chair. That was also reassuring.

Geoff had direct communication with Blankenship and was giving updates on the earthquake. "It appears to be a natural quake with an epicenter just off the coast of Gaza. Repeat—a natural quake!" Geoff said.

"How can they be sure?" asked Hellbent.

"A test hits hard and then tapers off. The real quake or natural quake is the opposite. But I know they will have the sniffers out—planes that can pick up even trace radiation. With the epicenter out in the Mediterranean, I'd say it was just a natural quake," Geoff said.

"We got company…" Hellbent announced. "Two bogies coming in hot! My guess is it's IRG or Russian MIG's trying to figure out who we are."

We were really hauling, but those two jets came by us as if we were standing still.

"They know who we are. Now begins the fun!" Hellbent said with a smile in his voice. He was quickly giving Alex instructions on this and that. "Okay, boys. They have a lock on us. Time for some fun. Counter measures ready!"

A rapid beeping began on the console. "Two missiles off—headed this way. Deploy counter measures!"

Lots of things were happening, but we could not see. I found myself praying for the first time in many years. While I was praying, Hellbent was busy explaining how the counter measures worked.

"Right now, we have two missiles bearing down on us at mach two. They lock onto a combination of exhaust, heat, and radar signatures. What the counter measures do is fly along behind us and put off the same signature. There are eight of them and they are fading away from our tail as we fly on.

"When the missiles get to within three hundred meters of the CM's, we will bank hard to the left to avoid any debris that may chase into us. That will happen—right now!"

With that, the chopper banked left hard, downward straining all of us against our seat harnesses. Then we felt the percussion of the two missiles somewhere behind us. It sounded far too close for comfort, I tell you that.

"What the MIGs don't know…" Hellbent continued, "is that flying above them at fourteen thousand feet are two drones carrying the latest SAM missiles, which use a signature that is unique to the MIG, a hum the jet puts out. The other thing is the SAM's won't alert the MIG's because there is no audible lock sensor that works on them. Plus, they are quiet and they literally won't know what hit them."

About that time, we were crossing into Turkey's airspace and felt two distinct explosions in the distance.

"Goodbye MIG's!" Hellbent yelled out. "Had to get that done in Iranian airspace or Turkey would be pissed."

Ten minutes later we were on the ground amid a gaggle of high brass. This debrief would not be routine and go well into the night. But we were alive. I still had some work to do, but my career as a spy was over. Praise God!

We were all separated and did the deep demobilization drill. Seventeen IRG lay dead, an Iranian police chopper carrying two pilots was disintegrated, and two of the IRG's top pilots were now part of the Iranian desert. It all went pretty much by the book. The arms deal was done, we made about $100 million on the bogus weapons. Our fellow team was able to track Sulaman back to a previously unknown office building, and IDs were taken off of the bullet-ridden IRG soldiers.

It was obvious to our team that the IRG had been there to wipe six of America's, England's, and Israel's top spooks out. I thanked Geoff for the fire extinguishers—"What amazing technology!"

"Yes, and the IRG is probably scratching their heads trying to figure out how six unarmed men shot seventeen of theirs ninety times in less than a second. That's why we couldn't leave them. America may be wounded, even irrelevant, but we still have some tricks up our sleeves!" Geoff said.

At dinner, we all got together and I shared with them that I had prayed for the first time in years.

"Yes, that was pretty intense…" Alex said.

"And we lived through it!" Jake said. "The question is, if Stone is outed, likely we are all outed. I mean, they were ready to kill all of us."

"I would say that we're all done—for covert stuff anyways. Although Stone could still pull off the girl, I'm pretty sure." Biggs adds. "Plus, we helped ID some of their boys."

"Yes, and now they are all dead. That is how spook legends are made," John added.

"The question is this," I said. "Do I get the girl in the end?"

"It's far from the end, my friend. And until you get the God, you won't get the girl," Alex said with a hand on my shoulder.

"I'm not sure what is holding me back. I know He exists. I know He was with us. It is a mystery," I told them.

"Yes, it is a mystery. You must be a Jew. Only a Jew could be this hard-headed," Jake added.

"By the way...who's the girl?" Geoff asked.

"Her name is Stephanie, a high school sweetie."

"High school? Stone, you haven't had much of a love life, have you?"

"No. None!"

The morning newspaper was broadcasting: "Tensions High over Iran Skirmish." The President was calling it a complicated mix-up. Iran's President Rouhani was calling it an act of war. Admiral Bryant from the G. W. Bush called it a desperate rescue of six American tourists. I wondered where all of this was going. I was called into the commander's office and told to show up in Whitehall, Virginia in three days. This was the NSA's temporary offices. The Navy would get me back to Marseille, then I was on my own. Time to resurrect Eliezer Abdullah Grollenberg from the dead.

I made it to Marseille, called my father and told him I was coming home.

"I'll be here with open arms, my son!"

That sounded really good. Chaos reigned in Iran. Russia was mad, Iran was mad, Syria was mad, and Turkey was mad. The good news was that the quake was a natural one and not a test. Besides, we still had a few more months before the timeline hit. Of course, I could be completely wrong about that. The hook in the jaw was close. I had just pushed the Iranians into a frenzy and probably elevated my photo to the center of Sulaman's dartboard.

After all, people don't just walk into Iran, sell them $120 million worth of bogus weapons, kill dozens of people, and leave the country by taking two of their MIG's out. I would not be getting an invitation to Sulaman's wedding, that's for sure. Israel had their finger on the trigger and Iran and its coalition was chomping at the bit to wipe them off the map. Now, it was all up to God's timing. He would put the hook in the jaw and draw them out. We were all just spectators of things to come.

chapter
TEN
✡✡✡✡✡✡✡

The long flight home had me thinking of upcoming lazy days at the lake, a nice dinner out with Stephanie, and maybe some fishing with dad. But first, I had to get my walking papers and final instructions. As we flew in over the devastated area of DC, Annapolis, and Northern Virginia, my entire mindset changed. Everything within the beltway was black. We were still fairly high as we headed to Richmond, the closest useable airport of any size, so I couldn't see many details. But I was moved. The devastation was overwhelming. I guess I had been living in my own world for too long. A huge part of America had been decimated.

I was met at the airport by two agents I did not know. They met me, asked to see my passport, and escorted me to a suburban. Not a word was said. I had a million questions about NSA headquarters and the Pentagon. No response. They wouldn't even share their names. I decided that I had become a hot potato. Most of the Arab world wanted me dead, I assumed, and the heat was on from the top. The ride was uncomfortable. In this part of the state, the only change appeared to be the lack of traffic. No need to head north anymore, I reasoned.

We presented IDs at the gate and entered a non-descript office building that couldn't have been more than five thousand square feet. I was escorted to the second level and told to sit in a waiting area. Rental offices, second-hand furniture…things had changed in the NSA. That fact was never more evident than when I was ushered into the plain office of the deputy secretary, Tom Sanger.

"Jeremy Stone—Tom Sanger. Nice to meet you." He held out a welcoming hand.

"Nice to meet you, sir."

"You are a highly decorated operative, Stone. One of our best. It's unfortunate we can't keep you. We have lost a huge number of agents."

"Thank you, sir. I'm sorry to hear of the loss."

"Yes, well, it wasn't just NSA. All the agencies are decimated. Of course, Langley was spared, but everything north of it was wiped out. I was out of town, but I lost my brother and many friends and coworkers."

"I'm sorry, sir. Nothing will be the same, I'm afraid."

"No. You're right. But a bit of good news out of Iran. Your weapons deal netted some very valuable and unexpected intel."

"Oh yeah?"

"Yes. It seems one of the dead IRG ended up being the brother of one of the Russian sub mutineers. We're not sure how complicit Russia was in the attacks, but Iran's fingerprints are all over it. That's the good news."

"There's bad news?"

"Yes. You, my friend, are done. Here is your gold watch."

He handed me a case of substantial size. I looked with an obvious question on my face. "Ill-gotten booty—profit from a gun deal. Sorry it has to be cash, but it's the only way. Prying eyes, you know?"

"Yes. So that's it?"

"No. There is more. A car in the lot—your Golden Parachute, if you will." He threw me the keys.

"Okay, what else do I need to know?"

"Stay low-profile, Stone. You are not a friend of Iran. Be safe. And we may need some of your expertise when we get closer."

"Closer to what?" I asked in earnest.

"The fulfilment of the Caliphate. That is what they are headed for. Let me ask you, Stone…what do you believe in?"

"As far as what?"

"You know, spiritually."

"Well, I'm mostly Jewish, so I believe in God. The God of the Bible."

"Is there any other one?" He asked somewhat sarcastically.

"No, but there is Jesus. You know, Messiah?"

"Yes, Jesus. Do you believe Jesus is God?"

"Not yet. But I am close. I see lots of good evidence. What is brewing in the Middle East—I'm seeing it gel with prophecy. It's hard to ignore."

"We're close to the end, Stone. Do your homework. Don't wait too long. When we go, it's going to get rough."

"Yes, I have read. What about you?"

"Oh, I'm gone. I would be hard-pressed to ignore it. Don't wait."

"Will do, sir. And thank you."

"Remember, Stone—low profile."

I smiled, shook his hand, and was off. The new Range Rover was sweet. The twenty-two million in cash wasn't too bad either. I could take Stephanie to dinner. First, I had to get to Smith Mountain Lake safely and somehow convince her to go out with me.

The drive through central Virginia was quite nice. As I wound through the rolling hills, fond memories of our trips here were vivid in my mind. Back then, we would rent a pontoon boat and camp on one of the many islands. Dad would say it was like the Jews in the desert, no toilets, no running water—camping. And very primitive camping at that. But I loved the fires, sleeping out under the stars and how quiet and peaceful it was. I liked the boats and the nice houses on the lake. My father wasn't a boater. In fact, the only reason he would rent the pontoon boat was to get us out to the island and for me to sleep any- where *but* in the tent with them.

Now we had all of the above: a house on the lake, the pontoon boat, and my favorite speed boat. We even had flushable toilets. "Spoiled," Dad would say. But to me it was just right, and I could go out to the boathouse and sleep in the hammock under the stars any- time I wanted. I wondered if Stephanie was a lake person. You know, you don't really make a person into a lake person, they just are. To be honest, thoughts of her consumed me. How would she look after all these years—almost thirty! It had flown by. And now it was time to wind down. I needed that.

When I pulled up to the gate, a wave of fatigue, loneliness, and want filled me. What had I done with my life? I had no wife, no kids, not much to show for my commitment to my country. I had a giant hole in my heart and a lack of any tangible peace. I hit the buzzer.

"Son! You're home, come in, come in!" The gate swung open and I drove along the twisting path through tall trees to the house. Then, there was my father, running toward me with open arms. I got out and we embraced. Marra stood at the doorstep, crying. I waved but wouldn't let my father go. It was good to be home.

"Look, Marra! The prodigal son comes home!"

We walked together to the porch and I pulled my sweet step-mom in. She cried and cried. I have to admit, I did too. It had been way too long and I didn't even fully realize it. They led me into my own house that I had built but barely recognized. It hadn't changed, but I had. Marra insisted on tea and we sat and talked. Fatigue was setting in fast. They could see it.

"So my world traveler, business big shot… You have worn yourself out, what have you to show for it?" Dad asked.

"Thanks, Dad, for reminding me." I went out to the Rover, pulled it into the garage, and grabbed my bags. Dad helped, of course, and I excused myself to my room. I had forgotten how great the view was, and the moon lit the deck looking out over a picture-perfect night. I stood, took in the fresh Virginia air, and thanked God. That was new. I had to smile. "Still working on me, huh?" I asked the star-filled sky. The answer was right in front of me in all its grandeur.

I grabbed the case, entered my walk-in closet, hit the keypad and entered the hidden elevator. I rode it down four levels, entered the control room and headed for the safe. The case went in. I locked up, scanned the vast array of security monitors and shook my head.

"DAVEO, set security to home."

"Security set to home. Welcome home, sir…"

I rode the elevator up, showered and crashed.

That night, my first night home and out of my trade, was like no other. I had visions of Christ on the cross, telling the man being crucified next to him that he would be with Him "this day" in Paradise. There was no confession, no acts of kindness, no jumping through hoops. The man simply believed that Jesus Christ was who He said

He was. John's reading of Romans 10:9 was in my head as I woke: "If you confess with your mouth that Jesus is Lord and believe in your heart that God raised Him from the dead, you will be saved." It spoke directly to me.

My mind reeled. I was exhausted, jet-lagged, and feeling emptied. It was bright, the morning sun high. I glanced at the clock—10:46. I had slept hard and needed it. Then it hit me. I was home. My jet-setting life was behind me—or so I thought. The Egyptian cotton sheets embraced me. My favorite pillow comforted me and for the first time in many years I felt a peace about my life. I reached out to my side. No one. It must not be a dream—Stephanie was not there.

For the first time in my life I thought, "I could change that." I wouldn't have to short-change someone I loved. My former life was in no way conducive to any relationships. Even my father treated me as the prodigal. "Special," I thought. I got up, not because I had to, but because I wanted to. With my pajamas on, I traveled to the kitchen, smelled the coffee, and headed to the fridge. Italian sweet cream... Thank you, Marra!

I joined Mom and Dad on the deck.

"Welcome home, sleepy-head. Tough year?" Marra asked jokingly.

"Yes, but it's finally over. I am home for good." They both looked at me.

"For good? What do you mean?" said Dad. "I was just going to ask when you had to go."

"I don't have to go. I don't have to do anything. The Range Rover was my retirement gift. I am done!"

"You're serious, son? How will you support yourself?"

"I'll be fine, Dad. I had a successful business. The payoff was good. I'll—we'll be fine."

"Now you need to find a girl…" Marra said.

"You read my mind, mamacita."

"You're nearly fifty, son. Who will you find?"

"God will find her for him."

"That's right, Marra. Couldn't have even been a husband in my old life."

"I'll second that!" Marra added with a smile.

"You better hurry, son. I think Jesus is coming back soon…"

I had been looking out at the lake, sipping my favorite coffee and cream. Now I was looking at two smiling faces who suddenly looked very different to me.

"It's the peace, son. You can see it, can't you? The world is falling apart, but we have a peace. If you want that girl, you better get some of your own…" Dad offered.

"How? When?"

"Let's see. How long have you been gone?" Dad asked.

Marra hit him lovingly. "Eight months now, son. We went to the synagogue for atonement and came out born-again Christians."

"You mean Messianic Jews?" I asked.

"Well, sort of. We're part of a new following. It's called 'The Way'," Marra explained.

"Isn't that what Paul called the early followers of Christ?"

"Yes. It's not Jewish or really any denomination. It's followers of Jesus," Dad added.

"Amazing!" was all I could say.

"You could go with us. Lots of nice ladies there." Dad said with a wink.

"I had a vision last night, Dad. Jesus was on the cross inviting the man next to Him to join Him in Paradise. John has been working me over, too…"

"Son, the prophet Joel says we will have dreams and see visions. We're in the last days."

"Okay. I'll come Sunday."

"No, son, Saturday—the Sabbath."

"Of course, the seventh day—keep it holy."

"Yes son. We're all Jews, you know—descendants of Abraham."

"Yes, I've considered that. And we could all be with Jesus in the Kingdom."

"Yes, that is what the Tabernacle is all about, the Kingdom."

"Jesus brings it all together, son," Marra added.

While I was gone, on my own search, God had moved in my folks. There was never a Jew more stiff-necked than my Father. If he could see the light, why couldn't I?

"What day is it?" I asked.

"It's Wednesday."

"Stephanie's day off," I muttered.

"What, son?"

"I need to make a phone call."

"That's not what you said. Did you say Stephanie?" Marra, never one to miss a thing, asked.

"Yes."

"That's interesting. We met a nice lady at home named Stephanie, about your age."

"Attractive, son. Very attractive." Dad had a look on his face that explained it all. If you were me…well, you know…

"Where did you meet her?" I asked.

"At church."

"The Way?"

"Yes, but the one in Front Royal. She's from there," Marra explained.

"What does she look like?"

"Brunette, green eyes, perfect teeth."

"Mom!"

"Curvy!" Dad added. Marra hit him and Dad lifted his eyebrows.

"Couldn't be the same one. What's the population of Front Royal now?"

"A hundred thousand at least."

"Couldn't be her…"

"Who?" Marra asked.

"Stephanie Skater—the girl from high school."

"Oh, the one from the dance?" Marra asked.

"Wait, what dance?" Dad prodded.

"1990, Dad. Sophomore Sadie Hawkins dance. Stephanie asked me, of all people."

"And you went, and…?"

"The kiss of a lifetime, as I recall," Marra said.

"Mom! I was fifteen."

"Yet you remember. I think God is busy orchestrating," Dad said.

More than you could know… I thought. "But it couldn't be her. Too much of a coincidence. Do you know her last name?" I asked.

"We didn't get that. But she's lovely."

We all took a deep breath and were smiling.

"You know, son, the teacher at The Way says as soon as you pray for something, God begins to orchestrate things to answer it. We're dealing with man's free will here, and He can't change that, but He uses it all for good."

"Romans 8:28," Marra adds.

"You two are learning a lot. Praise God."

"It is time for you, Eli. We aren't promised tomorrow."

"You're so right, Dad. I'm close. So very close."

We beat around the place, took in the perfect summer day and relaxed. I decided that I truly needed this break. I was just mesmerized by the whole Stephanie thing. But I couldn't ask about my folks. She would have no way of knowing they were my parents, even if she was the same Stephanie. But I did need to call her. I was simply amazed at Dad and Marra. They were like two peas in a pod. Their love and peace was obvious.

Jerusalem—Time of Jacob's Trouble

There were now around sixty people between me and the machine. Even to someone like myself who had been exposed to so much war, so much suffering and death, even at my own hands, the sounds, sights, and smells were horrifying. My mind was computing the scene, evaluating risk and reward, assessing the possibility of escaping this horror. I felt I needed help… God's help certainly, but human help as well. The woman ahead of me was no help. Her language was foreign, even to me. The man behind me was in his eighties. How he had survived this long was a mystery. He had only murmured, "God help us" a few times in German. Two behind him was a young woman. An Arab, possibly from Yemen. She looked fit, alert, and very composed. The scars on her face reflected a roughness and a war torn past. Most importantly, she appeared steadfast even under these circumstances. We made eye contact. I glanced at the guard who stood between us and the large crowd of spectators. She nodded. Perhaps we were on the same page.

chapter

ELEVEN

✡✡✡✡✡✡

At four o'clock I dialed Stephanie's number. I think she was excited to hear from me. She was grieving several acquaintances that had been lost in the attacks, but she mentioned that she was doing some work for a new church. They had a satellite church in Bedford and she had to travel there to deliver some paperwork and some Bibles.

"Where in the world are you, Eli?" she asked.

"In Virginia. Smith Mountain Lake. I have a place here."

"Let me look on the map," she said.

"Bedford is very close by."

There was a pause. It was shorter than it seemed. "Stephanie, what is the name of the church?"

She took her time answering. It seemed she was still studying the map. "The Way."

I swear I couldn't talk.

"It's very close to you. Where do you live at the lake?"

"Near the state park. It's a peninsula."

"So do you live on the lake?"

"Yes."

"Wow..." She giggled. "I love the water!"

Now I was shaking, unable to speak. I took a breath. "Stephanie, my folks just invited me to go to church this weekend."

"Oh really? What kind of church?"

"I'm not sure really. I've not been a church goer. It's non-denominational."

"Oh, what's the name of it?"

"The Way."

Now the phone was silent. I found myself praying. Had God really put all these pieces together? John always would say, "There are no accidents. God has purpose in everything."

"Well, Eli Grollenberg, it seems we will meet again much sooner than we thought."

I could tell she was smiling on the other end of the phone.

"Yes. I'm looking forward to it."

"Me too."

"See you then, Stephanie. Be safe, and I'm so sorry for the loss of your friends."

"Thank you Eli, I will. Until then, goodbye."

I hung up with Stephanie and felt like I had never felt in the past, not even that night of our kiss. Under normal circumstances, I would have given myself credit for my charm, wit, or likability. But for some strange reason, I could only give the credit to God. The orchestration John often talked about, God's work behind the scenes, was the only explanation. It was a supernatural work.

There was no doubt in my mind that it was Stephanie my parents had met, that she had been waiting for some unknown reason to marry and have the life she desperately wanted. All the details were falling into place. I felt a desire to do something that had always been difficult for me—to read. Stephanie had mentioned how she loved to read. I felt I needed something to tip me over, pull me out of my reluctance to offer my life to this amazing God. Why wasn't that enough? "God's will and timing"—that is what John would say.

I decided I would bless my folks with a summer cookout and tell them the Stephanie saga that evening. I had to go to the market, do some shopping, and find myself some motivation. The crossroads center would have to do in this small town. Oddly enough, I found all I needed: the food, a book for Stephanie entitled *Surrender: The Heart God Controls,* by Nancy Leigh DeMoss, and a book on faith for me. I had decided that I needed more faith. I would not discover it until much later, but God was working; orchestrating even on this seemingly insignificant trip to the store.

I went all out and refused to allow my parents to help. BBQ chicken breasts, boiled potatoes, grilled asparagus, fresh corn on the cob, and matzah. Dad said the blessing, we broke the bread and had a splash of wine.

"To what do we owe such a great occasion, son?" Marra asked.

"Yes, son. What has gotten into you?"

"Well, it's partly about that phone call. You see, Stephanie, my Stephanie from high school, will be joining us Saturday for church at The Way."

Both wore looks of astonishment. "Wow!" They said in unison.

"My life is changing. I can't say that I can take any credit for it. But I feel different."

"Did she convince you to confess to Jesus?"

"No, but there is hope. I need more faith. I picked up a book called *Perfect Faith*. It's a Christian book."

"You don't read, Eli. I could never get you to read as a child," Marra said.

"I need to change."

"Well, you certainly have learned to cook…"

"Thanks Dad. Let's hope I can impress the girl…"

"You have always been impressive, Eli. You just need the right girl to impress."

"You're right, Mom. And I somehow believe that it is all coming together. I want to invite her to come here, give her the guest suite, and stay a day or two. She says she loves the water. If it's all right with you?"

"No hanky panky?"

"Mom, I am not in that mindset at all."

"Okay, son. Go for it."

"Thanks, Dad."

I started in on the book. It was nothing like I thought. First of all, it was the second book, a sequel to a book called *Double Faith*. I kind of came in on the middle. But the orchestration was there. A young kid, talented in his sport, turned pro, and then things started coming together. It is clearly God. He was a dirt bike racer in the seventies. I got caught up in it and couldn't put it down. His girl from early on moves away, they rediscover each other, and things just take off. I found myself encouraged, my faith building. He realized he was missing God after a fellow racer who was a born-again Christ follower died. Light bulbs were going off in my head.

I read the entire book in one night and outrageous things were happening that could only be supernatural. The most important thing I learned from the book was that God doesn't care how bad you are or how many mistakes we make. His love is unconditional and He is busy trying to get our attention. Sadly, we are a stiff-necked people and I am the best at that. Now I could hardly wait to get the first book, and I knew there would be a third. The writer just seemed to move me.

On Saturday morning, I came out in my best. Marra said I looked like a keeper. We loaded up into the Range Rover and stopped at the gate.

"Does anyone know 'The Way'?"

"I do…" Dad said.

"So do I…" Marra added. We all laughed.

I had never felt more at peace. We arrived early and Dad and I escorted Marra in arm-in-arm. As soon as we walked in the door, I saw her. She recognized Dad and Mom and hurriedly came to greet them.

"What are you two doing here?"

She was so bright, full of joy, beautiful in every way I like.

"We brought our son to church…" Marra said.

"This is Eli, our son." Dad said proudly.

"You're Eli?"

"Yes." I extended my hand. "Nice to meet you…"

"But how? I met your folks months ago."

"They thought it might be you—The Way, Front Royal. I say it's supernatural."

She was just stunning. She had flowers in her wavy brown hair—I was in awe.

"I couldn't agree more." Stephanie was shaking her head, trying to grasp all the connections. We were all doing that. It couldn't have been more perfect. They served us coffee at the coffee bar.

"Italian sweet cream for me…" Stephanie said.

"Really?" I asked.

"Yes, I love it."

"Two please," I said. She just smiled.

We sat, sipping our coffee, chit-chatting and listening to the band warm up. The church was perfect with stained glass windows, a simple wooden cross at the front and a single chair on the stage. We sat in the middle on the aisle. I never liked being up front or way in the back. I liked everything about Stephanie and I could see that girl I first kissed inside. She had grown into a beautiful, smart, delightful woman and she was fluent in French and German, which excited me to no end.

The Pastor came out and welcomed the crowd of about three hundred. He prayed a powerful prayer and asked new-comers to stand and introduce themselves. I did, and he said he was grateful our Jewish friends had come. Then we worshiped. The songs were both touching and powerful: How Great is Our God, He Reigns, How He Loves Us. I was near tears, I was so moved. I could feel the Spirit in this place, and when it was time to teach, Pastor Richard sat and asked the congregation to open to Ezekiel 38.

"We begin a new study this week, venturing into God's prophetic Word." I knew the text well, but Richard put amazing tidbits of history, culture, and Jewish tradition into the mix. This was a church that wanted its congregation to know the truth and to know it well. It was a sermon and a teaching. Richard's title of pastor/teacher was fitting. He then answered questions. I bravely asked one—about the Prince of Rosh.

"Most Bible scholars believe that this is the underworld leader of Russia, also known as Gog. Perhaps he is an Oligarch or a former leader of the KGB. He would be operating in the shadows with Putin as his puppet leader. He would be an agent of Satan."

"You are familiar with a man named Sulaman?"

For a second, I thought he was asking me directly.

"He is the leader of the Iranian Republican Guard, a very evil man. In fact, he is not supposed to leave Iran for any reason. We know he recently traveled to a small province of Russia in a Russian military plane. Who he met with, we do not know. But the province is called Rosh. We can't be sure of the connection, but he could have met with the one referred to as the 'Prince of Rosh'. There are many references to princes, some good, some bad. There is the Prince of Persia, the prince of this world, and the Prince of the power of the air. These are all forms or names for Satan. We'll have more on this next week. Watch the news, my brothers and sisters. We are close."

I was blown away and wanted to talk to this man. First, he gave an invitation and many went forward. I was not one of them, but I had never seen this before. He led them through a prayer similar to the one John prayed at Marseille. Then he said something amazing: "If you prayed that prayer, the angels in heaven are rejoicing and your names are now written in the Book of Life—they can never be erased. Amen, Amen."

With that, the service was over and everyone stayed and talked while the band freestyled. It was awesome and we met many amazing people. There were huge families with polite children, couples of all ages, and young adults by the dozens. Everyone told us what a great couple we were. "You take after your parents," they would say. Of course, these people knew my folks. Stephanie and I were the newcomers and we both felt right at home.

Pastor Richard made it a point to come and talk. "You two are an amazing couple. Stephanie, I didn't know you were attached."

"We just reconnected, actually. We went to high school together."
She said.

"Well, I discern a closeness in you two…"

"Thank you, Pastor. And thank you for the great teaching. You
must have some connections for your insight. It's a favorite subject of
mine."

"Yes, a Rabbi friend of mine – former Mossad. Hits close to home
for you, I would think."

"Pardon?"

"You are Jewish? Born in the Holy Land I assume."

"Yes, in Tel Aviv," I said.

"You and your father share a namesake?"

"Yes. Eliezer."

"God is help," he said.

I looked at Dad.

"Yes, son of Moses," Dad said.

"I love the Old Testament—and the Jews. We are so blessed you
could come."

"Nice to meet you, Pastor."

"Call me Richard—please."

I invited Stephanie to come to lunch and to see the place. She
nodded enthusiastically. I walked her to her car and held the door.
Nothing had ever felt so natural. She loved the house, the lake, and my
folks. I asked her where she was staying.

"With a friend in Lynchburg."

"Could you stay here—a day or two?" We have a guest room."
Then I smiled and put on puppy-dog eyes.

"Oh, I couldn't impose," she said.

"Nonsense, girl. You're family," Dad said.

"I'll give you a ride in the boat..." I offered.

"Really? No imposition?"

"Of course not."

"Okay then. Thank you. I rather felt I was imposing on my friend," she said.

"She'll understand then," said Marra, always one to state the obvious.

"It's settled then," Dad said. "Marra and I will get dinner ready and you two can get a sunset cruise in. Now, off with you!"

"I should change," Stephanie said.

"Oh, don't change. We like you just the way you are..." Dad joked.

"Jewish humor," I offered. We all laughed.

The sunset cruise was spectacular and we turned off the boat, sat in the darkening sky, and talked.

"I'm not good at this, Eli."

"Good at what?"

"Relationships."

"Whoa now, we're just friends!" My huge smile and puppy-dog eyes were working.

"Will you hold me?" she asked.

I stretched out my arms and we embraced. It was a perfect setting. I had some tears—not like me. But it felt so good.

"God is so good," she said.

"Yes, it appears so. Only He could make a way."

"The Way. It's always the way and never halfway. My friends told me, 'God cares most about what we do while we wait.'"

"I think you are going to say He rewards us."

"Yes, in amazing ways. You are amazing…"

"You are as well. As amazing as I remember that first kiss."

"It was good, wasn't it?" She said with a smile.

"Oh yeah."

"Encore?"

And that was it. It all came back and it was even better under an orange-red sky with a cool lake breeze.

"I have a confession, Stephanie."

"Okay."

"I owe you this, I am not yet a believer."

"In us?"

"No, that's the easy part. You are perfect…"

"What then?"

"I have not confessed my faith in Christ."

She looked deeply into my eyes. "I would never have guessed."

"I'm a Jew—the whole stiff-necked thing."

"Well, after that kiss, you better get it together. He can't make it more perfect than this."

"I agree. Just be patient with me."

"I can do that. God has to draw you. In time."

chapter TWELVE

I spilled the beans, all of them, to this god-send of a lady. I told her she needed to hear the truth about who I am, who I was, and what I hoped to be with God's help and hers. She reciprocated by telling me she had never been with a man—she had remained pure. I was moved and my respect for her was off the charts. Then, I blew her mind by telling her that I had never been with a woman. I had been a woman, but not with one. I had to show her my passport.

"Wow, you're gorgeous, and I'm not kidding."

"What about a man?" She asked.

"Huh, what do you mean?"

She just smiled as it set in.

"No. Absolutely not!"

"I'm just kidding, silly. But really, all this spy stuff, world traveler—never?"

"No, never. It's a Jewish thing I suppose. But I have been in some uncomfortable spots a few times. Some men can be animals!"

"Don't I know it. Except for one—clear back in high school. You were special then. You are special now."

"Ditto!"

We both smiled.

Stephanie had read both *Double Faith* and *Perfect Faith*. "They are great, such a simple and beautiful love story. I can relate to Robin (the leading female character in the books) so much. People don't realize how hard it is to be young. If only we could go back…"

"Yes, but then we may not have this. This is pretty special too. And we have all that experience and knowledge God has given to us. So I need to read the first book?" I asked.

"Oh yeah. Plus, the third book is coming out in July, I think."

I had to stop and thank God for this last week. One door closed and another opened. Amazing!

"What are you thinking?" Steph asked.

"Thanking God for everything."

"We haven't seen anything yet…"

"You mean the prophecies, the promises, the return of Jesus?"

"No, us!"

We both laughed. Things were so easy with Stephanie. Mom and Dad just watched in awe. I couldn't believe it myself.

Two days passed and we had the time of our lives. Then she had to go work and tie up some loose ends. The goodbye was bittersweet.

"When will we see each other again?"

"God's time. You have things to get in order and so do I. God was orchestrating, yet I really never expected this… I am excited for what lies ahead. Call me…"

"You know I will."

"By the way, I love the place, and your folks, and…" She just smiled. Then she was gone.

Dad and Mom walked over to me and gave me a hug.

"Son, I'm not sure what you did, but you did it well…"

"Thanks, Dad. She's great, isn't she?"

"A match made in heaven," Mom said.

"Get your things in order, son. Your life has changed and you have work to do."

Of course, he meant that I needed my salvation. I decided to call John, who was getting some rays in Florida.

"Hey buddy… How ya doing?"

"Jeremy, where in the world are you?"

"The lake."

"Good. I need to come see you. I'll drive up. Got myself a new ride."

"Okay, John. See you in a few days?"

"More like tomorrow night. Put some ribs on for me."

"Will do. Be safe."

I told the folks my friend John was coming to visit.

"Do you need anything at the store?" Marra had a list, and I had my own. They had ordered me *Double Faith* and I had a pre-order in for *Extreme Faith*, which would be released in July. I got a text from Stephanie. She was home and missed me already. This was all so new. I had a best friend—and it wasn't John anymore. He would be so disappointed! I voice-texted back, "Thank you. Miss you too. I am very fond of you!"

"You're too much—fond of you also!"

I picked up the book and the girl behind the counter told me it was good.

"Best seller, you know." She said.

"I didn't know that, but I loved the second one."

"You read them out of order?"

"Guilty as charged."

"Then you missed out on the best parts. You'll love it…"

"Thank you."

I picked up the groceries and a six pack of Corona. John loved ribs and Corona, which reminded me to get a half-dozen limes. What a nut. I had missed him.

I read *Double Faith* in one evening and was moved to tears. Now I could see Robin and Ken in their early years, growing up too fast, losing each other and finding each other again. I texted Stephanie and she asked me to call. We stayed on the phone until two in the morning. I told her about John and our time at the Academy.

"It's gone now, you know," she said.

"The Academy? Yes, I heard. Sad indeed."

"My best friend had two sons there. Like many others, they could not get out in time."

"Oh, I'm sorry."

"The losses are just beginning to add up." She said. "If you're right on your dates, things will get ugly quick. But God is in full control."

"Yes. I hope we can be together in that time."

"Is that an invitation?"

"Yes, of course. Come stay with us."

"I'll think about it."

"Fair enough. Goodnight, precious one."

"Goodnight, precious man…"

John arrived in style with a new, slightly used Ferrari 458 in silver. Now, I had always been a Ferrari fan, and this thing was sweet. The ox-blood leather interior and awesome sounding V8 were inviting us to the open road. He met the folks and was so kind. But we had some man-talk to get to, and the car was the best place for it.

"So is this your Golden Parachute?" I asked.

"No, I'm still on the payroll. They told me to get lost for a few years, stay low profile and not to spend my bonus too fast. So I bought the car."

"This thing is amazing and sounds wicked."

"Oh, it's in quiet mode. Here…" He pushed a button on the dash and suddenly we were in a racecar.

"Hold on…" he said as he punched it and ripped through the tight and winding roads of the Blue Ridge mountains.

"Holy crap!" I gripped the seat as best I could.

"640 horses, baby…" John boasted.

"Awesome!" I was impressed. We made it to Roanoke in record time and managed to avoid any state troopers.

"So Jeremy, what's going on?"

"I met the girl…"

"No kidding. How hard did you have to look?"

"Not at all, really. We sort of found each other. At church."

"Holy cow, man. God's really been busy, huh?"

"Oh yeah."

"Are you convinced yet?"

"Yes, but still stiff-necked. She stayed at the house a few days."

"No kidding. That's sweet, man… When's the wedding?"

"No wedding until I'm a believer."

"Good for her."

"She's a god-send, John, let me tell you."

"Well, you better get with it. Time is short."

"Yeah, yeah, I know. I'm close."

"Close doesn't cut it, Jeremy."

"I know. And call me Eli—that's my name."

"Eli—that is a good Jew name. You haven't used that since the Academy."

"It means, 'God is help'."

"Good. You need all the help you can get... When do I get to meet the girl?"

"I don't know. How long are you staying?"

"Through the fourth, if that's okay."

"Sure, no problem. Saturday, maybe. She may come to church. She lives up north."

"Okay, looking forward to it. Now let me tell you about how much intel our last mission yielded." I got an hour's worth of updates as we wound through the mountains.

"So what's Sulaman up to?"

"Another trip to Russia. I don't think he's too happy with you. A raw deal, lost half of his body guards and two MIG's. Not to mention the police chopper. He can't be happy. And they are about to take it to Israel—all in your name."

"God will give him his due."

"Yes, let's hope he gets his before he can get us."

"We're small fish in a big pond, John."

"Let's hope so. I would keep an eye in the rear view."

"I am. But we have God."

"Correction, I have God. You are stalling..."

I gave him a sideways smile. We were home.

We enjoyed ribs, old times, outrageous stories of the Academy, and John being John. My folks loved him and they somehow knew I was alive because of this man. That's right, we owed each other for life-ending bail-outs in the field. I showed him the rest of the house—the command center, the bunker, the security system.

"I feel safe here." John said.

"What are you saying, John? Did you not feel safe in Florida?"

"I had a close call. That's all. I wanted to get the heat off, so I snuck out to Miami, bought the car, and headed up here."

"You could have gone with something a little less conspicuous. What does that thing go for?"

"You don't want to know."

"Did someone try to hit you?"

"Not exactly. More like run me into on-coming traffic on my bike!"

"Who was it?"

"I would guess it's Sulaman's henchman. You have to be on that list, you know."

"Great. All I need is to put my family in danger."

"I was really careful, Eli. No one followed me. What I can't say is if they know where *you* are," he said.

"Well, we just went to Defcon 1."

A few days went by with no problems. We went to church and met Stephanie there. We made John stay at the house, just out of caution. Steph couldn't stay, but agreed to come for the fourth. She loved the book I gave her and wondered how I knew what she would like.

"Just a wild guess," I said.

We hugged and sent her on her way. It was good to see her and gave me something to look forward to. It was clear that my folks loved her too.

When we got back, the first thing John asked me was, "Did you do it?"

"Not yet."

"What is your problem?"

"I don't know. Stubborn, I guess. I want God to move in me, not just accept it because of Stephanie. I want to do it for the right reasons."

"Okay, you got me there. Still, you are so stubborn."

Dad answered for me, "Stiff-necked Jew."

"There is good news though, Steph is coming next weekend for the fourth. We have fireworks here at the lake—spectacular. We'll take the pontoon boat out."

"Sounds good, bro."

We had a good week and it went by fast. John and I were diligent without being obvious. Everything was quiet and in order. We decided we would all go to church and John loved Steph, the church, and the teaching. There was also a woman, Steph's friend from Lynchburg. Her name was Renea Austin, an attractive woman of some stature. At least six-foot-one and athletic. She was introduced as Steph's best friend from college, a professor of European Language and martial arts instructor. Needless to say, John and Renea hit it off. John, of course, was born in Berlin and had lived there until age thirteen. Soon we were all conversing in German.

"It seems John and Renea have hit it off." I told Steph.

"Who could have known? Honestly, she wanted to come to see who it was that caused me to stand her up. And look!"

"God is good!"

We all sat together and listened to Richard in the heart of the Gog prophecies. He kept referring to the Armies of Gog. "They are being lured in and God will show the world who He is." It was a spectacular sermon and teaching. I held Steph's hand the entire time.

We had a huge lunch at the lake house and talked endlessly. Renea was very curious about our occupations, but we somehow diverted her by saying that we did business together but were in the process of retiring.

"Well, you must do well. This is an awesome place. No wonder Steph stood me up…"

"Renea, would you like to stay? We have a huge firework display here on the fourth," I offered.

"Oh, I would love to, but I didn't bring a bag and I really have to get back tonight."

"Could you come back tomorrow? Plan to stay a day or two with Steph in the guest suite?"

She looked at Steph, at John, at me. We all had puppy-dog eyes.

"Are you sure you have room?"

"Yes, absolutely…"

"Okay then."

She and Stephanie had a conversation in private before we all said goodbye, then John asked to walk her out. It took twenty minutes for him to come back in.

"Wow! Stephanie, how did you know?"

"I didn't even know about you… Let alone that you were here. Amazing!"

"Yes, she is. Did you hear Pastor Richard say we were a great couple?"

"We heard that, yes John…" I said.

"You two *are* a great couple… Just be on your best behavior. She is one tough girl."

"I for one would love to see that match…" I said.

"Okay, you two. Calm down. John, do you like her?" Steph asked.

"Yes. We have a lot in common, blonde, blue eyes, smart, tough. I guess God really has been orchestrating. And you two—well, it's unbelievable. Thank you for making an honest man out of him." John said.

"Renea really liked the church too," Steph said. "She goes to a huge church at Liberty University and she loves it. But she loved how Richard teaches. It's deep truth, and God-centered. Sometimes sermons are only designed to tickle our ears."

"I couldn't agree more. Eli and I had been studying Ezekiel 38 and 39, at least the political aspects, but Richard brings it to life. It could happen at any time." John said.

"That is true. Anyways, Renea will be back tomorrow…"

"Yes, I need to go to the store…" John said.

"Later… Let's go for a boat ride."

The big Wellcraft was made for off-shore and would run over a hundred on rough water. Out here on the lake, it was like a thrill ride. John had impressed me with the Ferrari. Now it was time to blow his mind. We headed out across the lake at about quarter throttle. Then I opened her up. Steph had a huge smile as we blasted to the far end of the lake. John was like a kid. This is what men did and we did it well. The good news was that Steph was right at home.

"Men and their toys!" Steph said as we pulled into the boathouse. John just shook his head.

"Wait until you see John's Ferrari…" I said.

"Oh, brother!"

She was shaking her head, but smiling. "Let's go see how well we get along in the kitchen."

"Now we're talking…" I said.

Steph and I threw together an amazing meal and we enjoyed a candlelight dinner on the deck with a full moon.

"It will be a perfect night for fireworks tomorrow." Dad said.

"Amen, Dad."

We finished the evening with Mom and Dad saying goodnight early, John watching baseball in the TV room, and Steph and I sharing a sweet goodnight kiss under that full moon.

"Turns out we're pretty darn good in the kitchen…" She whispered to me.

"Everywhere, so far."

"That must mean we have a trial coming."

"God's refining, huh?"

"Yes. Constantly, He chastises the ones He loves. It prepares us for this—the good part. We're close, you know?"

"It seems so. I trust God to draw me soon."

"It's His timing, Eli. He is never late. The challenge is not getting ahead of Him. We have no idea what He has in store for us. We just need to be ready."

"I like what He has delivered so far."

"Me too. Me too."

Jerusalem: Time of Jacob's Trouble

I assessed the situation and the mysterious woman. While many heads rolled, my mind drifted back to my home life in Virginia. It hadn't been a perfect childhood, but I also know that I had a lot to be grateful for. I knew that my father loved me and he did his very best to provide and retain a sense of my identity. He truly loved my mother, and in quiet moments he would tell the story of how they met, fell in love, and refused to acknowledge the difference between her culture and his. His kind words and passion for her were present in every story. They would always end the same, short of the final chapter, with my father frustrated and fighting painful memories of his loss.

He would get up and leave the room only to return a few minutes later, composed and wanting a hug. Though he had strayed from the Jewish religion, he had allowed Marra to teach me and carry on the Jewish traditions. One of my favorites was Purim. Father would join us in the fast and then the reading of the Megillah, the story of Esther from the book of Esther. Our favorite part was cheering and spinning the noise makers when Mordecai's name was read and then booing, hissing, and stomping our feet when the evil Haman's name was read. By the end, we were worn out from all the activity and humbled by the gravity of this epic account.

The moral of the Esther story was that our obedience to a God we can't see and don't always hear from is the difference in the world. Yes, I realize now that God was working behind the scenes, orchestrating all of the events while respecting man's free will to choose. Queen Esther could have played it safe, but God had put her in the very position she was to save the Jews. Looking back, I can see the times God wanted to have me do things I wasn't comfortable with. Marra, my stepmother, had us go to a Christian church after my freshman year in high school. It was all new to us, but I felt a connection.

Just prior to graduation from high school, God asked something of me. The idea came to me: Go to the hospital, to the ER. Take only my Bible and read and pray in the waiting room. Was it from God? Seemed straightforward enough, but kind of silly, embarrassing. Just walk in and sit down to read? But it was strong in me and I was motivated to go. When I arrived, I drove around the parking lot for a few minutes. Nowhere to park—I began to doubt, and it built. I grew impatient and left. When I got home, I sat in the car wondering. I opened my Bible. There in front of me was the verse from the book of Esther: "If you remain silent at this time, relief and deliverance will arise for the Jews from another place, but you and your father's house will perish. Yet who knows whether you have come to the kingdom for such a time as this."

It was clear to me: God had sent me on a mission, a simple one at that. As simple as Jesus' request of Peter at the shore of Galilee: "Put out a little from the land." A small request to test my obedience. Peter complied, I did not. Peter was being prepared for a huge catch. I was being tested. God had sent another into that hospital in my place. The mission was completed and I missed out on the blessing. Instead of drawing closer to God, I pulled back and stopped going to church. Summer and then college in Maryland completed my long list of excuses. There was no question, I was lost.

And now, as a tribulation saint, the choice was once again in front of me. I didn't know this woman behind me in line, but we were of one mind—the Holy Spirit. I could see it in her eyes. I could anticipate what was going to happen. It was clear to me—not the details, just that it was about to happen. God was about to make a way.

Even before I became a believer, God had rescued me from countless near-death experiences. I could trust Him and the Spirit which was binding me and this woman. Perhaps I was placed here for such a time as this. I evaluated the situation, the placement of the Global Constables, spectators, escape route options. The line was long and wound along the base of the Mount of Olives. The hill backdropped the stage for TV and the significant audience. The only real option was to overpower and kill the guard immediately in front of us, shoot as many others, take their weapons, and disappear into the huge crowd. I took a deep breath, looked behind me into the woman's steely eyes. She nodded, as if she had read every thought.

chapter
THIRTEEN
✡ ✡ ✡ ✡ ✡ ✡ ✡

I had pretty much decided that my heart's desire was to marry Stephanie. If all went well, I would ask her. I also knew the answer would be no unless I was a believer, so that we would be equally yoked. I would have to consider all of this and put some faith in God. Young Ken Sparks from the books made a lot of mistakes and blew it many times over. Still, God accepted him unconditionally. Why couldn't I have enough faith to go forward at church? The invitation was welcoming, but I still hung on to some doubt.

I toured Steph and John through the place into the deepest, remotest parts of the underground. I showed them the garage—not the normal garage, but the one where a quick escape could happen and exit way down the road. I guess I spent too many years living and working in secret bunkers. Steph was a little creeped out by all the weapons and defenses and technology.

"No, I don't have cameras in the guest suite. That would be weird. But they are everywhere else…"

"And needed, in some rare instances," John said.

"So you two have been spying together for years?" Steph asked.

"Sadly, we are consummate pros at spying, covert operations, and winning." John added.

"I hate to ask, but have you had to…you know…kill anyone?"

There was a huge pause and we both slowly slinked away.

"That would explain a lot!" Steph said. "You are dealing with guilt and forgiveness issues. Things like that are incredibly traumatic. You both probably have PTSD. That's why you compensate with fast cars and boats."

"You could be right," John conceded.

"I have an idea," Steph announced. "I'll go to work on it. Excuse me while I make a call."

Steph left John and I in the control room. While she was making her call, we watched the news. Fox News had some deep analysis going on regarding the Russians, the North Koreans, Iran, and many others. They called it a major storm brewing with a list of bad actors and power-hungry leaders pushing for power. On the US side, the same old arguments seemed to rage. People wanted autonomy. No one wanted to follow the rules and chaos was everywhere. Trump's war on lawlessness continued to arrest, deport, and kill lawbreakers. It didn't seem to matter. We were living in the end times.

"Second Timothy 3," John said.

"What's that, John?"

"It's a chapter in the Bible."

"I know that! What is the scripture?"

"I'm messing with you." He quoted it from memory, "But know this, that in the last days perilous times will come: For men will be lovers of themselves, lovers of money, boasters, proud, blasphemers, disobedient to parents, unthankful, unholy, unloving, unforgiving, slanderers, without self-control, brutal, despisers of good, traitors, headstrong, haughty, lovers of pleasure rather than lovers of God, having a form of godliness but denying its power. And from such people turn away!"

"Wow. I could see a little of myself in there," I said. "Headstrong, proud, unthankful."

"Yes, me too…" John said. "The reality is that at some point in my past, I have been all of those things."

"Yes, I'm afraid that goes for me too…" I said.

Perhaps Stephanie was on to something. There could be a whole host of demons inside of me. The truth was that I had killed many people, mostly bad guys, but there was always collateral—civilians in missile strikes, who knew? God knew. And perhaps Steph knew too. Maybe not all of the in's and out's, but she could imagine. I had opened up to her, and she knew it had to take a toll. Perhaps I was hardened and needed to be broken. When all of this began to set in, I felt weak, out of sorts. I knew it was time for change.

Stephanie had an idea. She handed John and me small sheets of paper and asked us to write down all those people whom we needed to forgive and all those whom we would like to forgive us. We were told to pray about it for ten minutes or half an hour and she would get back to us.

Each of us ended up with sizable lists and humble hearts. Both of us had caused a lot of pain and we ourselves had been hurt in many ways over the years. Coincidentally, we each included ourselves at the top of our lists. Mine included those who had killed my mother. We both agonized over our lists and were gripped by the overwhelming gravity of the exercise.

Stephanie then took our two lists and dropped them in a clear tub of water, and they dissolved right in front of our eyes. I broke down, and John hit his knees. Stephanie led me and then John to the sink, washed our hands, and prayed over us declaring that we were clean. At that moment, we were profoundly changed and it was clear to us that we needed it. Two tough guys yielded to humility that was long overdue. John and I felt an ever-present load lifted from our hearts.

None of this should have been a surprise to me. God was working on the churches. Even the cult churches that had been growing in previous decades were shrinking and disappearing. As Jesus said in the first three chapters of His revelation, "He who has ears to hear let him hear what the Spirit says to the churches." He was busy building truth-based churches and cutting off false churches. It was plain as day. Plus, He was dealing with governments that were persecuting His followers. This was the beginning of sorrows. The end was coming.

While prophecy gives us a lot of revelation and clues, we will not know the day or time of Jesus' return. He told us as much in Matthew 24:36. Like John had told me over and over, many steadfast religious people will believe that they will go in the Rapture, but instead will be left behind. He pointed to the Parable of the Ten Virgins in Matthew 25. Even though they were all together in the same place, waiting for the same coming of the bridegroom, some were ready and some not. I didn't have a chance. He told me plainly, "You must be born again!"

So I reasoned, if we were close and He was busy working on the preparations—the signs were everywhere—the warning of preparedness found in the virgin parable was for me. I couldn't buy it. I couldn't make a "head" decision. It had to be a heart decision. Again, John's reading of Romans 10:9 was at the forefront of my mind. Then, just then, Stephanie walked back into the room. He had sent me a sign, yet

He kept hardening my heart. Why? John reminded me so many times, "God's will. God's timing."

Apparently, there was work to do. Fortunately, I was surrounded by believers and knew, deep down inside, that soon I would join them. Stephanie was more than ample justification to give my life to Christ. John marveled at how well we fit together. He was hoping the same would develop between Renea and himself. We were all excited for what the Fourth of July weekend had in store.

We had a feast ready when Renea arrived. She looked amazing and was dressed to kill. My dad was having a field day with all of this. Of course, he and my step-mom were the perfect example of love at its best. We enjoyed dinner, had a lovely evening playing games and listening to Dad make Jewish jokes. We took the boat out for a moonlight cruise and shut it down in the middle of the lake to take in the warm night and star-filled sky.

Stephanie told the story of the Sadie Hawkins dance from her perspective. "I really liked Eli. He was a boy who didn't intimidate us girls. He was handsome, kind, and shy. To me, he was the perfect boy to ask, so I did. I about fell over when he said yes. Of course, girls are way ahead of boys at that stage. The proof was in the fact that Eli and I danced the night away while most of my friends ended up as wallflowers. I remember the song we danced to last. It was 'Faithfully' by Journey. We slow danced and all was perfect. Then it happened. We looked at each other, oblivious to the world, and we kissed. And we kissed, and we kissed."

"We heard it a million times in college," Renea said. "All Steph could talk about was Eli and the kiss."

"Is that true?" John asked.

Stephanie looked at me with a serious face and a tear. "Yes. It's true. I was moved by that kiss and haven't felt that way about a man since. Until the other night. I was fifteen again…"

"So was I…" I added enthusiastically.

We all gazed up at the amazing, star-filled sky. I reached out and took Steph's hand. I noticed Renea and John were embracing. Wow, I thought, if this is what God can do after a lifetime of wondering, what would we make of it? Steph squeezed my hand. I looked at her and the rest just flowed out of us.

An occasional aerial burst would light up the night here and there, although there were enough of those going off in my head. We talked for about an hour, then a slight breeze blew a chilling reminder that it was time to go in. We were ready for some coffee and Italian sweet cream. Oddly, Renea was a black coffee drinker, just like John. Weird… I turned the fire pit on and we roasted marshmallows.

Our goodnights were long and loving. I was sure John was thanking God for Renea. I was also sure I needed God. Stephanie, in classic style, assured me it would all come to me. "He never takes us halfway." she said.

"But what about that 'God's will' thing?"

"I guess we'll have to wait and see. In the meantime, I'm having a blast!"

"Me too, Steph. Me too."

I met John in the control room. I had been there a few minutes, catching up on the news.

"Iran is back to boasting, but the front is quiet."

"Too quiet, I would think. You know, a week ago I was ready for all this to go down."

"All what?"

"You know—the Gog war, the Antichrist, all that. I felt ready. Now, I feel like I want more time. I want to live a little"

"Yes, that would be nice. Well, there is no timeline between Gog and the covenant. Could be several years. We could be married and have traveled over the world."

"True. I guess we will see. There is little we can do to change God's plans."

"We can thank Him…for these amazing ladies."

"Yes, indeed. God really does have a plan. And you need to get with the program." John said.

"Yes, for me especially. I'm the lost one. He could come anytime. You know that many commentators believe the Gog prophecy will result in the revelation of the Antichrist and the Rapture. My time is short."

"I couldn't agree more. Shall we pray right now?"

"For world peace?"

"No, for your salvation."

"No, not yet."

Instead, John prayed for his stiff-necked Jewish friend to get a clue. I couldn't agree more, and we had a house full of guests who would also agree.

I had an email from the bookstore. My copy of *Extreme Faith* was in. Since Steph and I were early risers, I would shanghai her and sneak out for an early breakfast and coffee. As I opened the door to the Rover for her, she lifted herself in with a wince.

"You okay?"

"Oh, yeah. Leftovers from an accident two years ago."

"Oh no, what happened?"

"I'll explain at breakfast." she said with a smile.

The bookstore would not open until 8:00 AM so we settled into a nice booth at Lakeside Diner. I knew from experience the French toast was great, and they had our Italian sweet cream. We clinked our cups to new friends and another anniversary for our country.

"So you had a fender bender?" I asked.

"A little more than that," she began with a solemn look. "Young girl, texting, drove off the road, across the median of twenty-nine, and hit me head on. There was a big swale in between the lanes. She came out of nowhere. We were each doing at least sixty."

"Steph, you're fortunate to be alive…"

"That's what the firefighter kept saying. My car was a Chrysler 300, hers a Chevy Citation. She wasn't so lucky. It took them forever to get me out and all that was left of the car was the back of my seat and rearward. My knees went into the dash, or rather it came down to crush them. My feet were entangled in the brake pedal. And I mean entangled. Twenty-seven hours of surgery later, here I am."

"I'm so sorry. You have recovered well."

"Or so it would seem, praise God. I still live with a lot of pain and lack of movement. Otherwise, no worse for wear."

"Are you still in rehab?"

She looked at me a little sideways and replied, "Twice a week. Except when I have better plans." Now her smile was back.

"Fourth of July at the lake?"

"Fourth of July at the lake with you!"

"Why, thank you."

There was a quiet pause as we sipped coffee.

"The girl...?"

"Twenty-five, in a fight with her boyfriend. Her last text was, 'I can't do this right now.' Her family came to see me. They were grieving, but wanted to apologize to me. I was so out of it, but I do remember. I spent a lot of time in the hospital thinking about my life, God, my love life—or lack of it. I thought I was stuck, gimped up, beat up and alone. I shook my fist at Him a few times. My folks had split, but the one saving grace was that it brought them back together. A small price to pay for that blessing."

I didn't know what to say. The food saved the day. We ate, laughed, and moved on. I think God wanted me to know this detail, but not to dwell on it. It would be significant to the picture, I could feel it.

We enjoyed our breakfast, picked up the book, and headed home.

"Rock, paper, scissors for who gets to read it first," Steph said. I won, but still insisted she go first.

"Okay, I'll have it done in a day anyway..." she said.

We returned to a happy group of coffee-drinkers. Dad and Mom had started breakfast and everyone was still in pajamas. Steph excused herself to her room and Renea followed. John cornered me, "Eli, I got a text. We need to go downstairs..."

The elevator opened into the control room and we were greeted by bad news at every screen. France—three suicide attacks, at least 150 dead. UK—four deadly attacks, eighty-three dead and 190 injured. Stockholm—two huge resort hotels bombed, dozens dead, hundreds missing. Barcelona—a mall and a movie theater shooting, and two suicide bombers at a hotel and the airport. An Indian airline jet blown up over the Bay of Bengal. On and on it went.

"Global Jihad." John said. "It started early and is moving west. You know it's al-Qaeda, ISIS, the Taliban—an all-out war on the infidels. They want me at Quantico tomorrow morning. You better check yours." Sure enough, I was being asked to report to the new Whitehall complex at 1200 hours.

"It must be big. We're the last resort."

"No doubt. They are expecting a huge outbreak here. Remember the fourteen hundred cells and sixty-nine hundred bad guys that the former president had deleted from the database?" John said.

"Yeah, I think we may get to know them again in the next day or two."

"This could be ugly. Let's warn who we know. Large cities, parades, gatherings…ugh."

"No way to assess how bad this could be. Where are your folks now, John?"

"Tampa. Should be okay. We'll be fine here. They are going to be looking for high value targets. We need to get the girls to stay here."

I agreed. "We'd better tell them soon."

"Roger that…" John added.

The chaos was everywhere. It was small, pinpointed attacks all over the world. This was the Caliphate, blossoming from the branches. We knew it was global. With a month and some to go to my theoretical date, could this be a distraction or a first-volley? Regardless, it was ugly and once again proved that the enemy we were fighting was covert and everywhere.

We went upstairs and met up with the girls on the deck.

"A picture-perfect day…" said Renea.

"Unfortunately, we have some bad news from Europe and beyond. Perhaps we should eat in the TV room"

We gathered, John prayed, and I switched the TV's on. We were all in shock. I brought them all up to speed on the news as we watched coverage. It seemed every country but Israel had been hit with wave after wave of suicide bombers, suicide drivers, and hijackers.

"Nothing in the US yet, even though there are Independence Day parades in hundreds of cities coast to coast. All is quiet in America. You two should check in with your loved ones and tell them to avoid large, high profile gatherings in any big city. This could be trouble."

"Is this the Caliphate?" Dad asked.

"Could be, Dad. It seems they are going all out. We'll see in time," I said.

"We are going to be safe here, but Eli and I both are being summoned to our team headquarters," John said.

"You have to leave?" Renea asked.

"Yes, we need to report by noon tomorrow."

"Oh, I don't like that..." Steph said.

"Neither do we," John said.

We watched the news coverage off and on all day. Oddly, all was quiet in America. All the morning parades and celebrations, coast to coast, went off with excessive security, but without incident.

"Just like them to wait, lull us to sleep, then hit hard. I don't mean to be a doomsdayer," said John, "but this is their MO. We know they are here, thousands of them. But they are patient and know the psyche of the typical American: 'We will continue with our lives in spite of this adversity.'"

"You are so right, John," Renea added.

"We just don't believe it could happen to us. We think the government is protecting us. I don't like the quiet," Steph added.

"Yes, it is eerie," Marra commented.

"Well, we may as well follow the American psyche…when in Rome!" Dad interjected.

"Well said, Dad…"

"Plus, I do love fireworks!" Renea said.

We loaded up the boat with a picnic dinner, wine, candles, and all six of us, dropped anchor in our favorite spot, and enjoyed the dusk. By nine forty-five, the reports started to light up John's phone. Boston, Charlotte, Philadelphia, Atlanta, Orlando. All up and down the coast, there were suicide attacks in every major city. We prayed as our celebration went off as planned. No problem here, all our families were safe, but the wave was huge and moving west.

I explained to my family what John and I knew all too well. For the past twenty years, thousands of subversives had poured into the States through porous borders and began the long wait to Jihad. The global Caliphate—convert or die. Thousands more self-radicalized Muslim-Americans were joining the fight and thousands of families, couples, and innocents were dying. There was no way to stop it. No way to fight it. The cells sprang to life, rental cars and trucks were driven into crowds and blown up or their drivers got out and began to shoot.

We sat stunned at the huge banks of TV monitors in the control room. It was impossible to rationalize the horror before us. John and I excused ourselves to pack.

"How long will you be gone?" Steph asked.

"I'm not sure, sweet girl, but we'll be able to talk and text," I told her.

"Okay. I think we will stay a few days to make sure your folks are okay. Then I'd better go home and check up on things."

"Okay. If you must. I would feel a lot better if you stayed here."

"I'll be back. I have a doctor's appointment I really can't miss on Friday."

I pulled her in and held her tight.

"Not the best Fourth of July," I told her.

"No. But at least for now we are together."

"I'll be done before we know it. If it comes off the way I think it will, the leaders of ISIS, al-Qaeda, and others will ask for a surrender—convert or die. If we refuse, we could see another wave. But something concerns me."

"What is that?"

"Israel. The only country of significance left out of the fray. It doesn't add up. Or..."

"Or?"

"They could be setting the stage for the Gog war. This could be a ploy to get us sidetracked along with the rest of the world."

"I see...makes sense," she replied.

"Are you sure you have to go?"

"Yes."

"Listen to me. I sound like a school girl!"

"I like it. I miss you already."

"We live in some troubling times, my man. Pray hard about your salvation. We can't know the day or hour."

We hugged tight and said our goodnight.

John and I caught the west coast feeds late and discussed our strategy if all hell broke loose. The chaos was widespread and ranged from small incidents where the assailant was killed prior to inflicting any casualties to a huge four-point attack at a Fourth celebration in San Antonio that killed upwards of six hundred people.

"John, let's try to convince the girls to come back here as soon as possible, by the eighteenth or so of August at the latest. I want us to all be together if it goes down."

"I hear you, but you better focus on you…"

"I promise I will."

As we were leaving, there was Lech Manevetski calling for a halt to the attacks and for peace from a UN podium. He was slick, convincing, and had a traumatized, worldwide audience. He was the man, I'm afraid. There, in the background, was the former president and his pet flunkies whom he would use to elevate himself to world leader. Things were shaping up and it was beginning to wig us out. John and I watched with interest what was happening in the US. Islam had already placed major footholds in the government and politics in the UK and France. They had infiltrated their elections in small provinces and began to introduce Sharia law in brilliant political moves. Quietly, they had taken over these areas and under existing local statutes forced majority rule. Rather than fight, the governments of England and France allowed these changes in the name of tolerance.

The number of illegal Islamic immigrants and provinces governed by Sharia law had grown exponentially, nearly out of control in both countries. Germany had its own share of problems. Mosques were going up all over, as they were in America. But the US and Germany had strong-willed populations that were steadfast against Sharia law and Muslim advances. Interestingly, the media in all these countries and in places like Australia, Sweden, and other areas of Europe were beginning to push for tolerance and acceptance of Sharia law. Especially in the US, where the attacks were unrelenting and thousands were dying. The media began parroting talking points direct from the clerics, "Islam is a religion of peace. The best way to stop the violence is to submit—then we will have peace."

Statements like these were reported by news anchors and commentators speaking about the attacks. It was as if they were mesmerized.

"It is pure evil!" John said. "People see the tragedy of the attacks and they want to give in—surrender."

"And thousands are doing just that…" I said. It was also emphasized by the buildup of Islam in the coalition against Israel. It really seemed that Islam was at victory's doorstep. Many were just following mindlessly. Perhaps this was part of the lead up to the Antichrist and his power over weak minds. With heavy hearts, John and I promised to stay in touch and said our goodnights.

chapter
FOURTEEN
✡✡✡✡✡✡✡

John and I followed each other all the way to Quantico, where we waved and I continued on. The world was chaotic, and this was only just beginning. For the first time in my life, I felt I had more to live for than just myself. I missed my girl, my family, and my retirement. I was headed into the belly of the beast and could never have imagined how big a mess we were in as a country. The attacks went on into the second night and left a traumatized country, with some twenty-two thousand people dead. Then it all stopped. Hundreds of jihadists had been killed, but it was just a drop in the bucket. Now we had to try to predict what was next.

The first of the demands came from Taliban spokesman, Zabiullah Mujahid. "Infidels of the world, the prophet Muhammad has spoken. He has awakened the core of the worldwide Caliphate and the demise of the infidel is imminent. You have no option. You will convert or die. You have seen only the first round of our jihad. Prepare for the power of Islam to be unleashed on the world."

Iranian president Hassan Rouhani condemned the attacks as did Turkey's Erdogan, Afghanistan's president, Ashraf Ghani, and the Saudi King Salman.

This was little comfort to anyone, and we all knew—at least those of us who had our fingers on the pulse—that the condemnations were window dressing. The one thing most every Islamic state wanted was for the US, Europe, and eventually Israel to be at their mercy. My first system-wide teleconference was proof we were in trouble, as deep inside Cheyenne Mountain, the proverbial trigger-finger was itchy at best. Still, all was quiet. Throughout the day, one Islamic faction after another had someone on to give an ultimatum. For the first time in history, it seemed that all of Islam was at war as one. It truly was a global jihad.

World leaders were in a panic. "We are now facing an enemy that lurks in the very bowels of our neighborhoods and lives," one news anchor weighed in. "Who can lead us out of this disaster? Are we to succumb to the demands of this brutal group of extremists or will someone step up to make peace?"

It was sickening to watch the world's news media set the table for the Antichrist's grand entrance. He was certainly sounding like the only one who could understand and negotiate with these extremists. The world was starting to buy in.

The NSA and other agencies were looking at a single point of attack. Pinpoint the leadership of these groups as close as possible and carpet bomb the area of three to five miles in a radius around it. I added my two-cent's worth: "All you are going to do is trigger the next wave. They can turn it on and off like a light switch. Plus, there are hundreds of factions with leaders all over the world. They have done a great job of using civil war as a vehicle for getting their operatives out into the major cities. We are a compassionate people. Especially when it concerns families of refugees. They have used it against us."

"Well, what exactly do you suggest, Stone?" the director asked.

"Patience. Let's collect intel and stall. Go ahead and release the remnant at Gitmo to appease them—buy us some time. They are in the driver's seat. As long as there is a pause, we are not losing."

"What are you talking about, Stone?"

"Israel. They didn't touch Israel. We know that it is target number one. Yet they didn't even look that way. This is a distraction—you know, watch my army over here while I outflank you over there. It's all about Israel. This is a smokescreen."

Everyone took a breath. The pause was shorter than it seemed.

"Even if I wanted to hold back, the higher up's want some sort of definite plan of action," the director stated.

"Put a small team with me to monitor the movements and intercepts around Syria and Israel. We have a bunch of sat-phones and computers we can milk. But we can't ignore the real goal, which is to wipe Israel off the map. The rest of the team can go after the faction leaders. I don't agree with broad targeting. We're talking about potentially millions of civilian deaths," I concluded.

"It's not my call on that, Stone, but you have your team. You pick them—ten. Find something good and let's make some noise."

"Will do, sir."

Within twenty-four hours, I had my team and we were all over IRGC intercepts. This was the motherload. I was pretty sure God was setting the table for the hook in the jaw. It was also clear to me that God was allowing the judgment of America. My call to Steph was passionate. She had been putting a lot of prayer in and had come up with several Scriptures to share with me about God's judgment. She began reading from Leviticus 20: "Then the Lord spoke to Moses, saying, 'Again you shall say to the children of Israel; whoever of the children of Israel, or of the strangers who dwell in Israel, who gives any of his descendants to Molech…' Eli, that is child sacrifice. *We* call it abortion. Our modern society is willingly sacrificing our children to the gods of convenience." She continued, "'he shall surely be put to death.' Now jump down to verse four, 'And if the people of the land should in any way *hide their eyes* from the man, when he gives some of his descendants to Molech and they do not kill him, I will set My face against that man and his family.' You see how much He hates us killing our future generations—even those who see it and don't act to stop it will be judged," she said with a sigh.

"Now let's go to Jeremiah 18. Here God tells Jeremiah to go to the potter's house. He tells him to watch how the potter makes what he wills and if it doesn't come out right, he can tear it down and make something else. He tells the prophet that He can do this to any nation. He can lift them up and tear them down at His will. Now He is speaking here of Israel, but it is applicable to any nation. He has done just that to the great powers of the world. Jeremiah passes the message to the people, and their response is predictable. Verse 12 says, 'And [the people] said, That is hopeless! So we will walk according to our own plans, and we will every one obey the dictates of his own evil heart.'" she read.

"Wow! So that is why Israel—and America—have been judged."

"Yes. We, like Israel, were warned—the 9/11 attacks, the civil war, the missile attacks, now this. And we simply will not stop. We will obey the dictates of our own evil hearts."

"It is autonomy, plain and simple. The people want what they want," I added. "No accountability."

"Exactly. Now, we have chaos."

"And the chaos is allowed by God, a result of our bad choices."

"Listen, Steph, I have much to do. But I will be home on or before August 18. Will you come and stay for a few weeks?" I asked.

"That's over a month from now!" I could tell this pained her.

"Worst case—ok?"

"Okay. Just be safe."

"I will. What did the doctor say?"

"He upped my meds. I'm in a lot of pain."

This concerned me. I had done the math. Two years on this stuff. "Whatever you think is best," I said in a supportive tone.

"See you soon." Then she was gone.

Our team was focused on one thing—the buildup of troops around Israel. Everyone kept commenting on the huge volume of intercepts from the computers and sat-phones sold to the Iranians by Deandrea Perone. "Who was this agent, and how did she pull off such a sweet deal?" they would ask. I would just chuckle. It was clear that the factions, at least those in Europe, Asia, and all around the Middle East, were pulling fighters into Iran, Lebanon, Syria, Sinai, and Yemen. A second wave of attacks outside of the United States was unlikely or greatly minimized. We went to work with the teams evaluating US terrorist activity—no activity, no movement. They were hunkered down, waiting patiently for the next move.

Of course, travel into the US was halted altogether. Travel out of the US was far too risky. There was a flow of departures on the southern border, but not huge volumes. I supposed that ICE was happy to see them go. Still, there was a huge number of subversives scattered throughout the US. I asked Tom Sanger to get me the file that the former president had ordered purged. Sure, it was ten years old, but it had to be valuable even today. He cringed.

"You know we don't talk about that," he said.

"He did give Congress a copy prior to purging it, did he not?"

"You know I can't answer that. And it was the whistle-blower!"

"It would be helpful in tracking, what—seven, eight thousand terrorist operatives?"

"It's a moot point, Stone!" he said with a stern voice. I just walked away.

"Our own worst enemy." I muttered under my breath.

"What was that, Stone?" he barked.

"Have a nice day…"

"So," I briefed my team, "we have a massive pull-back of fighters from all over the world except the US. What do you, America's best, have to say about that?"

"They are holding the remnant in the US to implement another wave—it's leverage," said Stan Ballman, an NSA relic.

"Leverage for what?"

"For keeping the US out of the picture, focused on their own problems," added Steve Reed, a former strike teammate.

"Good, Steve. So where is the action?"

"Israel."

"Israel."

"Israel, no doubt about it."

"Israel."

"Israel is toast. They stand alone," Steve added.

"Okay, I concur. So that's what we go with."

"You'll get no support for Israel," Stan said.

"Yes, that is the plan," I concluded.

The entire team had questioning looks—except one, Terry Kaplan.

"Terry, you seem to have a thought."

"Yes. You may consider me crazy, but it's Ezekiel 38 and 39."

"What, the Bible? Come on, man," Steve quipped.

"You're dead on Terry. Good work."

"We cannot consider the Bible actionable intelligence in any way," Steve said.

"I don't know why not, it is evolving exactly as forecasted 2,600 years ago," Terry said.

"We can certainly use it as a possible path that is being followed, like Terry said. It's unfolding exactly as predicted," I agreed.

I met with Scott Crawley, who was leading the intel on Asia.

"Give me an update, Scott."

"Okay, here we go. First, it was the Philippines, then Japan— two major attacks in Tokyo and Sapporo. Three in China—Shanghai, Beijing, and Hong Kong. South Korea got hit at Seoul, North Korea was spared, India was hit at Bombay, Delhi, Calcutta, and Madras, all resorts. Lots of deaths—and the plane."

"What about Russia?" I asked.

"Stone, I am scratching my head on that one. Only two attacks, both in Moscow. Reports are still coming in, but our operatives there say no deaths, no explosions, no dead or captured assailants. We have Benny Pravchech over there and he says it looks staged. Vehicles driven into virtually abandoned buildings at slow speeds. The drivers just got out and fled."

"Fake attacks?"

"It appears so."

"That happen anywhere else?"

"No, nowhere. Everywhere else it was obvious they were going for broke—kill as many as possible in highly visible places."

I had what I needed. My confidence level was high that the coalition coming against Israel was providing cover to move troops into the region—a distraction. It never ceased to amaze how clever and patient the extremists were. I reported my findings to Tom Sanger. I left out the Bible talk, but he brought it up. We all knew what was coming, but had no way to stop it.

The borders around Israel were quiet. At the same time, commercial and military flights brought men, lots of men, into Egypt, Yemen, Syria, Iran, and Lebanon. This, of course, was on top of all the subversives already inside these countries. I encouraged Tom to pull our team out of Damascus. He knew I was right, but wanted to keep them there until the last minute.

"Finger on the pulse, Stone…" he said.

"Well, if there is the big one or word of an Israeli first strike, extract them quickly."

"I will, Jeremy. I read my Bible."

Days went by with only sporadic attacks in a few cities and only in the US. I put a call in to Steph after a particularly long day.

"Are you done yet? I miss you." she said.

"I miss you too. I would feel a lot better if you were at the lake house. How are your folks?"

"Terrified, but safe. Not a Muslim within a hundred miles of Bluefield, West Virginia."

"True enough."

"I'm not so good, though, Eli."

"What is it, precious one?"

"You always make me feel better. It's just anxiety. I am being attacked on a spiritual level. Doubts, fear, pain. This is how Satan gets to me."

"Would it help to be at the lake?"

"Not right now. I have Pastor Steve here at The Way. He and his wife have been having me over, praying, working on my trust. It's a lack of trust, you know?"

"Sounds like me. I can't even confess faith in Him."

"Well, that solves the big question of where you will live in the next life. But we still fight with our own free will and the prince of the power of the air in this life. He uses the physical pain to pull me away from my focus on Jesus."

"How can I help?" I asked.

"You are so sweet, Eli. These past weeks have been amazing. I have hope, even at this dark time. You know, hearing sermons and talking about the end times is a lot easier than actually living through it. I could use a hug."

"Me too, sweet girl. I will pray and we can look forward to next week. I have two priorities in life now: my salvation and you. I want to live for you and God."

"One foot in front of the other, my man. I can't wait for the hug."

"You know, I am only an hour or so away. I could come see you."

"Eli, you have a job to do. Do it and I'll see you soon. I need to work on me. Now pray for me. Read James 5:16 and pray for me."

"I will."

"And Eli?"

"Yes, sweet girl?"

"I love you."

These words hung with me. My mom and dad loved me and told me often, but it never sounded like this. My eyes welled up with tears, her pretty face filling my mind. "I love you too, Stephanie."

"I know you do."

I laughed, and she giggled. "Are you smiling?" She asked.

"Yes, of course."

"Me too. See you soon, special man. Oh, and I finished *Faith*. It was sad, but great. It moved me."

"I'm glad. We have it in common. Goodbye, precious one."

I was so tempted to drive to her and pull her into my arms. But I had work to do. I couldn't have her until I had God directing my life. This she had made clear. I prayed for her, for my salvation, and for God's guidance. John always said, "He knows what He is doing, always on time, never taking us halfway." I had to trust in Him. Bottom line.

The next day, a dozen big attacks happened in cities across the country. One in particular occurred at a veteran's parade in Minneapolis. A hijacked freightliner pulling a flatbed of steel careened into the end of the parade, killing four hundred and twenty. It was a particularly hard day. As I wrapped things up, I got a call to come into Tom's office.

"Jeremy, I'm afraid I have some bad news. I just got a call from the sheriff in Front Royal. Your friend Stephanie Skater was found dead this morning in her home, an apparent overdose. I'm so sorry, buddy."

I was stunned, emotions rushing through my head. It wasn't possible. "No!"

"I'm sorry Jeremy. It's true. You know we have to monitor all calls out, have to check contacts out. She was a great person. I know you two had become close."

I was swimming. What Tom was saying was not news to me. I knew they listened in, even the most trusted agents had to be monitored. But I was reeling from the news...she was dead. My hopes, my life, my best friend—dead.

"I have to go."

"I know. Go!"

A million thoughts went through my mind as I skirted around DC and headed to Front Royal. All I had was her address. The Rover got me there and I was met by Steve Hartman, pastor of The Way. He hugged me and told me how sorry he was for my loss.

"Where is she?" I asked.

"The morgue. They found her about two hours ago—the housekeeper. She died in her sleep, Eli. We know where she is now."

I looked at him in disbelief. "How, Pastor?"

"Not sure, Eli. She was struggling with an opioid addiction—the accident, you know."

My mind reeled. "She just had her prescription upped."

"Yes, she told me. Sally and I have been ministering to her. She was a cherished part of our congregation."

I stared. Visions of her sleeping filled my mind.

"She's meeting Jesus now, Eli," Steve said.

"Yes." This softened me and I breathed a deep breath.

"You were the bright spot in her life, Eli. Her parents are on their way. They would love to meet you. You are all she has talked about the past few weeks. They would like to know the man who brightened her life."

"I would like to meet them," I finally said.

"Eli, please come with me to the church."

"Could I walk through the house? I have never seen it, but I just feel I need to."

"Hold on." He went inside and brought out the sheriff. "This is Sheriff Lee. Sheriff, Eli… I don't know your last name."

"Grollenberg." I said with a dry throat.

"Mr. Grollenberg. Sorry to meet you under such difficult circumstances. Please, come in."

When I walked into the house, I began to cry. It was exactly as I had pictured in my mind: light, bright, ordered. There were pictures of her and Renea on the walls. Knick-knacks of sheep. She loved sheep for some reason.

"She is one of His flock," said the Pastor. "You may be interested in this one, Eli."

I walked to the hallway where a single eight-by-ten hung. It was our dance photo.

"Oh my goodness. That is us—all those years ago. Could I see her room?"

The sheriff looked at the pastor, who nodded.

"This way, Mr. Grollenberg."

I noticed her touches everywhere. It was like I had come home after a long absence. The walls were filled with art by Robert Lynn Nelson, a famous Hawaiian painter who specialized in half underwater, half above water scenes. Prints of Van Gogh's Starry Night and The Harbor at Arles. She loved the water, all right. My heart was aching. I was led down the hall to a modest room with a huge four-poster bed, colored in yellows and blues. There were pillows everywhere, the covers pulled back like someone had just gotten up and there, on the night-stand, the two books.

I dropped to my knees at the edge of her bed and crashed. "Why Lord? Why did You take her? We were so close. Why?"

I felt a soft hand on my shoulder. All I could think to do was pray. And I did. God filled my head with thoughts of our times together. It had been so short, so abbreviated, yet every memory was vivid and breathtaking in my mind. I felt anger at God for a moment more, then it was gone. I broke down and cried like I had never cried before. The love of my life had gone on and my dreams dashed, but I somehow felt a peace...that hand. It comforted me.

I spent time thinking, praying, and then I stood. I turned to see the pastor and an elegant older couple who embraced me and pulled me in. I felt their pain, their love, their connection to the woman I loved. I was telling them I was sorry, they were telling me they were sorry. We were all a sorry lot, but God was keeping us all together as well.

"Isn't the grace of God amazing? We have lost a daughter, but we have gained a son!"

The love and passion of Steph was everywhere, filling us, embracing us.

We moved to the kitchen and sat at the table. Mrs. Skater made coffee and sat while it brewed.

"What you said earlier, Mrs. Skater, about gaining a son. It was precious."

"We feel that way. You two had just reunited, yet there was no doubt you two were meant for each other," she said in the most loving voice.

"I believe that is true. But it is not to be."

"Nonsense!" Mr. Skater said boldly. "What God brings together no man can tear apart. You will be together in heaven. But you better hurry, son. We are in the last days."

"I agree. Our time was short, no matter what. Still, it is a bitter pill to swallow," I said.

When Mrs. Skater brought out the creamer from the fridge, I broke down again. This time it was my new parents comforting me.

"I'm sorry. Steph told me it was both of your favorites. I didn't think."

"It's okay. It just hit me like a wave."

We sat and talked for an hour. "Will you come to the lake house and meet my folks?" I offered.

"We would love to. We have some planning to do here, but we could come after the funeral," Mr. Skater offered.

"Yes, the funeral. It's hard to come to grips with."

"For us too, Eli," Mrs. Skater said with a hug.

Mom, Dad, and I drove to Front Royal for the funeral. Pastor Steve delivered the eulogy and both Steph's parents and Renea spoke. The gospel message was offered and many remarked how godly of a woman she had been. The gathering afterwards at Steph's house was very difficult. My mom loved the photo of Steph and me. My folks fell in love with hers. They agreed to come to the lake house, as well as Renea and John.

We all met up at the house and I gave the Skaters a tour. We all got to know each other and spoke of life back in Front Royal before it was a DC bedroom community.

"Eli, the art at Steph's house and the picture of you two belong here. They would be perfect," Mrs. Skater said.

"I agree," Mr. Skater added.

"I think Steph would want that," Renea chimed in.

We wound down early and everyone headed to bed. John cornered me and said he wanted to talk. We went to the command center. When we got there, we both stopped. The main monitor was running the silent headline: "7.8 MAGNITUDE QUAKE ROCKS IRAN."

chapter
FIFTEEN
✡✡✡✡✡✡✡

"Holy crap. Here we go!" John said.

I turned it up. "The huge quake, centered at Yazd near the center of Iran was measured at 7.8 on the seismic scale. It hit hard and then shook for nearly twenty seconds. There is no official word out of Tehran, but cities all over the Middle East were shaken hard at 2:35 PM, East Coast time. Damage is heavy and widespread despite the remote location of the quake. US officials would not speculate but the readings shew a seismic pattern consistent with a nuclear test. The quake was felt as far south as Ethiopia and as far east as Indonesia."

"What do you think?" John said.

"We have a day, maybe two," I said. "All of a sudden, I want to go there."

"Where?"

"To Jerusalem."

"Are you nuts? This is it, man. We could see first strikes as early as tomorrow."

"I think it will be a day or two. It's been three hours since the quake. Netanyahu will want to see how the world responds. But you can be guaranteed, the plan is already in motion."

"Why would you want to go there?"

"I'm a Jew. I want front-row seats to the greatest spectacle in history—so far. Now, what did you want to talk to me about?"

"Okay, I want to ask Renea to marry me. Look—I have the ring, and time is short. But the timing—with the funeral and all. I wanted to ask you. Are you okay?"

"John… I am all in. You two are perfect for each other. What's your timeframe?"

"Obviously, I need to ask, but two weeks. That's how long it takes to get a dress."

"You're the man, John… And I'll be back by then, Lord willing."

"You really are going?"

"Wild horses couldn't stop me. Do you still have that connection for the jet?"

"Yep, but you'd better come back alive."

"I will, don't worry."

I called Tom Sanger on my secure phone. "Tom, I need you to get word to Jake Schneiderman and have him email me. Have you moved the guys out of Damascus yet?"

"Aren't you full of questions. They'll be out today, but you didn't hear it from me. What are you up to, Stone? How are you?"

"I'm fine. The funeral was difficult. Her folks are amazing. Thanks for asking, and for sending the flowers."

"You're welcome. Now, what are you up to?"

"A little vacation. Just have Jake hit me up."

"Okay. Stay out of trouble. It's all over…"

In an hour, I had a Honda A-600 lined up to come at 6:00 AM, as well as Jake's number. I would call him in the morning. I said goodbye to my folks, Renea, and John. He was taking Renea out on the Wellcraft to propose during sunset.

"Didn't know you had it in you, big fella…" He just smiled.

By 5:00 AM, I was on the road in full alias mode. I would be flying to Spain and then on to Tel Aviv as Samantha DeVoss on one of the fastest private jets on earth.

I met my pilot, Ron Forester, at Bedford right at six o'clock and we were off. The Honda was an awesome little eight-seater in total luxury. We took off, banked east, and put the hammer down at 720 miles per hour. We filled up in Barcelona and I made a new friend in Ron, whom I had met before, but as one of my male aliases. I paid him in cash and agreed on a pick-up date one week later—if we were still among the living.

Jake picked me up at the small airport outside of Tel Aviv. He was looking all over for me. I went up to him, asked the time, and whispered in his ear, "I'm your man…"

"Oh man. I would never know… You are good. I just can't be seen with you, you know how people talk…"

"Yeah, I just couldn't risk coming as myself." He kept looking at me as we drove toward Jerusalem.

"Where are we, Jake?"

"You mean in the grand scheme of things?"

"Yes."

"I'll let you see for yourself. First, we go to my place so you can get out of those heels."

"Yes, they are killing me." We talked about the close call in Tehran.

"I am a local hero among the Mossad…" He said.

"Oh yeah?"

"Yes. Turns out we got some of the IRG's best bodyguards—Sulaman's own personal guys. They were there for two weeks studying the forensics. They just can't figure out how six of us got off ninety rounds in less than a second, killing off all seventeen of them and not one injury on our side. My buddies laughed and laughed when they broke that one. We are all superheroes. It's how I got you in."

"In?"

"In. All the way in. Mossad headquarters, top-level. But not in a dress. You are very attractive, however…"

"Why thank you, Jake."

"Hey, how is the girl?"

"Dead—sorry to say."

"Victim of the attacks?"

"No. Victim of the AMA."

"AMA?"

"Yes. She overdosed on pain killers. The doctors governed by the American Medical Association over-prescribed her and about twenty-million others."

"Oh, I am sorry, Jeremy. Affordable healthcare, huh?"

"Something like that."

In two hours, we were in Jake's humble abode near Hebrew University. I showered, changed, ate, and then slept. Far too soon, Jake woke me up.

"We have to go. It's about to hit the fan!"

We took the bus and walked to a non-descript building near President's Park.

"This is where the fun begins," Jake said. We passed through two low-security entrances, then into a full briefing room where I was put through the screening. They had me verify every step of my travel so far. If I was lying, they would know. Five more fingerprint and retina scan posts and we entered an elevator.

The trip down took seven minutes. I was about to ask.

"I could tell you, but I would have to kill you," Jake said with a serious look. Then he said, "Deep!" with a smile.

The doors opened to a room of around one hundred feet by one hundred feet. There was a round of applause to welcome us and then it was back to work. The room looked very much like a terraced movie theater. There were eight rows or levels, each with a curved row of desks with forty-eight-inch computer monitors on top. There were about forty people manning those stations and in front dozens of twelve foot monitors on the walls. Jake pointed out that each battle group had a communication monitor. That included voice, video, and missile tracking for each group.

"There are thirty-eight battle groups for this mission. The side monitors bring video from cameras at two hundred seventeen positions at the borders. We can observe all cockpit video, voice and missile operations. We can watch 100 percent of the northern and southern borders. They are quiet now, but not for long."

"The mission?" I asked.

"Hook in the Jaw."

"Holy…"

"Yes, He is!"

"So the quake?"

"The biggest, baddest bomb we are aware of. It seems it was built with Pakistani and probably Russian help. It's a monster. We simply cannot wait any longer."

"And the global jihad?"

"Just a distraction—a precursor to the overall plan. You notice, all the operatives are still in the US. Virtually everywhere else, they bolted and headed here, to the epicenter. This is where it all goes down…"

Jake introduced me to Levi Barstein, the head of communications monitoring.

"This room is mine," he said. "We have seventeen levels here, Mr. Stone. That is all I can tell you. But if the Prime Minister comes here, this is the room he will watch from. You have front-row seats to the biggest event in modern history. If it happens in the air, on the lines, on the TV, or the internet, we will have it."

"When?"

"No one knows the day or hour."

I smiled. Boy, was it good to use my Hebrew after so long. I felt right at home. It was close, I was sure. Even though all the normal and predictable military activities were going on, they were ready to go at any second. Israel had been at a high level of readiness since September 2001. The planes were full of fuel, the training state-of-the-art, it was all as good as it could get.

In all of this, my biggest concern was Damascus. I knew they had huge storehouses of chemical weapons there from the Saddam days. Israel was not going for an exercise. This was what they had planned for. Since the test came, it would be all out. Damascus was a city of about seven million people, and if the Bible prophecy was correct, it would be grazing land at some point. I did not know how it would happen or who would cause the eventual destruction, but I was sure it would come and it would be complete.

I also thought about Revelation, a quarter of earth's population gone, perhaps a billion raptured. Would I be one of those? That was a question only I could answer. Perhaps when God showed His mighty power, it would no longer be a question for me. Perhaps it would be me and millions of other fence-sitters. I didn't mind dying, I just wanted to be with Steph.

The thought occurred to me, "They may say they don't know the day or hour, but Jake had woken me up and dragged me down here in full jet-lag mode. If the Prime Minister showed up soon, I knew I was in for a treat."

Jake put his hand on my shoulder. "How you doing?"

"Tired, but amped up for this."

"Coffee or sleep?" he asked.

"Sleep, if it's available."

"Okay."

I was taken to a small room with a sink, toilet, and bed. Heaven, I thought.

Jake pointed to a light. "When that flashes and 'all posts' is announced, come to the floor. We'll have coffee and some food for you then."

"Thank you, Jake."

I slept hard and bolted awake to a flashing light and blaring PA. It was go time. I quickly peed, washed my face, and brushed my teeth. Within five minutes, I was in the communications room standing next to Prime Minister Benjamin Netanyahu. Jake introduced me and I told him we had met.

"Really?"

"Yes, July 2016 in Beersheba. In fact, Jake introduced us."

"Are you sure?" Netanyahu questioned.

"Yes, but he may have looked a little different. Back then he was Deandrea Perone," Jake added.

"Holy cow, a woman?" he exclaimed, which sounded awfully funny in Hebrew. "I do remember you. Very effective alias, I might add. And nice job in Tehran. We need the same kind of luck today, I think.

"Or something else... God's will," I said.

"Yes, indeed."

"Right now," Jake said, "four hundred F-22s and eighty-four F-18 Hornets are headed north along the coast of Lebanon. Soon, they will turn East and head toward Iran. A quarter of the F-22s and all of the F-18s will drop down into Syria to take out weapon storage and missile manufacturing facilities in seven cities. The F-22s will fly on to Iran and hit up to twelve facilities and two nuclear power plants. The goal is to decapitate the entire nuclear and chemical delivery programs of the Caliphate. On the way back, we will hit positions in southern Lebanon. Then, we wait and have a little surprise to boot."

"Can the F-22s make it back on fuel?"

"Great question... No. They won't have to. You'll see. The top row of big screens, up there, are our satellite feeds. We have six, and borrowed two more. Don't ask. I can't tell you any more than that. It's unlikely we can take out more than half their capability, but it's better than going on defense. Plus, we still have the unknown of the Russians and when they will join the fray."

We watched as the bogeys on the screen went north flying at less than one hundred feet off the surface. They were using radar jamming, satellite jamming, and all kinds of new technology. They all figured Iran knew they would be coming sooner or later. The sheer number of planes would certainly be a surprise. They turned right, skirting the border of Turkey and Syria, in enemy territory from here on. I began to pray, "God, I know I don't know You like I should, but I need to pray for my country, Israel. I have already lost so much and I still trust You. Be all You told the prophet Ezekiel You would be." It made me chuckle, as I had prayed in English. It was somewhat ironic, I guess. I knew John, Renea, and all four of my parents would be praying also.

"We have company!" came the radio of Israeli Defense Force 1, the group leader. "Sending Strike Team 2 to engage. Six bogies coming in hot, due west. Strike Team 2, engage." There was a pause. "That's odd. Com1, they just flew over the top of us, like they didn't see us. Strike Team 2, disengage and fall back."

"IDF1, did you have visual?"

"Affirmative. Six Turkish MIG's flying blind."

The one hundred F-22s and the F-18s peeled off into Syrian airspace. We watched as they made direct hits on every target they encountered. The first wave of F-22s also found their marks, dropping surface and bunker-buster bombs on appropriate targets. The sheer number of explosions was impossible to count. Huge buildings and facilities were being leveled one after another.

"IRG MIG's out in number—engaging for cover!"

It seemed obvious to me that Iran knew this was coming. They seemed content to let the Israeli's spend the munitions on their targets. They only sent a minimum number of MIG's up to engage. The screens were filled with images of cratered buildings and mountain sides blasted away

"IDF1 advance team returning to base."

To my surprise, they flew right into Iraqi air space and landed at a top-secret air base even we did not know about. Then we saw two hundred more F-22s take off in succession from that base.

"Wave number two, Jeremy. And look at what is happening in Syria and Lebanon. They're almost to Damascus, the final assault in the north."

"An air base in Iraq. Come on, how did you pull that one off?"

"Our secret. Now watch screen 3. It is satellite coverage of Damascus, the abandoned Qassam missile factory. It's not so much abandoned anymore. We think that is where two of the warheads are. The silo is shrouded by those old buildings, there and there," he pointed.

"IDF6, we have a lock on two prime targets. Requesting permission to proceed."

"Permission granted."

I know that the process was for high-value targets that had an 80 percent or better likelihood of destruction with minimal collateral damage. They had two drones surveying the area. It was a go.

"IDF6 payloads deployed—contact in 12, 11, 10, 9, 8, 7, 6, 5, 4, 3, 2, 1, contact."

The satellite screen erupted in light.

"IDF6, it appears we have a nuke in target 1. Clearing the area. Correction, both 1 and 2. This is getting ugly, let's get out of here, boys!"

As the satellite cameras backed out and the drones zoomed in, a dual mushroom cloud rose up from the two silos.

"We're getting huge seismic readings, sir!"

"Where are they originating?"

"Eastern part of Damascus. It peaked out at 9.7 at Dimona station."

The building began to shake, and shake hard. I held tight to the rail in front of me. While the building rocked and swayed, everything else stayed in place. It was amazing. Then it began to slow and eventually stopped.

"IDF6, we just barely got out of there. It is a set of mushroom clouds. Are the drones getting it? It's pretty spectacular from here, but Damascus will never be the same."

"We got it, IDF6. Come on home."

The second wave had finished in Iran and they all headed straight across Syria and into Israel.

"Two F-22s lost, sir, due to surface flack. Everyone else intact," IDF1 reported.

"What is your drop percentage, IDF1?"

"100 percent. We dropped them all, sir."

All the planes returned to Israel, even the three hundred F-22s from Iraq after they refueled.

"We will need them all here," Jake said.

Now the task of evaluating damage and success rates would begin. They hit their targets, but how badly did they hurt the nuclear weapons program? It only took one nuke properly placed to destroy Israel. Of course, the Caliphate did not want Jerusalem damaged, at least not with nukes. Operation Hook in the Jaw was complete. Now, how long would it take to amass the armies of Gog out of the North, and when would Russia engage the fight?

chapter

SIXTEEN
✡✡✡✡✡✡

Damascus was gone. The Isaiah prophecy fulfilled almost literally. Six and a half million people dead, with another million from Iran. As expected, most of the bomb sites had been filled with civilians. We were told that drawings were held, there were so many willing to be martyrs. I turned my attention to CNN news breaking in the US: "Massive Air Strike on Syria and Iran by Israel."

"Two nuclear bombs were dropped on the city of Damascus this morning in an apparent attack by Israeli air forces. The two explosions caused a 9.0 plus quake in Syria and thousands have been killed in Iran. In addition, forward missile bases in Lebanon were also struck by Israeli F-22s. Iran claims this is an unprovoked offensive strike that came in the early morning hours and has killed thousands, perhaps hundreds of thousands, of innocent civilians. 'Iran and its allies will not sit by and watch the aggressive Jews kill our women and children. We are preparing for counter measures,' said Iranian President Hassan Rouhani in a Tehran news release.

"The question remains, why would Israel use nuclear weapons on a city of six million people? At this early hour, it is unclear. What is clear is that a pair of mushroom clouds fill the sky over Damascus, Syria, a decimated city caught up in an ugly civil war."

"Not unlike the world to blame Israel for the destruction of Damascus. The truth will come out, but the press will insist, as long as they can, that we dropped nukes on an innocent city," Jake explained.

Meanwhile, the planes were landing, high-fives were given all around, and Prime Minister Netanyahu worked to refine his press release. It explained the quake several days ago, the purpose of the first strike, and the destruction of two missile silos in Damascus that were thought to contain chemical warhead missiles, but actually contained armed and ready to launch nuclear missiles. He had to try to convince the world, and in particular Israel's enemies, that it was a strike first or be destroyed decision. Israeli news was celebrating, while the world was condemning—nothing new under the sun...

As the planes landed at a dozen secret air bases, the control rooms burst into applause. The mission was a major success, even better than could have been anticipated. A long list of confirmations was streaming in, including the men lost in the two planes, the targets hit, and that Iranian, Russian, and Turkish satellites were dark because of the use of the newest technology. Only one Russian satellite had remained working, but it was over India and was useless to them.

Netanyahu himself called the families of the downed pilots to express his condolences and deep appreciation of their service. A film crew set up the map and flags of Israel and Jerusalem in the background for the news release. Within ten minutes, they had the speech finished and were ready to roll for a recorded release.

"Today, the nation of Israel undertook a mission of survival. Following the significant quake, which our scientists confirmed was a test of a massive nuclear warhead, and acting on verifiable evidence of two Hormuz 6 medium-range missiles in silos reported to have chemical warheads mounted, I made the decision to initiate a preemptive strike on Iran, Syria, and Lebanon. This decision did not come without debate, but was supported by confirmed, actionable intel obtained in all three countries. Our aircraft struck targets in Iran known to be production facilities for their nuclear weapons program and for the development of resources needed to produce the very bomb that was tested days ago. Aircraft hit the two silos at Damascus and several known chemical weapon storage facilities. We will soon release video that conclusively proves that our pilots had no way of knowing those missiles, locked and loaded, were tipped with nuclear warheads. Regardless, these strikes and subsequent strikes on Lebanon rocket-launching sites were more than justified for Israel's survival. These nations have made it clear that their goal is to wipe Israel off the map. Knowing what we know now, they were perhaps moments away from fulfilling that task. If anyone asks where those two nuclear-tipped missiles were destined for, our intel will prove that it was Tel Aviv and Haifa. We are deeply saddened by the loss of life, especially for our pilots who were lost over Syria. The coming days will show the world that our enemies were close to eliminating our nation and our people. We simply had to act. It is with tremendous sorrow that we report the current situation. We can only hope that we can now have peace."

The director cut the production and we erupted into applause. Netanyahu had said it all and stated the facts. Yes, the press would distort it, question Israel's actions, and call for more UN intervention. No one in this room cared at the moment. The fact was, Iran had been ready to light up the sky over Israel and only the hook in the jaw could stop it. Jake came and high-fived me.

"What's that for? I didn't do anything..."

"I'm afraid you did. Those computers are churning out all kinds of intel, including every bit of hard intel we had for this attack. All we had to do was verify it. When our guys on the ground confirmed the Hormuz 6s in the silos, we knew we had to go. Those rockets with chemical weapons would have been devastating, but a nuclear strike would have been terminal. They really did intend to light up the sky over Israel. And your computer sale stopped it."

"I hit the clock pretty close, too. We'll never know now since they are destroyed. Isaiah 17 fulfilled too—at such a cost."

"Jeremy, we knew the loss of Damascus would be tragic, whenever it came. The only thing that was certain was that it *would* come."

"Yes, I'm afraid so."

"Now, we wait for what Russia and Iran have left in the tank. We knew we could not get everything. The armies of Gog are coming."

We watched the US news reports condemning Israel and calling for the UN to step in. Every country in the world condemned the strikes as "acts of war." Then, Netanyahu was on, his quiet, somber spirit in evidence. He delivered his statement and let the chips fall where they would. He knew all too well that the world was against Israel. I just never could figure out why. CNN had thrown together panels of mostly anti-Israel commentators dissecting Netanyahu's speech. Fox had a mostly pro-Israel team explaining their dire circumstances and pointing out that Israel's greatest ally, the US, was impotent in light of current attacks.

Russian President Vladimir Putin condemned Israel and spoke of the tragic loss of Damascus. The Tashim News Agency, Iran's semi-official news office, blasted Israel as aggressive killers with no respect for human life. It seemed ironic given the fact that Iran had had not one, but two nuclear missiles aimed at Israel that were ready to launch. The simple fact was that if Israel had not done a precision preemptive strike on these known targets, Israel would be gone.

Israel had several anti-missile programs including Iron Dome, Lockheed Martin's Thaad ABM, and the Arrow III. But these systems took the missiles out as they closed in on their targets. A nuclear explosion of this size, even miles above Israel, would have been devastating to life, property, and technology. Israel had also deployed a new technology called BPI, or Boost-Phase Intercept. It was designed to take out medium and ICBM sized missiles in their boost phase, within a minute of launch. An unmanned aerial vehicle, basically a huge drone, carried four BPI anti-missile missiles at fifty-five thousand feet in international air space. In this case, Israel had this UAV flying out over the Mediterranean Sea and continuously patrolling for a launch. It had one minute to identify and lock onto the missile during boost phase. Then it was over. At least, that was the theory. It was sound but untested technology.

Jake and I both thought it would be well tested in the coming days. On top of that, we both trusted that Ezekiel, like Isaiah, would not miss the mark. The armies of Gog were coming out of the woodwork, like rats out of a burning building. Soon they would be on Israel's doorstep and it would be God's turn.

I told Jake I needed to go topside to make a call.

"Can't happen. But we have secure lines here. Just plug in where you want the origin to be. Be aware, we will be listening."

"I know." I logged Barcelona as my origin to throw any US agency off. I knew they would be on John's and my calls. They couldn't listen in, but they would certainly pick up the Barcelona part.

"John, good morning… Are you watching the news?"

"Yes, Renea and the folks are tuned in—amazing!"

"Did the Skater's go home?"

"Yes. All is well, considering. They are amazing people, buddy. I am so sorry."

"Thank you, John. So everything is good there, still moving forward?"

"You bet. Looking forward to your arrival."

"Okay. See you soon."

I moved back into the control room and got back with Jake. "Look at the CBS Morning News," he said. The coverage was of the Israel attack, of course. But also of the ongoing attacks by terrorists throughout the country. Surprisingly, thousands were going into mosques and converting to Islam.

"What has the world come to?" I asked.

"Just what Jesus said it would—the days of Noah. The Rapture is coming soon, buddy. You shouldn't wait."

"I know, but the loss of Steph just added to my confusion. God gave me peace, but it really made me angry to lose her."

"God has a plan for you. I hope it is not to be a tribulation saint, although you would be a heck of a good asset."

"Gee, thanks Jake!"

"Well, you're the one stalling."

The Mossad was pleased with all that had transpired and were preparing for the armies of Gog. Because the satellites were dark, none of Israel's secret bases had been revealed, including the Iraqi site. This was critical because if a protracted war was to ensue, the refueling capabilities of the Iraqi base was imperative to success. Jake told me I had some time to catch up on sleep. Instead, I pulled out *Extreme Faith*, retreated to my room, and dove in.

In an unforeseen twist, the young rider loses his girlfriend and is taken aback, just like me. He reads her eulogy at the funeral and dozens are saved. Then, his life takes a dramatic turn. I was stunned and enthralled at the twists and turns. Every step he took in the story was precisely laid in place by God, and he recognized it. His purpose was in full light ahead of him with God firmly at the helm. It moved me to no end.

Then, I saw it clearly—it was his faith. As he began to trust in faith, God blessed him. I wrote in my journal that when I got back to The Way, I would trust in God to make a way the angels would rejoice. The books had moved me in a way that was subtle, yet obvious. I decided he must be an incredible writer, or else have the Spirit—or both. I did thank God in my own way and then I slept.

Jerusalem: Time of Jacob's Trouble

The man holding the MA-67 machine gun just twelve yards from me was very real and under tremendous stress, not a fictional character in the least. And I was fairly certain that the bullets that spewed out at seventy rounds per second were quite real as well. I wasn't sure about my new female friend, just feet away. She seemed real, but the plan that was developing in my head could not be relayed to her. The one common thread, at this point, was the Holy Spirit. Because we were both standing in this line at the base of the Mount of Olives and facing imminent death, I was pretty sure she was a Christian, a tribulation saint, like me. I could see a love, a passion in her. It was Jesus, I had no doubt.

Unfortunately, I was a strategist, right down to the very last detail and this plan was not in my wheel-house. Albeit, now that I think about it, none of them had been really. All along, God had provided the way. I just did not, or refused to recognize it. At this point, I didn't have any other choice. I was putting my life in this woman's hands and hers in mine. We would have to trust God, simple as that. That didn't mean it wouldn't be scary...

As all this went through my head, I sized up the number of Global Constables in the vicinity. There were eight that I could see, three within forty feet between us and the crowd. Then there were two with weapons drawn at the machine, as well as a man sitting at a table who announced the names of those dying. Two more were tasked with operation of the ugly device. The good news was that only five of the eight had the MA's. All had side arms which I recognized as Daisy AG-225s. That's right, Daisy as in BB gun Daisy. These were special-ized CO_2 powered handguns with seven-inch barrels. Each carried one hundred rounds of BB's and a special six-inch long CO_2 cartridge that rode just under the barrel.

Much like other small caliber handguns, the AG-225 had a lim-ited range yet substantial velocity. Where they differed was ammo capacity and the ammo itself. While limited to CO_2 bottle capacity, these babies could fire all one hundred BBs on a bottle. The BBs them-selves were a dream right out of Satan's playbook. Each three-sixteenth-inch diameter BB was made of thin latex with a core of plastic explo-sive. As the BB hit its target it created a small explosion, immediately destroying anything it came into contact with. An upper body or head shot and you were dead, times one hundred. That was the bad news. The good news was that standard operating procedure for a Global Enforcer was that the safety strap on the holster must be undone when carrying another weapon.

The other thing about the Daisy was that it was light, all plastic, and almost silent. All of the eight constables in my view were well in range. I was almost convinced that I could pull this off. I made eye contact with my girl. It all clicked. Then, she was down on the ground. The enforcer nearest me was on his way. It was go time!

chapter

SEVENTEEN
✡✡✡✡✡✡

Following the hook in the jaw, Jesus visited me that night in a dream. I was directed by the radiant figure to "talk to the cloud, tell him the things of events to come, be selective and have the cloud take it to the man who moves you. This is your purpose and you will be rewarded with love." There was more, but it was cryptic. A young woman I thought I recognized, but could not pinpoint. There was a plane taking off, and I felt I needed to be on it. Then this: "All will be well, my son. I am with you. I will never leave you or forsake you. Your name is written on My hands. Have faith—perfect faith."

The message was in Hebrew and I remembered it completely when I woke. I quickly wrote it all down. I did not understand it, but I wrote what He gave me. I was in awe...

Jake too had slept and had good, thick Israeli coffee and Italian sweet cream ready. I thanked him and poured at least a half cup of my favorite creamer in to begin to turn it brown. "Wow, you like it strong in this land..."

"Yes, we do..." He answered, and we clinked cups.

"I've been evaluating the news—we have few supporters, and by and large, we are an island. The UN has already proposed a dozen condemnations and sanctions. Lech Manevetski has been on, speaking of peace and taking a primarily neutral stand on the event."

"Paving the way for the covenant…" I said.

"No doubt."

"Jake, I have something I need to share with you—in private."

"Sure, Jeremy. This way." He led me to a nice conference room and told me it was private.

"I had a dream—a Jesus dream."

"Now that's what I'm talking about," he said excitedly. "Go on."

"It's cryptic. I wrote it all down as best as I could. My brain is not photographic, but I do retain information well. This was very real…" I went through my notes, then filled in the rest from memory.

"We need to break this down. You're sure it was Jesus?"

"Yes, no doubt. Plus, look at His words—those are Jesus' words."

"Okay. The cloud. He said talk to the cloud?"

"Yes. Talk to the cloud. To tell him the things of events to come."

"He must mean the internet—cloud storage. Publish a paper?" We both paused and contemplated.

"Wait, what was the next part?"

"To be selective and to have the cloud take it to the man who moves you. Oh, and this is to be my purpose. 'And you will be rewarded with love.'"

"Okay, so your purpose is to take events to come to the man who moves you, by way of the cloud. Who is this man who moves you?"

"Well, last night I read a book, the third in a trilogy that I have been moved by."

"Could the author be the man?"

"I thought that he must be a good writer or have the Spirit, or both—he did move me, and he moved Stephanie as well. It helped me decide that, when I go back, I will surrender my life to Christ—in faith."

"Okay, that's progress. What is this author's name?"

"I'll be right back," I said.

I was back with the book in a matter of minutes. "R. K. Sparks."

"For now, let's plug that in. Let's go back to the events to come. I was thinking, you don't know the events to come—only prophecy, but not first-hand knowledge."

"Yes, so it must be events I know—like what?"

"Let's look at the cloud thing." He pulled up the internet and ran a search on R. K. Sparks.

"Here's a Reginald Kensington Sparks—just a bio. Wait, it does have a cloud-server link. This is odd. No social media accounts. You know, most authors have Facebook, blogs, anything they can to promote their books. Let's see, born in 1957 in California. Author of several books. That's it. All you can do from this is upload to his cloud. Weird. What would people upload?"

There was a long pause.

"How about events to come?" I say. We both had looks of astonishment and curiosity.

"What was the middle part again?" Jake asked.

"Let's see…to be selective. I guess selective in what I tell him about events to come."

"But why, and what events?"

"The Rapture, Revelation… I don't know."

"Anyone with a Bible knows that. And this guy is saved, right?"

"I would imagine so, he's writing Christian books."

"Hold on…" Jake went back to the internet. "When I search for him, only this file appears. Wait, this is a link to a ProtoCloud."

"What is that?"

"Lots of controversy about this. The founder claims it will exist forever—like cryogenics for your data. Frozen in time! It is claimed that human DNA is used to store all types of media. It's cutting edge and a bit on the fringe." Jake grinned.

I was shaking as a thought came to me. A thought and a chill. "Jake, what if the events I need to tell him about are still to come for him?"

That stopped him cold and his eyes practically rolled back in his head. "Do you mean he may be behind us in time?"

"Listen, talk to the cloud to tell him the things of events to come."

"To tell him the things of events to come—yes, events that will come in his future."

"Jesus wants me to send back a message, events to come, back in time via the ProtoCloud."

"Could this upload link be a pathway to his present, sometime in our past?" Jake asked.

"Look! There is nothing else about this man. Jesus doesn't want us to know anything about him. I mean, the Mossad internet search can't find but this one file. That is absurd!"

"Well, it is strange. And He doesn't want him to know all the details…we can't know the day or time," Jake said.

"I have questioned why I have documented everything, even my daily journal. Now I know why. It could be my purpose to alert the world through documenting notes about the chaos to come—but selective things only."

"He wants people prepared—the ten virgins!"

"Yes. Prepared but not perplexed. Living it is perplexing. The connection is his books—your link."

"To my faith. To my salvation as well, it seems."

"God is amazing, isn't he?"

"Now, what about the girl?" Jake asked.

"Oh, yes. The rest. It was like one of those rather opaque portraits. She looked a little like Steph, younger… Beautiful. Same hair, but not Steph. But first He said I would be rewarded with love."

"She possibly has something to do with that. And the plane?"

"Well, it was taking off, and I felt I should be on it."

"Hmm," he rubbed his chin. "No idea."

He knew darn well what it meant, and so did I. At least Jesus would be with me—always.

We began to hear from Islamic groups around the world. Most were internet posts, although some took to posting videos at various sites. The Muslim Brotherhood spokesman, Maha Azzman, said: "We stand with the Caliphate against Israel."

Taliban spokesman Zabiullah Mujahid announced, "We are with our brothers to defeat Israel!"

Iranian spiritual leader Ayatollah Ali Kahmenei proclaimed, "We embrace the Caliphate to crush Israel."

Zawahiri of AQAP said, "Israel will be gone in thirty days, crushed by the Caliphate."

Bashar Assad, the Syrian president speaking from an undisclosed location stated, "The infidel Zionists will be wiped off the map. We stand with the Caliphate. Israel will pay dearly for Damascus!"

Lastly, IRGC Brigadier General Amin Ali Hajizadah said, "Every Zionist pig will die and Israel will be no more. We will light up the sky over Israel."

The messages droned on and on. ISIS, al-Qaeda, the Taliban, and even King Salman of Saudi Arabia and Egyptian president Abdel Fattah al Sisi condemned Israel, but landed short of a pledge to join the Caliphate. We all knew, however, that their men would come to fight. This was the chance they had all been waiting for. Even at this early stage, troops from Libya, Somalia, Ethiopia, Yemen, and Algeria were gathering at the southern border in Sinai. Ever since Sinai splintered off from Egypt, the southern border of Israel was a hot zone. Now it was a staging ground for a seeming multi-lateral attack of this tiny country.

The drone video out of Damascus was eerie. The two craters looked like something seen on a distant planet. For ten to twelve miles in each direction, there was nothing but moonscape. Beyond that, the far western edge of the city had some evidence of a building or bridge here and there. The one common aspect in the entire region was the lack of life. The two huge mushroom clouds were gone, but layers of smoke and dust filled the sky. Condemnations continued from across the world, despite Netanyahu's press release.

"We are used to the worldview against us. Nothing will change that. Sadly, our only two friends are God and Lech Manevetski—and only because he must fulfill prophecy," Jake said.

"Yes, but you have the One who counts, and we already know the winner of this challenge," I said. "In fact, I'm perfectly comfortable being here. It is perhaps the safest place in the world."

Iran's president, Rouhani, had his own press release. With the Ayatollah sitting behind him, he railed against Israel and boldly declared that the attack by Israel had not compromised the power of Iran at all. "We are stronger than ever, and now have the support of all our brothers in Islam. Converts to Islam are coming forward from all over the world. Soon the Mahdi will come to claim the victory for Islam."

"Well, Jake, you have certainly stirred up a hornet's nest!"

"Yes, the hook in the jaw has rightfully emboldened our neighbors."

In the meantime, the attacks on Americans intensified to a fever pitch. The cries of *Allah Akbar* preceded hundreds of attacks each day. Trump had recalled all troops from every corner of the globe. Everyone who owned a gun was carrying it, and many times the attackers were killed before the attack could begin. Still, many were entering mosques and converting to Islam. They would come out briefly for interviews.

"I feel safe inside. America has corrupted the world. Our future is with Islam." Every interview was the same. The brain washing was working.

Two days after the Israel strike, Trump declared martial law in the US. The troops were home and out in force. The United States of America was no longer the police force of the world. The country had withdrawn into itself and was fighting for survival. I called John and asked how the folks were. The Skaters were back and they were all spending a lot of time praying in the underground. They felt the Rapture was close and encouraged me to confess my faith. I told him about the vision but asked him not to divulge it to the others. He said he would pray about the dream and see what God revealed to him about it.

"I'm sorry, buddy, it looks like I will miss the wedding."

There would be no going home now for a while. I would need to ride this out and review my journal entries and notes in preparation for sending them to the cloud. This was all too weird and fantastic. The image of the girl never left me, but my dreams that night were of war and people being beheaded. We were heading into a dark time in human history. Jesus had said to His disciples: "Unless those days were shortened, no flesh would be saved."

Lech Manevetski was on the air, asking for cooler heads to prevail—"Peace is the only answer. Mankind must put away the desire to make war, otherwise no flesh will be saved."

My mind reeled. I had studied this man. If he was, in fact, the Antichrist, he would be just that—the opposite of Christ. Quoting Scripture, seemingly godly and peace-loving. He was what you might call slick, like Bill Clinton. The stage was set, but for now, the world faced the threat of the Caliphate—global submission to Islam.

I knew different, or at least I believed it would turn out the way the prophets had described. God was good, and He would use all things for good to those who love Him. I had to admit, I felt drawn to Him. I was not sure why, but I felt strongly that I had to return to America and be saved at The Way. I also knew that that could cost me.

"God's will and timing," I thought.

Each day brought escalation in troop movements from the south and from the north. Satellite images of a huge convoy coming from the coastlands of Russia told of the size of the armies of Gog. There were huge numbers of tanks, transports with missiles and guns, Armored Personnel Carriers, and several hundred thousand men. The convoy stretched over two hundred miles from Russia into Turkey and ending inside Lebanon.

Since Israel had annexed the Golan Heights, they had a tiny buffer zone between the Syrian border. This wouldn't make much of a difference, except that anti-missile deployments could intercept enemy fire that much more quickly. Each day, Israel had a dozen unmanned Boost Phase Intercept aerial vehicles in the air at fifty-five thousand feet. They also had over two hundred reconnaissance drones in the air monitoring troop movements and alerting them to any attempts to disable the more than six thousand anti-missile batteries around the country.

"Jeremy, we even have two dozen Aegis intercept batteries underwater in the Sea of Galilee," Jake bragged.

"How does that work?" I asked.

"You'll see."

Jake and I found ourselves in the conference room praying often. I admired his faith and could feel the Holy Spirit in him.

"Jake," I asked one day, "could it be that I am one of those Jews who has to see Jesus, the One we pierced, before I can be saved?"

"No! I'm not. And you have had the dream Joel talks about… 'Your old men shall dream dreams and also your young men shall see visions when He pours out His Spirit in those days.' You, my friend, are ready, and stubborn as an ox. You have no excuse!"

chapter
EIGHTEEN
✡✡✡✡✡✡✡

In Ezekiel 39:21 God says to the prophet, "I will set my glory among the nations; all the world shall see My judgment which I have executed, and My hand which I have laid on them." There was no doubt that He was describing what was happening to this tiny country at the epicenter of world politics and religion. Every satellite, every possible news show and every camera available was focused on Israel. The sad thing was that the eulogy was already written, even as the details of their death were still to develop. An estimated eleven million troops, thugs, terrorists, and perhaps all remaining Nazi sympathizers were gathered to end Zionism in the world. Once the world was cleansed of their nation, the Jews around the world would be targets of every kind of hate group.

The predictions were dire, the anticipation high, and the whole world was tuned in. Benjamin Netanyahu, in a desperate cry for help, reached out to the UN for their very survival. The only one who picked up the phone was Lech Manevetski. His reply was, "I am with you. But it is me alone. If you survive, I will do all in my power as UN Secretary General to negotiate peace."

This caught Netanyahu off-guard. "Secretary General?" he asked in the private and secure call.

"That is correct. The emergency vote was held last night. It seems I have been promoted. Your country is fortunate, for I alone can negotiate peace. Even if you survive, many other countries desire your technology and your natural resources. Peace is the only way."

"I see," was all Netanyahu could muster. He knew their only hope of survival was the God of his forefathers: Abraham, Isaac, and Jacob. If he himself had never had faith, he would need some now.

The giant cloud of dust and the stream of Russian and Iranian naval ships came to a stop. The Armies of Gog had Israel surrounded on three sides. Only Jordan held out and would not allow troops on their land. It wouldn't last. Once the first shot was fired, the political will of Jordan would be lost to their Muslim brothers. As one commentator described, "We are waiting for a tiny nation to be mercifully destroyed, as the world watches."

The pivotal date arrived and the armies of Gog were massed at the borders. The launch of hundreds of Katusha and Kassam missiles began, destined for anti-missile battery locations that were known by the PLO and Lebanese armies. Exchanges of rocket fire on both sides of the border were plentiful, but no troops advanced into Israeli space. It was obvious that the coalition leaders were attempting to destroy as many of Israel's defenses as possible prior to advancing. On the surface, it appeared to be working. Many of the older Iron Dome and Arrow I and II sites were being hit. But these were essentially props, antiquated units left to draw fire from the enemy forces. Even so, many of these older missile batteries were working effectively and intercepting rockets prior to reaching their targets.

So far, the plan was working with Israeli troops far from the hail of rockets. Israeli's advanced satellite scrambling system was also giving coalition generals headaches. Netanyahu ordered the IDF Airwings to launch and take out rocket launching positions just inside Syria, Lebanon, and Sinai. Russian, Iranian, and Syrian MIG's were on the way, so Netanyahu ordered an all-out assault on the navy flotilla and the two Russian submarines lurking in the Mediterranean Sea.

As F-22s fired at the ships, the MIGs pursued. The two Russian subs got off six short-range missiles, but all were intercepted and destroyed by the BPI. Cheers were going up in the control room as Israel made headway against the Russian ships. Eight F-22s carrying air-to-surface, deep-penetrating torpedoes delivered their payloads and sunk both subs. There was heavy damage to the aircraft carrier, and two destroyers had been hit. Dogfights between MIG's and F-22s broke out all over the sky. The MIG's just kept coming in waves.

Every screen was displaying explosions and cockpit videos of strikes against ships and rocket launch sites. Then the alert sounded: four Hormuz missiles launched from western Syria, six more from Iran. Two of the Syrian missiles were picked up by BPI and terminated within seconds of launch. A UAV over the Caspian Sea took out one more before being shot down by Russian drones.

"Tracking seven, repeat, seven incoming."

"Targets?"

"Tel Aviv, Haifa, Dimona—two each. The single is headed for Bet Shean."

"Crap! Secret missile base there," Jake exclaimed.

For now, the F-22s outnumbered the MIGs, but more were on the way. The incoming missiles became the main priority. Dimona was the location of Israel's nuclear power plant. A direct hit there could be tragic, even though it was remotely located.

"Not a chance these are nukes," one tech said.

"Why is that?" Netanyahu asked.

"The targets are too close to their own troops. They are not going to amass troops on the border just to wipe them out with nukes," the tech responded.

The IDF F-22s, backed up by dozens of F-18s, had every ship in trouble. They were winning the air war as well, but losing many planes. The focus narrowed on the two remaining Syrian-launched missiles, one toward Tel Aviv and the other destined for Dimona. Arrow III had the Dimona missile locked and Iron Dome had the Tel Aviv Hormuz. These missiles had been proven very capable in testing and the defenses were imperative to Israel's survival. As the Tel Aviv missile came in hot, the Iron Dome fired six anti-missile rounds. The missile was destroyed eighty miles north of its target. Arrow III also proved itself, taking out the Dimona missile. So far, so good.

Now five more were inbound from Iran and determined to hit their marks. The newest technology, the Aegis anti-missile intercept system, sat on a platform sixty feet below the surface of the Sea of Galilee. It saved Haifa, knocking both birds out of the air. Arrow III missed the second Tel Aviv bird, but Iron Dome picked it off just over Ketel Sava. The second Dimona missile was destroyed by the Aegis system. Meanwhile, the IDF was battling to keep the MIG's from taking out the BPI drones. These would prove critical if a later launch from Syria or Iran occurred. F-22s also knocked out the majority of enemy drones, which were targeting anti-missile batteries.

I have to tell you, watching those anti-missile rockets explode out of the water, track toward their target, and intercept them in a ball of fire was spectacular. There was some bad news—a few of the debris fields showed toxic chemicals. These guys were serious, and Prime Minister Netanyahu knew the nuke was in the wings. They had already shown a willingness to use it. More missiles came, one right after another. Then the troops began to cross the borders.

A two-mile-wide buffer had been left between the advancing troops and Israeli front lines. From every possible position, the troops poured into Israel. Satellites were tracking tanks that were moving down into Jordan and approaching the West Bank. There would be few hold-outs on the Islamic side. The goal was clear, and it didn't include taking any Zionist prisoners. The precision advance was choreographed with huge numbers of rocket launches and mortar fire from the tanks. The inevitable conflict was heating up as hundreds of thousands advanced into Israel from every direction.

As the battle raged, the bunker we comfortably watched from began to move. It started slowly and in waves. Then everything began to rattle, before rolling like waves in the ocean. We hung on to bars positioned throughout the facility. Not a monitor moved Nothing fell off the walls, no signals lost. The shaking intensified and rolled on and on—one minute, two minutes, three minutes. It was everything I could do to hold on. Some fell, others plopped out of their chairs. This was a big one! God was stepping in.

Incoming rockets crashed to the ground or exploded in an empty sky. Enemy aircraft lost power and fell from the sky, pilots ejecting everywhere. The troops were confused, not sure how to get their bearings. Large groups were being swallowed up into huge crevices that opened in the earth. The burning ships sank, the tanks froze, and the troops began to turn on themselves in the confusion.

The massive quake lasted eleven minutes and twenty seconds. Dozens of Hormuz missiles were launched from Syria and Iran, and then the big ones, the ICBM, were detected. Twelve huge rockets tipped with who-knew what were headed toward Israel. BPI took out two, both nuclear. The others marched on. The armies of Gog dropped their weapons and began to retreat.

Even if these missiles could be stopped, it would mean the end of Israel. Netanyahu gave the order for a mass retreat. The enemy was on the run, heading back across the border. As the missiles advanced, the ground opened and swallowed hundreds of thousands of troops. No MIG's flew, no mechanized equipment ran. Men were left to run for their lives.

As the missiles approached their targets, they simply disintegrated, raining down debris on the retreating enemy troops. It was as if a force field had been turned on.

The communications center erupted in applause and cheers. God was showing the world how He would protect His people. His counter-measures, His confusion of enemy troops, and His protection lasted for several hours. Then, there was a lull—peace, quiet, and a moment of relief. The largest army ever assembled was no match for the God of Abraham, Isaac, and Jacob. Our God! Jake and I hugged, in awe of how it all went down. But we weren't done yet, and neither was God.

Damage reports, losses of planes and soldiers were being reported from all over Israel. Rocket debris had injured some, but very few. The damage from chemical contamination had been limited to remote areas. I can't say that for the retreating armies. Missile, airplane, and rocket debris rained down on the top of them for countless miles along the borders.

Everyone in the control room, and Israel, was taking a deep breath, wondering what had just transpired. Of course, Jake and I knew exactly. God had stepped in and protected Israel against unimaginable odds. What few coalition troops were left alive were in a full retreat to get out of Israel. Netanyahu had gathered his top advisors to assess the situation and get updates on the damage done by the quake.

One tech chimed in, "That was a real quake, a God-made quake, emanating from nature and shaking the world." No specific epicenter was recorded. No one had noticed, but during the earthquake a lone camera caught a giant fissure that opened up on Temple Mount and swallowed the Dome of the Rock and the Al Aska Mosque. Not a stone was moved in the Western Wall, nor was the synagogue nearby damaged. But the point of reference for Islam, their holiest site in Jerusalem, was gone.

Reports were coming in from seismic stations around the globe and the quake had indeed been felt in the remotest lands. The fish of the sea had come to the surface as if to see what was happening. Birds had taken cover anywhere possible, but none flew. The quake was the longest recorded in history, eleven minutes and twenty seconds. This eclipsed the old mark by over three minutes. Oddly, there were no aftershocks and the quake caused cataclysmic shifts in mountain ranges. It even caused Mt. Horeb to flatten into a high plateau. There was no question, the world was moved by the force of God's power. Drones flying over Damascus had picked up something very interesting—the huge quake had opened up a massive fissure that swallowed all of the remaining buildings and debris from the nukes. Then, like at the Temple Mount, the ground healed and it looked like an undisturbed field. There was simply no evidence that the bustling city had ever been there. The prophecy of Isaiah 17 was now fully fulfilled.

News feeds were buzzing and commentators were scrambling to find experts and scientists to try to explain the oddities. Netanyahu got on the video and laid it all out. He held nothing back. Quoting from the book of Ezekiel, the prophet, he read: "Behold, I am against you, O Gog, the Prince of Rosh, Meshech and Tubal; and I will turn you around and lead you on, bringing you out from the far north and bringing you against the mountains of Israel. Then I will knock the bow out of your left hand, and cause the arrows to fall out of your right hand.

"Surely in that day, there will be a great earthquake in the land of Israel, so that the fish of the sea, the birds of the heavens, the beasts of the field, all creeping things that creep on the earth, and all the men who are on the face of the earth shall shake at My presence. The mountains shall be thrown down, the steep places fall, and every wall shall fall to the ground. Every man's sword will be against his brother, and I will bring him to judgment with pestilence and bloodshed. You shall fall on the mountains of Israel, you and all of your troops and the peoples who are with you; I will give you to the birds of prey of every sort and to the beasts of the field to be devoured. You shall fall on the open field, for I have spoken, says the Lord God."

"These are the words written in the book, the Bible—prophecy of a future war and penned some 2,600 years ago. Today, that prophecy was fulfilled. Days ago, a lesser-known prophecy from Isaiah was fulfilled—the total and complete destruction of the oldest city in the world. Sadly, the prophecy written by Ezekiel is not complete. The power of the living God is still to be seen. I pray for those who will be affected. He has warned you from years past of the judgment to come. Now it is coming and we have no way to stop or minimize it.

"As the world watches, we mourn our losses and grieve the terrible things to come. To our enemies, it is not too late to repent of your evil and your desire to destroy God's chosen people. Repent, for the kingdom of God is at hand! Our prayers as a nation are with you. As for our Jewish friends dispersed throughout the world, it is time to complete the Ayala. We encourage you to come home to the safest place on earth, praise God."

The control room erupted into applause. Netanyahu, the Prime Minister of the tiny country of Israel, who himself had lost his brother and countless comrades in battle, years prior, quieted the crowd. "Please, please. God has given us a great victory. But it is still a dark day. Many of our brothers and sisters are dead. Our country is wounded and God's judgment of the coalition is still coming. Millions will die, and the religious face of the world will be changed forever. It is not a time for rejoicing. Still, we must give the God of Abraham, Isaac, and Jacob glory for His protection."

Many were praising God and giving Him glory for His love. I was in awe by the thought of billions of people throughout the world opening Bibles and reading the words of Ezekiel. It was fitting that Netanyahu chose to omit some of the words so that the world could see who God is, and how He is sovereign.

News shows had Bible scholars, rabbis, evangelists, and historians on non-stop. This pause God had built in was as astonishing and thought-provoking as the events themselves. Jake and I broke away to the conference room to pray and talk.

"Millions of Muslims know their fate at this moment." Jake said. "Ezekiel clearly states that He will send fire down on Magog and on those who live in security in the coastlands. The judgment is coming for those in the coalition. God will deal with radical Islam."

"It feels odd to me," I said, "that I am praying for the lost to know God, when I myself am lost."

"Yes, ironic, isn't it? But don't worry, you have at least one praying for you," he smiled.

"Thank you, Jake."

The dramatic events surrounding Israel had taken a pause, but as many had predicted, it was still not over for Israel. God waited in the wings. His judgments, like His promises are sure and will be completely fulfilled.

chapter
NINETEEN
✿✿✿✿✿✿✿

For two long days, the news media of the world tried to cast off any legitimacy of God's assistance in the war of Magog. Rabbis, scholars, professors, and Bible experts would come on the air and read the Ezekiel prophecy, which was an exact play-by-play of the events, but the media would shun it, protest it, explain it as a coincidence. What was really entertaining was when bold Bible scholars would finish with, "Well, let me read to you what is next, so when it comes you will know the source."

We would always laugh because the response was always the same. "What now, fairy dust?"

"How about: 'And I will bring him to judgment with pestilence and bloodshed; I will rain down on him, on his troops, and on the many peoples who are with him, flooding rain, great hailstones, fire and brimstone.' Can you account for fire from heaven as a natural act?" It was always the same.

"You are caught up in fantasies," the media would say. But millions had watched as the planes fell out of the sky, the ground opened and swallowed up men, tanks, APC's, and even the Dome of the Rock. It was obvious to anyone with half a brain. We could certainly see why Antichrist would have a huge following. People could not or would not accept the idea of a true God. Then I would think about my own beliefs, my own hesitation. How could I witness all this and still hold out? I knew better. I believed in God. Yet I still procrastinated. I knew somehow that it would cost me, yet I languished in my unbelief. Jake convinced me to go topside with him to see the Temple Mount. There were thousands of people out in town and many were there to see the remnants of the Islamic mosque.

In the distance, we could see the great Wailing Wall with the rabbis still inserting prayers into the cracks. We took the walking path around and came out on the Temple Mount. Sure enough, the Dome of the Rock was gone, and with it every Muslim in Israel. The buildings were not only gone, the earth had sealed up like a flat stone—a foundation. God had not only erased Islam from Jerusalem, He had placed His Son, the Chief Cornerstone in position to erect a new temple—the temple of prophecy.

"How does the media explain this off, Jake? I mean, even the Muslims know this is a bad sign. It's like it never existed. The mosque and every related structure, gone!" I asked.

"No way to explain this. It's God's work and soon the rains will come. I just wanted you to see it, to build your faith, brother."

"I know—I know… I feel ready, but I am compelled to have my folks with me, at The Way. Just seems right."

"So cheat death, fly home to Virginia, and confess to Christ. You are only in the most holy of places right here. And you may not make it home, my friend. The Rapture is imminent. God has made the world ready for the harvest."

"Yes, to that there is no doubt. I think we will see the rain of fire, rise of antichrist, covenant signed, and then the Rapture. Some even believe a mid-tribulation or even a post-tribulation rapture," I commented.

"You are full of excuses, my friend. What you need is yet another Bible lesson."

"I suppose it couldn't hurt. How about tonight?"

"You are on. Now let's go eat..."

The city was reeling from the quake and the aftermath of the war. It had only been a few days, and we decided it was safer and more practical to go back to the bunker. First, I snapped a shot of the new Temple Mount to show Dad and Mom. We watched more coverage, this time from the 700 Club out of America. Their coverage was non-stop evangelical. "This is the Word of God come to life. Don't hesitate, God is calling you. His desire is for you to not perish but have eternal life."

It was amazing to watch clips from an Iranian-based ministry of Christ. For years they had piped God's message of hope to millions of satellite dishes in Iran and other Islamic countries. In most of these countries, dishes were illegal. That is why everyone had one. And they preached the gospel message, along with testimonies from one Muslim then another, then another, all giving their lives to Christ. Jesus was appearing to thousands and they would tune in, hear the prayer, and confess. The harvest had begun and God's Word was always true. His desire is that *all* be saved.

Jake kept poking me as one after another confessed faith in Jesus. We were busy consuming chicken and matzah ball soup when the rain began. It was just a light rain. The communication center had several cameras outside and one on the Temple Mount. Rainbows appeared all over the world as the rain came. There was no question that God was in the rain. But now it was time for judgment. Muhammad's run was over. The long line of Ishmael would evaporate, either in salvation or in death.

For ten hours, it rained a steady, light rain on every corner of the earth. Then, it turned into a world-wide deluge. This kept up until midnight Jerusalem time. While the rain fell, reports began to trickle in. Russia's major cities, the affluent coastline along the Baltic Sea, Tehran, Istanbul, Mecca, Medina, Kabul, Cairo, Benghazi, Beirut— the hail was coming down. First, it was softball size, then basketball size, then the size of a small car. The destruction was focused on government buildings, military outposts, mosques, and even some private homes.

Then came the fire and brimstone, falling on these same targets, consuming them with fire. Every country involved in the coalition, their capitals, their military bases burned. Every extremist mosque, every extremist Islamic center, every seat of Islamic power worldwide, consumed.

Governments had buildings destroyed. North Korea's corrupt government was left smoldering in ruin. Oddly, very few human lives were lost. Only those who had persecuted Christ followers or were outspoken enemies of Israel perished. It was a horrendous spectacle. As the first light of day broke, the Middle East was changed forever. Every part of Islamic life was gone except its people. God had issued His judgment, yet as a loving God will do, preserved His children in order for them to choose.

Then there were the sores. John called it pestilence. Awful, itchy sores began to appear on those who were lost. This too was part of God's prophecy.

"It is time, Jeremy. The door is open for a short time. God has given the remainder of the lost a time to choose. You must not wait…"

"I know you are right, Jake. But I must go home. I see the writing on the wall, but I must go home."

"Suit yourself. You truly are a Jew…"

"Pray for me, Jake. I just need to make it home."

Forty days after we had left Virginia, Ron landed the Honda at Bedford with Samatha DeVoss on board. The world had changed since I left for Israel. I was anxious to see my Mom and Dad, as well as John and Renea. I couldn't wait to tell them the first-hand account of the events. I said goodbye to Ron, who would head to Florida to see his family. All the way back, we had shared our experiences through the Magog war. He too was convinced, but did not know what to do. I told him to go to a good Bible-believing church—The Way, if he could find one.

I pulled in through the gate and met my Dad skipping toward me. I loved this man with all my heart, and he was filled with the Spirit. The first thing he asked was if I were saved.

"Not yet, Dad—soon."

I got hugs all around and all of us had tears. Renea said I was a truly beautiful woman. We all laughed. The makeup and costume were removed and I became my normal, Eli self. I was exhausted but could not go to bed. Church was in four days. I just needed to make it until then.

We ate and visited until I crashed. They were fascinated by the stories and amazed that I had been right in the middle of the action. I slept for fifteen hours, and dreamt of waiting in line to have my head separated from my shoulders. I woke up terrified. I had never been that scared, especially of a dream. It was so real. However, that faded as I enjoyed the coffee and promised my trip to the altar at The Way. "I am ready."

John was insistent that I say the prayer now. No dice. I was going to do this my way. They all shared stories of how the terrorist attacks had continued right up to the fire. Muslim attackers were being leveled by twelve-inch diameter hailstones, mosques were crushed by huge rocks and fire which completely destroyed them. The terror had turned on them and after the rain stopped, so did the attacks. God had made His peace with Islam world-wide. It was no more.

The most incredible thing was the people. Muslims all over the word were turning to Jesus. Like me, they had seen glimpses of God's love for them. Then, there was nothing left but Jesus and His open arms. It was truly a miracle.

John and I spoke about the sores. "This is the pestilence God spoke of. Have you noticed that those affected are anti-Israel or anti-Jew? It's the heart that God sees. Very few of those affected are Muslims. It shows God's love and holiness. He is also using the sores as a warning to the apostate churches."

"What do you mean, John?"

"It's amazing… People are going into Bible-believing, Jesus-following churches and being healed and saved. But the apostate churches can't heal them. It's all over the news. Plus, He gave those who have the sores forty days of suffering. Just like He gave the Jews forty years to accept Jesus before the destruction of the Temple and their dispersion. It's been forty days, the number of consummation, and the pestilence is ending."

"Now I am afraid of what might come next."

"He had to warn the churches: the lukewarm churches, the idolatrous churches, the apostate churches. Again, He is so long-suffering…"

"So He is dividing with truth?"

"Yep. And your time is about up…"

We both thought it was interesting that Lech did not get sores, but his two cronies did. "Yes, and he is using it to lure Israel into his snare…" John said.

We made our own pilgrimage to church, and were greeted by Pastor Richard and many other new faces. The place was packed with those praising God and worshiping His name.

Pastor Richard took his seat, asked the congregation to open their Bibles to 1 Thessalonians 4:16. "Brothers and sisters in Christ, we have seen the miracles of God first hand. He told us the world would 'see My judgment which I have executed', and we did see. We know and trust His promises and the promises of end times are being fulfilled. Millions have seen the truth, false religions have been judged, and God has poured out His Spirit on the house of Israel. Folks, the house of Israel is all believers and all nations. So what is next?

"Today we look at an event that could happen at any time. Allow me to read the text, beginning in verse 16: 'For the Lord (that is, Jesus) Himself will descend from heaven with a shout, with the voice of the archangel, and with the trumpet of God. And the dead in Christ shall rise first. Then we who are alive and remain shall be caught up together with them in the clouds to meet the Lord in the air. And thus we shall always be with the Lord. Therefore, comfort one another with these words.'

"Congregation, are you comforted by these words? If not, you need salvation. Only true believers of Christ will go in what Jesus

Himself called a twinkling of an eye. It could happen right now!" He snapped his fingers and paused. "Well, that never works…but someday soon."

I was thinking about how everyone wanted it to be now. "God's time," John whispered.

Suddenly, a loud voice said, "Come up here!" followed by a long blast of the shofar. I could not tell where it was coming from. I turned left, then right. They were gone. Every single one—gone. Panic set in immediately. I stood. There were clothes, jewelry, glasses, Bibles—lots of Bibles. I was alone. I heard a voice, "You are my beloved son. Come to Me. I will use you in My Kingdom.—fear not." I hit my knees and fell to my face.

"I'm sorry, Lord. I am so sorry, Lord. I confess that You are my Savior and I am a sinner. I believe You died on the cross for my salvation. I believe your Father raised You from the dead and that You sit at His right hand. I accept the gift You have been offering to me. I am so sorry."

There were no more words from God. I lay prostrate, pleading for my salvation. Then, a peace came over me. I stood on my knees and looked at the cross. I could picture Him there, pierced for my transgressions. I had missed the moment. Jake was gone, Dad, Mom, John, Renea, Pastor Richard. All gone. The world would be in chaos. I felt my spirit praying to Jesus, "Give me strength, oh Lord." Then, I began to cry. All of my sins flashed before my eyes in an instant. Finally, I knew that I was the man that He had been trying to show me all these years. I fell back, laid on my side, and cried.

This brokenness, this humility would be a part of me from now on. I had everything ripped away from me. Now, I was alone. My stubborn will had cost me a wife, family, and friends. Now I had only one focus. That was Jesus and that old wooden cross. I gathered my loved ones' personal things and left the church. The six miles to the lake house were uneventful. Two cars off the road with no passengers. When I turned on the TV, the situation was quite different. News anchors and camera operators had vanished, planes were crashing, cars and buses piling up on streets and highways.

The entire world was affected. Eye witness accounts were all the same. "They just vanished." President Donald J. Trump was alive and well. He redeclared martial law and a national state of emergency. All travel was terminated as millions of people were gone—vanished without a trace. I had no idea what to do, so I read my Bible until I fell asleep in my recliner. I was safe, away from the chaos. I was also very much alone.

I awoke with the Bible open to Luke 24. The twenty-fifth verse jumped out at me. "How foolish you are, and how slow of heart to believe all that the prophets have declared." I really thought I had figured it out. I was going to do things my way—a show of my salvation to my friends and family in front of an audience. A half hour, I reasoned. I missed it by a half hour. But it may as well have been a lifetime.

I heard the voice of my DAVEO security system: "Breach in sector II." I darted up from my recliner and headed to the elevator. Two hooded individuals were climbing the fence deep in the woods. I waited to see how well my system would perform.

I expected this—only thugs left, and this was a prime place to pick up some booty.

"Warnings in progress!" DAVEO announced.

I watched as the two cleared the sizeable fence. They both stopped short as the loudspeaker blared, "You are in restricted space. Leave at once or suffer the consequences." They looked around and saw no one.

"Just a recording..." said one.

"Yeah, let's go!" They headed toward the house.

"You are about to be fired upon. Leave the property now!" They kept coming after a short pause.

The next step was significant. Automatic gunfire sprayed an area near the two criminals. This got their attention. They both hit the deck.

"You have two minutes to vacate the property. Perimeter fence electrification commences in two, 1:59, 1:58, 1:57..."

That was all it took. The two were gone, never to return. I left the fence hot to deter any more intruders. At least I still had DAVEO, my trusty security system.

Days went by and I grew sick of watching the news, the chaos and the depravity of man. The most amazing thing was that every child was gone. Even pregnant women who were not raptured had their child raptured. I knew it was about to get ugly, and God had taken steps to protect His children, young and old.

The Bible was becoming all new to me as passages came to life with meaning. In occasional news stories, it was clear to me that millions had missed the boat and had now sworn allegiance to Jesus. Days and weeks went by as my purpose was revealed to me. That is when I got a text from Steph's phone.

chapter
TWENTY
✡ ✡ ✡ ✡ ✡ ✡

J erusalem – Time of Jacob's Trouble

The guard moved cautiously toward the fallen woman. He was glancing in both directions, up and down the line. When he looked away from me, I made my move, kicking his legs out from under him and sending him on his back. I crushed his windpipe with my elbow and took the MA from him. My new friend had the Daisy off his hip and the female constable to our left was dead in a millisecond. Who was I dealing with, I wondered? I turned and squeezed off a group into the next closest enforcer. I stood and fired a burst at the machine, killing everyone in the vicinity. The girl had two more constables finished off and side arms in hand. We grabbed two MA's each and headed into the fleeing crowd. It couldn't have been more perfect. I snatched two abandoned backpacks and stuffed the extra Daisy's inside. I swung the extra MA onto my back with the backpack over top. My friend followed suit and we moved quickly.

It had to be divine intervention, because all the Global Constables were rushing to the area of the machine. We were becoming lost in the crowd. I stopped on a knoll and sized up our escape. I held out a hand. "Eli."

"Beth."

"Vehicles over there. Let's try to find a private one to get out of here."

"Copy."

I knew I was paired up with a pro. Not sure where from, but a pro.

"Let's go—stay low."

We were off, and within five minutes we stood at the edge of a huge parking lot. I walked up to a woman in a black BMW M5. I pushed the gun into the window and told her to get into the back, where Beth joined her. I got in and punched it. With a gun to her head, she was shaky. I drove purposefully, but not to draw attention.

"I'm a reporter—and on your side. I was on the knoll taking shots. I watched the whole thing go down. Who are you people?" The woman asked.

"Just the enemy, young lady. Just cooperate so that my partner doesn't have to shoot you."

"Was this planned? You two look like you are a team." She asked.

"What's your name, young lady?" I asked.

"Missy. Missy Waters."

"From the News Day?" Beth asked.

"Yes."

I looked questioningly at Beth.

"It's an underground paper for followers. Pull back your hair, Missy."

"Sure enough—the mark," Beth proclaimed.

"How could she be on our side?" I questioned.

"The mark of Christ. Look."

"I glanced in the mirror. Sure enough, a barely discernable cross on Missy's forehead. Then Beth showed me hers.

"I never saw it before," I said.

"I saw yours in line," Beth said. "I knew we were connected. Not all in that line had one. Many are dying lost.

"That is why I'm out here," Missy said. "The gospel needs to be heard."

"Well, for now, we just need to get somewhere safe. Do you have any ideas?"

"If you can trust me, I can get you to a place." Missy said.

"Where?"

"Twelve miles from here. The headquarters for the underground."

"And you trust us enough to expose your hideout?"

"I saw what you did. We need skilled people. People who can fight and know who the enemy is. We are at war—until the end."

"Okay. Let's go!"

Oddly enough the path to Jericho was obstruction-free. We didn't see constables or helicopters or even Jerusalem police. Entering an industrial area, we pulled in front of a huge warehouse, the door rolled open, and I drove in. We sat in a totally bare room with another huge door in front of us.

"I have to punch the keyboard and explain why I brought you here."

Beth kept the Daisy trained on her as she typed in a code, did a retina scan, and spoke into the speaker. Soon, the door opened and a man of about sixty years old emerged. He and Missy talked. Then they came to the car.

"I am Rabbi Yosef Edelman. Missy tells me you are a brother and sister in Christ. May I see your marks? Ah, yes. And a Jew as well. And you, young lady—where are you from?"

"I'm Egyptian. Coptic."

"I see. You were in the line for the machine?"

"Yes," we answered in unison.

"How dare they desecrate the Mount of Olives with such expositions!" he exclaimed.

"And the Temple," Beth added.

"What is your name, young lady?"

"Bethany Hourani, but please call me Beth."

"Very well. And you, young man?"

"Jeremy. Jeremy Stone," I said.

"Yes, but what is your real name?"

"Eliezer Grollenberg."

"Good, Eli. No reason to use your alias here. You are among friends. Now come, see our home."

The doors opened and we drove into what looked like an underground parking lot. There were about a dozen vehicles parked inside and an elevator on one side. I felt a peace about this man and this place. We rode the elevator down a few floors and it opened into a giant underground tech center. I immediately recognized it as an intel center complete with every high-tech device and hundreds of staff. I felt like we had been swept out of harm and directly into the center of the saints.

As Rabbi Yosef led us into the massive underground complex, thoughts rushed back into my head. The amazing war of Magog and the judgment that followed had led to this, a great underground of

Jesus-following saints determined to hold on until His return. The work was of survival and evangelism. World-wide campaigns to bring the lost to salvation were emanating from right here in this abandoned Mossad bunker. Had Jake not been a Messianic Jew, he too would be here, sharing his personal testimony like so many others.

To my surprise, Rabbi Yosef led us to a room, introduced us to a small production staff, and asked us to share our own testimonies. Many were in tears as I told my story, my birth as a Jewish-Palestinian, my mother's death, my work in the NSA, my love life, as it had been. Then my amazing conversion following Jesus' dream and the disappearances. I had missed the Rapture, but would not miss out on eternal life.

Then, it was Beth's turn. A freedom fighter in the KCA, she saw many Coptic Christians persecuted and killed for their beliefs. She had been a holdout, an Egyptian first and always. In her view, Jesus was a prophet, a good man, but not God. Not someone you would pledge your life to. She had seen and recognized many miracles of God, including healings and protection of her fellow fighters. Then, in the Magog war she had nearly been killed by the raining fire. Somehow, she and her comrades were protected. She drew closer to God, but not to Jesus. She was also blessed by a vision of Jesus, writing her name in the book. She knew she would be saved, but she fought the desire to confess her faith. She learned her lesson from the Rapture.

She encouraged those listening to refuse the mark, "but do not die in vain." Then she recited these familiar words: "Today is the day, Jesus is the way." She then gave a prayer of salvation, the gospel message, and I felt the Holy Spirit in her. I could imagine many repeating her words and joining the ranks of tribulation saints. We rejoiced as the angels did. The small group clapped loudly as they signed off. I now knew who my earthly partner would be until Jesus' return.

"How long have you been a couple?" asked the Rabbi. We both laughed.

"About an hour now!" she said. Our eyes met and I knew we had been placed in that line together for a reason. Missy Waters had downloaded the video from our escape. As we watched, I was amazed at the way we worked together. It was an incredible turn of events.

"An hour, huh?" the Rabbi asked in Hebrew.

"Praise God," I said. "Only He could orchestrate such a miracle."

"I would think some specialized training went along with that. You disarmed the man and took out all the others in less than ten seconds. And you, miss. You have some training of your own?" he asked.

"A bit, but even I wouldn't pick a fight with this one!" she said, pointing to me with a smile.

"Please consider joining us here. We do need qualified people in our efforts to keep Satan at bay."

"I will. For now, though, would it be too much to ask for a hot shower?" I asked. Beth seconded the request.

"Of course, follow me."

This group did not have a name. It was a mix of Jews, Arab Christians, Africans, and various westerners. How they all ended up in Jerusalem was a mystery at this point. But it seemed they had provision and God's support. It seemed to be a good place to land for the moment. The accommodations were first-rate and I needed sleep badly. I knew we were getting close to the end, and I had some very valuable assets to offer this group. First, ever since the Antichrist had initiated the mark, the underground switched to cash in good old American dollars for trade. There were huge distribution centers all over the world that dealt in goods and services needed by the saints. God had set up most of these well in advance of the Rapture.

The mark of the beast was an ingenious little bit of technology. It was both a mark and an electronic device, applied like a small tattoo. The mark consisted of three cryptic letters in dark green ink. The technology was in the ink itself, impregnated with tiny flecks of crushed silicon and recently discovered crystals. It contained a unique signal that was matched to you and you alone. Various types of readers were utilized to identify you by name or give your entire known history. Over the past ten years, the UN had collected data from Facebook, Twitter, and other popular social media sites to capture one's identity for future use. The mark contained a link to a cloud database that had all of that information—good, bad or indifferent—available to the Global Constables. You could be "turned off" to prevent you from purchasing things like food or water. These resources were only available through two sources: the global market or the Christian underground market.

If you didn't have the mark, you were put in line, as Beth and I were. If you did, the global community knew who you were, what you were buying, and how to control you. Worship of the beast was mandatory each and every day. Following the Rapture, my new friend and colleague Tanner Rossini and I worked to decipher the formula and duplicated the mark technology. We could not only apply it, but have it read in any way we wanted. I could apply a temporary, screen-on mark and be anyone I programmed in, then wipe it off with a light solvent. We had done testing, but it was dangerous, and in its early stages led to Tanner's death and my capture. Nevertheless, I felt confident that I could get the technology to this group to be perfected.

I also had a substantial nest egg of many millions of dollars at the lake house. I felt the need to get home, grab the money, and see how the saints in America were doing. There was a lot I could offer and much to do. But right now, I needed sleep.

I heard a knock at the door early in the morning. I had been up praying and asking God for a way to get home. It was Beth.

"We have been invited to breakfast with some of the leaders. They have a feeling about us," she said.

"I wanted to thank you. Because of you, I live another day, at least."

"Yes, thank you too! I owe my life to you as well. Perhaps we will have future missions together. Would you like to go to America with me?"

She had a look of astonishment on her face. "Yes, I would. But why America?"

"I have some connections there. Not to mention a home."

"Family?"

"No. All were taken in the Rapture. I lost the love of my life just prior to the Rapture and the second love of my life a few months ago in Jerusalem."

"I'm so sorry Eli."

"You?"

"No. Most of my family was killed in Sinai during the war. I just could not convince them to leave. I lost my parents and older brother. Many of my Coptic Christian Army team mates are stranded in the Negev, and I would love to get them to Petra somehow. They are the closest people I have to family."

"I'm sorry for your loss Beth. So, no man in your life?"

"Yes, Jesus!"

"Good call!"

"You?"

"No. But lost my good friend just days ago."

"How?"

"Gunfight in President's Park."

"Oh, you were the cause of all the commotion over there. That is where they picked me up. I guess I can blame you for us meeting."

"I'll accept the blame, in this case. I lost a friend and gained one."

"Thank you for considering me a friend."

I wouldn't invite you to America otherwise."

"Good. I'll go then. How are we going to get there?"

"We're about to find out. God never takes us halfway. And I have a few tricks up my sleeve to offer."

"This I have to see…"

We entered a small boardroom filled with people and food. "So this is how the underground eats…" I said. The small group erupted into laughter.

"Some of the best farmers are Jesus followers…" said Rabbi Yosef. He introduced us to the group leaders. I couldn't remember the names, but there were four women and three men, including the rabbi. They all mentioned how much they appreciated the testimonies and the film of our escape. They had decided not to make the escape film available to the public, but Missy wrote a great eye-witness story of the small victory over the Global Community to share on the underground blog.

I figured time was of the essence, so I got straight to the point. "I need something and I have something, well, two things to offer for it that are tangible."

They were anxious to hear it all.

"First, I have resources—money. Second, I have developed a way to duplicate and program the mark on a temporary basis, as needed."

"Eli, we have been actively working on a way to do that. What you are offering is much needed, and would be appreciated. What is it you need?" Rabbi Yosef asked.

"A ride to America for two." I glanced at Beth, and the rabbi understood.

Rabbi Yosef leaned forward and spoke into an intercom, "Please get Ron Forester and have him come to the boardroom."

I recognized the name, but it was a distant memory.

"While we wait for Ron, tell me about your mark technology," the Rabbi said.

I went through the process we used to develop and duplicate the silicon ink. "Rabbi, I have all the application, production, and data across town at my former friend's place," I offered. Several of the leaders had good technical questions about the faux mark, as I called it.

"Amazing," Miss Eschelman said. "Have you done testing on the GC system?"

"Yes, functional, but the screen-on needs some work. Once they started applying marks, they were stuck with the system as is. It can't be modified—we used that slip-up against them. Plus, God had to leave us a backdoor," I said with a chuckle. "The tweaks needed are minor."

"He is a God of some humor, isn't He?" said the Rabbi. "Amazing work, Eli. Now, about the resources?"

"Yes, the money. Good old American greenbacks—a few million of them to spare."

"Eli, you have just answered several prayers," Miss Eschelman said.

"God is amazing, isn't He?"

"Yes, indeed," Rabbi Yosef added.

There was a knock at the door and in came the Honda pilot who flew me to Jerusalem several years before. I stood and shook his hand.

"Mr. Forester, good to see you again."

"Do I know you?"

I then realized he had flown me as Samantha DeVoss. "I'm Samantha DeVoss." I smiled broadly. "You flew me from Bedford, Virginia, to Spain, and then here to Jerusalem. We landed near Tel Aviv." Again, I smiled. He was looking confused.

"I remember the flight, but… Samantha DeVoss is a woman," he said with a big swallow.

"Yes. That's one of my aliases."

"Apparently a very good one."

"Thank you. Now, can you fly me back to Bedford then on to Oregon?"

"Sure. You buying the fuel?"

"Yes."

He smiled. "Samantha DeVoss, a man. Really?"

"Yes."

"Okay. When are we going?"

"Day after tomorrow. We have a little work to do here." Just like that, we were set.

Since Jerusalem was hot, we had to go covert and move quickly. I took Beth with me in disguise and we made it to Tanner's. It was undisturbed, and all the goods were there. We were back to the underground safe and sound by mid-afternoon. We made a good team, and now Ron was a part. He would be our professional pilot. God does answer prayers.

"This technology needs to go to the underground," I explained. "I want to get it to my good friend T-Bone in Oregon," I told the group.

"Is that General T-Bone at Joseph's at The Dalles?" Rabbi Yosef asked.

"The very one."

"Amazing. The Agri-store is a huge part of our network," Miss Eschelman explained.

"How do you know him?" asked the Rabbi.

"Let's just say we have done business together in the past."

"Some government business?"

"Yes."

"You have our blessing, Eli," Rabbi Yosef said.

Ron, Beth and I got reacquainted, and I lined them both out on the plan for America. Beth asked, "What is this whole Samantha DeVoss business?"

"Oh, nothing," Ron said. "It's just that this man can be one beautiful woman. I can't believe he is a man. It took me a minute. Speak in your Samantha voice, Eli."

I told Beth that Ron was imagining things, in the voice of Samantha. She had a look of disbelief and wonder on her face. She was already starting to consider how valuable all this would be in our service to the Lord.

I lined the tech's out on the process and programming for connection to the database. "We have a password for the highest levels and put ourselves on the list to be notified of password changes. We even have a way to do a global verification of worship for all the saints in the system. With the temporary mark, one can buy and sell freely. The faux mark wearer looks like any other Global Community follower, worship records and all. We can even terminate someone so that the GC stops looking for them," I explained. The group applauded enthusiastically. Within four hours, we had access to the GC database, had marks applied, and were verifying the viability of the data. Sure enough, we had a system that would benefit the underground significantly in the days to come. There was only one issue with the faux mark—it creeped out whoever wore it. It represented something that was pure evil.

Missy drove Ron, Beth, and I to the small airfield in Bethlehem. I was expecting to board the Honda. Instead, Ron led us to a shiny new Gulfstream XII. This craft was almost as fast as the Honda, but far more luxurious.

"Lost the Honda," he said. 'The GC fired at us in London and hit us in the tail. I was able to get us to Scotland before I crash-landed her in a potato field. Somehow, we survived, but the plane was lost. Then T-Bone had this one donated to us. It's a nice bird. You won't be disappointed."

We weren't.

We were loaded with everything we needed for our mission and, if all went well, safe passage into Morocco; Charlotte, North Carolina; and Bedford. Ron knew how to get us around under the GC radar. To my surprise, Beth was also a pilot, but not jet-certified. In this time, that didn't mean a thing, so Ron lined her out and we sat up front most of the way so that she could get a feel for the Gulf. You could never be too prepared. The rest of the trip, we got to know one another better.

As soon as we touched down in Charlotte, I could see the transformation. It was not new to me, but I got a harsh reminder of how bad things had become. When we opened the gate and walked into the lake house, it all hit me. The loss was real and palpable. Had it only been six years? It seemed like a lifetime ago, and the miles and near-death experiences filled my mind. Beth hugged me, sensing my turmoil. I took her hand and went out onto the deck overlooking the lake. Nothing much had changed here. Peace took over and rapidly filled my heart. It was beautiful. Beth put her arm around me and I began to cry.

"God is so good," I said. "I have been the most stubborn, stiff-necked Jew to ever walk the planet and yet He keeps sending me beautiful, amazing people to comfort me, hold me up, protect me." I squeezed her hand and we both stared silently into the picturesque setting in front of us.

"I was just thinking the same thing, Eli. Well, except for the Jew part."

We both chuckled. Ron interrupted to ask if there was any food, as he shuffled through the cabinets and fridge.

"Let me show you two around."

"How long has it been since you were here?" Ron asked.

"Nearly a year."

"Amazing. It hasn't been touched by anyone. You must have a guardian angel…" he smiled.

I took them down the elevator and into the control room. We gathered provisions from the food bank and freezer. Steak, coffee, wine, rice, pasta… Ron just shook his head. I did a quick scan of the boathouse and property. All was well.

"Let's throw together some dinner…" I said.

We all jumped in and had succulent beef stroganoff, a nice vino, and coffee with my favorite cream. Even the powdered stuff was bringing back memories. Beth liked it to—God was so good.

"I think we should go to church in the morning," I offered.

Both Ron and Beth looked at me. "Church? How?" Ron asked.

"I still get service updates on my sat-phone. The Way will be holding church tomorrow. It's a depleted congregation, but still should be good fellowship."

"I'm in."

"Me too!"

Both dinner and our conversation were great. We even dared to take the Wellcraft out for a sunset run. I looked at Beth and saw a godly woman, tattered and worn from the fight. A woman who had lost as much as myself or perhaps more. But she was drawing me. I had to resist, time was short. Then it occurred to me, time is short—why not, if it is God's will? I prayed for God to confirm my desire as a heartfelt and proper one and not a selfish one. She glanced at me and smiled as we watched the sunset behind the mountains. I was sure I could get nothing by her—nothing. I decided I would tell her about Steph and Susan.

Beth and I were both up at 4:30 AM, a result of the jet-lag. Even in a luxury Gulfstream, jet-lag was a factor. We both sought coffee.

"Can I tell you a story, Beth?"

"Time is short, Eli. Get on with it." Her smile was wry and discerning. My hunch about her was correct. I told her the story of Steph, my first love, our high school dance and her loss.

"About three months after the Rapture, I got a text from Steph's phone. 'Eli, I'm not sure what to say. I feel compelled to talk to you.' It was signed SS. I was confused, angry, intrigued. I knew her folks were gone along with mine, as well as my best friend John, and his wife Renea. I could not imagine who could have her phone or who would play with me like this. Two days passed and it consumed me. I prayed about it and God gave me peace. I replied, 'Not sure who you are, but want to know.'"

"So you had a mystery on your hands—feeling alone, and now this?" Beth interjected.

"Yes. It was obvious they knew me, had Steph's phone, and perhaps access to all our text messages and email. They may even know that I was planning on asking her to marry me."

"She was the love of your life."

"Yes. And of course, the NSA agent in me questioned if someone was tracking me, wanting to know how to get me."

"Sure, I would have been careful too."

"Still, my intuition, which can be good at times, told me it was something else. I pondered the next move, then the phone rang."

"It was Steph's number and my heart leapt out of my chest. I pushed answer, but could not get my voice to operate. From the other end came a voice, so recognizable yet different. 'Eli?' I was stunned, and still could not utter a word. 'I'm so sorry. I knew this was a terrible idea. I'll go now.'

'No, wait!' I told her. 'Who is this?'

'I'm Susan Skater. Steph's sister.'

My mind reeled. A sister? It was as if it were Steph talking. 'I'm sorry, Eli. I'm—I'm just so alone and scared. I didn't know where else to turn. I saw your texts—I knew if you were still among us that I needed to call you.'

"I learned that Steph had a sister, thirty years old, the prodigal daughter, if you will. I was in shock, but let her talk. I was mesmerized by her voice. It made me long for Steph. It was all so unfair!"

"So you fell in love with her?"

There was a long pause as I gazed into Beth's perfect green eyes.

"Here, have some more coffee," she offered.

I took a sip and swallowed hard.

"I am right, am I not?"

I nodded. "She was a troubled girl, a wild child. Refused college, got involved with drugs and the party scene and the like. Her folks had constantly reached out to her and prayed for her. After the Gog war and the disappearances, she got it together, gave her life to Christ, and needed a place to live. She went to Steph's and found her phone and diary, and discovered my love for her sister."

"So you fell in love with her?"

"Yes. And we were inseparable. We married within a week and became partners in this crazy world."

"I know. We need partners. We need our help-meet," she said as she took my hand into hers. I had tears and so did Beth. She knew what was coming.

"What happened?"

"We went to Jerusalem to catch the whole two witnesses thing. I wanted to see them up close. We did. We got within forty feet. They looked at us and asked in unison, 'What have we to do with you, children of God?'

"I told them that they were in danger. They acknowledged this, but shrugged it off. The Global Constables drew down on us and told us we were under arrest. The two witnesses spoke toward the two lead guards, and they seemed to burst into fire spontaneously. Another guard who ran up from behind took a shot, hitting Susan. Sadly, she was killed instantly. More guards joined the battle, but they too were consumed by fire. I ran for my life.

"Susan and I had spent three years together. I had never been married, or even been with a woman. She was everything to me. Oddly, our relationship fulfilled my love for Steph as well. Susan gave me a slice of Steph in giving me herself." I was left gazing into Beth's caring, glistening eyes. She was so warm and inviting. I knew right at that moment that she would be my partner for the rest of our time on earth.

chapter
TWENTY-ONE
✿✿✿✿✿✿✿

I suppose one could imagine how difficult it was to see our loved ones vanish all around us, and then seeing the horror of worldly events that resulted from it. I was blessed to be in a small country church in a rural area at the time, away from the chaos. I also knew exactly what had happened and knew where my loved ones where. It was a glorious day for them. For the rest of us, especially the truly lost, it was devastating. Jesus spoke to me after to provide comfort and peace. I made it right with Him right then and there, prostrate on the floor staring at that old wooden cross. I can only hope that all those on earth heard a word from God in one form or another, as they were able.

It was estimated that a billion or so would go. The actual number was thought to be two and a half billion. Every true believer was taken. It seemed every child under the age of sixteen was taken, even the unborn in the womb of an unbelieving mother. Many of the elderly, those suffering with dementia and alzheimer's disease were taken. Another half billion died from incidents related to the disapperances—plane crashes, accidents, doctors vanishing in the middle of surgery, etc. Then there came the suicides, millions more gave up or were so stricken with fear that they felt it was their only option. That continues months later.

There were now three mindsets in the world; The largest group, by far, were the opportunists, those evil people who thought only of themselves and how they could take advantage. These were led by greed, envy, hatred and the desire for power. Lech Manevetski was at the head of this pack.

The next group is hard to categorize, but the best way to describe them was panicked and full of anxiety. These were those who had loved ones and children vanish and had no answers. We hoped they would find their way into churches and many would. The vast majority lived in fear and the unknown. Most would end their lives or fall into the opportunist mindset to survive, simply because they refused any suggestion of God or divine influence.

The third group was seekers, looking for answers and seeking what they knew they missed. I was one of these, but only briefly. God had dealt with the churches and many, like The Way found newly saved saints to step in and start fresh. Like me, they had a good knowledge of the Bible, but missed the plane. many had been pastors or church leaders who Jesus had talked about in the parable of the ten virgins—They appeared ready, but were lacking.

As for me, God had me in His word, studying, learning, receiving revelation, preparing to be a Tribulation Saint. As I prayed and began to see my purpose unfold in the pages of the Bible, the vision Jesus had given me came back to me. I had missed the plane, was still steadfast in my journaling and notes, knowing even they had purpose. I had yet to be rewarded with love, but Jesus had me anticipating what was to come. That is when I received the text from Steph's phone.

To be honest, I was a little leery of Steph's sister. There was no doubt that she was a Skater. She looked a lot like the girl in my Jesus dream and a younger Stephanie. But she had lived a hard life, rebellion, drugs, men, a riotous life—like the prodigal son. It took the disappearance of everyone she saw as valuable in her life. The leeches were still around, but had no appeal to her anymore.

My impression was that she had a lot of growing to do. I had no room to criticize. In fact, we all had our lot. That is why we were still here. In fact, I was very surprised at who all was left. The Mormons were still here, along with the Jehovah's Witnesses, the Scientoloists, the New-Agers, and many in the prosperity churches. As I read the first three chapters of the Revelation of Christ and saw what Jesus had to say to the churches, it was clear to me why. Churches who worshiped idols, believed Jesus was but a prophet or a good man, were lost. Many straddled the fence, trying to serve the Lord and the world. You can't serve two masters. The warning signs were all there.

A common denominator was idol worship, putting a man or woman or a book as their source and denying the deity of Christ, who said plainly, "I am the Way, the Truth, and the Life." His claim to deity was one of tangible truth, and those who denied His deity removed the only intercessor they had to everlasting life. The new pastor at The Way, himself a new convert, tried his best to explain it. The message to the seven churches contained all the things that prevented one from being raptured. He used the parable of the ten virgins from Matthew 25. All of them were waiting with good intentions, but half of them were not prepared. When the Bridegroom came, it was too late.

Speaking to a packed church, he said, "Ladies and gentlemen, afterward I went out seeking to buy oil for my lamp. I knocked on the door, but it was to no avail. My heart simply was not yet right, not fixed on Jesus. And God dealt with the churches. He dealt with Islam. Many Catholics were left because they were not born again. They were counting on their works and the eucharist to save them.

Turn to Romans 10:9 with me, 'If you confess with your mouth the Lord Jesus and believe in your heart that God has raised Him from the dead, you will be saved.'

"It is that simple. Come forward and give your heart to Jesus Christ. It is a free gift, but you must accept it. Today is the day. Jesus is the Way!"

Many went forward, including Susan. Even though I had confessed my faith in Him, I also went forward. I prayed the prayer and felt the Spirit. Then they baptized us all and it was a miracle. I felt reborn. Susan also felt reborn and I saw a newness in her. She was broken yet confident—the peace that defies all understanding.

Susan and I spent the afternoon talking and sharing life stories. I didn't know if it was her youth or the Holy Spirit, but something, many things about her were growing on me. She invited me to come and stay at Steph's.

"Separate rooms, of course..." she said.

I was alone. She was alone. I had waited all my life to have a real relationship. I knew it would be okay. Plus, in the days following the Rapture, it was a dangerous world. I thought it would be best. My answer was, "Yes."

Susan was a chef, a full-blown culinary genius, and it didn't go wasted. She treated me to a traditional Jewish feast of lamb, red potatoes, and asparagus. It was a good start. Then coffee with Italian sweet cream finished off the night. We stayed up late talking, hugged, then said goodnight. It was nice. I dreamed amazing dreams about Jesus and things to come. My sleep was sound and full of peace, despite the dreams. In the morning, we shared coffee and compared dreams. She looked out the kitchen window and saw that her car was gone, stolen in the night. It was all I needed. We packed up and loaded her things in the Rover. I was bringing her home.

Everything changed in those few days. Susan and I bonded in Jesus and the Word of God. It was so amazing. God took us to the book of Ruth and the story of Esther. Susan read Psalms to me, and cooked me lavish dinners. I read Revelation and we broke it down. To put it mildly, it was quite terrifying, and we knew we would have to face it. We both felt we could do it together. Somehow, we knew that our folks and Steph were looking down and blessing us.

We felt compelled to go back to Front Royal. There were still a few things at Steph's and the insurance company had a check for Susan's car. I called The Way and spoke to Pastor Rickford, the interim pastor, and he was willing to perform a last-minute wedding. I took Susan out in the Wellcraft and proposed Thursday night. She said yes. We were full of anticipation as we pulled into the church lot. Another packed house, but one in particular stood out. He was two rows in front of me, clean-cut, muscular, attentive. I had a hunch about him. He was alone, listening intently to the sermon, but aware of everything around him, including me. We could sense each other—it was a vibe, if you will.

I kept an eye on him and watched as he and a hundred more went forward. We made eye contact, I stepped out in front of him, extended a hand. "Stay for the wedding," I said.

"Whose?"

"Ours. This is Susan. I am Eli. A fellow...brother." I smiled. He smiled.

"You will want to be baptized as well," I said.

"Really?"

"Yes. Baptism of the Holy Spirit—image of Christ. Can't miss out on that. We did it last week!"

"And now you're getting married?"

"Time is short, my friend…"

"Tanner. I'm Tanner, nice to meet you."

"Tanner." A trustworthy name, I thought, and one I could remember.

The baptisms were inspiring and most stayed for the wedding, Tanner included. Afterward, we talked.

"Tanner, where are you living?"

"Winchester."

"Family?"

He began to tear up. I knew.

"What brought you to Front Royal?"

"I just jumped in the truck and drove—stir-crazy, I suppose. I drove by, saw the cross, and stopped. I knew God had something here for me."

"God is good. He never takes us halfway," I said.

I looked at Susan and she knew what I would be asking. She nodded her head.

"Tanner, I need some help. I have a place down at Smith Mountain Lake, just Susan and I. Things are sketchy. You look like a body guard. What do you say?"

"It's your honeymoon!" he said, shaking his head.

"It's a big house…"

He looked at Susan—she smiled. He looked at me. I had that, "We're going in…" look. He knew it was what God wanted. We all did.

"Have lunch with us, we'll head over to Winchester, pick up what you need, and you can follow us down 81. What do you say?"

"Will do."

The conversation Susan and I had on the way home was amazing.

"I know this man is a spook," I said.

"A spook?"

"Yes, an agent. Spy. Everybody in Winchester is a spy."

"So it takes one to know one?" I hadn't mentioned the spy thing—only that I was retired from business. "I knew there was something unique about you, Eli. Tanner could be a real asset to our ministry."

"No doubt. I am dying to see what he knows. He is probably retired, or a director. Still in solid shape though. Mid-fifties?"

"I think so. But I'm more concerned with what kind of shape you are in…" Then I got the eyebrows. I knew what came with the eyebrows. This was going to be good…

Tanner followed us through the gate. He was checking out everything, including any possible way we could have been tailed. I knew we hadn't. He pulled his huge 3500 Ram Hybrid into the drive next to us and got out. He was smiling from ear to ear.

"What is it, Tanner?" I asked.

"It's DAVEO, the world's most advanced security system. NSA would be my educated guess."

"Takes one to know one!" Susan chimed in. Tanner shook his head. When I opened the garage and the 458 was there, he stopped.

"Jeremy Stone!" he said.

"I can neither confirm nor deny."

"How do you know these things?" Susan asked.

"He's a legend. Biggest arms deal ever. Pulled it off without getting killed and got the money too. Slick! Have you told her about Samantha DeVoss?" Tanner asked.

I looked guilty and Susan looked concerned.

"One of his aliases."

"A woman. You pulled off being a woman?"

"Again, I can neither confirm nor deny."

We all laughed. It was lightest our moods had been in weeks. God had given us each other. And we would be a formidable team. It seemed the skills of all three of us would soon be revealed. Susan and I had other things on our mind. The honeymoon would be short, but extremely memorable.

We gave Tanner a quick tour, electrified the fence, and bowed out early. He made himself comfortable in the control room, getting familiar with all my toys. Susan and I got familiar as well. I was praising God for my help-meet. He really does know best. What came to mind was Romans 8:28: "All things work together for good to those who love God, to those who are called according to His purpose." Yes, I had missed the call, as had Tanner and Susan. But if He had taken everyone, He would not have us. "His purpose," I kept reminding myself.

The events of Revelation had unfolded. God had dealt with the churches, Islam, and soon, Israel. Antichrist, the rider on the white horse, was revealed, and war was everywhere. It was plain to see that the disappearances had set in motion at least the first seven seals. Morning coffee never tasted so good and we were about to discover how formidable of a team we had. Of course, God knew and He would use us in His time.

chapter
TWENTY-TWO
✡ ✡ ✡ ✡ ✡ ✡ ✡

T anner was a man in his mid-fifties, a director at the CIA in charge of operations in China. Since the election of Trump, the trade wars, problems in North Korea, and lots of Chinese saber-rattling led to wide-spread intel operations. Tanner's team had predicted inevitable war between the US and China prior to the Magog event. Now a huge chunk of the US was gone, devastated by nuclear attacks, the civil war, and terrorist activity.

Tanner had given his life to his trade at the expense of his wife, his kids, and his own peace of mind. His marriage, nearing the end of its rope, was what drew him out of DC the morning of the Russian sub attack.

"I was working at the Pentagon for a few days. The intel was hopping and I wasn't going to leave. But Joan, my wife, called. My daughter had been in a severe car accident. I had to go. Then, the Pentagon was destroyed. I should be dead, but God orchestrated that accident to save me.

"I should have given my life to Christ right then. Joan and I picked at each other as my daughter came through the surgery. She was going to be all right. Us, not so much. Then the attack. I was spared. I began to rethink every aspect of my life. We tried to reconcile, and had glimpses. I decided I was going back to work, but she lost it. There was an ultimatum. I decided to retire. Eli, you know how much the spy thing becomes a part of your life. I really thought that I had to be there, or else the world would end," he finished with a sigh.

"Did you go back?" I asked.

"No, but I was a mess. I started drinking, wouldn't go to church, fought hard with my wife. Then they were all gone. Joan, the kids, my grandkids. I was truly alone. I was in a fog until I got to The Way. Now I have some hope. I am ready to serve God."

"Good. We need the help," Susan said.

Tanner stood. He towered over the two of us, a formidable man. He began, "I was up late last night. I made a list. First on the agenda is to establish communications with some of our old friends, if they are still with us."

"Good plan. If the Bible is correct, and we know it is, we will have a dogfight on our hands. Lech Manevetski has positioned himself to do what prophecy says he will do. Soon, he will make a covenant with Israel. An agreement to make peace and build the new temple. Then we have seven years of hell."

"We need to establish our team fast. What is left?"

"Cheyenne Mountain, and whoever is left there to man the switches. T-Bone, a friend of mine. You know of him, Eli, I'm sure."

"Yes. Is he at Cheyenne?"

"No, a secret base near Portland. There are five others, but I don't know who the principals are. We'll start with T-Bone. He is stubborn as a mule. Good chance he is still around. I'll begin a list of my military contacts. I suggest you do the same. I see we have good security here, plenty of weapons and food. You've done well to prepare."

"You can thank paranoia, living alone all these years, and a fascination with tech. We can do it all right from here. I have a desire to stay alive now for a while at least."

"Amen to that, brother."

I squeezed Susan's hand and asked her what she was going to get started on.

"Dinner…"

"Good call…"

By the day's end, we knew where all six secret bases were, what their capabilities were, and who was running them.

"T-Bone is alive and well in The Dalles, Oregon. They lost a few at Cheyenne Mountain, but McMaster, Trump, and several big wigs are there. They are at Defcon 1 and operating under martial law. Apparently, Pence gave all kinds of advice to Trump on this before it happened, even tried to get him to confess. His whole family went, but he, like us, was too hard-headed and stubborn."

"You know, it's almost comical. All of us who thought we had it all figured out are the ones who missed the boat," I added.

"Yes, but we are left with a lot of good, solid fighting men and leaders. We'll be fine."

America still had a huge supply of nuclear missiles and the means to launch them. In fact, now with Trump in Colorado, everyone needed to give the order and launch the missiles were all in the same facility, one thousand feet below the surface of the planet. T-Bone had a huge facility to distribute food and was equipped with drones, anti-missile batteries, and some F-22s. Despite the fact that the US was severely wounded and in chaos, we still had amazing capability for defense.

The Japanese and Chinese were in the best shape. Most of their population had been left behind, their militaries intact. I wondered what kind of leverage Lech would have over them. Of course, he was put in that position by God Himself. God would make a way for all of the prophecies to be fulfilled. We would be smart to focus on staying alive, avoiding the wave of depravity and the natural and supernatural events that were to come and evangelize. That would be our purpose.

I put Susan in charge of organizing my memoirs and journal entries. I told her of my vision, the books, and what I believed my purpose would be. She didn't understand at first. Then, she read the *Faith* trilogy.

"I see. He needs to write your story. Warn the world of what will come without giving away too much."

Much of it had to remain a mystery. Many books had been written on the end times, but none had first-hand accounts.

"It will lead people to the Bible, confirm the prophecies, and prepare even more." I explained.

"I get it. And it is proof that it really happens."

"Here is what Jesus says; 'And now I have told you before it comes, that when it does come to pass, you may believe.'"

"Amen."

Susan was a great wife and a whiz on the computer. She had hung out with some very advanced hackers that did it for sport. She had skills that Tanner and I could only dream of.

"God is good…" she said.

"All the time…" Tanner and I said in unison.

"By the way, guys, do you think we will need access to emails and secure phone calls from, say, the UN or the former president's office in Brussels?"

"Uh, yeah!" Tanner said with the "duh" look.

"I know a guy in Southern Maryland. He is still around. Pothead, loser, wouldn't be able to keep a job doing anything. But he is good—the best."

"We're listening."

"Russell Brown."

"You know Russell Brown, hacker extraordinaire?"

"Yeah, I know him. He does his own thing and costs a bit, but he knows all the back doors."

"And you happen to have Russell Brown's email?"

"Yes."

"God really is good."

Within weeks, we were listening in on the former president and Lech Manevetski. There was some huge money behind his power, no doubt. He seemed to be able to get done whatever he wanted. Of course, before anything happened, we knew about it. T-Bone put together a small meeting of leaders of the underground in Joliet, Illinois, six months after the Rapture. We met General McHenry, Bradley Carter, General McMaster, Admiral Benjamin Phipps, USN Gregory Leman, and a dozen others whose principal role was surviving and keeping some semblance of peace in the United States.

We all knew that famine, rationing, war, death, and Lech Manevetski were upon us. We had to go underground, set up our own money exchanges, purchases, and distribute and provide food and medicine and fight if we had to. Chicago had been the very epicenter of corruption in the US and the Boros teams were flush with money to support the globalization the antichrist was busy setting in place. We were here to spy on them. The one thing the underground had in common was the military and God. We were all believers now and we felt we had to evangelize as best as God allowed. We had endless technical resources, access to the inside of the power structure of Satan and the ability to track his puppet masters. One of our team, Art Pimmerton of Kansas City, thought we should take out the former president and his Chicago-based crony organization, now located in Joliet.

"Leave that up to God," I said. "Psalm 37." After I read it, they all understood. We didn't have to fret about evil-doers, God would deal with them. And He did. It seemed Lech had his own ideas and began to ignore the former president and his deep pockets. This infuriated the former President, and he publicly chastised the UN Secretary General. After that, the two men who had aided Lech Manevetski to rise to the top simply vanished, never to be seen again.

The demise of these two, along with their leader Gregory Boros, had to happen. They weren't serving good or evil, they were just unfortunate facilitators whom God had placed as President and mayor of the most corrupt city in America—possibly the world. They took the teaching of a madman and pushed forward with an agenda that was not only self-serving, but detrimental to the entire world. One of the very powerful lessons I had learned was that humans are their own worst enemy.

As the events of the last seven years of this age progressed, Tanner, Susan, and I frequently discussed what tidbits could be shared with those who would experience it in their future. After all, this was my purpose. Susan set up a program that allowed us to store my notes and journals. It had a preset for time. If we didn't come back to it, it would upload to Sparks' ProtoCloud account on its own.

We had many close calls as we served God through this time, and it was always nice when we made it out to add to the queue. We knew there would be a day when it would be sent to the cloud in its last—although unfinished—form. I was almost certain it would be incomplete, but the more we could provide the author, albeit selectively, the better.

Some sound advice; If you do not own a Bible, obtain one now, while they are widely available. Very soon, they will be banned and confiscated in most areas. We recommend a quality study Bible with as much historical, cultural and language teachings as possible.

We also decided that there were some inescapable truths that had to be sent back as we discerned them. Since all three of us had the perspective of missing out on the Rapture, we felt we could relay some valuable knowledge for those receptive to it. Every time we ventured out to help build the co-op, prevent a disaster, or throw a monkey wrench in Antichrist's plans, we added to or refined this list.

I can tell you this, the events of the first three and a half years happen pretty much the way the Bible reads. Yes, you have to take into account the text, the context, and the entire text. That means you have to read it and evaluate it in the context of the text prior, the text after, and the general narrative of the Bible. The first eleven chapters of Genesis are about the creation. The entire balance of the Bible is about redemption. The years of tribulation we are experiencing in these last days will be the greatest and final chapter of the redemption of the world. All of the characters and events no matter how seemingly insignificant factor into this narrative. It is also critical to do word studies so one can discern the intent of the writer in the language it was written. For example, the English word *love* can be *agape,* Greek for unconditional love; *phileo,* brotherly love; or *eros,* erotic love. Since the original was written in Hebrew, Aramaic, and Greek, with some exceptions, one must seek the original intent and meaning of the word.

It is also important to factor in the history, culture, traditions, geography, and other variables. Ezekiel could in no way imagine tanks, helicopters, rockets, TV, satellites, or airplanes. Therefore, a chariot is how he would describe a tank. The descriptions of events have to be filtered through the eyes and knowledge of the writer. Also, events are not necessarily in chronological order. You may say, "Well, Eli, why don't you just tell us? You have seen and witnessed it first-hand…

No. Doing so would deprive you of the most important part—seeking God and the mysteries of the Bible.

For two thousand years, people read the Word of God and dismissed the possibility of a third temple described in Ezekiel 40. After May 14th, 1948, readers could not only see it as possible, but likely. One miracle led to another. God promised He would make Israel a nation again. He delivered, and continues to deliver on all the rest—this we can assure you. Each step has its purpose.

The 144,000 are real. The two witnesses are real and awesome. Only God could think of having two of His beloved come back to do His preaching of Jesus. So captivated were we with them that it cost Susan her life. Looking back, it was for the better because things got very ugly after that. Once the prophecy of Daniel 9:27 came to be fulfilled, everything changed. I am lucky to be alive to tell you about it. The great tribulation is indeed God's wrath. He holds nothing back. You don't want to be here then—trust me!

Stars falling from the sky—yep, gone. Sky rolling up like a scroll—just like a play being enacted on a stage in front of you. You had to see it to believe it. Earthquakes—terrifying, and seeming like they would never end. You get the idea. Do everything you can to avoid it. It's not hard, and it's a free gift. Accept it! This may be the only warning you get outside of the Bible.

The saddest thing I think about is the billions of people who don't ever get it. Paul says we have no excuse. Still, people run from the light. Post-Rapture, the Holy Spirit is reserved to helping those of us who are left behind. The darkness is thick and ever-present. The depravity of man and his desire for power and dominance is in full bloom. Instead of viewing the chaos as a warning, many view it as opportunity for evil.

I remember one time I asked Jake why God chose to put all the horrible stuff in Leviticus. It seems like overkill to explain that people should not sleep with animals, or even men with men. His answer was somewhat obvious: "God put it in there so man would have no excuse. We are truly capable of anything and He knew some would do it." Much of it existed in every corner of the world in great abundance. The Antichrist had his agenda, and it didn't include any moral limitations. Even his church was a complete perversion of God's will for us. What a contrast to the underground church of Jesus-followers who had taken on The Way as their name and identity. No one knew or cared who the leaders of The Way were. In fact, Jesus was considered our only leader. The Way is a church of one—each of us individually abiding in Christ and coming together in fellowship of one accord. The GC church was operated like a government with a Pope-like man identified as the False Prophet. Full of pride and self, he is all about pomp and circumstance. He is also all about power and money—private planes, gold chains, people bowing and worshiping him. It was sickening.

Tanner, Susan, and I developed our own unique ministry. From the underground control center below the lake house, we broadcast to the world truths about Jesus and His saving grace. In gathering the lessons learned from our experiences, we have compiled some great information that we considered as valuable during the tribulation as well as prior to it. We set up a mini studio, something that looked like a newscast set, and had Susan recording half-hour-long videos that went out on Russell Brown's non-traceable RSS feeds. He routinely pirated GC programming and ran our stuff in place of some propaganda message or GC church service. She always closed it with an invitation, prayer, and the now famous line, created by author Ken Sparks: "Today is the day, Jesus is The Way." And it was working.

We figured that since Sparks had helped us, we would help him and it would all come together for the glory of God. We were receiving thousands of email messages with testimonies. Entire groups of terrified Antichrist haters were confessing faith in Jesus from all over the world.

These lessons were our observations taken from living out the tribulation, at least the first few years. These were truths that cannot be disputed and were proven out in our lives as witnesses. I will continue to document them and will upload them at the last possible time frame. My hope and prayer in sharing this with the world is that I myself, a Jew, an agnostic Jew for most of my life, was able to learn these lessons. They are backed by Scripture and confirmed in the experiences of Susan, Tanner, and millions of tribulation saints.

Please give these truths considerable consideration and confess faith in Christ now.

chapter
TWENTY-THREE
✧✧✧✧✧✧✧

Lesson #1: There is only one God, the God of Abraham, Isaac, and Jacob, the God of Israel, of Jesus and the Christian movement. There is none other—none. He exists in triune form as the Father, the Son, and the Holy Spirit. They are one God. This is referred to as the Trinity. It is beyond our comprehension, but is discernable from Biblical accounts and confirmed in personal experience once one is connected to Him by redemption. Nearly a billion true Christian followers disappeared in the Rapture. The common factor between these billion souls was that they had accepted the gift of redemption freely offered to everyone by God the Father, through His Son, Jesus Christ. Billions more who died prior to the Rapture and were saved after Christ's death on the cross were also resurrected and have joined Jesus in heaven in glorified bodies.

The promises of these events are all outlined in the Bible. John 3:16 says, "For God so loved the world that He gave His one and only Son, that whoever believes in Him should not perish but have eternal life."

His desire is that all should be saved. As I said before, this is a gift of God's grace, His way of allowing those who choose to be saved. You don't have to work for it, pay for it, or do anything other than accept the gift. We do have to choose to receive the free gift with a willing heart.

Because He is the only true God and has proven it time and time again, He is the only one that can offer true salvation and eternal life. His promises and His prophecies have been fulfilled over thousands of years, but none more than recently. Since Israel became a nation again, one prophecy after another has been fulfilled. As we air this video, more prophecy has come to light and has been fulfilled. Only the one true God can deliver exactly what He promised and fulfill the declarations His own prophets made centuries ago.

God asks us to have faith—to believe. Hebrews 11:6 tells us that it is impossible to please God without faith. The one true God is alive, active, and ready to send His Son as the final fulfillment of His prophecies in the book of Revelation. One might ask, "Why do these horrible things have to be?" The answer is this: He allowed us—that is, the ones He created—to choose and to exercise our free will. The ones who chose Him are with Him. The ones who did not have been left behind to endure the wrath of God.

Those of us that remain can also choose. He is repeatedly asking us to repent and follow Him. That is what these lessons are about. He waits in loving anticipation for all to be saved. Many have and will choose this path to have eternal life. Those who do not will suffer throughout this turbulent period then face death and eternal judgment. There is no escape. The one God has promised to give you ample opportunity. But if you die in your sin, if you wait until Jesus returns, you will give an account and suffer the consequences of your decision.

I know this sounds ominous. It is. God destroyed the world once, saving only Noah and his family. He can do it again. He is a sovereign

God that makes the rules. He made a way, a way for us to be saved. It is now your choice. Read the Bible and see for yourself that God loves you and wants you to be redeemed. It is a free gift. It is your choice, and you must make it before you die. With what is coming, that may be any minute.

The life of a Jesus-follower, a true child of God, is one of peace, confidence, and love. We are loved, we are not alone, and our God never leaves us or forsakes us. Those of us who have chosen to follow Jesus invite you to eternal life. If you would like to receive the free gift of salvation, pray along with me.

"Heavenly Father, I know that I am a sinner in need of salvation. I recognize that you sent your Son, Jesus Christ, to die on the cross for my redemption. I confess with my mouth that Jesus is Lord and that God, His Father, raised Him from the dead. I accept the free gift of God's grace and receive Jesus into my life. In the name of Jesus, I pray. Amen."

If you said that prayer, you now have your name written in the book of life, and the angels in heaven are rejoicing. I pray that you receive the Holy Spirit to guide and strengthen you. I pray that you have the opportunity to be baptized into the image of Christ. This is not necessary for your salvation, but it is a confirmation of your transformation into the family of God. Many churches offer baptisms and counselling.

If you did not say that prayer, you can at any time, in the quiet of your heart. Look for a church gathering to join and do not take the mark. It is an irreversible death sentence. Our ministry will be praying for all of you. God waits with open arms for His children to come home and be reconciled to Him. Today is the day, Jesus is the Way.

Susan's first lesson was out and seen all over the world. I told her it was amazing and that she was filled with the Spirit.

"Many will be saved..." I told her with a hug.

She took a deep breath and smiled. "God is good..."

We got an email from Russell Brown, who raved about the video. "We ran it on three of the GC stations and I said the prayer," he said with an enthusiasm rarely evident in this reserved man.

"That's awesome, Russell! We are so glad for you. Now about a billion more would be good."

"Couldn't agree more. I'll run it a few more times prior to lesson #2."

"Good call, Russell. And thank you..."

"No, thank Jesus!"

"Amen."

Susan and I celebrated and prepared for the next lesson: "God, the Only Thing that Matters." It was a beautiful day and we sat on the deck overlooking the lake, the mountains, and the wildlife. We enjoyed our favorite coffee and talked about how all of this would be going away, as outlined in the Bible. A third of the trees and all of the green grass burned up. We couldn't imagine. In a place as beautiful and forested as this, we couldn't imagine.

But God points us repeatedly to the things that matter, the things, the riches of heaven. The truth is, nothing matters but the things of God. Or better said, nothing matters but God. Solomon says in the book of Ecclesiastes: "Remember now your Creator in the days of your youth, before the difficult days come, and the years draw near when you say, 'I have no pleasure in them': while the sun and the light, the moon and the stars, are not darkened, and the clouds do not return after the rain; in the day when the keepers of the house tremble, and the strong men bow down; when the grinders cease because they are few, and those that look through the windows grow dim; when the doors are shut in the streets, and the sound of grinding is low; when one rises up at the sound of a bird, and all the daughters of music are brought low. Also they are afraid of height, and of terrors in the way; when the almond tree blossoms, the grasshopper is a burden, and desire fails. For man goes to his eternal home, and the mourners go about the streets. *Remember your Creator* before the silver cord is loosed, or the golden bowl is broken, or the pitcher shattered at the fountain, or the wheel broken at the well. Then the dust will return to the earth as it was, and the spirit will return to God who gave it. 'Vanity of vanities,' says the Preacher, 'All *is* vanity.' And moreover, because the Preacher was wise, he still taught the people knowledge; yes, he pondered and sought out *and* set in order many proverbs. The Preacher sought to find acceptable words; and *what was* written *was* upright—words of truth. The words of the wise are like goads, and the words of scholars are like well-driven nails, given by one Shepherd. And further, my son, be admonished by these. Of making many books *there is* no end, and much study *is* wearisome to the flesh. Let us hear the conclusion of the whole matter: fear God and keep His commandments, for this is man's all. For God will bring every work into judgment, including every secret thing, whether good or evil" (Eccl. 12:1–14).

Picture it like this: your life ends and you are in a theater with a huge screen. On the screen, your life runs—all the good and all the bad before your eyes. Your sins of commission, all you ever did against God and man. Your sins of omission, all you should have done and did not.

Your life is an open book. Nothing is hidden. However, another book is open—the book of Life. And your name is written in it. The sins of commission, the sins of omission, all wiped out and God judges you as righteous through the Savior's blood. It is the only thing that matters.

Within the film of your life is your career, your accomplishments, your bank account, and your retirement. It was all left behind. It has no value here. God's desire for His children is no different than any parent—obedience. Serving God in His kingdom work, sharing your testimony, acts of kindness. We are really nothing but beggars looking for bread. And now that we have found it, we want to take others to that place.

A rich young ruler asked Jesus what He lacked to inherit eternal life. Jesus said, "You know the commandments; Do not commit adultery, do not murder, do not steal, do not bear false witness, honor your father and your mother." The man said, "All these things have I kept from my youth." So when Jesus heard these things, He said to Him, "You still lack one thing; sell all that you have and distribute it to the poor, and you will have treasure in heaven; and come, follow me."

In Matthew, Jesus says, "Do not lay up for yourselves treasures on earth, where moth and rust destroy and where thieves break in and steal: instead, lay up for yourselves treasures in heaven, where neither moth nor rust destroy and where thieves do not break in and steal. For where your treasure is, there your heart will be also." There it is—your heart. God doesn't care about your stuff. He cares about your heart. The rich young ruler had the stuff and all the right words and even followed the Law, but his heart was his own. It was all for him and he walked away sorrowful.

We have heard that there is never a rental truck following a hearse. You cannot take it with you. None of it matters. If you consider that deeply, you will realize that your loved ones and family are included in that. Your goal should be to never put anyone above God. It should be to bring them to the Word and pray for God to draw them in to heaven also. If not, you will lose even them.

Jesus was clear that if the choice is family or Him, choose Him. That is a truth that cuts like a two-edged sword. In the Gospel of Luke, Jesus says, "If anyone comes to me and does not hate his father and mother, wife and children, brothers and sisters, yes and his own life also, he cannot be my disciple." This does not mean that you must hate your family and loved ones. Luke is using hyperbole to emphasize that we must love Jesus more, so much more, than even loved ones. This is Jesus' way of saying that God is the only thing that matters.

When God's children received His Ten Commandments, He emphasized our relationship with Him in the commands: you shall have no other gods before Me, you shall not worship idols, you shall not use vain oaths against Me, you shall honor My Sabbath, you shall honor your mother and father. Yes, this also means your earthly parents, but God is our true Father.

It is clear that God is who we live for and this is what He commands us to do. The second group of commands emphasize our relationship with others. Do not commit murder, do not commit adultery, do not steal, do not lie, do not covet. We may ask ourselves why these commands are important, and whether or not they still apply to our lives in the twenty-first century.

Just glancing over the list of commands gives us pause. It is, indeed, everything we need to know. Jesus went even further and reduced it down to two. Call it a summary that He and He alone was able to give. That is because it is found in Scripture. The first is called the Shema, found in Deuteronomy 6:4: "Hear, O Israel, the Lord our God is One! You shall love the Lord with all your heart and with all your soul and with all your strength."

The second comes from Leviticus 19:18: "You shall not take vengeance, nor bear any grudge against the children of your people, but you shall love your neighbor as yourself, I am the Lord." These are from the Torah, directly from God. Jesus sums it up in Mark 12:29–31 when He answers a question from a scribe: "Which is the first commandment of all?" Jesus answered him, "The first of all the commandments is: 'Hear, O Israel, the Lord our God the Lord is One. And you shall love the Lord with all your heart, with all your soul, with all your mind, and with all your strength.' This is the first commandment. And the second, like it, is this: 'You shall love your neighbor as yourself.' There is no greater commandment than these." God gives it, the Bible records it, and Jesus quotes it. If we make God the only thing that matters, the rest falls into place.

And what do you get from this? The answer is found in Galatians 5:22: love, joy, peace, patience, kindness, goodness, faithfulness, gentleness, self-control. Against such there is no law. Yes, we are rewarded exceedingly when we make God the only thing that matters. This is how our transformation is described in Ephesians 2:1–9: "And you *He made alive,* who were dead in trespasses and sins, in which you once walked according to the course of this world, according to the prince of the power of the air, the spirit who now works in the sons of disobedience, among whom also we all once conducted ourselves in the lusts of our flesh, fulfilling the desires of the flesh and of the mind, and were by nature children of wrath, just as the others. But God, who is rich in mercy, because of His great love with which He loved us, even when we were dead in trespasses, made us alive together with Christ (by grace you have been saved), and raised *us* up together, and made *us* sit together in the heavenly *places* in Christ Jesus, that in the ages to come He might show the exceeding riches of His grace in *His* kindness toward us in Christ Jesus. For by grace you have been saved through faith, and that not of yourselves; *it is* the gift of God, not of works, lest anyone should boast."

So far, we have learned that there is only one God, and He is the only thing that matters. As you have seen, I have used God and Jesus interchangeably. That may seem odd, until we get to the next lesson: Jesus Himself is God, part of the Trinity.

Susan closed with an invitation and directions to download the previous lesson. She was a hit, and many were commenting that they were coming to faith in Christ and sharing the testimonies of visions and dreams. The harvest was in full swing.

Susan, Tanner, and I worked as an information hub for the underground, confirming Lech's latest movements, orders, and pursuits of his foes. We knew from Scripture that he had plans to be in Jerusalem at the halfway point, three and a half years into the signing of the covenant to rebuild the Temple. The Temple was indeed built on Temple Mount, and the two witnesses were an ever-present mouthpiece for Jesus there.

The two constantly quoted Scripture to large crowds of spectators and Global Constables. Lech hated that they were there, and frequently tried to get rid of them. We knew that they would be there for one thousand, two hundred and sixty days before they were killed by the Beast himself. Dozens of GC had sacrificed their lives in an effort to exterminate them. All perished. No one could force a timeline other than God's.

Their message, all Scripture about Jesus, was not well received in Jerusalem. The Jews had their Temple back and were steadfast in their desire to re-establish all of the Old Testament observances. The descendants of the Levites were back to performing sacrifices and burning incense. However, the two prophets only spoke of Old Testament scripture that pointed to Jesus. This was what God had appointed them to do and they did it well.

Half the spectators would cheer and half would boo and hiss. They were relentless in their message. As their time approached, almost everyone, including Lech, was tired of hearing them. Susan and I had decided we needed to go there, to see the two and warn them of their death sentence. We had lost track of Ron, so I chartered a plane and we flew to Tel Aviv. Of course, this was pre-mark and pre-abomination of desolation, so we weren't in much danger. We just had to worry about not bringing too much attention to ourselves.

I would return alone, regretting that we had ever desired to go. I lost my help-meet, which was a major blow. Now I was on the run, having caused the deaths of nine GC. I assumed one of my aliases, made some valuable connections, and rented a small place in Jerusalem to work from. I stayed and watched the Antichrist desecrate the Temple, claim to be God, and kill the two preachers. I was there, an eyewitness to it all. I saw them lie in the street, decomposing on 24-7 video feeds. People were celebrating in the streets and making merry.

Following the killings, Lech made an impassioned speech: "Only God could kill these men. Mere mortals had no chance. But I have delivered the city from their endless rhetoric. Their God is dead. I am alive! I declare this a national holiday. Give gifts and make merry. For the true and living god of this world demonstrates his power on earth!"

It was all too surreal, playing out as yet another event laid out in Bible prophecy. After three and a half days, and I mean exactly eighty-four hours of lying dead in the street, they stirred, got up, and shook the maggots off of themselves. Then the voice: "Come up here!"

Fear gripped me, as well as everyone else. They ascended into a cloud as the cameras rolled. It was the last thing covered by any public television. Lech took control of it all and only allowed propaganda that he wanted to show. That five-day span changed everything. It was as though God had given the world a final chance to repent, a real and tangible opportunity to be saved. Now, all who would come to Christ would have to diligently seek it. Satan had been revealed, the Temple was desecrated, and the great and powerful wrath of God was on its way.

I had lost my help-meet, and the love I found was now in heaven. I somehow knew that Tanner and I still had work to do here. It would become more and more dangerous for us. But this was where the technology was being developed. Tanner and I would have to return to Jerusalem. It would be the only way.

chapter

TWENTY-FOUR
✿✿✿✿✿✿✿

I flew home and found that Tanner had been busy. He had listened to a call between Lech and his tech team in Jerusalem. They were within weeks of implementing the mark. They were also busy producing effigies of Lech for worship. Bowing to Satan would soon be mandatory in every part of the world. He also had some good news to try and cheer me up. He had been studying the hacked technical documents on the mark. He was close to a duplication method. He had also been busy with his Bible study. His intention was to help with the lessons by writing what he called "nuggets", little tidbits of godly wisdom that could be shared with the lost world.

The nuggets were exceptional, and it was good to be home. The Robert Lynn Nelson prints hit me hard. I missed Susan and I missed Steph. No time to fret now, though, we had work to do. Tanner shared the information on the mark.

"We'll need to get samples of the ink," he said.

"I figured we would need to go back, so I rented a little place in town. When you're ready we'll go."

"What about the lessons? Susan was a natural."

"How about we share some nuggets and see how it goes?" I suggested.

"You or me?"

"Rock, paper, scissors?"

"Sure."

I lost.

"You could do it as Samantha DeVoss…"

"Very funny." Then I lost it. I cried for half a day. Afterwards, we prayed and God gave me peace. I was thankful for three years of loving and sharing what God intended for His creation. How sad it would have been for me to miss it. Like David, I got up, ate, and moved on with God's plan.

God reminded me of His conversation with Joshua: "After the death of Moses the servant of the Lord, it came to pass that the Lord spoke to Joshua the son of Nun, Moses' assistant, saying: 'Moses My servant is dead. Now therefore, arise, go over this Jordan, you and all this people, to the land which I am giving to them—the children of Israel. Every place that the sole of your foot will tread upon I have given you, as I said to Moses. From the wilderness and this Lebanon as far as the great river, the River Euphrates, all the land of the Hittites, and to the Great Sea toward the going down of the sun, shall be your territory. No man shall *be able to* stand before you all the days of your life; as I was with Moses, *so* I will be with you. I will not leave you nor forsake you. Be strong and of good courage, for to this people you shall divide as an inheritance the land which I swore to their fathers to give them. Only be strong and very courageous, that you may observe to do according to all the law which Moses My servant commanded you; do not turn from it to the right hand or to the left, that you may prosper wherever you go. This Book of the Law shall not depart from your mouth, but you shall meditate in it day and night, that you may observe to do according to all that is written in it. For then you will make your way prosperous, and then you will have good success. Have I not commanded you? Be strong and of good courage; do not be afraid, nor be dismayed, for the Lord your God *is* with you wherever you go'" (Josh 1:1–9).

I had to be strong and courageous. This had been God's message to all His servants. And how did they respond? They got up early in the morning. Susan, my love, was dead. It was my time to step up. I had lost something I cherished and depended on. Now, God wanted my dependence to be on Him. And how did God reward His obedient servants? He restored them. He always restored them.

So I got up early in the morning and sat down with a cup of coffee and Tanner's list of nuggets.

"Let's start with 'Jesus is God', and I believe it could use a woman's touch—Samantha DeVoss," I suggested.

"Good choice, boss. Samantha DeVoss and Jesus. When you're ready let's roll..." An hour later we were ready to record.

"Hello my fellow earthlings. What I will be sharing with you today are some golden nuggets from the Bible. Be sure to take notes on the passages so you can go back to your Bibles and meditate on them. Okay, let's go...

"When Jesus stood in front of Pilate and asked, 'what is truth?' It would have paid Pilate well to wait for the answer. The truth was, in fact, standing in front of him. How shocking it must have been for him when he died and had to give an account of his life to the One whom he ordered to be crucified. Pilate was a believer, but it came too late.

"When Jesus was baptized in Luke 3, the heaven opened and the Holy Spirit descended in a form like a dove upon Him. A voice came from heaven which said, 'You are My Beloved Son; in You I am well pleased.' This is a beautiful picture of the Trinity. The Father in heaven, the Holy Spirit descending from His place and filling the Son. He went from carpenter to Lord; being fully man and then being baptized to receive the image of Christ, just as we do through our testing, our salvation, and our baptism of the Spirit.

"Then He was able to begin His ministry, a beautiful transformation that we can experience also, and do when we confess our faith in Jesus Christ, the Lamb of God.

"The next lesson on our list of biblical truth nuggets is the fact that observational science confirms that the Bible is true. What is meant by that statement is the fact that the modern scientific evidence we have is consistent with what the Bible teaches. For example, consider just a few major scientific discoveries that have been confirmed in the past few hundred years that is consistent with what the Bible taught thousands of years ago:"

- Life is in the blood.
  - Man discovered this in 1628.
  - Moses said it in 1400 BC (Leviticus 17:11)
- First Law of Thermodynamics
  - Man discovered this in 1842.
  - The Bible stated it in the first century AD (Hebrews 4:3–4)
- Second Law of Thermodynamics
  - Man discovered this in 1850.
  - Isaiah said it in 720 BC (Isaiah 51:6)
- Air has weight
  - Man discovered this in 1643.
  - Job said it in 1550 BC (Job 28:24–25)

- Washing hands prevents illness
  - Man discovered this in 1872
  - Moses said it in 1400 BC (Leviticus 15:13)
- The cycle of water
  - Man discovered this in 1580
  - Solomon said it in 950 BC (Ecclesiastes 1:7)
- The universe is expanding
  - Man discovered this in 1929
  - Isaiah said it in 720 BC (Isaiah 45:12)
- The earth is a sphere suspended in space
  - Man discovered this in the 1600s
  - Job said it in 1550 BC (Job 26:7)
- Avoid mold and bacteria
  - Man discovered this in the 1800s
  - Moses said it in 1400 BC (Numbers 19:3–22)
- Countless stars
  - Man discovered this in 1608
  - Jeremiah said it in 580 BC (Jeremiah 33:22)
- Ocean currents affect earth's weather
  - Man discovered this in the 1800s
  - David said it in 1000 BC (Psalm 8:8)
- Every element of man is found in soil
  - Man discovered this in the 1800s
  - Moses said it in 1400 BC (Genesis 2:7)
- Let the land rest
  - Man discovered this in 1840
  - Moses said it in 1400 BC (Leviticus 25:4).

"As we can see from these truths, God, the Creator and Maker of all things, gave His people the truth hundreds, and in some cases thousands, of years prior to science's ability to prove it. God used man's desire to pursue their own intellect and free will to reach this point, the time of judgment. As Jesus said, 'Unless those days were shortened, no flesh would be saved: but for the elect's sake, those days will be shortened.'

"Darwin's evolutionary theory has been adopted and taught as science. It has worked to take the creator God out of our schools, our minds, and our hearts. God tells His children not to forget Him and to pass His promises on to the next generation (Deuteronomy 6:6–9). We did not. God did not regret giving us free will because He created us for pure, true fellowship. Adam chose poorly and it put the entire redemption plan into action, starting in Genesis 12.

"Our free will and dependence on our own intellect is what has separated us from God. It has caused earthly corruption and the deterioration of all things. What a far cry our world is from what God had intended in the Garden of Eden. The devil came along and planted a lie right in the midst of us. Since we were disconnected and wanted to do our own thing, we bought into it.

"We truly are our own worst enemy, and I wonder what our world would look like without disease, death, and evil. Well, we are just a few short years away from finding out. In the meantime, I would give heed to the words of our true source: the God of Abraham, Isaac, and Jacob, who created all things and His Son who holds it all together The invitation to repent has been repeated billions of times, first by the prophets, then John the Baptist, Jesus, the apostles, the church, the 144,000, and most recently, the two witnesses.

"Say this prayer with me: 'Father in heaven, I know I am a sinner, in need of a Savior. You gave your Son to be that Savior and He was the ultimate sacrifice for our redemption. I ask today to receive the gift, the free gift of salvation. In Jesus' name I pray, Amen.' Today is the day, Jesus is the Way."

We had Russell Brown get the video out and he let us know that people were quite sad about Susan, but loved Samantha DeVoss. "The nuggets are good, too. People don't know much about the Bible, especially the world's population as it is now." He was airing the lessons over the most important programming he could, just to frustrate Lech. Now he had the underground to deal with, and our message was powerful.

Tanner and I flew out to Jerusalem and went to work on the mark. Our first goal was to break into the tech center and steal a small amount of ink and an applicator. We were now just a few weeks from implementation. As soon as we landed, we knew we were in trouble. We were escorted to a small office and interrogated. This was Mossad at their best, and we would be lucky to get past this. We were handcuffed and taken by car to Jerusalem.

Not a word was said between the two agents or to us. We were thrown into holding cells and left alone. For two hours, we did our best to communicate without revealing anything. Then, we were escorted by gunpoint to a lower level and into an interrogation room. We were left alone until a man and a woman came in. They spoke in Hebrew, asking each other a few pointless questions. This exercise was to see if we gave any indication of knowing the language. I knew the drill and played dumb.

"Miss DeVoss," the woman addressed me in English.

"Yes."

"What is your business in Israel?"

"We have business with the GC software."

"Software? So you sell computers to the GC."

I took a chance. "No, we are here to steal software from the GC," I said in Hebrew. Both of them smiled.

"Excellent response, Mr. Stone. Who is your associate?"

I nodded my head for him to acknowledge. "Tanner Rossini."

"It's an honor to meet both of you. Do you remember me from the control room?"

"Yes. I didn't remember your name, but I am good with faces."

"Fortunately, so am I. You pull off the lady very well. I'm Levi Barstein, Mossad."

"Good to meet you. And you know Mr. Rossini as well?"

"Yes, we are familiar. Nice to meet you. This is my associate Melania Kohn. For now, gentlemen, we are on the same side. And we need help. Are you interested?"

"Always glad to cooperate with Mossad. What do you need?"

"This mark thing. They hijacked some of our best techs from the University. They are afraid to help us, but they might assist with intel and leave the door open—if you know what I mean."

"So you need some unknown operatives to go in?"

"And help us replicate it, analyze the software, establish a back door, etc."

"Okay. We'll need some equipment."

"You got it. What about a place to work?"

"We've already got that handled. I'll get the list to you. Here is where we will be. We could use wheels, as well as information about which areas of the city are best to avoid."

"Our peace deal with Manevetski allows us some latitude. But they are closing in fast. Once the statues are up and they start applying the mark, it will all change. And as you know, we have had some bizarre weather and other phenomena."

"Yes, it's unavoidable and becoming worse."

"So let's move on this." He threw me a set of keys and led us out. Soon we were on the road.

"Get the list together. We'll need phones and hardware too."

"Already working on it. I thought we were dead there for a minute…"

"Things work out when you're on the right side."

"Amen, brother."

Meanwhile, we were in a pause between the seven seals and the seven trumpets. No one wanted it to start, but almost everyone knew it would begin at any time. Due to Lech's transformation into a so-called deity, most Bible scholars believed this and the desecration of the Temple would usher in the great tribulation. We anticipated terror, because the Bible says that when the Lord Jesus opens the seventh seal and reveals the seven trumpets, there is silence in heaven for half an hour.

Considering the fact that all is silent in awe of what is to come and the descriptions we read in Revelation, we wanted to get our work done and high-tail it out of Israel. Jewish scholars thought the big rock which we knew was coming would likely hit the Mediterranean Sea.

But the scientists said no, the likely impact point based on the trajectory would be the Pacific, north of Hawaii. Time would tell. Either way, Virginia seemed safe in either scenario.

With the Mossad's cooperation, Tanner and I pulled off every aspect of the break-in, the acquisition of the desired ingredients, and installation of our backdoor access to the main database for mark monitoring. I could share the details of our mission and they would certainly rank up there with any Mission Impossible storyline. But that would be boasting, and this is not about us. It is all about God and His orchestration. The underground needed to have a faux mark and the ability to verify that we were worshiping Lech's effigy when in reality, that would never happen.

We did mock-ups of the software and the temporary, printed mark we referred to as the faux mark. It took some fine-tuning, but we got it worked out. We also had to go deep into the existing database and hijack some souls that were no longer among the living but had extensive positive background data. These we would resurrect to create our fake accounts for our people who needed to be on the grid.

In the beginning, there were two faux marks. One was a sticker or decal that would work for store check-out or buying gas. The other was a direct ink screen on the skin, but not a true tattoo like the real deal. Only a doctor could tell the difference, and both came off with a mild solvent. It took two months to get all the bugs out and we were about ready to show the package to Mossad.

Tanner and I went into town with the sticker marks, ate at a restaurant, and bought some bread and coffee. The marks worked perfectly and our aliases were in the-system and viable humans—though not us. All was well until we ran into a bunch of GC idiots who had been drinking in excess. It was early in the implementation process, and they just had to pick on us.

All went well until a sober sergeant intervened. He insisted on seeing the marks that were on our right hands. First, he wanded them. Then he looked closely. As he drew down on us, all hell broke loose. Tanner and I fought off most of them. I hit the sergeant hard and he landed on the floor. We were winning until the sergeant came to, pulled his Daisy, and hit Tanner in the forehead. He was dead and I was taken into custody.

If the sergeant hadn't been so zealous, they would have discovered all our plans. Instead, they led me right to the death line. That was where I met Beth. I had experienced all the loss I cared to endure in this life. We were just past the mid-point of the seven-year covenant, and much had happened leading up to that transition. I can't tell you much, but I can confirm some events and give you a few things to think about.

First, let me say that you do not want to miss the Rapture, and there were plenty of "good Christian people" who did. Study the parables, such as the Ten Virgins. It is not enough to be prepared physically or mentally. Your heart must be right. And Jesus knows your heart. If you play around the edges or try to serve two masters, you are doomed. Doomed to what, you ask? There is no escape from the awful events to come. Only death will get you out, and God needs His tribulation saints to be evangelists. Once one converts, God will keep you alive unless you do something stupid.

The Antichrist spends most of the run-up to the midpoint gaining power, crushing his enemies, rebuilding Babylon, and establishing his government, church, and military. There is a single church under the False Prophet, and it will not be Islam. God deals with Islam during Magog. Because he is Antichrist, he will do everything possible to try and look like Christ. In the beginning, he easily deceived millions. Then, he fulfilled prophecy by dying and resurrecting. This caused millions more to follow him.

At the midpoint of the seven years, the antichrist will become manifest at the abomination of desolation. I've talked a lot about the mark, but consider this: in the Bible, Deuteronomy 6, Moses tells us that we are to bind the commands of God as a sign on our hands and they shall be as frontlets between your eyes. Similarly, the Antichrist will require his mark on your hand or forehead.

There is something very special about the 144,000 Jewish evangelists. There is something even more special about the 144,000 in chapter 14. Pray and ask God to reveal these things to you. He doesn't want me to tell you, but He loves to throw us a bone. Read and meditate on the letters to the churches. Lots of clues as to what will happen to the apostate churches in the last days. What about your church?

Since I am writing this, I am still alive. I don't hold out much hope for seeing Jesus' return, except to be with Him. I look forward to the Marriage Supper of the Lamb as described in Revelation 19. If I live through to see Him return, I will see Him come and all of you with Him. That is my prayer, and the purpose Jesus gave me. I have to tell you this now: trust in Him because He is trustworthy. Every step of the way, I experienced the evidence of His orchestration. He has supplied everything I needed along the way, even love—His and my own shared with my help-meet. God's glorious institution of marriage between a man and a woman is the most wonderful and God-honoring thing we can do. I give Him praise!

The gift of the Holy Spirit is amazingly beautiful. In prayer, I can just give it to Him and He will go to work delivering what I had asked, wanting to make it happen, or orchestrating something even better for the final outcome. One thing has become clear to me. God hates to see anyone perish, especially a lost person. But He views life and death in a way we cannot imagine and He uses it all for good.

All of this had led me to Beth and she had the ability to read my mind. When she came out for church, she was gorgeous, wearing a beautiful spring-yellow dress and white sandals to accent her dark Egyptian skin. I wondered if this was what Marra had looked like in her early days. Beth had a wonderful familiarity about her. The three of us showed up at The Way in the Rover. The place was packed and I met Richard's replacement, Pastor Peter, two pastors removed.

"Bible teachers don't last long around here," he said. "The Global Community figures that when they take the pastor out, the rest will give up. Too bad they don't know the way of Jesus."

Pastor Peter had heard of Susan and me, the two 'dynamos of the saints.' He said, "Your reputation is large in the underground, and I am so sorry to hear of your loss."

"Thank you, Pastor." I pulled him aside, told him what I was thinking, and he made a way. After the service, which included a guitar solo of "I Still Believe", an amazing teaching on 2 Corinthians 5:12–21—our roles as ministers of reconciliation—and a dozen people giving their lives to Christ, I turned to face Beth, took both her hands in mine, dropped to one knee, and asked her to spend the rest of her life with me.

She smiled and said, "Of course I will." Then she kissed me, right there in the middle of the church. Pastor Peter brought us forward and married us then and there. Everyone clapped and wished us well. I left Peter and the church a million-dollar tip, and we were off for our honeymoon. I insisted we sleep under the stars on the boathouse deck, and it was amazing. There was nothing like getting to know each other under the awesome grandeur of God's universe.

Of course, we both knew that those stars could come crashing down at any moment. I had often told myself I didn't want to be around to witness that. But now, it seemed somehow okay. The next morning, we would be in The Dalles, Oregon, and I would be introducing Beth as Mrs. Eli Grollenberg. We loaded up the heavy arms and said goodbye to the lake house, as I always did. It had been a source of fond memories, and last night was no exception. I grabbed the money and we were off. The country looked a lot larger than I remembered. Beth had a million questions about my folks, and me about hers. We got to know each other well. She joked about my name, telling me she wouldn't order any stationary. We all got a laugh out of that. But the new Mrs. Grollenberg and I were bonding.

We flew over the Rockies, dropped down below twenty thousand feet at Pendleton, Oregon, and chased the Columbia River westward. Soon, Ron had the Gulf at four thousand feet and was flying right down the river. We saw the silos on our left, swept out to the north, turned and landed to the southeast. It was a beautiful day in Oregon, and we taxied in. We were waved into a huge warehouse where the tow truck hooked us up and pulled us inside. We rode a huge elevator that dropped the entire plane down about forty feet into a hangar. We deplaned amid tight security, met up with Bradley Carter, and were welcomed in.

Bradley looked like he had aged twenty years since we met in Illinois after the Rapture. He had told us the Agri-store was unique, and we were about to discover just how unique it truly was. On the surface, it was a distribution facility that served the GC with fresh fruits, nuts, vegetables, and dry goods like rice and wheat brought in from China. They had their own ships, millions of square feet of storage, and distribution sites all over the west. It was one of six in the US.

What lay on the surface, as far as the GC could tell, was the Agri-store, a somewhat innocuous food distribution facility that served the Northwest region. In reality, the store was the breadbasket of the co-op, the Christian underground, and a key secret military base. I had seen dozens of secret facilities like this around the world, but couldn't imagine how incredible this place was. Bradley Carter was the operations manager for the facility. It appeared to be GC orders in, GC orders out, but Joseph's Agri-store distributed provisions of every kind to saints unable to buy from the GC. This included weapons and ammunition for the fight to stay alive and to counter GC gestapo tactics.

After leaving the plane, we rode the elevator up to the tower, camouflaged as a rooftop vent system on the top of the biggest warehouse. There, we met General Thomas B. McHenry, the infamous T-Bone. T-Bone was the chief military officer, in charge of covert operations in harmony with Cheyenne Mountain and four other secret bases across the country.

First, they had satellite intercept technology. Simply put, they could upload and run video from uneventful days or block the signal entirely in the event of a large operation that needed to escape the view of GC headquarters. McHenry toured us through the facility on top and then took us to the secret part. Externally, five to six hundred people worked in the warehouses, offices, or drove trucks. Because of its remote location, mark monitoring was rare and usually only needed for drivers who delivered GC goods to Portland, Seattle, Boise, etc. These employees were loyal to the Antichrist, bore the marks of Satan, and functioned as employees for the store. They showed up in the morning, had their own administrators and foreman, left in the evening, and had no knowledge of Carter, T-Bone, or the saints. The sprawling facility covered hundreds of acres along the river and was connected by underground passageways that the GC knew nothing about.

The saints would work in the underground, beneath the offices, communicating with the underground church and other facilities around the world. Below the Agri-store offices was a tech center, hospital, and communications hub. There were also military offices on the bottom floor, some one hundred and eighty feet below the ground. Passageways connected the huge warehouses below the above-ground warehouses that lined the airstrip. Above ground—GC. Below ground—saints' food distribution, support for military shipments, arms, uniforms, ammunition, medical supplies, etc.

West of the airstrip was a former rock quarry of granite that was eight hundred feet deep. This was the heart of Joseph's underground facility. Over six thousand lived here in plush, modern housing on the first two levels. Below that was the mall, grocery center, school, hospital, church, and power plant.

"Water and steam!" General McHenry said. "We power it all with hot water coming from the bottom of the quarry and hydroelectric turbines in the river. Joseph was a genius and discovered steam discharges from the depths of the abandoned quarry. The city fathers agreed to give him the property if he would fill it in. He did.

"Joseph ran it and flourished until his death. Then along came his successor, an author whom God led here. He bought the facility and with the help of the caretaker, Bob Chamberlain, resurrected the whole project, finished the western section, and revitalized and expanded the operation. He and his wife also began the Project 180 disaster relief ministry and founded The Way. The first church is here, six hundred feet below us."

"Wait! An author? Which author?" I asked.

"Why, Ken Sparks, of course. Everyone knows that," T-Bone said.

"R. K. Sparks, writer of the *Faith* trilogy? He started The Way and Project 180?" I asked.

"Yes. And all this was his mission until the Rapture. He even hired Bradley and me, knowing somehow we would be left behind to serve the saints. He was a phenomenal man."

Lightbulbs were going off in my head.

"What's wrong, Eli?" Beth asked.

"It's a connection. One that has been there all along, yet I wasn't allowed to see it until now."

"A good connection?"

"Yes, a very good connection!" I told her.

"General, why isn't Sparks better promoted? He doesn't seem to exist, even when looking for him."

"A sordid past. His testimony is incredible, but he preferred to let his godly work speak for him. And it did just that…"

"So this was all his?"

"Yes. Joseph laid the foundation, Sparks took it where God wanted it. So far, it is invisible to Satan. God is truly good. But like all of us, we came to that conclusion very late."

"Yes, we did…" My mind was reeling and I had a lot to explain to Beth. The Way, the books—he had been so close, yet so distant. Revealed finally to me in God's time. All along I was thinking that I would upload my memoirs to an author, one who wrote a couple of Christian books. But he did all this. Now I knew just how selective I had to be in what I would send him. I could very easily allow him to see his entire future. I knew that is not what God wanted. Suddenly, years later, Jesus' vision had meat to it.

When we toured the school, the hospital, the shopping centers, and the church, it became clear to me that R. K. Sparks was no ordinary man. God used him during the many tragic natural disasters, the earthquake in San Francisco, the civil war, the nuclear attacks. His team, the Project 180 team, was there, preparing meals, aiding in the rescue attempts, having emergency shelters available and huge church services for displaced folks. Bradley said Sparks referred to it as "large scale revival." Not only did they provide physical revival, but spiritual revival as well. Apparently, hundreds of thousands came to Christ in the midst of tragedy prior to the Rapture.

That night, the GC workers went home and the underground sprung to life. Flights were going out to provide food and supplies all over the West. It was like an entire city with one objective. We got called to the tower and watched a GC patrol drone slowly fly down the river. By looking at the feed, there was no activity at all. All was quiet on the front as far as Antichrist and his cronies were concerned.

I shared with Carter and McHenry the process for applying and programming the faux mark. It was slick, quick, and the answer to a lot of logistical questions. Now saints could mingle, work, and buy provisions right along with their lost-forever counterparts. This would be a game-changer and give us the upper hand without Satan being the wiser. I personally would not take it. Instead, the temporary application, which worked just as well, was much more practical for us chameleons. But we knew it was practical for those existing in the mix. We also dropped a cool five million on them and attended church at the original church—The Way.

Over the days we were there, we saw the day-to-day operations. There were wars going on all over the world between Satan and the saints. We were all waiting for the next big event. The seven angels would receive the seven trumpets. This would launch the trumpet judgments, and we knew that they would begin with another huge earthquake. None of us looked forward to the coming events. For several years now, the 144,000 Jewish evangelists had been covering the world with good news, saving many. It was the lull before the storm. Wormwood was coming, and a huge rock the size of a mountain, hurling its way through space. This all followed the earthquake and fire like hail from heaven. The underground church was keeping the saints and potential saints updated on the judgments as they came and explained what to expect. It was daunting but inescapable.

chapter

TWENTY-FIVE
✡✡✡✡✡✡✡

Beth, Ron, and I left Oregon as different people than we were before. We had new missions ahead and questions about how it would all work. Well, you know most of it. Beth became my bride, my mission partner, and my best friend. She took up where Susan had left off, in more ways than one. She had seen one of Susan's lessons and knew she could continue them. She fell in love with the lake house, Virginia, and me. I hoped it would be to the end, but only God knew for sure and I trusted Him. For now, we had a mission to serve Him and our fellow saints. Ron said goodbye and flew on to Florida to check up on his family. He had become an integral part of our ministry team.

I looked at Beth, this wonderful woman who God had brought into my life.

"You know, I thank God every day for you," I told her.

"You should. Neither of us would be here if we hadn't met. We were meant to be there together, to help the underground and to do this. I never thought I would be an on-air teacher."

"I believe God has equipped us to do all this. Like Esther, we were put in place for such a time as this," I told her with a hug.

"I love you, Eli. I don't feel like I tell you that enough. Who would have thought that an Egyptian girl fighting in the Coptic Christian

Army would marry a Jewish-Palestinian spy in America after standing in line to have our heads chopped off?"

"Yes, and now we are the ultimate thorn in Lech's side. He will be coming for us as soon as he figures out where we are."

"I'm not afraid to die—as long as I'm in your arms," she said. I smiled and pulled her closer. The sky was turning a beautiful red-orange as the sun settled behind the mountain.

"We'd better enjoy this. Soon the sun will go dark and all hell will break loose. I'm not looking forward to that!" I told her with a kiss.

"You're still pretty romantic for an old guy!"

"You haven't seen anything yet. Let me get a bottle of wine and some MRE's…"

She laughed. "It may come to that soon."

"We'll be gone by then."

"We'll see. We have work to do. The harvest is ready and the laborers are few."

We set up for lesson number three and I told Beth she looked great. Ron called from Florida to tell us things were dicey. The faux marks were working, but he and his Christian family were very nervous and extremely uncomfortable doing business with the GC.

"It's just creepy…" he said.

"Time is short," I told him. "And you are welcome back here anytime."

"Thanks. I love the teachings—and they are always interrupting some stupid GC public service program. They must be really happy with you…"

"Don't care. Thousands are coming to Christ. Even more will come. We already know—Lech loses."

"Yeah, that's a wrap. But he is inflicting lots of pain."

"Part of the program, Ron. Sad but true. We'll keep up the fight as long as we can."

Beth touched up her notes and we began the next lesson—"All About Jesus."

"'For unto us a child is born, unto us a Son is given; and the government will be upon His shoulders, and His name will be called Wonderful, Counselor, Mighty God, Everlasting Father, Prince of Peace.' The child is the son of Joseph and Mary, a virgin. He would be called Emmanuel, God with us. He would be born in Bethlehem, raised in Nazareth, and He would be a carpenter—for a time.

"Three hundred and twenty-two Old Testament prophecies told of His coming, His ministry, His crucifixion, and His position. Jesus Christ is the incarnate God, fully God, fully man. During His ministry on earth, He unquestionably claimed to be God, and repeatedly said that He would be killed and raised from the dead. Then, He pulled it off. He was nailed to the cross, and the tomb that held Him afterwards was heavily guarded, but still it was found empty. He was out doing what Jesus did, being God on earth. In His glorified body, He appeared to the women, to two men on the road to Emmaus, and to the disciples multiple times. He appeared to five hundred on a mountainside, then He simply ascended into the heavens.

"Jesus Christ was who He said He was. So who is He? God. God come to earth to complete a mission for His Father—to be the propitiation for all the world's sins. There is far more to it than that, but it shouldn't be a surprise to us that He came, or what He came for. It was all laid out in prophecy, and He fulfilled all prophecy regarding His first coming. To add to that, He also is prepared to fulfill numerous other prophecies regarding His second coming.

"There is one thing we need to know about Jesus the Christ. To accomplish what He had to do, that is, be able and willing to be our Savior, then pull it all off, He had to be God. Nothing less, God with us. So they—that is, the Trinity: God the Father, Jesus the Son, and the Holy Spirit—made a way for us as fallen human beings to be redeemed back to Them. They created us in Their own image, we fell to temptation, and the plan for our redemption went into motion.

"I don't ask that one God in the form of three unique and individual Persons be understood. We don't need to fully understand, we just need to be grateful that they love us enough to offer a way. And as John 3:16 tells us, God's desire is for us all to be saved. The only limitation is our disbelief and our free will. Just as Adam and Eve had a choice to obey or not, so do each of us.

"If you think, 'Well, this is all very difficult to believe,' don't feel alone. Virtually every person alive following the Rapture had that in common. I will tell you this: you need to choose and you need to choose now, before you die and certainly before you take the mark. Those two will be the end of you. There are no second chances after death or serving the Antichrist who we all know now as Satan. You cannot serve two masters. The choice is God or Satan. It's as simple as that.

"As far as other gods, who is it that is viable or valuable? God dealt with Islam, Mormonism, Scientologists, Jehovah's Witnesses, and the Dalai Lama. They were all left behind or are dead—bodies rotting in the ground. Jesus' tomb is empty. He is alive! Joseph Stalin was considered a god among the Russian people.

"Some god he is—dead! He is no different than those the true and living God describes: 'They have mouths but they do not speak; Eyes they have, but they do not see; they have ears, but they hear not; noses they have but they do not smell; they have hands, but they do not handle; feet they have, but they do not walk; nor do they mutter through their throat; those who make them are like them; so is everyone who trusts in them.'

"Jesus is not only alive, He has promised to return to earth to conquer Satan and usher in His kingdom. Jesus is God and every knee will bow. Three hundred twenty-two prophecies said He would come as Messiah and die on the cross. He Himself predicted His death and resurrection three days later. For each prophecy of His first coming, there are many more regarding His second coming. He also fulfilled His promise to take His people up to meet them in the clouds and to forever be with Him. We all witnessed it and it terrified us because we knew it was true—His statements, the promises, the Scripture—all true and documented.

"Jesus is God, the Son of God, the incarnate God who came to earth in the flesh. The Scriptures confirm it, history confirms it, and for many of us it is confirmed by personal experience. He is God and He is alive. Today is the day—Jesus is the Way!"

Beth, like Susan before her, closed with the invitation and prayer of salvation. The angels in heaven were rejoicing at the harvest... She promised to be on again soon with the next lesson: "The Bible is 100 percent True." We got a thankful email from Russell: "Perfect and spectacular. You are reaching the common man and the lost. We will run it soon..."

She led me by hand to the deck where we embraced. "You know, I think you should give your testimony at some point, perhaps near the end of the lessons."

"How about at the end of 'We are our own Worst Enemy'? I could be the poster-child for that one..."

"That is true for all of us. We missed it because we are our own worst enemy. I was mad at God, you were the classic procrastinator."

"Yes, indeed. And it was so unnecessary. But I did meet you and I am eternally grateful for that."

We enjoyed the day and watched some TV. Lech was on with one of his cronies.

"Hey, I know him. That's Qussam Sulaman, the Republican Guard leader of Iran. Why did he survive?"

"To be Lech's right-hand man, it appears. How do you know him?"

I told her the story of Said Imam, the arms dealer that turned the tables on the man.

"It all went well until the end—the delivery. He was there with others, nineteen body guards. Six of us agents, all unarmed. The deal was done and Sulaman and my arms-deal contact left. On his way out the door, he said, 'Very well, Mr. Stone, I bid you farewell,' in Farsi. We knew we had been blown. There we were in the middle of this old textile warehouse surrounded by seventeen of the IRG's best men. I'm sure they drew straws for this one. The IRG loves to kill spies, especially Jewish spies." I took a deep breath.

"How are you still here?"

"Geoff Hess, our advance team leader. He had built in a little surprise for just such a circumstance. At my command, all six of us moved and in less than a second all seventeen IRG were dead!"

"Wow!"

"Wow is right. Then we high-tailed it out of there, jumped on a Sikorski, blew up a police helicopter and two MIG's, and were gone."

"You must be on the center of his dartboard in his office."

"Oh, it's been years. I'm sure he has forgotten by now."

Beth took my hand. She knew that only by the grace of God were we still here. Both of us should have been dead dozens of times over.

"I'm curious. How do six unarmed men kill seventeen trained killers in less than a second?"

"Fire extinguishers!"

"Oh really? Fire extinguishers?"

I told her the story and she cringed. "Praise God for Geoff and the advance team."

"Yes, indeed."

Lech had Sulaman by his side as he spoke of cracking down on the underground. Then it went blank and there was Beth with lesson number three.

"Good job, Russell... Interrupt his speech about cracking down on the underground—perfect..." Beth said. Every effort to cut off the transmissions had failed. Russell Brown was the master and we were happy to have him on God's side.

Beth worked on the next lesson while I provided input, encouragement, and nutrition. We were a great team, brought together by God's eternal orchestration. We had learned a lot together and God was revealing truths to us as we went. It was amazing and provided us with extra stamina.

"'The Bible is 100 percent true.' It is said that the Bible is the anvil that has worn out the hammers of criticism for two thousand years. What seems to be a contradiction is always proven to be a truth It is supported by science and archaeology, as well as history. It has endured not only criticism, but deep study by millions of readers. It truly is the Word of God…

"It is the greatest selling, most printed, and most distributed book of all time since its beginning, some three thousand years ago. The first five books of the Bible, referred to by the Jews as the Torah, was penned by Moses under God's divine guidance. It begins with the creation account and ends with Deuteronomy, which means repetition of the law. These books provide the account of creation for all things, including man, and explains that God is overseer to them. Man begins well, with Adam and his wife Eve fellowshipping with God in the Garden of Eden. However, Eve was deceived and convinces Adam to go along. They had made a terrible choice. Man had fallen to temptation and found himself separated from God. It is the true story of all of us—bad choices and all. The first eleven chapters of the Bible in Genesis are about the creation and the fall. The entire rest of the Bible is about God's plan of redemption. Along the way, prophets, kings, and religious leaders of the Jews documented their journey from Egypt through the Red Sea, into the desert, and eventually into the Promised Land.

"Throughout the Bible, God's promises hold true. His plan for redemption unfolds, and glimpses and types of Christ show up all along the way. Unlike any other book, the characters are not elevated to something they are not. In story after story, we see people's failures, flaws, sins, and unholy desires. The Bible makes no effort to glamorize anyone. God's chosen people were disobedient, complaining, obstinate, selfish, and brutal. But God was patient and caring, slow to react, and just.

"As the story develops, the orchestration of God is evident throughout. As these stories highlight epic struggles, love, hate, war, and personal failure, everything points to the coming Messiah. The Old Testament ends before four hundred years of silence, the calm before the storm.

"Much of the Old Testament is supported by history, archaeology, and extra-biblical writings. Many Old Testament prophecies were fulfilled and confirmed in numerous ways over the centuries. It must be looked at as a history book that people constantly challenge until proven accurate. One must admit that many miracles, judgments, and events documented in the Bible are supernatural. The prophecy of Ezekiel 38 and 39, the War of Gog and Magog, was one of those— until it unfolded just as documented by the prophet Ezekiel.

"Just the fact that Israel is back in the land after nearly two thousand years should be enough. The destruction of Damascus, as sad as it was, matched the predictions of Isaiah twenty-seven hundred years earlier. These are not just lucky guesses. These are men writing down God's words and telling what God knows and wants us to know. And now He's telling us through the Revelation of Christ, the final book in His Word, that these things are coming. Shouldn't we pay attention?

"If one studies the finely orchestrated circumstances of World War I and World War II regarding Israel, it is clear that God used those events to put Israel back in the land as a nation, using people, governments, politics, droughts, famines, war, culture, and language to do so. The entire process is one miracle after another.

"Jesus was born of a virgin—miracle. He predicted and pulled off His own trial, scourging, death, resurrection, and ascension—miracle. He encouraged His disciples, converted Paul, used the incredible infrastructure of Rome to launch His church and spread His gospel. Now He sits at the right hand of God, where He has prepared a place for us. He came and got His church, and will come back to judge the world and usher in His kingdom on earth for a thousand years. All miracles, for us.

"We have been witnesses to just some of this, but it's all a miracle. All supernatural and undoable except by a loving God. Yes, the Bible is the Word of God because it is His—His story, His people, His creation, His Son, His plan. Even the earth will be saved so the kingdom can flourish here on earth after Jesus' return.

"But He also promises this: His Son, Jesus Christ, the Messiah, is the Way. He is the only way. Jesus Himself said, 'I am the Way, the Truth, and the Life. No one comes to the Father except through Me.' That may sound exclusive, and it is. We have to understand, He did not have to redeem us. But He made a way. We have a way. The choice is ours.

"I encourage you to read the Bible again in light of it being historical, prophetic, and absolute truth. It will change your life. It will save your life. The apostle John said that Jesus is the Word of God. He and the written word of God are your guide to eternal life. For God so loved the world that He gave His only begotten son that whoever believes on Him should not perish, but have eternal life. It's not too late, but it's close. Do not die unsaved. Do not take the mark. Today is the day—Jesus is the Way!"

Another video in the books and another wave in the harvest reaped by Christ. "In the Parable of the Wheat and the Tares, found in Matthew 13:24–30, Jesus tells us that the good wheat will grow up along with the tares, or weeds. When they are harvested, He will separate them and cast the tares into the fire. These lessons are designed to show there is a distinction. We can't escape, God knows everything about us—everything! Beth said it with such enthusiasm that I had to hug her after.

"Well said, sweet girl, well said…"

"I'm just so excited… Knowing that our lesson interrupted what the Antichrist had to say was thrilling. These lessons fire me up!"

"That's good. It's passion. What is up next?"

"I think we should combine 'Free Will', 'We are Appointed to Die Once, then Judgment', and 'We are our Own Worst Enemy.' It may go longer than a half-hour, but it keeps Lech off the air…" she said.

"Praise God! He is in all of this and I bet it brings a grin to His face."

We had to make a run into Bedford to meet Ron, who was flying in with supplies. It was a little creepy out in the world, even here in the country. Most businesses were abandoned and shuttered. Nobody was out, and it seemed unsafe. Even for a short trip like this, we still took the time to put on temporary faux marks. We both refused to do the more permanent marks. Even though they weren't real, it just didn't feel right, as if we were part his. But being caught out here in no-man's land without the mark could have us back in line.

We made it to the airport and met up with Ron. He had food-stuffs and coffee, always a necessary item. No one was around, but it felt eerie, so we hurried to load up and said our goodbyes. Ron, too, could feel it. Soon, the Gulf was rocketing down the Bedford runway and off into the blue sky. That's when we noticed the drone. Beth caught a glimmer and once we had an eye on it, we could tell what it was. They flew at around four thousand feet and were silent.

The bad thing was that they saw us. So we followed our evasion plan, driving into Lynchburg and around the abandoned Liberty University campus. It was weird, hardly anyone out. We stopped at one of the few stores that were open, looking like we knew what we were doing and then took the back way into the lake. We had parked the pontoon boat at King's Pub and Marina, loaded the supplies and waited to see if there was any sign of the drone. We skirted the shore, staying close for tree cover, and pulled into the boathouse. We unloaded through the tunnel. I checked radar from the control room and found it clear.

The King's Pub was owned by a friend of mine who had taken the mark but hated Lech. Everyone in the area and anyone with half a brain avoided any potential contact with the GC. Steve let me park, keep the boat there, and have free run of the place. I, in turn, kept him supplied with Irish whiskey, which was a tough get even under Lech, who encouraged drinking. I called Ron and he had made it back safely. He had picked up the drone, sent his identifier so that they would know he was okay, and flew on. All was well—for now.

We had an email from Russell. The salvation chart was pointing up steeply, so we were pleased.

"What was that you cut off today, Russell?" I asked.

"Oh, nothing much. Just an international news conference to tell the world how he was busy exterminating co-op members and anyone who would dare to defy his order to worship his likeness. He says he is on the verge of destroying any trace of the co-op."

"Well, good job Russell. We thank you, and God bless you."

"Thank you, Eli. Tell Beth the lessons are superb."

"I will. Keep up the good work."

It had been a full and challenging day. We could not wait to get the creepy faux marks off of us and crawl into bed. Tomorrow was to be another full day as we closed in on the terrible events to come.

The morning spent with my wife, the Word of God, a beautiful sunrise, and a sweet cup of coffee was precious. We were counting down the days now and would soon be sequestered to the control room, safely tucked away. We would try to get two lessons in today along with my testimony. Beth said that it was time. "People can relate to you, a Jew, stubborn and stiff-necked, who procrastinated until too late. Now you're saved. It will be powerful."

"Okay, okay. I'll do it."

We picked up a drone on the radar making a pass out over the airport. They were keeping an eye on something, but it was far from us. For now, we had to remain stealthy.

We set up and fired up the camera. It was time to tell the world that they were their own worst enemy. I was ready to roll and stopped, looked at Beth, and told her how beautiful she was. She blushed and told me I was crazy. "My face looks like I went ten rounds with a tiger."

"Still beautiful!" I said. She just smiled.

"So you have probably considered how all this came about: the judgment of God, the Rapture of the church, being left behind, and ultimately what is to come. We know it will be ugly, the words in the book of the Revelation of Jesus Christ are terrifying. And those are just words. We are about to live them out—the great and awful wrath of God... What did we do to deserve it?

"The answer is two words: free will. God created us with free will. He honors it, and won't change it or remove us from its consequences. To live godly lives, we simply must choose to do so. So when faced with temptation, whatever it was or is, we just could not or would not say no. James tells us that we are drawn away and enticed by our own desires. Then, when desire has conceived, it gives birth to sin, and sin, when it is full grown, brings forth death (James 1:14–15; Romans 6:23).

"Our sin nature is imputed on us. That is because Adam and Eve failed in the garden, which changed the entire world. God had to create us with free will or else He could never have children who were truly committed to and really loved Him. He wanted our love and fellowship, but He wanted us to willingly choose it. Adam chose badly and in a way, we all failed that test. We all have free will, and can choose to live our lives as we wish. God only encourages, warns, and at times chastises us just as we would a child.

"If your child continually ran into a busy street, you would have to do something to teach them not to. Because we love them, we chastise them. God does this with us. It is proportional to the degree of harm we do to others, and our sin always harms others. It goes out like a wave, affecting others outwardly depending on how big the wave is.

God gave us the commandments as a template of obedience. There is purpose behind every one of these ten commandments.

"We often begin with something small, a little shoplifting or getting high, pre-marital sex, or fornication, coveting the neighbor's new car, his house, or his wife. A classic example is David of the Bible. God called him a man after His own heart. Yet he walked out on his balcony, saw a woman bathing, and called for her. She was the wife of one of his soldiers who was away at war. Now, she was with child—David's child. He was the king, so he covered it up. Her husband was sent to the front lines to put him in harm's way, and he was killed. Problem solved.

"David took her as his wife and suddenly had a son coming. But God knows all things. He commissioned Nathan, the local prophet, to trap David in his sin. It was the beginning of the end for David, and while He didn't destroy David, the consequences were far-reaching. On top of that, the woman lost her husband and would lose her child as well. You see, it goes out like a wave.

"We are our own worst enemy. Now is the time we all need to do some soul searching. What is it that has control of you? Or is it more than one? In 2 Timothy, Paul tells his protégé, 'In the last days perilous times will come; for men will be lovers of themselves, lovers of money, boasters, proud, blasphemers, disobedient, unforgiving, slanderers, without self-control, brutal, despisers of good, traitors, headstrong, haughty, lovers of pleasure rather than lovers of God, having a form of godliness but denying its power.'

"We can all relate to at least some of these traits, or perhaps all of them. We tend to want what we want and don't even consider the consequences. There is certainly nothing new under the sun, but in the past one hundred years World War I, the industrial age, the wars, and the feminist movement have all contributed to the decline of the family. Satan knew that by destroying the family, the human race would also distort deep-seeded institutions God put in place like marriage, worship, obedience, and honoring Him. We are as bad as Sodom and Gomorrah, sacrificing our children to the gods of convenience.

"God has been warning us and we neglect to change, loving our sin and holding on to it until the end. Now Satan, who is running this world, makes sure everyone has all the perversion that they want. He wants nothing more than to keep you from God while he positions himself for a showdown with Jesus. Well, we know who wins, and what Satan's future will be. But he will try to take as many with him as possible.

"There is hope. If you are breathing and have not taken the mark, you can still choose. Repent, for the kingdom of God has come. The end and the ultimatum are coming. This may be your last chance. Time is short and God's desire is that you choose the free gift of grace. He made a way through Jesus' death on the cross. The price of redemption has been paid. All you must do is accept it. You missed it once and were left behind. The choice is heaven for eternity or eternity in the lake of fire where there is eternal torment. Today is the day—Jesus is the Way!

"Close your eyes and in the quiet of your heart, pray this prayer. 'Heavenly Father, I know I am a sinner in need of a Savior. I realize now that Jesus died on the cross to pay the price for my sin. I receive the gift, the free gift of salvation. I confess with my mouth the Lord Jesus and believe in my heart that God raised Him from the dead. In Jesus' name I pray, Amen.'

"If you prayed that prayer, the angels in heaven are rejoicing and you answered the prayers of millions who are praying for you. You will now live with Christ in heaven for eternity. Hallelujah! Tune in for a special testimony and lessons coming soon. God bless you..."

"That was amazing, Beth..." I said. "Can I tell you something I learned?"

"Of course..."

"God answers prayers in three ways. One, He says yes and delivers immediately. Two, He asks us to wait. Or three, He orchestrates an even better answer and delivers it at the perfect time. He is always orchestrating!"

"That is beautiful. And He brought me you!"

chapter

TWENTY-SIX
✡✡✡✡✡✡✡

I had a surprise for Beth and I would spring it on her at sundown that night. I set all the preparations in motion while she worked on lesson eight. Ron had filled my shopping list with all the key ingredients and I had done all my traditional exercises. It was the thirteenth of Nissan on the Jewish calendar and, as I had done every year of my life, I cleaned and searched for every bit of leaven in the house.

Sundown would usher in Passover and I had not missed a Seder meal in my entire life. The one obvious difference from the past was the absence of an empty chair and place set for Elijah. Jesus would be filling that seat now. The Messiah had come in more ways than one. I had the best china, the schmurah matzah, the lamb, the bitter herbs, the egg, and the wine.

The house had been cleaned of all chametz by the appointed time and everything put in place. I went down and put my arms around Beth's shoulders and kissed her on the forehead.

"Wow. Such a show of affection. What's the occasion?"

"Come and see. You need a break."

She used the powder room and we rode the elevator to the main level. Holding her hand, I led her to the dining room. Her eyes were wide, her nose taking in the smell of fresh out of the oven, bone-in leg of lamb.

"What is this, silly man?"

"You will see."

Beth lit the candles at exactly 7:36 PM and the fun began.

"As a child, Marra made this a special and fun event we looked forward to each year. Because I was the only child and therefore the youngest, I played every role in the Seder meal," I explained. "This, my love and my only family, is a celebration of Passover, the eve of the four-teenth of Nissan, that great and terrible day when all of Israel followed closely Moses' instructions. A lamb, the choice lamb, the unblemished lamb, was sacrificed and prepared. The house was cleansed of all impu-rities. The word is chametz—leaven or sin. All bread right down to the crumbs, any food with wheat, barley, rye, oats, and anything not kosher is cleansed from the house. It represents the cleansing of sin from our lives."

"I've heard of this, but have never participated. Am I, being an Egyptian, allowed?"

"Yes, as long as you are circumcised."

She laughed.

"Plus, you are my family and this is about family and passing it on to future generations." I suddenly felt sad that a future Grollenberg was not in the cards. Beth sensed this and came to me. A wave of peace came over me. Suddenly I was free of that sadness. God had brought her to me late in life, but I was so grateful to have her. I couldn't imag-ine having a Seder by myself.

"This festival is in remembrance of the Exodus from Egypt. Of course, we now know what the lamb is all about. The blood needed to be placed on the doorposts and lintel. We'll do that later, because the death angel is coming. The blood of the lamb causes the death angel to pass over. The wine is for the blessings, the egg for new beginnings, the bitter herbs to signify our strife as slaves in Goshen. I will show you the significance of the matzah when we get to it. For now, let's sit."

I explained the empty chair and setting traditionally reserved for Elijah, but now occupied by Jesus Himself, God with us. I showed her how my father would stack the matzah, three pieces representing the Father, the Holy Ghost, and the Messiah. "He would break off a piece from the middle piece—which represented Messiah—wrap it in white linen, and hide it. Then I would go and search for it. Now, of course, Jewish families are usually big, so the children would spread out to find the piece so it could be restored to the stack. The child who found it was rewarded. It was always me, and I didn't mind. I also got to ask the four questions, because I was the youngest."

"Four questions?"

"Yes. Four questions regarding why we do this. It is for teaching future generations. It was my favorite part, because as my father gave the answers, I could envision myself packing up, leaving Egypt, and trusting the provision of God. The children of Israel would be headed into the desert with not much more than the clothes on their backs. And it was not a small group. I put myself right there, on the edge of the Red Sea, waiting for God's deliverance from the coming army of Egypt. I guess I had a vivid imagination, or else it was the way my father would make the answers come alive."

I began to tear up and Beth got up to hold me.

"He has delivered us, Eli. Our families too. Soon we will see them and be rejoicing."

"You are so good for me, sweet girl. Thank you for being a part of my life."

"Thank Jesus. He's right there, smiling…"

I looked and had no doubt. "The Passover Lamb. Thank you, Lord Jesus…"

We went through all the steps I remembered so well. We dipped parsley in salt water twice. First, to recall Israel going through the Red Sea unharmed and on dry ground. Then, to recall the Egyptian army who tried to chase them. The parsley was then eaten to remember their destruction at the hands of God. We reclined when we drank to represent the freedom we now have.

"Of course, father brought it all to life—bigger than life. After all, this has been a Jewish tradition for three thousand years… Now, the matzah, especially the middle piece, was broken and eaten. The wine was used for the blessings. Sound familiar?" I asked.

"The bread and the wine. Jesus and the disciples in the Upper Room."

"Yes. Celebrating the Passover. It was Nissan 13, the eve of Passover."

"Communion!"

"Exactly."

Now it was time to place the blood on the doorposts and lintel. Using a mixture of barbeque sauce and water, I took the bowl and we went outside. I set the bowl down, went to the hyssop tree I had planted years ago, broke off a branch and brought it back to the porch. Now, the hyssop branch has hundreds of small leaves, more like a bush. Having Beth stand back a bit, I dipped the leaves into the mix and, following God's instructions, I struck the lintel in the center above the door. Then, I dipped again, striking first the left door post and then the right at about eye level.

As the mixture ran down the door, we stood back and observed the near-perfect cross on the door in "lamb's blood". We were in awe.

"How did they miss it?" I said. "Prior to Jesus' coming, I could understand. But after—the blood of the lamb, the cross. We really are a stiff-necked people, hard-headed as can possibly be."

"That may be true, but you have a lot of very nice qualities as well," Beth said. I knew something else was coming. "Jews are great fathers."

That hung in the air for a moment as we took in the cross forming on our door.

"And you'll be no different…"

I swallowed hard. "What?"

"You will be a great father, Eli."

I scanned her beautiful, scarred face for some clue.

"I'm pregnant, Eli!"

The joy on my face said it all as I tried to process. We were both too old, the timing—we had no time left. Beth knew all this was going through my mind. "We will have our child in heaven, Eli. Or perhaps we will make it through and we will be one of the very few tribulation saints to see Jesus in our human bodies with our child. God knows all of this. He has blessed us by opening my womb. And our child has just experienced their first Passover."

I was shaking my head in disbelief. Then we began to dance and I sang the song "Dayenu"—it would have been enough. It was truly a joyous occasion. We finished with a toast: "Next year, Jerusalem!"

The Grollenberg household was rejoicing late into the night. We continued on the second Seder night and praised God for blessing us. No matter what, we would have a child. We were in awe. On the third day of the Passover, or the Festival of Unleavened Bread, Beth queued up for lesson eight, and I prepared to give my testimony. It would be two separate recordings so that Russell could keep the flow going.

Ultimately, there are only two kinds of people: sheep and goats. Matthew 25:31–46 says, "When the Son of Man comes in His glory, and all the holy angels with Him, then He will sit on the throne of His glory. All the nations will be gathered before Him, and He will separate them one from another, as a shepherd divides *his* sheep from the goats. And He will set the sheep on His right hand, but the goats on the left. Then the King will say to those on His right hand, 'Come, you blessed of My Father, inherit the kingdom prepared for you from the foundation of the world: for I was hungry and you gave Me food; I was thirsty and you gave Me drink; I was a stranger and you took Me in; I *was* naked and you clothed Me; I was sick and you visited Me; I was in prison and you came to Me.'"

"Then the righteous will answer Him, saying, 'Lord, when did we see You hungry and feed *You,* or thirsty and give *You* drink? When did we see You a stranger and take *You* in, or naked and clothe *You?* Or when did we see You sick, or in prison, and come to You?' And the King will answer and say to them, 'Assuredly, I say to you, inasmuch as you did *it* to one of the least of these My brethren, you did *it* to Me.'

"Then He will also say to those on the left hand, 'Depart from Me, you cursed, into the everlasting fire prepared for the devil and his angels: for I was hungry and you gave Me no food; I was thirsty and you gave Me no drink; I was a stranger and you did not take Me in, naked and you did not clothe Me, sick and in prison and you did not visit Me.'

"Then they also will answer Him, saying, 'Lord, when did we see You hungry or thirsty or a stranger or naked or sick or in prison, and did not minister to You?' Then He will answer them, saying, 'Assuredly, I say to you, inasmuch as you did not do *it* to one of the least of these, you did not do *it* to Me.' And these will go away into everlasting punishment, but the righteous into eternal life."

"The Son of Man is Jesus, to whom God has given all authority for judgment. He has returned to take His place as both Judge and King on earth. The nations, both Jew and Gentile, are gathered and judged. Jesus separates the sheep from the goats—the wheat from the tares. His judgments and His words are straightforward and ominous. He knows every minute of each of our lives. He knows who has accepted Him and who has not. There is no escape and we have no excuse.

"Perhaps billions of people will be there, the sheep on His right hand, the goats on His left. It will feel as intimate as a courtroom with Jesus sitting at the bench. Nothing can be hidden. His explanation of His judgment, the criteria for His discernment pronounced in simple terms: 'How did you serve Me in My Kingdom during your life?'

"The righteous will answer in humble regard, 'Lord, when did we see you hungry or thirsty and give you a drink?' Then He will say to those on the left hand, 'Depart from me you cursed, into the everlasting fire.' It is that simple. The believers will be at once separated from the others, just as the wheat and tares. Everlasting fire or eternal life. That is the choice.

"It is also somewhat silly to elaborate on this. Jesus gave many examples throughout His ministry but the result was always the same. Some chose correctly, some chose to go their own way. There are eternal consequences that are inescapable. You don't go in a box. Even if

347

you could make a logical argument to that statement, and you do end up in a box, then you simply have nothing to lose. But denying Jesus is a very risky proposition. Jesus Himself said this: 'If you do not believe that I am the one I claim to be, you will indeed die in your sins' (John 8:24).

"You may say 'That is not fair. I lived a good life, didn't hurt anyone, gave to the needy, went to church on occasions.' All good things, but that is not the qualifier. Paul tells us in Romans 3:23 that all have sinned and fall short of the glory of God. The wages of sin is death, but God demonstrates His own love toward us in that while we were still sinners, Christ died for us (Romans 6:23, 5:8).

"We have no excuse and any excuse you thought you had just evaporated like a mist in the desert. I am telling you something you already know. The only thing that will keep you from the right hand of God is your own selfish desires. I suggest you put away such foolishness. You have already missed your first opportunity, don't miss your last. Today is the day—Jesus is the Way."

Beth closed this lesson with a list of Scripture she had assembled highlighting the separation and judgment. This was a short, hard-hitting lesson. Two choices—our choice. You have no one to blame but yourself! I was struggling with the fact that millions would choose a life sentence in the lake of fire and millions had already. Then I thought of myself, master procrastinator, stiff-necked Jew. I had put it off and put it off. Now, I had a chance to share it with the world.

Beth manned the camera and I fumbled with notes. Then, it came to me from the Holy Spirit—pray. I asked God to bless these words and to fill me with the Holy Spirit. Beth's smile gave me joy and the thought of God knitting together a child in her womb gave me a great peace.

"My name is Eliezer and I am a Jew and a Palestinian. My father met my mother in Tel Aviv, where they fell in love. Since both of their parents were dead, no one objected to their marriage and I was born two years later. It was a nurse at the hospital of my birth in Tel Aviv that informed the PLO of the situation. Two years later, my mother was dead and my father, angry and frustrated, scooped me up and brought me to America. He hired an Egyptian nanny and asked her to keep my Arab heritage intact. She taught me Arabic and my father maintained Hebrew as the household language.

"My father eventually married Marra, the nanny, and she insisted on keeping my Jewish heritage alive as well. Angry at God over the loss of my mother, we never stepped foot in a synagogue, but we did celebrate all the festivals. I was a Jew, circumcised and all. We just didn't have God in our lives. My step-mother was certainly a gift from Him. I seemed to know it. She loved my father and she loved me. She made sure I had everything a young man would need in life—outside of God.

"I met a wonderful girl in tenth grade and went to a dance with her, then we lost touch as I went on to college. I somehow knew I had missed an opportunity. But where I was headed, a woman had no place—Seal Team 10. I had always been a bit feminine and my dad encouraged me through years of bullying. He told me that men like me made great fathers—it pulled me through and gave me some additional incentive in the Academy. I pushed hard and with my tech and language skills, was a shoe-in for the team and later mission bound. Let's just say I was deep, very deep, and had plenty I needed to be forgiven for. I wouldn't wish it on anyone but it was my job.

"I had a best friend who was a born-again Christian and another who was a Messianic Jew. We were working together during the build-up of the Magog war. Since we were in Syria, the conversations were focused on how short our time was, how we were in the worst possible place to be, and how I was a lost soul.

"They took me through Scripture prophecy and showed how perfectly Jesus fit into the entire picture. God was drawing me in and I could feel it. We survived a certain-death experience. I had been through many, many near-death moments, but this was different in that only a supernatural rescue could save us. Daniel in the lion's den, the boys in the furnace, all of that and more. God rescued us, took us out of Syria, allowed me to reunite with my high-school love, and sent me back to Jerusalem for a front seat to the war. As my Messianic Jew friend tried to convert me prior to the Magog war, I found every excuse in the book. I did not feel worthy of God's love, let alone His salvation. I was confused by my Jewish roots and my stiff-necked heritage.

"Even after seeing God's miraculous protection of Israel and how accurately the events of the war matched up to prophecy, as well as watching my parents confess to Christ, I had a hard heart. I lost the girl, dead of an overdose, and became angry. Afterwards, I felt peace. Then I decided that I really did need God. I was preparing to go to the altar, sitting in the center of church when Jesus came for His own. I was left alone, my folks gone, my best friend gone. I hit my knees right there and told God how sorry I was and how I wanted Him in my life. I was saved thirty minutes too late. I was destined to be a tribulation saint, and God forgave me for all the lives I had taken, all the lives I had destroyed along the way. He restored me and made me new again. He gave me a mission, a wife, and now a child. Once this stiff-necked Jew saw Jesus in a vision and showed me all that I had, I can never thank Him enough. I am the worst of the worst and He loves me. He loves you too and He can save and restore anyone. It is His desire to do so.

"If you feel the pull of Him on your life, do not wait. Do not take the mark. Act now! Pray with me. 'Dear Father, you know every act we have ever committed. We know we need a Savior, because we are all sinners. I believe that Your Son died on the cross to pay for my redemption. I believe that Jesus is God and He rose and is alive and with You in heaven on the throne. I ask to receive the gift of grace, my undeserved salvation. I confess these things to you, precious Father. In the name of Jesus Christ, amen.'"

As soon as Beth turned off the camera, I was done. I broke down in tears and fell prostrate on the floor. What He had forgiven me for, I could hardly forgive myself for. He is such a good and loving God. Beth took me in her arms and we lay on the floor, sobbing. I kept saying, "Thank you, God…" in short whispers. An hour went by and we just lay there. It was good Friday, the day Jesus hung on the cross. He showed me visions of it, the three crosses on the hill. The sun was turned dark and the earth shook.

"Did you see that?" Beth asked.

"Yes. The crosses."

"Yes, on the hill, Jesus and the men. It was dark, like dusk."

"Yes. Amazing."

We curled up and held each other on the floor, tears running down our faces.

"Do you suppose Jesus is appearing to many?"

"It could be—those who are the elect. The harvest is winding down, soon He will be coming. The door of redemption will be open until He returns."

"Yes. We are close."

We were startled by *bing*. An email from Russell. "It's in the can. Powerful stuff. I saw a vision of the crosses, and it was moving. An amazing testimony, Eli… I know you skirted many of the ugly details. But I can imagine. It's like Tour of Duty, but real. Love you two. God bless and Happy Resurrection Day."

"God is using us to change people's lives, Eli."

"Yes. It's so humbling. Do you feel that wave of peace?"

"Yes. You know what is awesome?"

"What, sweetie?"

"We are the joy that was set before Him."

"Yes…unreal…"

We would do the last lesson, "We are Ministers of Reconciliation", tomorrow. Russell would run it over the top of the World Church Service on Resurrection Sunday. That would make Lech very happy. Although the church was just a front for idol worship and Lech's way of having poor suckers send him money, they did take it seriously. The False Prophet, a well-known and beloved figurehead of a very large church prior to the Rapture, was left behind and was the perfect fit for Satan's church. It was all very surreal.

Russell did know how to anger them, and typically interjected godly programming over ungodly programming. Slowly but surely, the battle lines were being drawn between Jesus' followers and Satan's minions. God could not have laid it out better with John's Revelation, supported by the books of Daniel and Isaiah. We kept thinking that decisions this pressing should have been made months ago, but that was not true. Thousands were still coming to Christ and, sadly, thousands were dying lost.

"Russell saw the vision of the crosses," I told Beth.

"It must be our Good Friday gift, directly from Jesus Himself—a reward for our work."

"I think you may be right..."

"He also said he is getting some heat from the GC. They've been coming around, kicking the tires."

"What do you mean?"

"Feeling things out. Like when you test drive a car, checking to see if they have air in them. It's an agent term."

"Would that mean that Russell was an agent?"

"It just hit me. That would make sense. If it's true, he will have redundancy."

"Oh gosh. What does that mean?"

"Someone trained to do his job in another place and everything duplicated, just in case. It also means he would have termination protocol."

Beth just looked at me, knowing she didn't have to ask.

"That would mean he has a way to nuke the place if they out him."

"Like blow it up?"

"Yep. Standard protocol. Leave nothing in which to trace anything or anyone."

"Oh, how awful."

"Part of the game, my love. Part of the game."

"Well, I'm glad you're retired."

"Me too."

We decided we would work on and deliver the last lesson together. It was not an evangelistic message, but one of discipleship. "Everyone who converts to The Way needs to be doing what we are doing," I said.

"Yes, dear."

We talked about how the Romans would have wanted to get the bodies off the crosses prior to sundown—the start of Sabbath. That is why they broke the criminal's legs, so they couldn't lift themselves to get another breath. It was truly a cruel way to die. Jesus, of course, died on His own terms and nary a bone was broken. That fulfilled yet another prophecy. In Psalm 34, David says, "He guards all His bones. Not one of them is broken," and in Numbers 9:12, Moses writes, "They shall leave none of it until morning, nor break one of its bones, according to the ordinances of the Passover."

"It's eerie, really. How God is foretelling His Son's death as the Lamb in the instructions for Passover," Beth said.

"Yes, and that is just a tiny example. It is astonishing. All Christians should become intimately familiar with the seven feasts of Israel."

"Spoken like a true Jew..."

"Thank you—I think," I smiled.

"So they got the bodies down and Joseph of Arimathea convinced Pilate to give it to Him. He was part of Jesus' followers who would become The Way. Even more interesting is that Nicodemus was there, the Pharisee that had come to Jesus at night. Jesus told him that he must be born again."

"It seems he took Jesus' advice."

"Yes, neither man as a pure Pharisee would have gone near a dead body. However, they were among the first true Christians and gave Him a respectful burial after the disgraceful crucifixion."

"I never thought if it that way."

"Numbered with the transgressors…

Beth just shook her head, her eyes welling up with emotion. I held her and we gave thanks to our Lord for making us His joy in such an awful time.

"The really sad part is that He died for all, not just His followers," I said.

"Thank you Jesus." Beth said.

And we went back to work. Time was short.

It had been a long and emotional day, and we headed to bed early. Just as we were shutting down, an email came in from Russell. "If the wheels fall off, my shadow will hit you up. Hope to talk tomorrow. If not, see you on the other side. His code word is Stephen's fellow. Pray for me! RB out."

"Susan was all wrong about him. She thought he was a stoner, a gamer, a hack. This man is an agent, and a darn good one at that. Let's pray for him." We prayed, and Beth thought we should reply.

"No good—out means out. No further contact. He is a smart man. Very smart."

"If he makes it through the weekend, we should invite him to come here."

"That's not a bad plan. He could do it all from here. Plus, it would cause the GC to start at point A to find him again.

Then we prayed and prayed.

chapter
TWENTY-SEVEN
✡✡✡✡✡✡

I got up early and checked our email. I ran back to tell Beth that Russell was still alive and still in business. "Close call but good to go…" was his message. This inspired us to get our coffee out of the way and get to the lesson. Many people go through life with no clear idea what their purpose in this life is. We wanted to clear that up. We also wanted people to know that even Paul the apostle hated and persecuted Christians before his conversion. Perhaps it could soften some of the GC who seemed hell-bent on ridding the world of us.

"We begin today with a question. What is the purpose in this life? In the present time, we seem to be focused on survival. But for what? Do you really know if the future is bleak? We are living in a world with two certainties. First, Satan is the dark angel who claims to be God, but is not. His goal is to steal, kill, and destroy. He's doing a pretty good job of that. With Lech Manevetski, who is Satan, in case you aren't aware, your future is hell on earth. Survive but prepare to die. Then, eternal torment.

"The second certainty is Jesus. All of His promises in the Bible have come to fruition. Care to wager on His return? It's a life and death bet. In the Revelation of Christ, John the apostle writes: "And I heard, as it were, the voice of a great multitude, as the sound of many waters and as the sound of mighty thunderings, saying, 'Alleluia! For the Lord

God Omnipotent reigns! Let us be glad and rejoice and give Him glory, for the marriage of the Lamb has come, and His wife has made herself ready.' And to her it was granted to be arrayed in fine linen, clean and bright, for the fine linen is the righteous acts of the saints.

"Then he said to me, 'Write: 'Blessed *are* those who are called to the marriage supper of the Lamb!'" And he said to me, 'These are the true sayings of God.' And I fell at his feet to worship him. But he said to me, 'See *that you do* not *do that!* I am your fellow servant, and of your brethren who have the testimony of Jesus. Worship God! For the testimony of Jesus is the spirit of prophecy.'

"Now I saw heaven opened, and behold, a white horse. And He who sat on him *was* called Faithful and True, and in righteousness He judges and makes war. His eyes *were* like a flame of fire, and on His head *were* many crowns. He had a name written that no one knew except Himself. He *was* clothed with a robe dipped in blood, and His name is called The Word of God. And the armies in heaven, clothed in fine linen, white and clean, followed Him on white horses. Now out of His mouth goes a sharp sword, that with it He should strike the nations. And He Himself will rule them with a rod of iron. He Himself treads the winepress of the fierceness and wrath of Almighty God. And He has on *His* robe and on His thigh a name written: KING OF KINGS AND LORD OF LORDS.

"Then I saw an angel standing in the sun; and he cried with a loud voice, saying to all the birds that fly in the midst of heaven, 'Come and gather together for the supper of the great God, that you may eat the flesh of kings, the flesh of captains, the flesh of mighty men, the flesh of horses and of those who sit on them, and the flesh of all *people,* free and slave, both small and great.'

"And I saw the beast, the kings of the earth, and their armies, gathered together to make war against Him who sat on the horse and against His army. Then the beast was captured, and with him the false prophet who worked signs in his presence, by which he deceived those who received the mark of the beast and those who worshiped his image. These two were cast alive into the lake of fire burning with brimstone. And the rest were killed with the sword which proceeded from the mouth of Him who sat on the horse. And all the birds were filled with their flesh."

"The people in heaven are those raptured and those resurrected from the dead. They will attend and be the Bride of Christ at the marriage supper of the lamb. Oh, how we would all love to be there for that... Then He returns with His Bride to do battle with Satan and his armies. There will be another feast—the Supper of the Great God. This supper is for the birds, who will eat the dead bodies of Satan's army. The beast and his False Prophet will be captured and cast alive into the lake of fire. All the rest are killed. This is Armageddon.

"If you follow Satan, you have no chance. Your purpose then is singular—death. You can read it for yourself in Revelation 20, but I'll sum it up by quoting verse 15: 'And anyone not found written in the Book of Life was cast into the lake of fire.' You won't die there, you will live in torment forever. This is the second death!

"Jesus followers, that is anyone who confesses faith in Jesus, will have eternal life in heaven. But what about now, our life as Christ-followers here on earth and living, perhaps until His return? We have a very specific purpose. Paul the apostle describes it in detail in his letter to the church at Corinth. He says, 'Therefore, if anyone *is* in Christ, *he is* a new creation; old things have passed away; behold, all things have become new. Now all things *are* of God, who has reconciled us to Himself through Jesus Christ, and has given us the ministry of reconciliation, that is, that God was in Christ reconciling the world to Himself, not imputing their trespasses to them, and has committed to us the word of reconciliation.

'Now then, we are ambassadors for Christ, as though God were pleading through us: we implore *you* on Christ's behalf, be reconciled to God.'

"Now Paul was a persecutor of Christians in the first century, a Pharisee and a Jewish zealot. He felt he was fighting a heresy against Judaism. On his way to Damascus to arrest Jesus-followers, Paul was struck down by a great light: 'Saul, Saul, why are you persecuting Me?' Jesus' words cut like a knife.

'Who are You, Lord?' Paul, then called Saul, asked.

'I am Jesus, whom you are persecuting.' Then Jesus instructed him to go to Damascus and learn what he must do. Blinded and convicted by his recent actions, Paul is broken before becoming the greatest evangelist of all time.

"Now Paul tells us what our purpose is: ministers of reconciliation. That purpose is highlighted in Jesus' final words to His apostles: 'All authority has been given to Me in heaven and on earth. Go therefore and make disciples of all the nations, baptizing them in the name of the Father and of the Son and of the Holy Spirit, teaching them to observe all things that I have commanded you; and lo, I am with you always, *even* to the end of the age. Amen.'

"Our purpose is to share the good news with every living, breathing human being. God gifts us through the Holy Spirit with purposeful abilities and talents to accomplish this. The time is short. Pray with us, 'Heavenly Father, You have known me from before time, before I was knit together in my mother's womb. You tell me that my name is written on the palms of Your hands. You know my life, my experiences, my personality, my skills, my sins, my bad habits. You love me unconditionally, because and despite these things. You desire that I be reconciled to You into a loving relationship. Your Son's death on the cross paid the price of my redemption.

"'Father, I confess with my mouth the Lord Jesus and believe in my heart that you raised Him from the dead. I receive my free gift of salvation and anticipate the filling of the Holy Spirit. Make me a minister of reconciliation and equip me to reach the lost souls in the world. Protect me from the evil one and prepare me for my meeting with your Son very soon. I am prepared to give my life to the great commission— to make disciples of all I encounter. In Jesus' name I pray. Amen.'

"God answers prayer. Whether you prayed for salvation or you asked for a way to reach lost souls, He is busy orchestrating. Jesus told us, 'Seek ye first the kingdom of God and His righteousness and all these things will be added to you. Therefore, do not worry about tomorrow, for tomorrow will worry about its own things. Sufficient for the day is its own trouble.'

"'Ask and it will be given to you, seek and you will find, knock and it will be opened to you. For everyone who asks receives, and he who seeks finds, and to him who knocks it will be opened.' Let's ask, let's seek, let's knock. Our friend and Lord, Jesus Christ, is waiting with open arms. 'The harvest is plentiful; the laborers are few.' Today is the day—Jesus is the Way. God bless you!"

I sent off the file along with a message. "Glad you are still with us. Loved that you saw the vision of the crosses. I believe it was a special reward for those who persevere to the end. If things get too hot there, you can come here. We're equipped and have room. Happy Resurrection Day my fellow brother in Christ."

The response came quickly. "Still hot, but we have fellows here. I'll have the videos up tomorrow. Happy Resurrection Day to you. RB."

"What's with the 'fellow' thing?" Beth asked.

"Fellow workers—agents. I would love to meet them. I'll bet they are kicking Lech's butt day and night."

"What do you mean?"

"Disruption of communications, hacking of his files, planting viruses, denial of access, gathering intel and being a thorn in their side. He probably knows they are close because they are intercepting his calls, emails, sat transmissions. If they find him, they will want him gone."

"What do you make of this Stephen's fellow character?"

"We'll wait and see. I hope we don't have to find out. If we do, it means Russell and his team are dead. Or they may show up here or out west. Who knows. Sounds like they want to stick it out as long as possible."

"We better pray again for them…"

"Yes."

We woke up Sunday morning feeling resurrected. It had been two thousand years since Jesus left the tomb and we still felt His newness of life on Resurrection Sunday. Of course, He tells us that we were resurrected right along with Him. It was an amazing spring day at the lake and the coffee and Italian sweet cream were exceptional.

"Do you suppose our child would like to do an Easter egg hunt?"

"Funny you would ask. It is a pagan practice, but we did it in Egypt when I was a little girl."

"Wait, you were a little girl?"

"A few years ago, but it seems like yesterday."

I smiled and we clinked cups. "Coffee's good…"

"Yes, and the company. It's been nice to meet you, Eli Grollenberg."

"It's very nice to meet you, sweetheart. I can't believe you are pregnant. My father would be jumping for joy."

"Is jumping for joy… I'm sure he knows by now."

"Yes. Marra and your family too. Today is first fruits."

"What is that?"

"Another Jewish holiday. It is the Sunday that falls within Passover. Jesus was raised on first fruits. It represents the completion of the harvest. A perfect time for announcing a new son or daughter."

"Sounds like a good reason to celebrate. Maybe we can go out on the boat?"

"We'll see. For now, how about some more of this delicious coffee…"

Beth's eyes were welling up as I returned with the coffee.

"I will never leave you or forsake you, Beth."

"I know, silly. I just feel such peace amidst all the chaos. And it will get worse, much worse…"

"One step at a time, darling. I'm still swimming from the whole 'with child' thing."

"I know. It's just…they'll likely never see this world. I guess that is best. I wonder how it will be—you know, in the kingdom."

"We'll just have to trust. He is trustworthy."

"I know. And so are you. We just need to stay together…to the end."

"Yes, of course." We drank, smiled, thanked God, and took in the beautiful day. We stayed outside until noon and basked in the sun, the sun that God made and ordered to praise Him. We were praising Him right along, knowing days like this were not long for this world.

The days passed and we did a few more lessons. Russell had to be infuriating Lech with the videos and interrupting lots of Lech's programming. Russell sent me a message one day and said I was the topic of discussion around Lech's dinner table.

"Apparently, you and Sulaman know each other, because you really ticked him off with the testimony and lesson. He has put a 'find Stone at all costs' notice out. He's gunning for you, my friend. Just a heads up. Hey, you weren't a part of that Tehran incident, were you? It's legendary!"

My reply was short. "This guy is serious. Let us know if he gets close." I was more concerned than he was. I knew he had taken a few shots at my friend John after the incident. I was really surprised he was still alive. Of course, he was known as the most ruthless person on earth, right up there with Hitler and Stalin—at least, until Lech came along.

"Everything okay?" Beth asked.

"Yes, for now. We just need to be prepared for anything. I'll get the place buttoned up around here." I turned and hugged my girl. "Time is short…"

Late that night we got a message from Russell. "We're at Defcon1 here. GC crawling all around us. Love you, brother. Hug Beth. God bless. RB out." That was it. We had to pray and know that they were in God's hands.

TWENTY-EIGHT

✡✡✡✡✡✡✡

W e stayed close to the satellite and saw nothing about a raid of any kind. Of course, Lech's news was vigorously censored. No news from Russell either. Beth and I prayed. One bit of good news was the interruption of programming by our lessons and sermons out of The Way in The Dalles, as well as the general annoyance of Lech when he spoke of the underground.

Two days later we got an email from Stephen's fellow. We knew it was over for our friend. "I'm Nicolas from out west. RB is done, took ninety-two GC with him. Sulaman was leading, but got out somehow. You are in his sights. We are continuing from here. The heat is on—be alert. TB and BC send regards."

"Oh no! Russell?"

"Yes. It's over for him. Sulaman came for him. I hope I didn't lead him there."

"No, they were close all along. Who's the contact?"

"Nicolas from out west. He's at The Dalles."

"How do you know?"

"TB and BC send regards. That's T-Bone and Bradley Carter. And the broadcasts continue as does the intel. He's coming, Beth. It's only a matter of time. If I'm right, they will get nothing from Russell's place. They know how to purge. Plus, the only link is the video with us in it.

No way to trace our feeds. They bounce all over the world, off of three satellites, and are carried in on a laser signal from that mountain over there. No way."

"Well, that's good news."

"That doesn't mean they can't find us. We need to be alert." I ran one more cycle with DAVEO. All the cameras were up and working, all the guns loaded, the fence was on, the tunnel sealed. We moved everything downstairs and made everything look like we had been gone for months. No more deck days, no more sunsets—at least for a while. If it came down to it, we could seal ourselves in by closing a hatch in the elevator shaft. Water tight and air tight at eighty-five feet deep, with power coming from six sources, we could hold out for some time. Only a sizable bunker buster could reach us. Then it would be lights out…

We had the whole bank of monitors on the grid. The fortified gate was closed and the fence of five thousand volts turned on. It would take a team of men a week just to find the power source. I had built this house for a circumstance like this. Many would want a man like me dead, and even more would be willing to pay to take me out. Welcome to my life…

We got news from Nicolas on the raid at Russell's. I knew the names of most of the nine agents working there. Among them was Geoff Hess, the advance team leader in Tehran.

"There is the connection," I told Beth. "They found Geoff. He was part of our Tehran team. This is a huge loss to the underground."

Nicolas also told us that things were humming out west. Lower profile, but still humming. They still had their intel links and the ability to override the satellite transmissions. He would continue airing the lessons and The Way sermons.

"Send more if you can. People love them. You know, over seven hundred thousand have checked in so far. Saved by the broadcasts and the visions of Jesus. God is so good!"

Two weeks went by, and we made a half dozen more videos and saw them air. Nicolas sent us a message: "Ron says he is coming to get you. We have supplies for you and your pursuer is in Italy for the next two weeks. TB and BC need to see you. Meet Ron at 0900 tomorrow."

I had to admit, we were ready to get out and we needed supplies badly. Plus, Beth could use a doctor's visit, and there were some good ones in Oregon. She was thrilled. We checked the cameras and radar, found it all clear and took the boat to Kings. In half an hour, we were on board with Ron and our new contact, Nicolas.

Nicolas Sorenson was a young guy in his thirties, built like a linebacker. A former ICE turned Homeland Security guy, he had been an intel guy for US/ISIS communications. He nearly bought the farm during the civil war when the border was flooded around Nogales, Texas. Then, he had close calls on two of the terrorist attacks, one in Dallas, one in New Orleans.

"But what nearly took me down was the Rapture. I was on a small plane over Phoenix and the pilot disappeared. I had little experience at the sticks, but landed it somehow. My family was gone and I was alone. My only play was the agency, and they took me in."

We could see the burden of being left behind in his soul. His green eyes filled with tears. He apologized and swore that he had never been an emotional person until he was saved.

"And how did that come about?" Beth asked.

"I wandered around Phoenix for a few days, not seeing anyone I knew. I stumbled into a church full of people singing and praising

God. It was a Thursday! I had never been to church, and certainly not on a Thursday. I was drawn in and my heart just gave up. I fell to my knees and several laid hands on me and prayed. A man encouraged me to go to the altar and give up what I was carrying. It was a heavy weight, and when I confessed to Jesus, it came off of me."

"Guess what the name of the church was," Ron called from the cockpit. We both looked at Nicolas.

"The Way. Just like at Joseph's. It's like it swallowed me up," he said with tears.

Ron was laughing. "Today is the day—Jesus is the Way!" We all laughed.

"Now I go four times a week. Pastor Craig is awesome…"

"I'll second that…" Ron added. "You'll find out Saturday. Everything stops for church."

"Good, we haven't been in weeks," Beth said.

"So, guys, how is the co-op doing?" I asked.

"Still moving a lot of stuff. GC keeps a tight leash on us, but we're still getting it done. Everything gets packed at night and our first flights in are co-op. So far, so good," Ron answered.

"Time is short though. The rock is on the way. We are going to evacuate the entire place, button down the hatches, and see how it holds up. The wave will be huge, they say," Nicolas added.

"The wave?" Beth asked.

"When the asteroid hits just north of Hawaii, they predict it will make a wave hundreds of feet high, moving fast."

"Wow. And how high is the facility?" she asked.

"About two hundred feet above sea level. We are right in its path. At least we know when it's coming."

"Very soon!" Ron added.

We flew fast and low over the last of the Rockies, then dropped in over Idaho. "Spudville!" I commented. We all laughed.

"Don't laugh, we bring in about a million tons of potatoes from Idaho. Lots of Mormon farmers there. They were all left behind," said Ron. "They grow an awesome spud… Many have converted by now, thanks to the videos."

Ron had the tower at Joseph's on the line. "What have you got?" he asked.

"All clear. Come right down the river. Stay low."

"Lots of drones out," Nicolas said. "Trolling for us. But we can jam them, thanks to our boy Russell."

Then it was quiet. We had all lost a lot in the past years: family, friends, co-workers. It was all a part of living in the time of Jacob's trouble. The worst was still on its way. But it was good to get out, and we still needed to see a doctor. We all felt a little exposed out here. However, it was quite scenic flying into the sun late in the day, having the river as our guide.

We flew by Joseph's on our left and made a huge circle, landing back toward the east. Then we disappeared into the hanger and were taken to our quarters. I was surprised when we came up in the huge Victorian house near the river.

"They decided you needed the executive quarters. Joseph built this house and lived in it for a few years. Then Sparks and his wife lived here until the Rapture," Ron said.

"They lived here? How weird is this…" I said to Beth. "It's amazing, Ron. Thank you."

The evening is yours. You can call for food or cook. The kitchen has been stocked for you. There is a honeymoon suite, top floor, facing west. If you hurry, you can catch the sunset. See you at 1000 hours, sir, miss."

"Thank you guys."

Then they were gone. We headed upstairs and walked out on a picture-perfect Oregon evening. There was nothing but river looking west, and the sun was just touching down. I held Beth's hand and we stood in awe. The river was about a half-mile wide here and headed straight west into the sun.

"Watch for the flash," I told Beth. The huge red orb eased downward, reflecting off the water and turning the sky a brilliant orange. It moved slowly into the river, and then—the flash.

"Sparks wrote in the books about the flash. It was always a special moment of oneness with God. I felt it. Did you?"

"Oh, yes. It was breathtaking. I wonder how many times they stood here and saw what we just saw?" Beth said.

We stood in awe as the sky did its God-praising dance of clouds and light.

"I would like to know more about this man whom you will entrust your story to."

"So would I. Carter knew him, and worked with him. We'll ask."

"Suddenly, I'm hungry. Let's see what they have for us." We went downstairs and opened the fridge.

"Italian Sweet Cream—yes! Look at this. We couldn't have stocked it better ourselves. Even some pickles!" I said.

"Good. Let me have a pickle and a bath. Did you see the tub up there?" Beth asked.

"Yes. I'll cook while you relax and get rid of some jet-lag. Look, some fresh-caught striped bass…"

"That sounds delightful," Beth said with a smile.

I got busy and spoiled my girl. We had a great night and slept with the windows open, a breeze blowing in from the river. It was heaven-sent. The coffee and sunrise on the other side of the house were equally impressive. We could see dozens of planes coming and going. What a vision Joseph had had. Thousands were being fed and supplied.

We got an email with our schedule at nine forty-five. Ten o'clock breakfast and eleven-thirty doctor's appointment. We checked out the rest of the house and could not believe it.

"They must have been living their dream. A beautiful home and view, plus the business is only a stone's throw away. Incredible!"

"It is amazing," Beth said as she snuggled under my arm in the morning sun.

Just to the south of us was an underground city of six thousand people. They worked, shopped, went out to dinner, to school, and even to church. I couldn't wait to see it again and go to church at the original The Way, Beth was a little nervous about the doctor's appointment.

"I am pretty old, you know."

"No, I don't know. Last night was like a honeymoon for me."

"Me too."

We met Bradley and Tom at the bottom of the elevator. We hopped into the golf cart and were at the complex in no time. Over breakfast, we discussed the place, the mission it served, and the owners who were now in heaven.

"The house is fantastic, guys… We can't thank you enough. Five stars all the way…"

"And the sunset…wow!" Beth added.

"We thought you would enjoy the wide-open space after being in that bunker for so long," Bradley said.

"Well, we would love to stay here, but I hear the surf's up."

"Yes. We *will* all evacuate. Sparks had a plan already designed for just such an unforeseen event." Tom adds.

"Amazing! His vision was twenty-twenty! What was he like?" I asked.

"He was seventy-two when he came here. He found a girl in Portland and they fell in love. Her name was Abby. He drove down here one day and saw this place. It was up for auction and he bought it. He had money from his books. Where we are right now was empty, a quarry that Joseph had filled with this huge structure. Sparks finished it and built the housing on top, the church, the shopping, the hospital. You'll see it," Tom said.

"This place was hopping back then. Sparks created the Project 180 emergency response team, which is still out there feeding hungry souls and evangelizing. Lech has tried to shut it down, but it is super-naturally protected," Bradley added. "He was an amazing, energetic man. There is something you have in common. He and his wife got pregnant with twins right before the Rapture. The doctor that gave Abby her news is the same one you will see today."

"Oh my goodness. Are you serious?" Beth asked.

"Oh yes. He is excited to meet you…" Tom said.

"How does he know us?" I asked.

"He doesn't. But he's heard about you. Ron tells everyone about you. Plus, you two are celebrities now…" Bradley said. We let that soak in over coffee.

"This place is amazing. You would never know we are…how many feet down are we, Bradley?"

"Five hundred feet here in the restaurant. The church is seven hundred feet, but still a light unto the world…" he boasted.

"Wow!" was all Beth could say.

People were bustling here and there, some with small children. This had both Beth's and my attention.

"Kids. We haven't seen kids for a while…" Beth said.

"Born since the Rapture. God took them all home," Bradley said.

"They look so happy," I said.

"Most haven't seen above. It's just too dangerous. We have GC working here on the surface, you know." Tom added.

"Amazing."

We met Gerald Rosner, MD, in the clinic on level 4. He greeted us warmly and hugged Beth, ushering us into his office.

"Nice to meet you, finally… Ron speaks highly of you. He is my pilot as well. I grew up in Roanoke and know Smith Mountain Lake well. I hear you have quite a place there."

"Thank you, Dr. Rosner. We would invite you, but…"

"Yes, time is short."

We chit-chatted as he examined Beth. "You are in amazing physical condition, young lady!"

"Hardly young… But thank you."

Based on all the factors, he estimated that Beth was eleven weeks along and doing just fine. "Would you like to do a static scan?" he asked.

Beth and I looked at each other. Did we want to know the sex of the baby? She shook her head. "No, doctor. We want to be surprised…"

"Okay. We're done then…except for two things. He left the room and returned with two boxes. "These are for you. The blue box you may open on the plane going back. The white box may only be opened after you reach home and are safely tucked away in the basement."

"How do you know…"

"Just trust me," he interrupted. "I am a very discerning man!" Remember, blue—plane. White—home. Don't mix them up, please. You will know why when you open them. Your trip here is not by accident," he smiled reassuringly, "and congratulations."

"Thank you, Doctor." we both said in unison.

Bradley was waiting for us. "Tom had to attend to some business. How did things go?"

"Perfect," Beth said.

"Would you like to have lunch now, or rest? We will have dinner as a group tonight here at the restaurant."

"Okay. We'll go for the rest," I said.

Soon, we were back at the house enjoying the views up and down the river and a perfect day. We napped and I rubbed Beth's baby bump.

"I am a little curious," I said.

"Yeah, me too. But it's best to see her in heaven," she smiled.

"Her?"

"I don't know, but I have a feeling."

I held her tight and told her how much I loved her. It felt like a lull before the storm. The inhabitants were stocking up on the co-op side with orders flying out all night. The above ground warehouses were being depleted. The wave was coming.

Dinner was fantastic and we discussed the logistics of the next few months. I told them we had room for a few. But Sparks had prepared everything. He constructed a huge hotel in the mountains north of the store. They would be safe there and close by to return, if that was God's will. The entire underground was water tight when sealed up. There was still the question of the damage and if the wave could reach them this far inland. It was in God's hands. The hope was that the wave would only do surface damage and the GC would abandon it. Lech may have been close and perhaps on to them, but with the rock coming and all the work that the store had done for the GC they didn't feel there was much danger. So we headed out with a load of supplies and the two boxes.

Beth and Ron encouraged me as I opened the box. It was a book: *Forever Young* by Reginald Kensington Sparks. I was in awe.

"Have you read it?" Ron asked.

"I didn't know he wrote beyond the trilogy."

"I think you will like it."

On the cover was an illustration of the house, their house with the river running alongside.

"It's the house..." Beth said.

Ron flew while Beth and I read about this man leaving Georgia at age seventy-two and moving to Portland. He met Abby and found Joseph's. It was all too surreal. We took a break while Beth used the bathroom.

"He wrote the *Faith* trilogy and *Forever Young* in prison, fifteen years before he moved to Oregon," Ron said.

"In prison? But the house on the cover. It's identical to…" I shook my head as I realized that what he had written before he was released perfectly matched his life after his release.

Beth came out. "Did you say he wrote this while he was in prison?"

"Yes. Fifteen years prior to his release. He was a visionary. Wait until you get into it a ways. He saw it, and it became a reality."

"Whoa! But the house looks just like the real house…" Beth said. "Fifteen years?"

"Yep. Fifteen years."

With that bit of information, every page was a revelation. "Talk about calling your shot…" I said.

"You haven't seen anything yet…" Ron said. We could not put the book down, and we had a hundred and seventy pages down by the time we made it back to Virginia. Ron scanned the skies, set down, and helped us offload the stuff. We were sent on our way with hugs and well wishes. The trip home was uneventful, and all was intact. We unloaded and dove back into the book.

Not only did the book match up closely with reality, it was filled with Christian teachings and some Jewish ones as well. At one point, Sparks told the story of how the baby growing in the womb followed the timeline of the seven feasts. Beth and I were fascinated with this amazing revelation. We even looked at how eleven weeks along matched up to the feasts. We were blown away. The book ended with Abby's pregnancy, which was in itself a miracle, and then the Rapture. They were gone, along with his entire family, including the twins she was carrying. The descriptions of the underground, the Project 180 emergency response team, the food operation—it was uncanny. Beth and I agreed that God had picked the best person to send the files to. We were very excited about the baby too!

It wasn't until morning that we went down into the control room. There had been visitors. Someone had pushed the button on the gate intercom. I went back to pick it up on the hard drive. There in the camera was the ugly mug of Qussam Sulaman.

"Mr. Stone, we have a package for you, but your barriers to delivery are, well…robust. So I'll be back…"

I didn't bother telling Beth. It wouldn't matter at this point. I did button up a bit and asked DAVEO to go to Defcon 1.

We had coffee and discussed the book. It was all too surreal. "What do you suppose is in the other box?" Beth asked.

"I decided I would pray about opening it. I think I know, but I don't want to know."

Instead, we got the Bible out and began to read in Revelation. It was clear that everything was tracking along as the prophecies foretold. Of course, the details that happen in real life were left out. "Selective," I thought. Is this how I needed to be? We slept and had coffee in the morning.

We needed to go over my notes, journals, and memoirs selectively. I needed to be very careful, check it over one more time, and be ready to upload it on a moment's notice. Beth agreed and we went to work. The words were alive in my mind, "events to come", "selective", "the man who moves you." Now, he had moved me even more. I knew it had to get to him. It was God's supernatural plan.

We were all focused on the big rock and the events of the first trumpet—blood, hail, and fire. The rock was due in eleven days. The scientists had named it "Wormwood". It was all very terrifying to think about, but all I could think about was Sulaman's ugly face.

I looked outside and a storm was brewing. I told Beth we should go downstairs and she agreed. It was an ominous feeling. Then, we heard it in the distance. A trumpet. It filled all space and was everywhere. Then the rain, the hail, and bolts of lightning. Then came the fire, like balls of molten lava coming down in golf-ball sized globs.

All that was left to do was pray. Virginia being a humid state this time of year, we only had some spot fires for DAVEO to extinguish. We never saw blood, but we saw it on the satellite. The west was burning, Mexico was burning, Central and South America were burning. Oddly, Europe, Australia, and Asia were mostly spared, as was Canada. As the reports poured in, the devastation was clear. Now we would wait for the rock.

As with all the seals, the trumpets were holding to Bible descriptions. The next two could be the knock-out punch. We decided to finish up the notes and journals and be prepared to upload the file to Sparks. If we could get the events of the second trumpet in, we would. Otherwise, it would end here. It was certainly enough for Ken Sparks to go on. Our biggest challenge was not giving him too much. We were very careful about dates and times. "Selective," the vision said. Also, we knew Sparks would be discerning on this once he figured out what he had. I was thinking that I would have liked to meet him and Abby.

We had done everything we could think to do. It did occur to us to try to get some last-ditch converts. Time was running out. We had eight days and counting. Beth and I set up one last news cast to alert the world to the ominous rock's approach. Beth would encourage the world that it was time to accept Jesus. It was a loving, yet desperate, attempt at what could very well be the last evangelistic video. I thought it was awesome that Nicolas chose to run it right over Cardinal Victor II's Sunday service.

"Today is the day—Jesus is the Way," Beth concluded. "Hope to see you in heaven... Don't hesitate. It is time..." Suddenly, we had activity at the fences. Six GC, two by two in three locations. We watched as the DAVEO system sent out the warnings, fired the warning shots, and saw them head to the exits. These measures worked well on local thugs, but Sulaman wanted me and there would be no stopping him. I told Beth, "Looks like we have some serious company. Let's pray."

Several quiet hours went by. I ventured out to reload the stations. We may well be in for a fight. If GC knew we were here, it would only be a matter of time before they came in numbers, especially now that they had seen my defenses.

"It may be our last night in human bodies, let's take advantage of it..." Beth said. I smiled.

We loaded the recent entries and set up the upload timer. If the timer kicked in or the power went out, or I hit send, all of my files, memoirs, journal entries, and lessons would upload to the ProtoCloud. I had no idea how it would get to Sparks or when. But that was in God's hands now. I called Ron. He had gotten his family out of Florida, but it was hot there. Maybe Greenbriar would take him. I thanked him and told him we would see him on the other side.

chapter
TWENTY-NINE
✡✡✡✡✡✡

You are seeing these additions because several days have gone by. On the past nights, drones have flown over to check us out. I was sure they were using infrared to try and see how many we had here. They would learn nothing. In fact, the place looked abandoned. The rock was two days out. Cameras had been set up in Hawaii and along the west coast to try and capture the event.

Beth and I were lying low, praying for many to come to faith in Jesus. The reports were that it was working. We were almost convinced that the GC had given up on the lake house. There was no sign of them after the last drone pass. We re-watched Beth's last video on the coming rock and let Nicolas know to run it one more time.

"Will do... Hold onto your hats down there," he said. "See you on the other side..."

"God bless you, Nicolas. You have been a life saver."

"God provides the increase..." he added.

"Amen!" we said in unison.

We watched the feed from Cheyenne Mountain tracking the rock. With two hours to go, Lech Manevetski chose to run a Friday the thirteenth marathon on the GC station. He had no interest in telling his unfortunate followers of the impending disaster. In fact, his propaganda machine was working to call the underground reports "Bible nonsense."

The "Bible nonsense" hit the Pacific Ocean just as predicted. The wall of water headed for the Pacific coast of the US was a thousand feet high, traveling at fourteen hundred miles per hour. In two hours, it would be over for most of the western states. The hatches at Joseph's were battened down and everyone was gone. At two hundred feet above sea level, it didn't stand a chance. We felt the earth shake minutes after the rock hit the ocean.

With fifteen minutes to go, the entire Pacific shelf was dry. The water was being sucked back into the oncoming wave. The sun was coming up and the gleam of the sun off the blood-red wave spectacu- lar. The drone shots were amazing. All of our underground command watched the wave hit. It was terrifying. Like models, cities were obliter- ated. The earth shook with the force of impact on the west coast.

Our view from a camera near Crescent City, California, showed the huge wave in bright red. The sea had turned to blood and hit the coast with such force that it wiped the states clean right up to the Sierra Nevada Mountains. California, Oregon, Washington, British Columbia, Alaska—devastated. The Hawaiian Islands were obliter- ated, as was Japan, the Philippines, and western Canada. Alaska had blood a hundred feet deep all the way to Anchorage.

Nothing on the coastline was spared, and the tremors on the earth continued for hours. Beth and I were fascinated, but something dis- tracted us. The monitors showed uniformed GC, hundreds of them, outside the fence. This time they were serious, very serious. They had portable bridges to get over the fence and shoulder-fired rocket launchers. We knew this could very well be the end. They may not be able to get to us down here, but they could wipe the house out.

We decided to write this final entry into my journal and describe the onslaught, then upload it to the cloud. Eventually, the auto-cannons and trip-grenades would run out. They would eventually get into the house and find the elevator. I had already anticipated the siege and the tactical strategy, planning well for it. There was simply no way to reach us without a lot of effort.

I told Beth it was likely they would not stop, thinking there must be something very valuable here. I calculated that they would try, give up, and order an air strike. Bunker busters could end our run. We prayed it wouldn't come to that. We watched the first assault on the house with the DAVEO system at Defcon 1. Not one bullet would be wasted and, unlike in scare mode, DAVEO would take perhaps a hundred or so out just in the yard.

The object, of course, was to protect us and deter the attackers. A loss of that many should do that, but it was late in the game. I wondered how serious they would be. With one monitor on the prophesied events and a half-dozen on the property, we sat back and anxiously awaited our fate. As instructed by DAVEO's unique program, he allowed nearly all of the troops to cross over the fence before he began firing. Beth and I prayed. It was truly ugly. Most had no chance. DAVEO blew up the two bridges they brought, cutting off their escape. Then he began selecting and targeting one at a time in each sector. He was conserving ammunition, just as designed. They fired rockets at the gun posts and DAVEO sent grenades back at them.

The man who invented the DAVEO system was a Seal Team 10 member, an expert in counter-measures and guerilla tactics. Right now, it was outthinking its enemy. The GC were dying by the dozens and it wasn't pretty. They had nowhere to go. Sure, DAVEO did not have unlimited ammo, but he was a great shot. Their laser-guided grenade launchers were also having their effect. They began firing rockets at the house and that seemed to inspire them. But soon they were all dead.

I could not risk going out and reloading. Honestly, we both felt it had gone on long enough. We would fight until the end, leaving behind all the information to warn the next generation behind us. We had done our part. All was quiet on the property for now. They would not be done. In an hour, they were setting up 200mm cannons on elevated platforms from outside the fence. It was clear that they were serious.

We quickly finished the last entry and Beth was about to hit upload when the secure line came in from Cheyenne Mountain. It was Bradley Carter. "Eli, I am glad you mentioned Sparks to me. I have a book here that you may be interested in. It was written several years ago and mentions someone who sounds a lot like you. I just received it, but I thought you should know."

"What's the name of the book, Bradley?"

"The Armies of Gog. A best seller. I never knew…"

"Thank you, Bradley. You all safe?""

"Yep. Cameras show the underground is dry. We may be able to go back."

"We are under attack here and it looks bleak. Sulaman, I'm afraid."

"He'll get his…"

"Yes, indeed… See you, buddy. God bless."

I ran to get the white box. Beth and I cut the tape and opened the box. *The Armies of Gog.*

"Amazing. He actually wrote it. Bradley says it's a best seller...or was. I wonder why I never knew about it. It's been out there. I would have benefitted greatly to have read it myself."

"Just curious, what is the copyright date on *The Armies of Gog?*"

"2019."

"And *Forever Young?*"

"Two years prior."

"Amazing. So it is likely I had no influence on his writing. Go ahead and hit send..."

We close with this: Thank you, Mr. Sparks. God bless you. Eli and Beth...out!

EPILOGUE
✡ ✡ ✡ ✡ ✡ ✡ ✡

How humbling for me to be chosen to tell this story. I have always been fascinated by God's prophecies and His love for His creation. Many of us read the words, and perhaps we are even so brave as to marinate in them, but they feel distant and obscure. As Steph told Eli, it is much easier to read the passages than to experience them first hand.

Soon, the harsh reality of the end times will be upon us. Even now, it is manifesting into our daily reality. The statistics of war, earthquakes, famines, pestilence, and even false Christs show a steady increase in numbers and intensity. Birth pangs. "Lawlessness will abound and the love of many will grow cold," says Jesus.

People are not the problem. God sees the qualities He has gifted to each. It is the sin nature, the free will, our pride and evil desires. The word is Sa'tan: an adversary, opposing spirit. What the world will be, and virtually is now, is the antithesis of what God intended for us in the Garden of Eden. That is why He had to judge and destroy Sodom and Gomorrah, Nineveh, Tyre, and Sidon.

In all of this, I discern that you should not delay. Do your homework. Study, read, investigate, question, and find a good Bible-believing, Bible-teaching, Jesus-following church. As the writer Blaise Pascal once said, "If you are right in believing, you will die, go in a box, and it is over, you have nothing to lose by giving your life to Christ.

But if I am right and you will suffer eternal torment in hell if you do not give your life to Christ, then you have much to lose."

If you ignore the signs and continue as is, you have no one to blame. You are without excuse! Choose wisely.

Your friend,
R. K. Sparks

One last thought—if you are alone and are about to die, just drop to your knees and say, "Save me!" He will make a way, because He is the Way!

BIBLIOGRAPHY

✡✡✡✡✡✡✡

Chapter 6

Head, David. *Jerusalem Rising: Countdown to Armageddon*. Vine-Dresser
    Publishing, 2018, pp. 7, 8.

Chapter 7

Meier, Paul. *The Third Millennium*. Thomas Nelson Publishers, 1993,
    pp. 304–305.

Jeffery, Grant. *Armageddon, Appointment with Destiny*. Bantam Books,
    1990. pp. 40, 41.

Why I Am a Christ Follower

Christ is Truth
I need forgiveness
Jesus died for us
It works

"For all have sinned and fall short of the glory of God." (Romans 3:23)

"For the wages of sin is death, but the gift of God is eternal life in Christ Jesus our Lord." (Romans 6:23)

"For God so loved the world that He gave His only begotten Son, that whoever believes in Him should not perish but have everlasting life." (John 3:16)

"Jesus said to him, 'I am the way, the truth, and the life. No one comes to the Father except through Me.'" (John 14:6)

"That if you confess with your mouth the Lord Jesus and believe in your heart that God has raised Him from the dead, you will be saved." (Romans 10:9)

Today is the day, Jesus is the way.

The Way

Connection – Abide in Him
Obedience – Get up early in the morning
Commitment – Complete the work
Desire – To do His will in all things
Perseverance – Never give up or in
Prayer – Unceasing
Peace – Eternal Life

Recommended Reading

The Bible

The Shack, William Paul Young

The Harbinger, Jonathan Kahn

Miracles from Heaven, Christy Wilson Beam

Left Behind—The Series, Tim LaHaye

A History of Israel, Dr. Howard M. Sachar

A Case for Christ, Lee Strobel

The Faith Trilogy, R. K. Sparks (Future Release)

Forever Young, R. K. Sparks

Jesus Calling, Sarah Young

Jerusalem Rising: Countdown to Armageddon, David Head

Infamous Quotes Notorious Notes, D.G. Lester

All Books, Joel C. Rosenberg

Surrender: The Heart God Controls, Nancy Leigh DeMoss

The Miracle of Passover, Zola Levitt

The Seven Feasts of Israel, Zola Levitt

A Christian Love Story, Zola Levitt

The Seven Churches, Zola Levitt

Jerusalem Forever, Zola Levitt

Just because the creator of the universe loves us, forgives us, and tolerates being called by His first name, doesn't mean His patience is endless. D.G. Lester

Printed in the USA
CPSIA information can be obtained
at www.ICGtesting.com
LVHW041413241023
761876LV00038B/35

9 781645 152750